Moonlady Falls

STONES OF THE KINGDOM

Falcon Pass

Moonlady Falls

Moonlady Falls

Stones of the Kingdom: Book Two

M. C. Foster

A Leaf It To Me Book

ISBN 978-0-9864581-2-5

Published by Leaf It To Me Publishing

Cover design by Leaf It To Me.

CHAPTER ONE

A hard rain beat down on the Watchtower of the West, accompanied by a howling southwest wind that moaned around the tower and whined at the shuttered windows. The rain hammered in a steady rhythm. Farren Blackarrow glanced up as the candle beside him guttered and waned briefly in a cold draught, then burned steadily once more. He ran one hand through his short red hair, moving the tickling tip of his forelock back. He took a better grip on his quill pen as he dipped it into the inkpot beside the candle, then drew a long, curving line on the thin scrap of parchment in front of him.

The fire crackled, sending sparks dancing upwards, then something thudded heavily and softly, and he smelt smoke. He looked up at the open fire burning in the common room hearth. A small log had rolled from the top of the heap of ashes onto the hearthstone. The tall, slender woman who had been lying reading on the deerskin in front of the fire scrambled to her feet and reached for the fire-irons. She coughed as she hoisted and levered the charred and smouldering log back into the fireplace. "Azariel Stormwolf, you've moved," he said, half reproachfully, quill poised in his left hand. "When you lie down, you'd better take exactly the same position you had before."

She brushed a few smears of ash off her black leather uniform trousers and shook her long raven-black hair back over her shoulder. "What, down to the exact fall of my cloak and everything?" Her dark grey-blue eyes flashed at him and she smiled. "You'll have to correct me if I go back into a different one." She dropped to her knees and picked up a lump of charcoal from the deerskin.

"You won't have that problem when you're married, will you?" chuckled one of the other soldiers from her chair against the wall by the fire. "Then you'll be able to sketch her without her cloak and without anything on at all. I know you want to."

"Not in the common room of the Watchtower with everybody who's not on duty sitting around and watching, Shadira," he replied, feeling a warm flush spread across his cheeks. *Why is the truth so embarrassing? My face must match my cloak by now. If I didn't want Azariel, then I'd really have something to be ashamed of.* He rubbed his face with his hand, then fidgeted with the betrothal earring through his left ear. "Get on with your knitting, woman, and let me sketch my lady in peace."

He looked away from the other woman and back to Azariel, who lay leaning on her elbows on the skin again. Her horse's mane of hair tumbled over her shoulders and one lock fell beside her face. The red-orange firelight washed over her, gleaming off the heavy silver armbands encircling her wrists and the chainmail where it showed beneath her red wool cloak. "Tweak your cloak back a bit further and stop it bunching up on the floor, Stormwolf," he said, watching her. "That's about right. Don't move again. I'm down to the details."

He bent back over his sketch of her, tracing the tousled lines of her hair and cloak as they draped across her shoulders and down her long back. The small sounds of the Watchtower surrounded him: the whispering of the fire, the rhythmic click of Shadira's knitting needles, the muttered table-talk of the other two off-duty guards playing cards on the other side of the round room. Behind the small sounds came the howls and moans of the late autumn night as the rain and wind battled in fitful gusts outside.

A heavy pounding on the door cut across the small sounds. Azariel started, shaking the lock of hair he was sketching back from her face. He sighed and laid his pen down. "Who's that?" he asked. "They're mad to be out tonight in this weather." He heard the voices of the guards on the roof, muffled by the rain, but no reply.

"Let's go down," Azariel said, scrambling to her feet. "Anyone out on a night like this won't be much of a menace. If it is an enemy, we'll be able to drive them off, even a sorcerer."

He pushed his chair back across the floorboards and picked up his candle. She slipped her hand into his free hand and smiled at him, sapphire eyes sparkling. "You've got ink-blots on your nose, beloved."

He groaned. "I was trying very hard not to smear myself. It's all Shadira's fault for embarrassing me." He fell into step with her long stride, walking smoothly to avoid spilling hot wax from the candle. She opened the hatch that led down to the circular stairs, making the candleflame dance. He let go of her hand to shield the flame from the draught and she slid her arm snugly around his waist, pressing closely against him as they stepped down the hatch and walked briskly down the stairs.

The pounding on the door began again as they reached the beaten dirt and stable-smells of the ground floor. One of the horses stabled in the stalls lifted its head and whickered at him as he passed. Azariel let go of him and lifted the heavy beam barring the door out of its place and dropped it down beside the door. He stepped back, keeping one hand cupped around the flickering flame. One or two drops of hot wax trickled onto his hand. She shot back the bolt and turned the doorhandle.

The door flew open, blown by the strong southwest wind. Rain and wind burst through the door, lightly stinging his hands and face. For half a heartbeat, he saw somebody in a red cloak and hood standing in the doorway. Then the candle guttered out to darkness. The wind spattered more hot wax onto his hand. He heard shuffling feet and hooves, and the hinges creaking. "Sorry," he said. "Give me a moment and I'll get this re-lit. Come in, if you can find the way."

He stepped out of the wind and knelt, balancing the candlestick on the dirt floor. He unbuckled the pouch at his belt and found his tinderbox. He scraped sparks from it several times until one caught on the cotton wadding about the flint. He re-lit the candle with the small blue and yellow flame, then stood up and turned towards the door. The hooded stranger was leading a spotted horse through the doorway. A black dog, tongue hanging out and tail wagging, stood beside the newcomer. The strange man shook back the hood, revealing a weather-beaten face and dark hair slick with rain. The man wore the usual Kingdom uniform of red cloak, high-necked chainmail, black leather trousers and black riding boots. He grinned at them, showing a mouthful of large white teeth, and shook some of the rain out of his hair. "Bit wet out there, eh?" he said.

"That's putting it mildly," said Azariel as she shut the door behind the bedraggled horse. "Who are you? If it wasn't for your uniform, I'd say you were a farm labourer caught by the downpour."

"Call me Adam – Swordsman Adam of Illinlebh-yan. And by the looks of the rings on your fingers and the armbands, you must be the two *minyasti* I've been sent to get."

"We are." Farren turned, knocking into Azariel and spilling another trickle of hot wax onto himself. *You'd be able to make a candle from what I've got on my hands,* he thought. He looked back up at the newcomer. "You look wet to the bone and your animals are drenched. Go on upstairs to the common room. There's a good fire burning up there and we should have something boiling over the fire for you to drink. I'll take care of your animals."

"And we'll find you something dry to put on," said Azariel. She replaced the heavy beam with a solid, secure thud. "Morgan's about your size, so ask him. You'll recognize him by his fair hair and the way you'll only get grunts in answer out of him. I'll show you up."

"That'd be champion," Adam said. "I'm a bit peckish, not having eaten since I set out this morning from the capital. Thanks for seeing to my four-legged friends, redhead."

"I'll see you back up in the common room, Stormwolf," he said. "Will you be all right on the stairs in the dark?" He leaned over and pressed a kiss onto her cheek as she passed him.

"Of course I will. Have fun with the animals." She walked into the black opening of the stairwell, Adam following her and trailing a line of drips across the beaten dirt floor after him.

He watched her go, then set the candle on a window ledge. "Now, horse, come here and let's get your gear off. We'll find a stall for you and a nibble or two." He held out his hand to the spotted horse. It pricked its ears and stepped towards him, nostrils quivering. He rubbed his hand over its warm wet neck and felt for the bridle buckles. The horse bent its head and let him slip it off easily. "You sense my animal tamer's Gift, don't you, horse? But I'm sure you're friendly even without that." He slung the bridle over his shoulder, ran the stirrups up and unbuckled the girths. Sliding the saddle off the horse's back, he inhaled the rich mixed smell of horse-sweat and leather. *I guess that fellow will want his saddlebags brought up.* He took the bulging bags off the saddle and stowed the tack on the empty pegs and racks outside the stalls.

He stepped backwards and stumbled over the dog. It whined at him and jumped up, scrabbling at his thighs with its large hard paws. "You're friendly too, aren't you?" he said, rumpling the dog's ears and gently pushing it back down. The smell of wet dog rose from the animal. "You don't need my Gift to draw you over at all. Good dog." He stepped around it and chirruped to the horse. It stepped daintily towards him and he caught it by the forelock. He led it past the stalls ringing one wall to one of the empty ones at the end. Princess, his fine-boned chestnut mare turned her head and neighed at him, tugging at her tether. "Hello there, my lady," he said to the mare. "I'll bring you a titbit when I've finished seeing to your wet friend here." He led the spotted horse into the narrow stall and found a rope to hitch it to the iron ring in the wall.

He fetched an armload of hay and filled a bucket with water from the pump opposite the privy closet. "There you go," he said, stuffing the hay into the wooden manger hanging on the wall. In the flickering light of the candle, he ran his eyes over the horse. Its legs and belly were spattered with mud and it had a small line of white sweat on its breast. *Careless, letting a horse get too hot in this weather.* He walked smartly out of the stall and found a stiff brush, a hoofpick and a spare horseblanket. A nest of mice rolled out of the horseblanket. Small animals scampered about at his feet and one ran onto his boot. "Off you go, and stay out of the feed bins," he said before it turned with a flick of its tail and vanished into the shadows. He carried the gear to the spotted horse, then set to work grooming and rubbing the horse down.

I wonder why that soldier's here, he thought as he prised a stone loose from the horse's hoof. *He mentioned something about coming to get us* minyasti. *But why?* He let the hoof drop and moved to the horse's hindquarters. He slid his hand down the knobs and sinews of its spotted leg and bent it up, cupping the grit-covered warm hoof in his right hand while he worked the hoofpick with his left. *Has something happened to Janna Greyhawk? Last I heard, he was riding around the country looking for new acolytes to train up.* He finished the hoof and let the horse lower it. *I'll find out when I finish here and go upstairs, I hope.*

He finished grooming the spotted horse and spread the blanket over it. The black dog greeted him as he turned away from the stall. "Now for you," he said. "Let me wash my hands and I'll cut you a bit of that pig we slaughtered."

He clanked the pump up and down, half filling a bucket with water. He knelt beside it and dipped his hands into the water, knuckles aching from the chill. He gritted his teeth and began washing the mud and horsehair from his hands. *Better cold than filthy.* He went to the meat safe and cut a rough chunk off the hanging carcass. "Make yourself comfortable in the hay," he said as he tossed it to the dog and shut the safe door firmly. He washed his hands again, then emptied the dirty water down the privy. A few horsehairs clung to his trousers. He brushed them off before he took the warm stub of candle and climbed back up the echoing stone steps to the common room.

He found Adam seated at the table, Azariel and the other five guards grouped around him. The delicious savoury smell of hot soup filled the round room at the top of the Watchtower. He breathed it in and gave a small sigh of pleasure as the warm air wafted over him. "Something smells tasty," he said. "I hope you enjoy it."

Azariel got to her feet and came over to him. "Do you want a bit of it too?" she said, squeezing his hand and winking. "I know how much you like bacon soup."

"Oh, sweetheart, you're trying to spoil me. I've already had my dinner." He sat down on the end of the bench at the table where his quill, parchment and ink were. Her arms wrapped around his neck, warm above the high neck of his chainmail, and he felt her press a kiss onto his scalp.

Adam clattered his spoon down beside his empty bowl and picked up what was left of a large, thickly buttered slice of bread. "Now that I've finished your excellent soup, I guess I'd better tell you why I'm here and feeding my face. I've come from the capital and I've been sent to get the two *minyasti*. The Greyhawk's back and he's retiring."

Azariel's arms uncoiled from his neck. "What? Retiring? What about the acolytes?"

"I don't know about any acolytes," said Adam. "All I know is that he's retiring and you, Azariel, are taking his place. Officially and permanently."

Farren twisted his head around to look up at her. Her eyes were wide and her eyebrows raised. The armour around her throat moved as she swallowed. He smiled and his hand went up to touch her bare forearms. *Good for you, sweetheart.*

"Do you mean to say that she's the arch *minyaster* now?" asked Shadira, shaking her brown curls and taking one hand off her ample hips.

"She's going to be," said the messenger. "And after the way she faced that head sorcerer and all during that little skirmish last spring, it doesn't surprise me at all." He glanced above Farren's head at her. "And why a common soldier like me's here and not another of you wonder-workers is because they've all got to be there to see you installed, or whatever they call it."

"That's against the regulations, though." A grizzle-haired guard at the other end of the table shot a look at the two *minyasti*. "There's supposed to be at least one *minyast* here and a lot more guards if there's only one."

"There really isn't any point in that, though, is there, Arturus?" Farren picked up the quill pen and twisted it back and forth between the fingers of his left hand. Idly, he dipped it into the inkwell and added a few lines of shading in his sketch of Azariel. "Those rules are there to ensure that the Stones of Protection – that got stolen at least two hundred years ago – are kept safe. So it doesn't really matter if there aren't any *minyasti* here for a few days. When do we have to return to the capital, Adam?"

"Oh, as soon as possible. Tomorrow, as a matter of fact." Adam stretched his arms and yawned. "I just hope you don't have to ride through the rain like I did. It's a wee bit unpleasant out there."

"Tomorrow," Farren heard Azariel whisper. "King of Heaven, it's so sudden." Her hands shifted on his shoulders. "Is the road through Falcon Pass open or has snow closed it?" she said more clearly.

Adam chuckled. "It's not, fortunately. I don't think there's a soldier in the Kingdom who doesn't know the danger of going through there when there's a bit of snow. Not after what happened at the battle!"

"We'd better pack our gear ready for riding out, beloved." Her arms circled his neck again and her hair tumbled down and tickled his cheeks. He brushed his face against the fine strands of black, inhaling the scent of rosemary in them.

"I'll finish this drawing first," he said, cocking his head on one side and looking down at the parchment. "It's just about my best I've done of you yet."

***

The rain was still falling the next morning, although the wind had dropped. Farren led Princess out of the Watchtower and let her drop her head to graze among the puddles. He pulled his thick red wool cloak closer about him and looked northeastwards towards the mountains. They were hidden behind a thick sheet of soft grey that hazed the trees dotted about the plains. He heard the door close behind him and looked around. Azariel let go of the latch, leading her black gelding, Storm. She reached up and pulled the hood of her cloak over her head, shivering. "I can think of better weather to be riding in," she said.

"At least it's decent rain and not drizzle," he replied. From the corner of his eye, he saw his big hunter's bow hanging slightly awry from its rest by the high saddlehorn. He carefully slid it back into place. "Come on. Let's get the journey over and done with. If we get there in good time, there'll be some hot water still in the boilers at headquarters." He put one hand on the saddlehorn, placed his toe in the stirrup and swung himself onto the mare's back. "On the march, Princess, my lady," he said to the mare, tapping her sides lightly with his heels.

They rode steadily through the rain along the cobbled highway that led eastwards through the Seranyai-y-Taranar mountains to the east of the Watchtower and down to the plains on the other side. By nightfall, they had reached the stone wall and wooden gates of Lebhern-y-Domastin, the capital of the Kingdom. The gates were closed, but a sentry let them through into the echoing plaza streets. The horses splashed through the puddles lying on the cobbles, heading for the central plaza where the army barracks stood. The windows in the houses lining the narrow streets shone with a warm golden light that was reflected from the rainwashed stones. He looked into one and glimpsed a family seated around a table for a meal. Suddenly, he grew aware of the damp chill of his rainsoaked clothes and the dull ache of hunger in his belly. *Only three more corners to pass until we get there. And I wish there weren't as many*

They reached the plaza and rode over to the set of grey stone slabby buildings that contrasted with the more elaborate architecture of the other chief buildings that ringed the plaza, still dimly visible. They rode up to the iron gate and let their weary horses halt. "Who rides there?" challenged a sentry from above them. A lantern appeared at the top of the wall, casting odd shadows across the face of the woman who held it. "Well, by the looks of your uniforms, you're some of us, but who are you?"

Azariel swung herself off Storm's back and landed heavily. One heel of her riding boots splashed into a puddle and she gave a small hiss of irritation. "Azariel Stormwolf and Farren Blackarrow from the Watchtower of the West," she called up to the sentry.

"Oh." The face and the lantern disappeared, and Farren heard the sound of boots striking stone then squelching through mud. The gate creaked open, and the sentry and her lantern reappeared. "I was told to look out for *minyasti*. You two in particular." Her face creased into a frown as she pulled the gate wide. "That's right. You're not to go and report in to the main block. You're to go over to your own headquarters straight away. Leave your horses with me and I'll see to them. He's waiting for you."

Farren swung himself off Princess's back. In the dull light of the sentry's lantern, he saw, to his disgust, that his hands were covered in mud, grit and horsehair. He brushed them off on his trousers as best he could. "Thanks, sentry," he said. "We'll take our saddlebags off them first. Who's waiting? Janna Greyhawk?"

"No. Himself. The boss. General Alpherastin. He's waiting for you."

"We'd better step smartly, then," said Azariel. The buckles of her saddlebag jingled faintly, then she swung the bulging leather bag down.

He swung his saddlebag over his shoulder and lifted his bow from its place. "I'm ready. Goodbye for now, my lady," he said to his mare. "The grooms will look after you – and I hope they get all that mud off you."

"They will. Don't worry." The sentry took both horses by their bridles and walked away, carrying the thin handle of the lantern between her teeth.

He fell into step beside Azariel and trudged through the rain across the muddy courtyard and around some buildings to the whitewashed two-storied *minyasti* headquarters with the small round tower jutting out from the centre. Yawning and stretching his stiff shoulder muscles, he opened the door and stepped into the dry shelter of the corridor. "Back again," he said, lowering his burden onto the floor beside the door. Footsteps pattered at the far end of the corridor and voices rose and fell cheerfully. "And now to meet the General. I wish I had time to tidy myself up properly before we do."

"You know him. He won't mind as long as we're prompt." Azariel thumped her saddlebag down. "We'll take these to our rooms afterwards." She straightened her back and reached for the sword hanging at her left hip.

He stood back and she brushed past him into the common room. A fire was blazing in the hearth at one side of the room, ringed by a collection of comfortable chairs, including a thickly padded armchair where one of the older *minyasti* was dozing. Several candles burnt in a candelabra above the fireplace, casting yellow light around the square room. A broad-shouldered man wearing a red uniform cloak stood by the fire, staring into it with his hands behind his back. The candles beside him guttered as Farren shut the door behind Azariel and the man looked around. "Hello, you two," he said, his weather-reddened face crinkling into a smile. "You look like a pair of drowned rats."

Farren twitched his cloak out of the way, drew his sword from his side and flourished it in salute. "Greetings, General," he said. "We have come."

"Cut the fancy stuff and come and warm up," the grizzle-headed soldier grunted. "I don't want to lose good fighters to exposure, especially when one of them's about to be the arch *minyaster*." He shifted to one side of the fire and beckoned. "Janna will be here before too long and some of the other *minyasti*, too. He's just showing the new acolytes their rooms."

"Remember those days?" Farren asked Azariel, sheathing his sword and reaching out to take her hand as they walked around the chairs and the small card-table to the fire. "It does and it doesn't seem like ten years ago."

"And now look where you are," said the General, winking. "Both of you. Before anyone comes, I've got something for you,

Farren. A little memento of the war six months ago." The big old soldier fumbled at the pouch at his side and pulled something out that flashed in the firelight. "Take it."

The General opened his large hand and Farren leaned over. A small silver star winked and sparkled in the other man's palm. He breathed in sharply and his heart began to pound. He looked up at the General again, a warm flush flooding his face. "Sir..." he faltered. "What's this for?"

"For killing that Wayasti general, of course, Farren. Put it on your cloak. Start a collection like mine. Who knows? One day, you might get the whole lot." His other hand pointed to the array of silver badges on the shoulder of his cloak. "I thought I'd put you straight up to this rank, rather than making you fool around with cadets as a sergeant." He lifted the star and his thick fingers tugged at Farren's cloak. "Here you are – Lieutenant Farren Blackarrow." He fastened the clasp of the silver star and patted him hard on the shoulder.

Considering I only killed that man when I had actually been sent to kill the head sorcerer – with the threat of forty lashes if I didn't – it's ironic that I'm getting rewarded for it. He smiled widely and stepped back. Azariel was smiling at him, her stormy sapphire eyes flashing lightning at him. He reached for the sword at his side and brandished it in salute over his head. "Thank you, sir. Thank you." He lowered his eyes, breathing hard, and sheathed his sword.

"Congratulations, beloved." Azariel stepped forwards, her hands held out. She stopped and bit her lip, turning her head towards the General.

"Oh, go ahead and kiss him, lass. I'd say he deserves it."

Farren opened his arms to her and drew her close as her arms encircled him. He bent his head and his lips met hers gratefully. Reluctantly, he drew his lips off hers as she dropped her head down to rest on his shoulder. She jerked up suddenly.

"Ouch," she said, rubbing her cheek. "I'll have to watch out for your lieutenant's star now."

The door creaked and a slightly-built man with silver hair and a black cloak walked in. "So you're here, now," he said. "Welcome back to the capital, Farren and Azariel."

Azariel wriggled out of his arms and turned towards the newcomer. "Janna!" she said, walking to him and throwing her arms about his neck. "It's good to see you again." She let the older man go, then walked back to the fireplace and slid her arm around Farren's waist.

Farren smiled and draped his arm around her shoulders, her cloak and hair still damp underneath his bare forearm. "When did you get back from your ride around the Kingdom?" he asked Janna Greyhawk. "I hear you've found some new *minyasti*. How many and who are they?"

"Oh, I have, I have. Two of them." Janna sank down onto one of the armchairs and stretched out his legs, pulling up sharply with a hiss of pain and rubbing the small of his back. "I found two youngsters with the hand of the Power on them. One of them you know already: Kiihaon, your sister's love-child girl."

"Was that the little brunette with the bright blue eyes I saw tagging around after you this afternoon?" the General asked. "I thought she looked a bit familiar. This *minyasti* business must run in families, then."

"Indeed it does, it does," said Janna. "But now I've got to train her and the boy from Sersaran, too. You'll meet them in the morning – if you've got time to before the ceremony. We're all here now."

"Ceremony?" asked Azariel.

"The ceremony to pass my authority on to you, of course. You'll be busy tomorrow! But if you don't meet them then, you'll see them around. It's time you two had some time back here in the

14

capital. There – that's my last order to you. Stay and spend some time with the old books. See if they can tell you where the Stones of Protection might be."

"Your last order…" she bowed her head. "I'm not sure I'm ready for this, Janna; you haven't told me anything of my duties as the leader. And the acolytes – do I train them? I don't have half your wisdom. I don't know the way to use any Gifts but my own – and Farren's, of course." Her fingers dug into his waist. "Why did you choose me to replace you?"

The old man tilted his head to one side and looked at her with his piercing blue eyes. "You are the strongest of the *minyasti* – my equal, if not more. It must be you who takes my place and no other. If we ride to war again…"

"You'll have to put up with me," put in the General. "I don't know much about *minyasti* business, but I do know you'll have to protect me on the battlefield." He scratched the mole on his nose. "And turn up to High Council."

"Don't make her nervous," Janna laughed. "High Council's too much to worry about for now. Don't panic, Azariel. It's only my body that's unfit for my position, not my mind, and I'll use that, if you'll let me."

"It will be the first order I'll give you," she replied coolly. "I'll probably be too busy fulfilling your last order to worry about anything else."

"Back to the books again, is it?" groaned Farren. The heat of the fire grew uncomfortable on the backs of his legs and he shuffled a few inches away from the blaze. "What about the Watchtower?"

"I'll take care of that," he replied. "I'll take the acolytes with me. And there are others knocking about who can take your place out there for a while." He closed his eyes and bowed his head. "Don't worry about that. We've got more immediate things to think about at the moment. Have you two dined this evening? I thought not. Go and get some dry clothes on and then come back here. There's food left still. How about you, General? Will you join us?"

"Thanks, Janna." The General smiled and winked. "I won't say no to that."

***

The shrill blast of the barracks bugler woke Azariel. She rolled over in her bed and pulled the covers closer under her chin for a few lingering moments. *The air's so cold and I'm going to have to get out of this warmth into it. The ceremony's today. When I next sleep here, I'll be the arch* minyaster. She brushed a strand of her black hair out of her eyes and looked around her room in the *minyasti* headquarters. Sounds drifted in from outside: cocks crowing, the bell chiming in the abbey next door to the barracks, the rumbles of the city. She breathed out slowly, watching her breath steam up in the cold morning air. A faint crack of light shone between the thick green curtains, shining on her armour piled on the trunk beside her bed then onto the mirror, catching rainbows on the bevelled edge.

A brisk knock sounded on the door. *Good. An excuse not to get out of bed yet, seeing as I'm naked.* "Who is it?" she called. "You can come in if you're female."

The doorhandle turned and a woman with honey-coloured hair falling smoothly to her shoulders walked in, a tray balanced on one hand and a towel hanging over one shoulder. "Good morning, Azariel," the woman said. "I've volunteered to lady's-maid you this morning. I've brought some breakfast for the two of us."

"Thank you, Taramaritan," she replied, sitting up slightly and holding the covers around her chest. "When did you wake up?"

"About when the bugler did, I guess." She set the tray down on the writing desk in the corner of the square room and turned to draw the curtains. Sunlight sparkled off the large ruby ring on

Taramaritan's finger as it flooded the room. "It was so cold that I couldn't get comfortable. You look nice and warm, though."

"Too warm," she chuckled, wriggling backwards and sitting up a little further. "It's hard to leave a warm bed on a cold morning. Pass me my cloak, please, if it's dry."

Taramaritan fingered the red cloak draped over the chair in front of the tiny fireplace and tossed it over. "Catch," she said.

Azariel gritted her teeth against the frigid air as she sat up fully and tossed the cloak around her shoulders. "I may as well get up and dressed enough to go to the washroom for a bath."

"No, you won't," the other woman said, green eyes flashing with mischief. "I'm going to bring a bath through here and bucket the water in. I am supposed to be your lady-in-waiting this morning. Here's your breakfast – bread rolls and jam." Taramaritan held out a full plate and sat beside her on the bed.

"Oh, honestly, Taramaritan!" She took one of the round bread rolls from the plate. "I don't need help having a bath! And thank the King of Heaven for His gift of food." She broke a piece off the roll, wincing as crumbs and a few poppy seeds fell down into the sheets.

"So be it," replied the other woman, taking a roll from the plate and raising it. "But it's part of the fun. Today's your day to be fussed over and you may as well enjoy it."

Azariel swallowed her mouthful of bread, savouring the sweet, tangy taste of the plum jam. "Very well then," she said. "Have fun. I'll do the same for you one day."

"I doubt I'll ever get to be arch *minyaster*. You're younger than I am and the only way I'll be it is if you're killed. Or disgraced, but that's unlikely. You wouldn't be around to doll me up."

"For your wedding then." Azariel felt a smile attempting to shape itself on her lips and she suppressed it. *I shouldn't tease, but it's irresistible.*

"Oh, I'm not planning to hitch myself to some man!" She ripped her roll in two. "Not me."

"Not even to what's-his-name – Colonel Annan?"

Taramaritan flushed. "Finish your breakfast, Azariel Stormwolf, and stop repeating gossip."

Azariel finished eating and lay back on the pillows. Taramaritan left the room and came back with an oval tin bath. Azariel watched her as she took a few things out of it, then closed her eyes. *Arch* minyaster *until the day I die. Which could be sooner or later, depending on where the road leads me and when the Power will call me home. I've stared death in the eye before now.* The sound of pouring water came from the other side of the room, followed by footsteps. *I wonder where our search for the Stones of Protection will lead us. That traitor – Jaime... Jachim... Jamin; that's who he was – stole them and took them northwards, and they've never been heard of since. Who has treasures like that in their keeping? And how do we, how do I get them back?*

"Asleep again?" Taramaritan's voice held a hint of laughter. "Your bath's ready." Azariel opened her eyes in time to see the other woman pour another large steaming bucket of water into the bath. "Now you'll have to get up and get into it."

"And I'll be glad to," she replied, unbuckling her cloak and throwing back the covers. She stood up, feeling pale and awkward as she stood naked in front of the other woman, then walked across to the bath, shivering slightly in the cold morning air. She climbed into the hot water, closing her eyes as it lapped deliciously around her limbs. A heavy fall of water poured over her head, making her gasp. As the water fell away, she heard Taramaritan's chuckle. The other woman knelt beside her and began busily scrubbing and lathering her with a large bar of lemongrass-scented soap.

Taramaritan poured another jugful of water over her chest, then paused. "Is that where that sorcerer stabbed you?" she asked. "That is a nasty scar."

Azariel looked thoughtfully down at the six-inch line of silver scar tissue that ran from her collarbone to between her breasts. *The legacy of some unfinished business. One day, I'll face Izar Gardweil again. And on that day, I won't go down or grapple with him.* "It looked worse when the stitches were still in," she said aloud. "Have you finished flaying me with your scrubbing brush?"

"Not quite." The brush rasped up down the line of her spine and up again. "There. All done. Now, I know it's not quite the proper thing, but I'll leave you to dress yourself while I go and empty the soapy water down the sluices. And from what I know of you, you'll prefer to do it yourself, anyway."

"You do know me," Azariel replied. She stepped out of the bath and wrapped a rough towel around herself. *I'm glad I set my dress uniform out last night,* she thought, seeing the pile of black clothes on the wooden trunk. Taramaritan nodded and scooped a bucket of water out of the bath, then left the room, trailing drips and little splashes behind her.

Azariel dried herself and wrapped her long black hair up in the towel. She pulled her clothes on, neatly tucking her woollen underclothing and black leather tunic about her slender waist into her trousers. Taramaritan returned and dragged the bath out of the room behind her as she left again. Azariel finished lacing up the neck of her tunic and waited, sitting on the bed, until Taramaritan came back. "All ready?" the other woman said. She looked slightly flushed. "Good. Now to dress your hair and face." She turned towards the washstand that stood beside the door underneath the mirror. "What's this little bottle beside your hairbrush?"

"Rosemary oil. Put a few drops on the brush and run it through. That'll do for today. My hair's dry and it needs it, especially in summer. What about yours?" She sat on the bed and twitched the towel off her head, letting the hair fall in a hot damp cascade around her face and shoulders. Quickly, she pulled her chainmail on and the other woman pulled it firmly around her neck and laced it. She bent her head as Taramaritan began to tug and tease at the tangles in her hair, gritting her teeth as one strand was yanked sharply. The other woman took a lock of her hair by her temple and began to braid a silver thread through it.

"There," Taramaritan said, standing back and critically flicking her green-gold eyes up and down her. "That's your hair. Now for your face." She stooped and took a small jar from the pile of things she had brought into the room. "Hold still and look at me."

"My face?" Azariel raised her hand as the other woman bent over her. "I don't want to be painted up like a whore! How much are you planning on smearing over me?

"Don't panic," the other woman said, grinning. "With your pale skin, you don't need much improvement. Just a touch. Haven't you worn cosmetics before?"

"Not much these days. I did when I was in my teens – didn't we all? But they're a chore to make and expensive to buy."

"Well, here's some. Keep quiet and don't grimace unless I tell you to."

Thankfully, this won't take long, she thought as she let Taramaritan dab and daub at her lips and eyelids. *But I wish she'd hurry up!*

"Right, you're all ready," Taramaritan said at last. "Open your eyes and take a look at yourself in the mirror. You're fit to meet the King now."

"Not quite." She stood and reached for her dress uniform belt. She fastened the silver clasp of the ornate belt and slid her own sword into the decorated scabbard. Pins and needles began to prickle at her wrists and nerves danced in her stomach. Glancing in the mirror, she buckled her cloak around her neck and let it drape down her back and long legs. Belt secure, she took a moment to study her face. A thin line of kohl rimmed her eyes, accented by a smudge of silver, and her lips had been stained a glossy wine-red. She ran her tongue across the front of her teeth to remove any traces of the gloss. *Well, the make-up doesn't look too bad. Quite nice, actually. King of Heaven, be with me in this ceremony and afterwards. Especially afterwards.* Her reflection looked back at her from the mirror. The silver thread in her black hair flashed like lightning through thick thundercloud as the sunlight caught it from behind. *But if you chose me for this, then you must have made me for it.* A small shiver of energy travelled down her spine, banishing the nervous tremors. "I'm ready," she said aloud. "Ready for anything." She swept her long hair back from her eyes and walked with the other woman to the door.

CHAPTER TWO

She stepped into the passageway, cloak sweeping behind her. Her skin still tingled from the brisk scrubbing Taramaritan had given her and her hair lay damply against her face. The common room door opened ahead of her, and Farren looked around the door, his short red hair neat apart from a few rumpled locks above his forehead. His eyes opened wide as he looked at her, flicking up and down along the length of her body before looking into her eyes. "Stormwolf!" he said, walking forwards with his hands held out to her and smiling widely. "You look splendid. Are you ready to go to the chapel now? The rest of us are."

She strode forwards and sank into his warm embrace eagerly. For a few seconds, she rested her face against his shoulder, the star on his cloak cold and hard against her cheek. She straightened up and looked into his dark brown eyes. "I'm ready," she said. "Walk with me to the chapel."

She linked her hands with him, feeling the ring on his right hand hard between her fingers. The other *minyasti* drifted out of the common room and wandered behind them talking as she walked with him through the barracks, across the muddy courtyard and to the small walled chapel. A light cool breeze stirred her cloak and hair, and spun white and grey clouds through the sky. The garden gate clanged behind them and they strolled up the small path to the open door. A light frost lingered on the grass, turning it to burnished silver in the sunlight, and raggedy brown and gold leaves clung to the trees. She stepped across the threshold into the chapel and waited, breathing in the sweet scents of wood, incense and beeswax while her eyes adjusted to the dimness.

A few of the green-robed monks from the neighbouring monastery were inside and she recognised the Abbot among them. He must be here to lead the ceremony. *This really is important, even though it's me who it's happening to. I still can hardly believe it.* Two other people were sitting in the pews with their backs to the door. "To judge by the back, that one on the left's General Alpherastin," she whispered to Farren, pointing at one of the two. "But who's the fair-haired person in the civilian clothes?"

"I don't know," he replied. "But you'd better keep quiet. He'll hear you."

Janna Greyhawk came up beside her and laid a hand on her arm. "We'll begin soon. Caph Domastin is here and we can't keep him waiting."

A cold thrill plunged through her chest and stomach, and her legs suddenly felt weak. *The King! Here to watch me, the daughter of a widowed Zenifi weaver from a tiny mountain village. How did I get here?* Her hand tightened around Farren's and she set her teeth, fighting to master the urge to crawl away and hide from the eyes. *It's the gift of the Power that brought me here,* she lectured herself. *I am the Stormwolf and the servant of the King of Heaven. If I can talk to Him, a mere mortal king shouldn't cow me.* She flicked the braided strand of her hair back from her face and strode forwards one pace. *And I'm going to make my nerves believe it!*

The Abbot came down from the altar, a red leather-bound book in his hands. "Here are the words of the rite," he said softly. "Read it and prepare yourself." He smiled and handed the book to her. "But don't worry if you don't remember your part. Your man can hold the book for you and stand by your side."

"I'll be glad to help you, sweetheart," Farren said. "May the Power go with you."

She ran her eyes over the words written in the Old Tongue, swiftly translating them into Common Speech as she read. Only the rustle of quiet breathing from the seated *minyasti* filled the chapel. The Abbot padded on bare feet across the carpet to the altar and lit the two tall candles on the altar. She drew herself up to her full height and stiffened her back. Then he turned to face the small congregation. "Azariel Stormwolf, *ilnasa talan lahava*," he said, the words of the Old Tongue rolling smoothly and easily from his mouth.

She handed the heavy book to Farren and walked towards the altar in response to the Abbot's command. Her mouth felt dry and her wrists tingled with nervous excitement. She reached the altar rail and her eyes met the Abbot's. "I am here," she replied in the same language.

"Take off your weapons of war and lay them at the altar, for no foes dare approach this sanctuary. Take off your shoes also, for you are standing on holy ground."

She unbuckled her cloak and belt and handed them to the Abbot. He took them and as she unlaced the high neck of her chainmail, she heard him draw the sword from the decorated ceremonial scabbard. For one excruciating moment, she pictured her shirt peeling up from her body along with her armour. A sick thrill plunged through her body and she felt a warm rush of blood in her cheeks. *Master, help me not to make a fool of myself with all the eyes on me.* Holding her breath, she drew the heavy, clinking tunic smoothly over her head then knelt to pull off her riding boots. She stood on the stone aisle near the altar carpet, the chill biting through the thin woollen socks on her feet. *I don't know how those monks can bear to walk barefoot all the time, even in winter. This stone's freezing! Why couldn't we be standing one pace closer to the altar on the carpet?* She slipped the lapis lazuli ring from her right hand and unclasped the heavy silver bands from her wrists.

The Abbot laid the collection of arms and armour on the altar. She watched him, feeling half-dressed without her armbands and rings. The green-robed monk turned and faced her again, speaking in the Old Tongue. "Azariel Stormwolf, chosen by the Power, God Incarnate and the High King of Heaven, the Triune God for His especial service, are you willing to accept the mantle of the arch *minyaster*, the leader and servant of the ones He set apart to battle the hosts of hell?"

She glanced at the book, then bowed her head. *If I want to shirk this, this is my last chance. But I won't. I can't. Now the burden's going to rest on me.* She swallowed down the lump in her throat, then raised her head, meeting the Abbot's eyes squarely. "I am willing," she said.

"Receive, then, the tools of your task, the weapons of a warrior." The Abbot lifted her chainmail from the altar. "Azariel Stormwolf, take this armour to guard your heart from weapons of steel. Wear it and remember to guard your heart, keeping it innocent of evil. Yet not by your own virtue alone, but that of God Incarnate, bought with His blood. Do you swear to keep yourself, with His strength and your own, from the stains of sin?"

"I swear it." She held out her hands as he handed the armour back to her. Pulse pumping at her ears and wrists, she pulled it on and fastened the high neck.

The Abbot raised her belt, the scabbard dangling empty from the left side of it. The silver clasp winked in the gleam of the candles as he held it in both hands. "Take this belt to bind your waist, to brace your back, to hold your armour close to your heart and to keep your sword at your side. Wear it and remember to bind and brace yourself with the truth, keeping virtue and the One who is the Word of Truth incarnate close to you at all times. Do you swear to live and speak the truth at all times?"

She held out her hands for the belt. "I swear it." She fastened the big shield-shaped clasp and set it straight around her. *That's better,* she thought as the firm leather settled snugly into the small of her back. *I feel so slovenly without my belt on.*

"Azariel Stormwolf, take this cloak. Draw the hood over your head to hide and warm you from the elements. Wear it and remember that you have been bought with the blood of God Incarnate, blood that is your shield and hiding place. Will you remember this each time a cloak drapes your shoulders, this and any other?"

"I will." *This is starting to sound like a marriage ceremony.* She took the cloak and cast it about herself, the familiar smell of wool, sweat, smoke and horses rising from it as she fastened the clasp.

The Abbot stood holding her boots. *Oh, at last! My feet are freezing.* "Azariel Stormwolf," he continued, using the Old Tongue, "these shoes protect and comfort your feet and hold you firm in your place as you ride and march. Take them and stand firm in them as you stand firm in the precepts of the Holy Book, the words of the King of Heaven. Do you swear to always walk in the Way, His word in your heart and mind?"

"I swear it." She glanced over at Farren and caught his eye, a pang of longing shooting through her. *You know how much we want our own copy of the Holy Book. And I know how hard you're working to make one in time for our wedding.* She swiftly pulled the boots back on and stood wriggling her toes inside them to get the warm blood moving through them again.

The Abbot coughed, catching her attention. She looked up again and saw him holding her silver armbands, one in each hand. The candlelight shone on the garnets, picking out the blood-red stones from the thick damasked silver. "Azariel Stormwolf, take your armbands of protection, shields by virtue of your faith in the Power's might, to protect you from the firebolts from the servants of evil. Take them and never forget."

"I will remember and trust the King of Heaven each time I use them." She held out her hands for the bracelets, then started slightly as instead of handing them to her, he clasped one about her wrist, the catch softly clicking closed. "Take them also to remember that as leader you are a slave to all." The second silver bracelet closed and the Abbot stepped back. She lowered her arms, quick rushes of breath filling her lungs with the sweet waxy air as she waited. Another monk handed him her sword and lapis lazuli ring from the altar. "Take these also, your weapons for your fight against evil, to strive against not merely flesh and blood abut also against the renegade rulers of the world above, below, beside and behind this. Fight fire with fire, steel with steel, justice and mercy ever in your hand. Take them and use them, fighter for the King of Heaven."

The Abbot caught her hand and she spread her fingers towards him. He looked at her hands and his eyebrows shot up. *He's seen how my ring finger is as long as the middle one – the main mark of a shapeshifter. Will he say anything?* His breath hissed out slowly as he slid the ring onto her fingers. He raised his head and presented her sword to her. Her hand closed around the worn leather bindings on the hilt. She tossed a wandering strand of hair back behind her shoulders and raised the sword in salute, watching the yellow light glint off the polished steel blade.

"Now, Azariel Stormwolf," the Abbot asked as she sheathed her sword, "do you take the full responsibility of the arch *minyaster?* Will you take up the burden of guiding the Guild and, by guiding, serving? Will you be the first in the attack and the last in the retreat? Will you stand firm in the face of all foes? Will you stand by your General and defend him in battle? Will you give counsel to Caph Domastin your king? Do you swear to all this?"

She swallowed. *Can I swear to giving counsel and guiding others? Master, I'm the youngest of the minyasti. How can I tell them what to do – and how am I going to be an advisor to the King?* She held her voice level to control the shakiness and tried to moisten her dry mouth as she glanced at the words in the book Farren held. "I do, with the help of the King of Heaven, God Incarnate and the Power."

From the corner of her eye, she saw Janna Greyhawk striding towards her. She half-turned to face him as he unbuckled his black cloak. "Take yours off," he mouthed at her in the Common Speech. She nodded and her fingers felt for the clasp of the cloak. She let the red wool broadcloth fall to the ground as Janna stepped forwards and threw the black cloak about her shoulders. "Azariel Stormwolf, you are now the arch *minyaster*," he said in the Old Tongue. "Receive the mantle of your authority. Wear it and bear it until injury, old age or death forbids you from the battlefield." She swept her hair out from between the collar of her armour and the black wool and held her head high to let the old man fasten the clasp. She shook her hair down and shrugged the cloak into place on and around her shoulders.

Energy prickled and coursed down the length of her spine from the cloak, the familiar shimmering touch of the Power. She gasped slightly at the intense prickling and clenched her hands into fists. Her ring flared with sudden heat and as she looked down at it, the dark blue lapis lazuli flashed with blue flame. The flame spiralled and swirled like a vine around her hand and arm then reached tendrils of warm light around her whole body. The light shimmered across her skin in stars and diamonds of blue, and a sharp clean smell, floral and slightly spicy, rose around her. She raised her hands and the light swirled into two pillars of flame, one balancing and swaying on each hand. Then the columns of light leaped from her hands towards the ceiling, where they burst into multicoloured stars before vanishing. She watched the colours fade, heart racing and lips parted. *A sign. I've been accepted.*

Soft garments rustled from the front of the nave and she turned to see Caph Domastin on his feet. Janna took her by the hand and led her to the young king. He had sleek blond hair and his slight frame was dressed in rich deep red trimmed with black fur. She dropped to one knee before him and brandished her sword in salute, fighting to hold her hand steady.

"My lord Caph Domastin of the Kingdom, may I present Azariel Stormwolf, the new arch *minyaster*, as member of the High Council," Janna said, one hand resting on her shoulder.

The king nodded. "Rise, arch *minyaster*," he said softly. She got to her feet and Caph Domastin kissed her lightly and formally on each cheek. "Welcome, Azariel Stormwolf."

"I am honoured, my lord," she said, bowing her head.

The Abbot padded down the steps and down the aisle to the middle of the chapel. "The rite is done. Go your ways and may the King of Heaven, God Incarnate and the Power watch over you always."

She smiled and followed the king and the Abbot out of the chapel into the garden. The footsteps of the others followed her and she felt Farren take her hand and squeeze it. "Congratulations, sweetheart," he said. "I'm sure you'll lead us well."

"Thank you, beloved," she replied softly. "But at the moment, I'm not sure what happens next."

"Well, for a start, those of us who were in the common room this morning know that there's an excellent luncheon waiting for us. And after that, well, how about sword drill and then over to the library to start this research about the Stones?" His brown eyes flashed. "Does that please my mistress?"

She laughed, jabbing him lightly in the ribs with her elbow. "Mistress? That sounds wanton. A shame there's no true feminine to 'master'. But it's an excellent idea – especially about the luncheon. My nerves must have used up all I broke my fast with."

"I'm not surprised." He let go of her hand and circled his arm around her waist. "Come on."

***

Several hours later, she stood with Farren in the thick dusty air of the monastery library. Hot blood coursed through her veins after the exercise of sword drill, and the celebratory luncheon was only a pleasant memory. She looked around the lines of shelves in the rectangular room, brushing back a strand of her hair, kinked from where it had been braided. She heard the soft padding of feet coming from one shadowy corner and looked around. A young blond monk, the monastery librarian, came towards them. "Greetings," he said in his rich baritone voice. "I've been wondering when you two would return here."

"We're back, Brother Claran," Farren said, leaning on the sill of one of the square windows. "Although not altogether sure of exactly we're looking for. Did Janna say anything?"

"Not the Book of Lore this time," the blond monk said, shaking his tonsured head. "I did talk to Janna about it when he was recovering from his injuries after the war and he said a few things. Now our task is to search through all of the books, both in here and the palace library, for any clues as to what happened to the Stones of Protection after the traitor Jamin Bluecloak took them."

Azariel ran her eyes over the shelves of books lining the small dark room. "What, looking through the records of the time to see if jackdaw dragons inhabited the northern mountains then, and so forth?"

Brother Claran beamed at her. "I hadn't thought of that. I was thinking more of researching Jamin Bluecloak's background, if we can find it. They do keep a record of the *minyasti*, you know, even you two rascals. I only hope the arch *minyast* of his time didn't delete him from the books when he betrayed the Kingdom."

"Sounds like any book could hold a clue," groaned Farren, running one hand through his hair. "How many books does this library hold, Brother Claran?"

"A mere five thousand. But don't forget – only the books from around that time will be of any real use. When we find them."

"You ought to tell each *minyast* to take ten each back to wherever they're going and read them, Azariel," cut in Farren.

Brother Claran chuckled and continued. "And then there's the ones in the palace. For all I know, even the lists of imports and exports could give us a clue." He put his hands on his hips and fidgeted with the knotted cord girding his waist. "I pray that the Power will give us the wisdom to know a clue when we see it."

"So be it," said Azariel, turning towards the shelves. "Let's start searching instead of talking. Reading through all these will take months."

"I'm only sorry our reading room isn't as comfortable as the one in the palace with its big padded leather chairs and all." Brother Claran's bare feet shuffled on the carpet. "However, we've got a good fire burning. I dare say that in the depths of winter, we'll all be glad to have a task that keeps us inside."

She walked to the shelves and pulled out a thick brown-covered volume. The smell of dust and old leather rose from it as she wiped a cobweb from the gilt-leafed pages. *This looks old enough, but I'll soon find out if it isn't.* She blew the dust off it and tucked it under her arm. She waited for the two men to choose their books and walked with them to the small reading room at the far end of the library. Windows dominated the northern wall, letting plenty of the autumn sunlight onto the wooden chairs with their threadbare cushions and the ink-stained writing tables. A sheepskin lay invitingly in front of a crackling fire. She threw herself down on the soft wool and shuffled about, finding a comfortable place for her hips and elbows. The large stone at the end of her dagger pressed into her stomach and she moved it to one side. She drew a deep breath, carefully opened the tome and began to read.

***

Farren turned another page and yawned, leaning back against the high-backed wooden chair. A brisk wind whistled outside, muffling the sounds of the city beyond the monastery. *Words, words, words. We've been reading nearly all day for at least a week now, and still nothing. I doubt I'll ever forget that script I've been reading.* He looked through the rain-streaked windows, seeking the ghost-disk of the sun through the clouds. *How much longer until midday?* He sighed, imagining and anticipating a good gallop through the cold autumn air outside the city. *Not long. About an hour or so, if the sundial could cast a shadow in this. Princess, I'll be with you before long, and the sooner, the better. This chair's so hard that in spite of the cushion it almost feels like I've got no backside left.* He rubbed an aching muscle in his neck and bent his head back over the bestiary he was reading.

He heard a sharp intake of breath and looked up. Azariel was on her feet, playing with a strand of her long hair. She stared down at the book lying open on the floor, then began to pace about the hearth, head bowed.

"What's up, Stormwolf?" he asked, slipping a tattered strip of cloth between the pages of his book before closing it. "Found something?"

She paused in front of the fire, looking at him. "I think I have. At least, I've found an account of an incident involving both Jamin Bluecloak and one of the Stones from before the time he turned traitor." She turned her head to look towards the window. "It may be all the hints we need," she said softly. "And I don't like where it's pointing us."

"Let me hear it," he said, laying his book down open face down and coming over to stand beside the fire. He twitched his cloak over his arm away from the gently lapping flames and leaned back against the mantelpiece, stretching his cramped neck.

She sat down cross-legged on the sheepskin and picked up the thin book. "I've been reading a journal kept by a *minyaster* at the Watchtower of the North – Narya Fivering," she said.

"Wasn't that the one Jamin murdered when he stole the Stones?" Brother Claran asked.

She shook her head. "I don't remember. I hope not. They were sweethearts. Anyway, translating from the Old Tongue, this is how it reads. And don't ask me why she used the Old Tongue for her journal. She uses it really well.

'*As I write, day is dawning. It was bitterly cold last night, and a hard one. Jamin and I were keeping watch together, the southwest wind gnawing at us. A storm broke over the mountains and as we watched, it proved to be a demon-storm. We fought them off, but as they retreated, she came. She, Crajaval, the Moon Lady and great goddess of the Wayasti. She came and I collapsed with terror. Jamin, dear brave man that he is, shielded me from her and stood against her. She spoke to him in a voice of sweet ice. "Give it me," she said. "Give me your black jewel." Jamin refused. I watched as she reached out and touched him, her pale glowing hand brushing over his cheek. She is beautiful! Evil as she is, she is so beautiful a woman that any man would desire her and any woman envy. He shivered, then stepped towards her like a man in a trance. I saw his eyes – wide and fixed on her as she seized him. She whispered things to him, then let him go. I got to my feet, praying and readying my rings. Then she left, her ruby lips parted in a smile. Poor Jamin! He was shaking and sweating and his eyes kept searching the place where she vanished. I asked, but he would not tell even me what she said to him. The memory must pain him, poor darling. But the Stone of Wind is safe still and the border about the Kingdom remains. Now I shall sleep, duty done.*'"

Farren whistled slowly between his teeth and stared down at the thick wool pile of the sheepskin. A cold knot tied and untied itself in his stomach. "She asked him for them," he mused. "And later, he stole them."

Azariel half-closed the book and looked up at him, eyes wide and glinting. "I'll wager that Jamin gave them to her after he stole them – the treacherous scum. He fled to the Seranyai-Cheli where she lives."

"At the source of the Illin-Ast, isn't it?" he asked. His mouth twisted into a wry grin. "That's not the only story I've heard about the source of that river." He turned and bent to feed another log into the fire.

"What did she promise him in return, I wonder," said Azariel, firelight flickering on her pale face as she studied the flames.

"She's a love-goddess, isn't she?" he chuckled. "What do you think she gave him?" The fire began to grow unbearably hot on the back of his legs and he dropped down onto the sheepskin beside her. "And I'd wager the same as you, Stormwolf. It makes sense."

"You realise what you'd be staking on that wager, don't you?" said Brother Claran from his corner of the reading room. "You're staking your lives on it. Crajaval must be a mighty spirit if she's the great White Goddess of the Wayasti – and an evil one."

She closed her eyes and leaned her head onto his shoulder. "And if she doesn't have the Stones, then it's a heavy penalty to pay."

Farren slipped his arm around her shoulders and stared into the flames. His mind swam with the stories he had heard about Crajaval, what he knew of her rites and the brief glimpse he had had three years past of another of the Wayasti gods. *Staking our lives on a wager*, he thought. *Gambling with them. Master, I'm no gambler, even with cards. Is that what you demand us to do? I'm willing enough to lay down my life for you, but I wouldn't want to throw it away on a wild hazard. King of Heaven, you know. What do you say? Does she have the Stones? And what do we do?*

"If Janna were here, he'd tell you to go and do something and let the Power speak," said the young monk, cutting through his thoughts. "Let your minds clear."

"And what are we to do?" Azariel's head moved, her chin pushing his cloak forwards over his chest. "Go on reading, even though we think we've found what we're looking for?"

Farren dropped a kiss onto the crown of her head, breathing in the scent of rosemary that always lingered there. "We can take the horses out for today's gallop, Stormwolf. Fresh air to clear our heads. What does the arch *minyaster* say to that?"

"Don't call me that." She raised her head and turned to look at him. "But it's a good idea, Lieutenant Farren Blackarrow." She jumped to her feet and held her hand out to him. "Let's go."

"I hope you come back settled in your minds as to what you're going to do," said Brother Claran. "Have a good ride. Some days, I almost envy your roles in the drama written by the Great Playwright, but not on a rainy day like this one!"

"Enjoy the warmth of your library fire." He threaded his fingers through hers, feeling the tacky dust and grime from the books on her forefinger. She reads quickly and doesn't bother to blow the dust off like I do. Which is why she found that journal and I didn't. She tugged him to his feet and together, they walked out of the library, out of the stone corridors of the monastery and back through the rain to the barracks.

He led the way to the stables and creaked the door open, standing back. She stepped in and he followed her. The stable air was warm and heavy with the smells of horses, manure and hay. He walked down the far right aisle between the hundreds of looseboxes and put his fingers to his lips to whistle shrilly. Two loud neighs came in answer and two heads appeared at the door of a double loosebox halfway down the row. "Princess, Storm, we're here," he called to the two horses. He half ran to the stall and pressed his cheek against Princess's velvety muzzle. "Come on, my lady. Take us out of the city to where we can find some quiet."

"Do you want to talk this business about the Stones and Crajaval through now?" Azariel looked at him over Storm's neck, her black hair almost indistinguishable from the gelding's black mane.

"Yes." He unhooked Princess's bridle from where it hung beside the stall door. "What questions are in your mind?"

She sighed and her stormcloud-blue eyes seemed distant. "I think there's very little question about what happened to the Stones. If we were to read all the books in the Kingdom or out of it, we'd find no heavier hint. It's what to do next that I'm uneasy about."

He opened the stall door and walked in between the hot, pushing bodies of the horses. Princess turned her head and he slipped the bridle over her pricked ears, crooning softly to the chestnut mare. "Well, if Crajaval does have the lost Stones of Protection and we're supposed to bring them back to the Kingdom, then…" His voice trailed off. Then we've got to go and take them back from her, he added mentally. From her! The one they worship as the Great White Goddess. I'm just a man, even if the Power does work through me. What can I do against her?

"We'll discuss it outside the city." She fastened Storm's bridle and tossed the reins over his neck. "I don't want the grooms overhearing us and the gossip spreading before we have decided."

"Especially if I raise my voice," he chuckled. A small pang of shame shot through him. "I'm sorry about my temper, Stormwolf. I hope it won't come to argument." He took Princess by the bridle and led her out of the loosebox to the room where the saddles and other tack were kept. Behind him, Storm's big hooves thudded into the dirt, burying the sound of Azariel's boots.

He quickly saddled Princess and led her outdoors into the cold wind. He swung himself into the saddle and waited while Azariel brought Storm out and mounted. He shot a smile at Azariel, then nudged the mare's sides with his heels. They rode through the jumble of barracks buildings, across the muddy courtyard and out of the gate. Light rain spattered onto his cheeks and bare arms, raising the fine red hairs like the back of an angry cat with the cold. The two horses clopped along the cobbled streets to the city gates, then out into the plains. He reined Princess in and glanced at Azariel. "Where shall we race to today? The three-mile mark again?"

She tossed back the flurry of dark hair across her face and swept her black cloak back from her arm as she pointed across the tree-studded plains. "See the big pine standing alone to the northwest? It's far enough to mark the end of a good race."

"Then, charge!" He stood in the stirrups and clapped heels to Princess. The mare reared and neighed, then sprang into a gallop like an arrow from the bow. He rocked with her smooth swift gait, blending with the horse's motions. Her mane blew back in his face as he bent low and his eyes stung with the cold air and flying rain. The ground blurred green-brown beneath him. He blinked the tears from his eyes and looked between Princess's pricked ears at the massive pine. The thunder of hooves filled his ears, mixed with the squeak and jingle of tack keeping time with the mare's rhythm.

A black shape entered the edge of his vision and Princess snorted. He turned his head and saw Azariel ride past him, hair and cloak streaming like a black river behind her. Mud flew in the air from Storm's hooves as he passed and a cold clod hit him in the arm. He shook it off and urged Princess on.

He ducked under the broken branches of the jagged old pine and drew the mare to a halt. Azariel had dismounted and stood looking up at him, eyes and cheeks brilliant with excitement. He tumbled off the panting mare's back and threw his arms around her. "Well ridden, sweetheart. You and Storm beat us again."

"You gave that fine horse to me," she said, snuggling against him. A pine needle was sticking in her hair and he gently eased it out. "Thank you."

"You deserve him." He bent his head and kissed her cheek. "Now to talk alone together. We can let the horses graze, if they can find much grass worth eating. Come, sit with me under the tree."

He released her and sat with his back against the gnarled trunk of the old pine. He shifted around between the tree roots to find a place where they stopped digging into his legs and leaned back. She flicked her black cloak out behind her and sat down cross-legged on the bed of faded chestnut needles. "Well," she said, looking at him from behind a curtain of hair that half-covered her face, "tell me your thoughts."

He slid his hand down onto her silky hair, catching a glimpse of the onyx and diamond betrothal earring in her left ear as he stroked the black curtain back from her face. A sharp pang of longing shot through him as he sensed the curves of her body calling his hand down. *Not yet,* he told himself. *There's a year and a half yet to wait before I can do that.* He sighed and buried his chilly fingertips in the warmth and damp of her hair. "Stormwolf, it's fair to assume that Jamin gave the Stones to his goddess before they caught him. I don't doubt it and I don't think you do either. Which means we've got to go and get them back somehow. I don't think there's any other way."

"And that's a hard task for just two of us," she interrupted.

"Yes." He twisted a lock of her hair between his fingertips. "A hard task for all of us *minyasti,* even if we all went together."

"Are you suggesting all fifteen of us go and take them from her?"

"It would make sense. Many hounds pull down the boar that gores one hunter, as the proverb says."

Her brow furrowed slightly, then smoothed again. "We're the ones who have been given the task of getting them back, Farren, my beloved. The others have their own duties to perform."

"But what good is guarding the Watchtowers when there's no Stones in them to guard? Soldiers can watch the border. You're the arch *minyaster*. You can order them all to come with us."

She put her forefinger and thumb against her temples and closed her eyes. "I had forgotten that," she said softly. "Why was I given this responsibility? I've got the authority to send all of us to our deaths if I choose to."

"It's less likely to be our deaths if we all go together." A flicker of impatience stirred inside him. *Can't she see that? I know she's proud, independent and stubborn, but I hope she doesn't take it too far.*

"And if it does prove to be the death of us all? Where does that leave the Kingdom if Wayast attacks again with its sorcerers? Can some half-trained acolytes defend it? Who'll tend to the wounded if the healers are dead?" She looked sharply at him. "And you know how the *minyasti* abilities run in the blood. If we all die, then there'll be no others. I've got the potential to pull down all the *minyasti* and the Kingdom with them. I can't do that. I won't. I mustn't."

"You are stubborn, aren't you Stormwolf? But I won't let you throw our lives away. I love you too much for that."

Her eyes rolled and a frown creased her forehead. "I'm not made of porcelain, Farren. I know it's risky, but it's our risk to take." She sat up and stared to one side, toying with a lock of her hair.

He reached for her, running his hand over her knee. "I don't want to see you killed. And if there's some way that I can prevent that happening..."

"We've been in danger before. And we've got to do it again."

"But we don't need to put ourselves at such great risk. There's no need to race into a Yellow Claw unit dressed only in your skin if you can wear armour. Take some others with us."

She dropped the strand she was playing with and whipped her hair behind her shoulders. Her stormcloud-blue eyes glanced at his sharply. "Who? Shall I take all the fighters and leave the Kingdom helpless? I can't do that."

The flicker of impatience inside him grew to a small fire, tightening his chest. *Keep your temper, Blackarrow.* He slid one hand through his hair and roughly grabbed and tugged at it slightly. *I don't want to go off alone and die unless I have to.* "You've sworn to lead the *minyasti*. Who's going to lead them if you die? Janna says you're the strongest fighter."

"Which is why I should go." She shrugged.

He cupped both his hands under her chin and turned her head towards him, trying to control his mounting irritation and to keep his touch gentle. "Don't you dare go off alone," he said softly between bared teeth.

She raised her chin out of his hands as her back stiffened proudly. "I've no intention of going alone. I'm not that reckless."

He smiled. "You're being sensible at last. Now, take a horse-breeder's advice. If you're concerned about losing the abilities that run in the blood – this may sound insulting, but no breeder would butcher his best broodmare to feed the guard dogs."

"I'm not a mare; you're not a stallion," she said indignantly. "Horses don't care who they breed with. People do. *Minyasti* do. The King of Heaven does. Otherwise, I'd have been married off to Arruran Silverhand and borne him a dozen children by now. So I'm glad about that."

He ground his teeth to stop himself wincing. *I know I've got no need to be jealous and think she's been eyeing up Arruran. I'm not that stupid. But why did she have to remind me that he's a better* minyastin *than I am?* "Sorry," he said, slightly sulkily. "I won't say that again. But still, don't throw your life away. Don't throw mine away."

Her eyes blazed at him. "So who's going to do it?" she said in a voice of iron. "Shall I order some of the others off and keep us behind all snug and safe in our cosy little Watchtower? What sort of coward would that make me – and you? Would you rather throw someone else's life away?"

He felt his blood thicken and heat behind his temples. *Stubborn, comparing me with Arruran and now this.* He laid his hand firmly on her shoulder, digging his fingers into her chainmail. "Are you calling me a coward?" he growled.

"It's what you'd be if you sent somebody off to die in your place merely because you're too scared to do it." She pulled back from his hand. Her lips curled back, baring her teeth.

He seized her shoulder again and gripped her tightly. "You dare call me that," he snarled. "Just you dare."

"Let go, will you?" She tossed her head and her eyes burned. "Are you going to be a bully as well? You won't change my mind like that."

He growled wordlessly. Briefly, an urge to slap her on the cheek shot through his mind and his other hand gripped her arm, half from anger and half to stop himself from striking out. *How can she say that? How can she call me a coward like that?* His breath hissed in and out over his bared teeth and the blood pounded at his temples.

"I said to stop that! You're hurting me." Her eyes narrowed. "You reminded me that I am the arch *minyaster*," she said coolly. "You know what will happen to you if you finish losing your temper and hit me, don't you?"

He folded his arms and jerked his head back violently into the trunk of the pine. *That hurt*, he thought, trying to stop the pain showing on his face. *But I'm damned if I'm going to say anything about it now.* "You would say that, wouldn't you?" he said sulkily. "Damn it! You are and you can order me off with you, in spite of what I say. I suppose my opinion doesn't count now that you're up there as one of the High Council."

"Farren – don't say that. Why do you think I'm asking you what you think?" Her voice had lost its hard edge and he looked down at her. Her eyes were lowered and the line of her mouth had relaxed. "I shouldn't have said that about my rank. I don't like having it, and I don't want it to change things between us. I'm sorry."

He let his breath out slowly, anger slowly ebbing away. A small flame of shame burned in his cheeks. "I'm sorry I even thought of hitting you. But you shouldn't have called me that."

She hugged her knees to her chest and laid her head on them, eyes closed. "I'm sorry if you took it that way. I didn't want to call you anything and I know you're not one. All the same, sending someone else off to fight Crajaval while we stayed back would be cowardice. And I'd be the bigger coward of the two."

He let go of her shoulder. "Sweetheart, forgive me. I've got a hell of a temper." He let his arms fall open at his sides and he smiled at her. Her eyes met his and she shuffled over so that she sat sideways in his lap. One of her arms went around his neck and she kissed him on the cheek. He wrapped his arms around her and crushed her tightly against his chest for a few heartbeats. He relaxed, then sat twining his fingers through her hair. "To be honest, I am afraid. I'm afraid of going to face her alone – alone apart from you, that is."

She slid over and sat sideways on his lap, her weight pressing heavily onto his thighs. "We won't be alone, don't forget. We're never alone. And I don't mean the horses. Look at the ring on your finger."

"You're right. Maybe going alone is what we're supposed to do." He wrapped his arms around her and drew her close to his chest so that their chainmail tunics grated together. "But I'm still afraid."

The weight of her head dropped down onto his shoulder. "So am I. But I've got to – we've got to keep remembering that we won't be alone. If the Power has dropped us into this cauldron of hot water – and I'm certain that this is what we're supposed to do – then He'll pull us out again. I have to tell myself that and it's hard having to tell you as well. But how we're to do this, I don't know. That's what I want to think about."

He shrugged and the folds of his cloak fell forwards over his shoulder. "You're right. The Power's with us. But you remember that Horned One, Shayim, back in the Ulfskin-Aza? Even the faint touch of his anger made my blood run cold. And she's more powerful than he is – and more *here*, if you know what I mean. What are we going to face this time?"

"Not sorcerers, at least. They were our chief danger back then." She played with a lock of her hair and her grey-blue eyes stared at a point near his left shoulder. Once or twice her mouth twitched before she looked back up at him and spoke. "I'm afraid of the phantoms. The night I spent fleeing them still chills my blood. It comes back to me in nightmares: the stench, the cold and poor Cloud screaming and running wild with me through the pines. This time, though, we have to ride through them, not away from them…"

"You survived that and you'll have me to keep the horses under control with my gift." He glanced over at the chestnut mare and the black gelding grazing a little way from the sheltering branches of the old pine. A few windblown raindrops hit him on his bare forearms. "I can hold them steady in the face of fear – more or less."

"You're alarming me, quelling my greatest fear as quickly as that." Her eyes flashed at him and her lips, what he could see of them, curved into a smile. "But you'd never be able to do that with all the horses of the *minyasti,* could you? We'll be heading for Moonlady Falls tonight if we keep on like this."

He slid his right hand under her hair while the others linked fingers with hers. The bright blue lapis lazuli stone on her ring was crooked and he nudged it straight. "You make it sound so easy, Stormwolf."

"Not easy. But if there's the faintest flicker of hope that we can return alive and loyal, then we know our duty."

"Loyal?" A cold stray drop of rain fell onto his hand as it wrapped around her.

"Well, Jamin Bluecloak defied her and stayed alive, but he didn't remain loyal long. She may have ways of twisting minds."

"I know you well enough to know that you'd never bend from the path you've chosen. And if you think she can seduce me stupid, she won't. But to return alive – that's possibly another story." He gripped her hand tightly, feeling her callused path against his own. "But we've been set the task by the Power, like you said." He sighed and looked up. "There must be hope that we'll get there and back with them. There must be."

Her eyes fixed his. Fighting lightning played in the stormcloud blue depths. "There is, Farren Blackarrow, my beloved. And you know it." Her breath hissed slowly out of her mouth and she looked down. "It's settled. I wasn't in much doubt, but I had to make myself sure. We're going. Just the two of us."

He let go of her hand and took her face between his hands, turning her face up to look at him. "The two of us. And I'll fight beside you as I promised." He kissed her hard and felt the ferocity of her response. He drew back, feeling the lift and fall of her chest against his own. A sliver of desire screamed at him to kiss and caress her more and more, but he willed it silent. "It's settled." Lightly, he tugged a lock of her hair. "Come on. Let's put the horses through their paces and have a quick duel before we go back."

***

"You're going to what?" Janna stared at them, his knuckles white about his goblet as he sat at the table in the *minyasti* common room. "May the King of Heaven watch over you if you do! Are you mad? The Great White Goddess of the Wayasti! I've warned you about the phantoms, Azariel, and they're enemies enough. What about their mistress?"

"I faced and escaped the phantoms, and I could have stood firm and fought them if poor old Cloud hadn't been so afraid." She looked up from her cup and caught Farren's eye. "That won't be so dangerous now that I'm riding out against them with Farren."

"I still think you're walking to your deaths." He put his goblet down, puffed out his cheeks, then let his breath out slowly. "But if the Master has sent you, you must, you must. But I still mean it – may the King of Heaven watch over you. You'll never do it without Him."

"I agree," she replied. "I'm not that much of a fool."

"Definitely not." Taramaritan came out of her corner, one hand on her hip. "You're the arch *minyaster*. If anyone can do it – and somebody's got to – it's you." She folded her arms across her full bosom. "But don't go unprepared. I've been meaning to make you a new attack ring, Azariel, now that you're our leader. Now I can't put it off any longer. The afternoon is young; I've got time to do it today if I work like a madwoman." She turned her head and smiled at Farren, deepening the small furrows around her green eyes. "I'll make one for you, too. You'll both need rings of as high a calibre and purity as you can manage. Come here, both of you."

Farren drained his cup of the last half-cold dregs of the camomile tisane and put it down on the table. His chair squeaked as he pushed it back and went to stand beside Azariel in front of the guild Ringsmith. The blonde woman put both hands on Azariel's shoulders. "Look at me," she said. "Let me read you." Taramaritan looked intently at Azariel, then her thick lips parted in a smile. "No question about what yours will be, arch *minyaster*. Opal set in silver – the strongest. And I've got a gem ready that I think you'll like. Now for you, Farren."

Her hands rested on his shoulders and he raised his eyes to her. She gazed piercingly at him and he shifted his feet uncomfortably. *I don't like women I don't know well looking at me like this.* At last, the green-gold irises of her eyes flicked away from him and her hands left his shoulders. He reached past Azariel's cloak and felt for her hand. "Emerald for you this time, Farren," the Ringsmith said. "You've grown since you were a new-made *minyastin*. And silver. I've never had to make a gold ring yet. I don't know why I keep the ingots in the Ringsmith's chest. However, I'd better get to work and light the furnaces for the crucible. At least I don't have to cut anything and I've got your measurements. You two go and pack. I'll try to have them ready this evening after supper. I suppose you'll want to be on the march as soon as you can."

"Of course." Azariel shrugged her shoulders, stirring the folds of black about her shoulders. "What else is there for us to do here in the capital now? We'll leave you to your work while we do ours." She cocked her head to one side and smiled at him. "Come on, beloved."

He drew her arm through his and walked towards the door. "I'll race you in packing our bags with our winter gear. Then I'll meet you over at the warehouse to get the other odds and ends we'll need."

For the rest of the afternoon, he worked hard, folding gear, stowing gear in saddlebags and strapping them to Princess's saddle. He pulled the last strap tight and stood back. He looked at the heavily laden saddle and picked vaguely at a fragment of dirt under his fingernails. *All done. I hope Princess can travel fast enough with all the extra gear as well as me. A spare quiver of arrows, warm clothing, blankets, ropes, plenty of food and all the rest of it. She's a strong mare and she'll have to be. At least Storm's carrying the lighter rider as well as the tent.* He watched Azariel hoist up the roll of canvas tent and strap it behind the saddle. *She's right that we'll need to keep watch at all times in the night, so we only need the one.* "I hope the quartermaster in the warehouse isn't getting filthy ideas about what we'll be doing, seeing as we only asked for one tent."

"Oh, let him think what he likes," she said, slipping the tongue of the buckle into place. If we die, then it doesn't matter what people say, because we won't hear them. And if we return, then it's proof we haven't been indulging in a bit of slap and tickle. I trust you to behave yourself and you can trust me." She dusted her hands off and rested one on the hilt of her sword. "Now we've finished – or at least we're ready to begin."

***

He stood alone in his bedroom, bare to the waist and shivering slightly. He looked up at the branched and spiked antlers of the elk's head displayed on the wall as the yellow light of a single candle caught them. Somewhere outside, a dog barked. *Taking that trophy gave us that brief glimpse of Shayim the Horned, Crajaval's consort. And I survived that.* He turned his new emerald ring towards the candle and watched the golden light glint off and through the facets of the arrowhead-shaped stone and the silver couching it. He took it off his left hand, then drew off the onyx ring from his right and swapped them over. *Now I can use one hand for my sword and one for the emerald if it comes to a fight. When it comes.* He looked again at the trophy head on the wall. *When it comes. And, Master, help us both then!*

CHAPTER THREE

Azariel pulled her cloak closer about her as the light rain spattered about her. The gates on the western wall of the city thudded closed behind her, followed by the soft snick of the bolts closing. A strong wind was blowing from the southwest, pushing her cloak against her body, and streaming her hair out on either side of her face and chilling the back of her head. She swept her hair around her left shoulder and looked across at Farren on her right. He nodded to her and they nudged their horses on. She turned Storm northwards and followed the wall around the city. The heavily laden gearbags pressed into the backs of her legs. They rounded the end of the wall into the shelter of the north side of the city and began to ride eastwards towards the Illin-Ast. Grey clouds swirled in a thick writhing mantle between the earth and the sun, and the mountains to the north were hidden in a dark grey cloak of cloud.

She worked her fingers around inside her black fur-trimmed gloves. *I'm glad to have them, but I half wish I could feel the leather of the reins between my fingers instead.* She reached behind her shoulder and pulled the hood of her black cloak over her head. The warm wool blanketed her chilled ears pleasantly, warming feeling back into them. She peered around the edge of her cloak at Farren and saw that he also had his face hidden inside his red cloak. "So much for the warmer weather we thought would come today," she said to the sharp tip of his nose, all she could see of his face. "What is it going to be like in the mountains?"

"Worse." He turned his head and looked at her. "Perhaps we're crazy, setting out into the mountains with winter approaching." He raised one hand and pushed the edge of his hood back from his forehead and shrugged. "Mind you, hunters do it all the time – it's the season for stags. We're hunting too, in a way."

Storm tossed his head and snorted, tugging at the reins. Through the gloves, she felt the gelding's impatience. Smiling, she patted his neck, then looked back at Farren. "We'll have reached the depths of winter by the time we reach the mountains if we keep the horses at a walk like this. Storm's eager to run. Shall we give them their heads and let them run to warm themselves up?"

His hood fell across his eyes again and he pushed it back up. "I'd love a good gallop, but we'd better not. We can't let them sweat; they'd chill off too much in this wind once they'd stopped running. Let's give them an easy canter for a bit, but not for too long."

She tapped Storm's sides with her heels. The black gelding whinnied and strode into a trot, pulling against her hands. "Steady, Storm," she said, rising and falling with his big steps. "Don't charge off into a gallop now. You've a long road to take us on, and few or no stables on the way." She clapped him on the neck, longing for the touch of horsehair and living flesh under her hands instead of the gloves. "Save your strength for the mountains – but you can run for a bit." She slackened the reins a little and swung with him into a canter.

They reached the eastern edge of the city and rode onto the main road leading to the eastern border, still keeping the horses at a brisk pace. The cold south wind, clean with the scent of rain, whipped about them. Ahead, she saw another traveller along the King's Highway coming the other way and heard the rumble of iron cartwheels over the cobblestones. She checked Storm to a trot and turned him onto the bare beaten earth beside the road, splattering through the broad puddles lying in the dips and ruts in the mud. Farren looked up at her then turned Princess in beside her, dodging around a milestone. Side by side, they checked their horses to a walk. The pony-cart drew near them, piled high with hides. The driver looked up and raised his heavily gloved hand to them in greeting. "A nasty morning, soldiers," he called. 'I'd better warn you that there's a herd of cattle being driven to market the other way, and they're all over the road and skittish. Driver's in a foul mood, too. Watch out."

"Thank you," Farren said in answer as the cart rumbled past. "I hope your hides fetch a good price in the markets."

They rode along the edge of the highway, dodging the herd of cattlebeasts and the other livestock being driven along the King's Highway to the markets in the capital. Other carts passed, the heavy iron wheels almost drowning the steady thud of horsehooves on mud with their dull thunder. The rain grew heavier, changing from light drizzle to heavy driving beads of water that battered the cobblestones and swelled slick, dark puddles on the road. The reeking muck left by the beasts began to wash off the stones into the weedy cracks and coarse grass at the road's edge. She glanced down and saw Storm's legs plastered with mud and filth.

Around midday, they entered a small village. "Let's find an inn," said Farren. "Time for a halt and something hot to eat as well. We'll ask them to send something hot out to the horses as well."

She shook the hood back from her head, rain pelting her face as she scanned the village streets. A large building with a sign hanging by the door stood by the side of the highway, a trough and hitching posts beside it. "Well, there's the inn," she said, pointing to it. "And the smoke from the chimney's a welcome sight. I hope it's not just the kitchen fire and they've got a fire in the taproom as well."

She reined Storm in and dismounted by the trough. She opened one of the saddlebags and found a rope to hitch the gelding to one of the metal rings in the hitching-post. She closed the leather bag and heaved the saddle off his back. "You'll need to stay warm, old fellow," she said, clapping him on the withers. "I'll open your saddleblanket over your back for you and I hope you don't try to eat it like poor old Cloud used to do." She unfolded the warm, grimy blanket that had been underneath the saddle, inhaling the sweet-sharp nutty aroma of horse-sweat. She yanked her gloves off with her teeth and spread the blanket over his back, feeling the short, jabby hairs caught in it prickle her hands, and knotted the blanket around his neck. "There."

She stood back from the gelding and watched Farren and Princess. He was still petting and crooning to the mare as he unsaddled and blanketed her, his cheek pressed against the mare's neck so that her mane blended with his red hair. *The red rider and his red horse,* she thought, smiling. "I'll see you inside, beloved," she said, then walked towards the steps that led up to the inn door.

She ducked under the brightly painted inn sign, quickly taking in the picture of a bundle of full-eared grain and the words "The Wheatsheaf." As she put her hand on the doorhandle, she heard footsteps behind her. She turned, hearing a thud and a yelp. Farren stood beside her, rubbing his head. "What happened to you?" she asked.

"A strong wind and a sturdy inn-sign," he replied. Some of the skin on his forehead was reddened. "Let's go inside." He drew off his gloves and slipped his hand into hers.

She turned the handle and pushed the door open. Blissfully warm air, sweet with the scent of ale, wrapped around her as she stepped inside. A large open fire crackled on the hearth in one corner and the warm light shone off the blue glassware and pottery-ware arranged on the windowsills and round tables. A grey-haired woman sat in a large horsehide armchair by the fire, busily crocheting lace with a tabby cat curled at her feet. She looked up as they came in and put the lace down on the blanket spread over her knees. "Good day to you, soldiers," she said. 'What can Magda Brewer do for you?"

"A hot meal for two and something warm for two horses, thank you," Farren said. The tabby by the woman's feet uncurled itself and stretched its fore and hind legs, then came over purring to wind itself about his legs.

"Certainly." Magda put her lacework in a basket by the chair and heaved herself up. "Take a seat and I'll see what I've got in the pots. I'll send Tom out to see to your steeds." She cupped her hands to her mouth and turned towards the bar. "Tom! Tom! Customers with horses that need hot bran mash!" She smiled at them as thuds and clatters came from the back rooms. "Will you take a drink with your meal, soldiers? I've got some good Sersaran wine mulling – just the thing to warm you up on a rainy day. And there's ale, both light and strong, not to mention our cider. What will you have?"

Azariel caught Farren's eye. "Hot spiced wine sounds delicious to me. What about you? Or will you choose the cider, as usual?"

He bent down to stroke the tabby under the chin. "It's a close race between those horses, but I think the wine wins, thank you." The cat raised its head, exposing as much throat as it could and whiskers quivering ecstatically. "How much will that come to? We'll pay you now."

"Let me see..." Magda's face crinkled into a frown and one eyebrow arched as she vaguely counted on her fingers and stared into the distance. "Three stars and eight crowns, all told." She smiled and winked at Azariel. "You've caught a good man there, lass. Always trust a man who likes cats to be a good husband. We've seven at the Wheatsheaf, and we need every one of them to keep down the rats and mice."

Azariel loosened the strings of the pouch hanging at her belt beside her dagger and fished around for her share of the money. She paid the innkeeper and sat down at one of the tables near the fire. She leaned across the table to take Farren's hand as he sat down opposite her. A black and white cat emerged from behind the bar and joined the tabby in winding itself around Farren's legs.

"Yes, I have caught a good man indeed," she said, looking into his dark eyes as the firelight flickered on them. A smile played on his lips and a warm rush of longing flooded her. "Handsome," she whispered.

Magda Brewer brought them a large helping each of thick, steaming mutton broth with plenty of slices of warm bread spread generously with butter. "Thank you and thank the King of Heaven," she said as the old woman set it before them. She ate gratefully, feeling the warmth of the salty broth spread throughout her body. She lingered over the meal, then sat back in her chair, sipping at her beaker of hot spiced wine as she stared into the fire.

Farren set down his beaker and gently placed his hand over hers. "Well, Stormwolf, we can't stay here forever in front of the fire. We won't get to Illinlebh-Yan until nightfall if we linger on. We started out late, too." He waited while she gulped down the rest of the sweet wine and chuckled as she stifled a sneeze as too much spice washed around the back of her mouth. He squeezed her hand then got to his feet, disturbing three ginger cats and a fat, fluffy tortoiseshell. "Thank you for an excellent meal and drink, Magda Brewer. We must ride on – though your fireside's tempting."

"Thank you for your custom, soldiers." She stood up from her armchair, hands on hips. "Make sure you tell our cats to stay here instead of following you. They look fit to tag at your heels to the ends of the earth and back again."

Azariel led the way outside, a pleasant glow of warmth burning deep inside her. Cold air struck her in the face and she shivered briefly, drawing her gloves back on. The rain had stopped falling and the dark cloud had dragged its trailing pillars away. Hurriedly, they resaddled their horses and set off along the rain-slick highway towards the Illin-Ast and the twin towns of Illinlebh-Yan and Illinlebh-Zan. She pulled her cloak about her and settled into the gentle rocking rhythm of Storm's walk.

Dark was falling and the clouds had dragged the rain over them often by the time they reached Illinlebh-yan, the town on the western bank of the river. Through the town gates they saw the lights of houses burning against the cold and darkness. "Time to find a place for the night," she said, stretching a cramped muscle in her shoulder. "The barracks, I suppose. They're in the centre of town."

"At last. My cloak's wet through." He shook his hood back from his head and it slumped down in thick folds around his neck.

They followed the straight streets through the houses to the town square. She reined Storm in under the barracks gates and waited, hugging warmth to herself while Farren dismounted and knocked at the solid wooden gate. A peephole in the centre of the gate was pulled open and a soldier looked through. "Who are you and what do you want?" he asked.

"Lieutenant Farren Blackarrow and Azariel Stormwolf come from the capital," he replied. "We're looking for beds for the night."

"It's not up to me, sir," the soldier replied. The peephole closed and the gate opened. The soldier saluted as Farren and Azariel rode in. "I'll take you to the Lieutenant-Colonel and you can report in. Follow me."

Azariel rode through the gate behind the sentry. "Where are the stables?" she asked as she dismounted beside a hitching-post. "Our horses are cold and tired too." She hitched Storm to it and folded the blanket out over him.

The sentry paused, one hand on the door of the main building. "Leave them out here and I'll see them stabled. If you're staying. I think we've got stalls free – but I'm not sure." They followed him into the big limestone building and down the dimly lit corridor. He knocked at a door and waited for the answer.

The sentry drew his sword in salute as he opened the door with his other hand. "Lieutenant-Colonel Ahren – Lieutenant Farren Blackarrow and Azariel Stormwolf."

"Thank you, David," answered a voice inside the office. "You may go."

"Will they be staying, sir? Their horses..?"

"Stable them, thanks,"

The sentry left and Azariel took Farren's hand as they pressed through the door into the room. Lieutenant-Colonel Ahren was on his feet, a wide smile spread over his freckled face and his sandy hair ruffled. "It's a pleasure to see you both again," he said. He shook Farren's hand, on hand on his shoulder, then gave her a light embrace of welcome. She shook her hair back from her face and smiled at him as he let go and she pulled back. Ahren glanced at Farren, eyes flicking quickly down, then up again. "When did you get your silver star, Farren? And what for?"

"Four days ago for that business during the war with the Wayasti general," Farren replied, reaching out an arm and coiling it snugly around Azariel's waist. "I'm surprised you haven't been given the Colonel's laurels for your work with the firewall."

He shook his head. "Not yet, Farren." He grinned again and looked up at Azariel. "And where did this black cloak come from? Don't tell me you're the..."

"The arch *minyaster*. I am." She drew herself up to her full height and twitched the cloak back as the damp wool brushed her forearms.

"Congratulations, Azariel," he said softly. "You've come a long way from the shy girl you were five years ago when I first met you."

Her shoulders slumped. "Don't dig up too much of the past," she said, setting her teeth on edge. "I'm sorry you had to put up with a raw, highly-strung chit like me in your division."

"And I'm sorry you had the blundering fool I was as a commander. But I won't dig it all up, as you've said." He smoothed his sandy hair flat with one hand. "Now, what brings you here?"

"We're on our way to accomplish something," she said. "It's dangerous. Possibly the most dangerous anyone could go on." She gazed at the collection of smooth stones on his desk and let out a long slow breath between her teeth. *And maybe this is the last time we meet.*

"And we need a place for the night," cut in Farren. "Not that that's the dangerous undertaking!"

"You haven't seen some of my lads and lasses, obviously," chuckled Ahren. "I bet you want some dinner, too. Anyway, I'll arrange places for the two of you. You can eat in here and tell me what you're up to while you're having it. Excuse me." He walked past them into the corridor, half-closing the door behind him. She heard his footsteps on the stone floor, then his voice calling. After a pause, the muffled sound of talking and footsteps came through the door, then Ahren reappeared. "All sorted out," he said. "I hope you don't mind cold meat and bread."

"Not at all," Farren's arm tightened around her waist and his fingers kneaded the links of her chainmail into her stomach as he talked. "As long as there's something to drink as well."

"There is; don't worry." Ahren sat behind the desk and began fidgeting with the collection of pebbles. After a while, a soldier dashed into the room with a tray, panting. "Here y'are, sir," he said, then set the tray down and left the room as quickly as he had come.

"Well, here's your dinner," Ahren said. "Thank the King of Heaven for his gifts." He got up from behind his desk and fetched a couple of three-legged stools from one corner. "Sit down, you two, and help yourselves." He waited while she slipped out of Farren's embrace and sat on one of the stools. "Now, what are you up to? Have the Nightravens dug up another Yellow Claw headquarters in the woods?"

"Not this time." Farren paused, a slice of meat and bread halfway to his mouth. "We've told you about the lost Stones of Protection that used to guard the Kingdom's borders, haven't we? We think Crajaval has them in the Seranyai-Cheli at the source of the Illin-ast where she is. We've got to get the Stones back."

The blood drained from Ahren's face, making his freckles stand out even more, and he dropped the pebble he was toying with. "You're mad," he said quietly. "Haven't you heard what they say about her? Or have you lived too far west or south? But surely – you've had dealings with the Wayasti. You know that she's their goddess?"

"I grew up not far from 'Yan," said Farren. "I know the stories around. But I've also learned that the tales children tell to send shivers up each others' spines aren't always true." He caught Azariel's eye and chuckled. "All those gruesome tales about werewolves – or shapeshifters! – for example."

"Don't brush it off lightly." Ahren's shoulders shuddered, stirring his cloak. "I've heard enough as a grown man about the phantoms that roam the foothills at night. Everyone knows not to go near the mountains east of the Ulfskin-aza after dark. I've heard them myself – the phantoms, not the tales –and the sound comes back to me in nightmares. Even memories of the war aren't that frightening, and they're bad enough."

Azariel gulped down her mouthful of meat and bread. *He didn't see Shayim that time three years ago.* She tossed a wandering strand of hair back from her face, a small, reckless lightning-shiver of courage flashing down her backbone. "I have seen and heard them," she said. "And fought them. And I'm alive enough to talk about them. We're not taking it lightly." She sighed and closed her eyes for a few seconds. *The sound of them. That horrible shrieking that never stops. I remember that only too well.* "But we've been set the task and we can't turn back from it. Not if we want to keep any honour." She bent her head over the bread and meat she held and tore at it with her teeth. *All the same, I hope we come back alive.*

Ahren fell silent. "I suppose you're right," he said at last, picking up the pebble he had dropped. "The Power protect you both."

She shot a glance at Farren and he smiled back at her. "We're counting on that," she said. She winked, then ate the last morsel of food.

Ahren sighed and shook his head. Then he looked up again quickly. "If you've finished eating, I shouldn't keep you standing around talking when you're wet and tired. I'll get someone to show you to the dorms. We've got a lot of married couples here, so the beds in the single dorms are hardly ever full. You'll find places easily – at least this time. If you come back looking for a room when you're married, it may be a different story."

He went out into the corridor again and called loudly. A red-headed lad in a very new uniform came through the door with him, finishing a salute. "Stefan," said Ahren, "take these two to the dorms."

"Yes, sir!" said Stefan, saluting again, then sheathing his sword awkwardly. He led them out of the office and down a long series of corridors. He paused by a big set of double doors. "Here's the ladies' room, ma'am," he said, looking up at her. "I'll bid you goodnight here, then I'll take you, sir, to ours." He turned to Farren and grinned nervously.

Farren caught her gently by the arm and drew her to himself. One arm coiled warm and supporting around her back and his other hand cupped lightly under her chin. "Goodnight, sweetheart," he said softly. She pressed against him, locking her arms about him as he drew her close and pressed his lips tenderly against hers.

"Sleep well, beloved, she replied in a whisper, gently running a finger over the short stubble on his cheeks. She looked into his dark brown eyes and felt the blood at her temples and wrists pulse momentarily with desire. *King of Heaven, how did such a handsome man choose me?* "Enjoy the last night in a proper bed with sheets you'll have for a while." A picture filled her mind of Farren lying bare-chested beside her, his arms around her and cool sheets over them both. *Later,* she told herself. She kissed him warmly again, then turned and went into the women's dorms.

She looked around her at the other women in the bunk-lined hall as she closed the door behind her. There were between forty and fifty other women, all turning towards her, curiosity and welcome in their eyes. She walked slowly towards them, her clothes warm and wet against her. *Why is it that I can face hostile people bravely, but my heart sinks when confronted with friendly ones?* She swallowed and her eyes flicked around the circle as the women ringed her.

"You must be the woman staying here overnight," said one. "News gets around quickly here. Who are you? I'm Laurelin."

"And what are you doing here?" asked another.

"My name is Azariel Stormwolf," she answered. "I'm lodging here tonight on my way up the river with my betrothed Farren Blackarrow."

"With him?" said a third woman. "Not in here, you won't!"

"Shut your mouth, Gwennis," said Laurelin. "She's a *minyaster*. Don't mind her, Azariel. I remember seeing you in those battles against Wayast back in the springtime. I remember your face – and your hair. Except you had a normal cloak on, not that black one you've got on now."

Azariel tugged the damp wool on her shoulders and looked down at it, a twinge of pride shooting through her. *Master, forgive me, but I am proud of the cloak I wear.* "It's the arch *minyaster's* cloak," she said aloud. "Janna Greyhawk has given up the post."

"Well, congratulations," said Laurelin. "Come and join us. There's at least three decks of cards somewhere, or you can just sit and talk."

"Thank you," she replied, smiling.

***

Farren looked at the array of cards in his hand and studied them. *Ace of shields, Ace of stars, King, Queen and nine of crowns and the other five are low crescents. Six No Trumps, maybe, or I'll leave it for my partner to bid.* He sat back and looked at the other three men about the card table. "So where are you off to, Farren?" asked the middle-aged soldier partnering him.

Farren grinned at him over his hand of cards. *Is that an attempt at table-talk, or only conversation?* "Oh, I'm just off up the river to do something."

"What are you doing?" asked another man. "After Claws?"

"Don't push him, Zorfa," said the older soldier. "He might not be allowed to tell you."

"It's nothing secret," said Farren lightly, playing with his earring with his free hand and watching the faces of the other men. "I'm not a Nightraven. I'm only going to steal the lost Stones of Protection off Crajaval in the Seranyai-Cheli."

The card players and the few watchers stared at him. A wave of silence rippled out, drowning the talk in the dormitory. "You're joking, right?" said Zorfa, breaking the silence.

"No, I'm dead serious."

"You'll be dead, all right," said another man. "You'll never get past the phantoms. And even if you do, who knows what you'll find beyond them?"

"Nobody escapes the phantoms if they go into the hills at night," said a man outside the circle of players, coming closer. "Nobody goes into the hills at night at all. Maybe one or two have by accident. But nobody ever went there deliberately – or returned if they did. Ask anyone from the guardposts on the northeastern borders."

He looked at the man. "My wife-to-be, Azariel, has been there at night, met the phantoms and fought them. And she's riding with me."

"She's brave! Braver than all others I've heard of."

"You sure you want to marry her still?" called somebody. "You'll never teach a woman like that who's master." A roar of laughter went up and he grinned wryly. *Azariel, Azariel, of course I want you*, he thought.

"I've heard of one that went a second time," said a soldier with the rolling accent of Helmn, the country to the east of the Kingdom. "It was when I was stationed in one of the northern guardposts near the Illin-Ast..."

"Tell us a good one, Bryhtnoth," said one of the card players. "Shove the cards down. They can wait."

"As I was saying," Bryhtnoth continued, "when I was up there, we knew this hunter. He was going into the mountains during the daytime – which is safe enough; it's only after dark that the danger begins. Anyway, one day, he stayed too long. We heard him at midnight, battering on the door of the guardpost and screaming for help. We let him in. He was half-mad with fright – pale as a ghost, he'd wet himself and he sat there gibbering for the rest of the night. But he was off into the mountains again the next day – in the late afternoon, of all times to go! Said that he'd left a good day's bag up there. Well, we never saw him again, but some of our lot went to look. We found a knife, a few bearskins and a set of footprints running south. Then nothing. They must have got him, poor beggar."

"Well, I've heard another story about the phantoms," another soldier said, coming out of one corner. He began to tell his tale, then others joined in.

Farren listened, head and eyelids growing heavy with sleep. *I don't know what to make of all these tales about headless men, people turned into stone, packs of burning hellhounds and so forth, but I want to go to sleep.* He quietly got to his feet and slipped out unnoticed from the circle of taletellers. He found a spare bunk and made himself comfortable, then drifted into sleep, the rise and fall of the storytellers' voices lulling him.

***

The next morning, the southwesterly wind still whined across the rooftops and pushed torn grey clouds across the sky. It blew coldly through his hair and across the bare skin on his forearms. He rubbed the cold metal of the thick silver bracelets around his wrists as he sat astride Princess, waiting for the city gates to open. His cloak, mostly dry after being spread out overnight, sat comfortingly warm about his shoulders and neck. He pulled it around his body. He glanced at the sentry who busily worked the bars and bolts, then looked back up at Azariel beside him. The wind blew a flurry of black hair across her face and he felt his heart turn to water inside him. *My love, my beauty,* he thought, edging Princess towards her slightly. *Such pale skin and such dark hair, with lips curved as a bow and red like sunset. And eyes like lightning!* She tossed her head and the hair flicked back from her face as she turned to look at him. He smiled at her, letting his breath out slowly, hearing the creak of the gate swinging open.

He turned Princess towards the gate and the mare walked through it into the grass, heading around the city towards the bank of the Illin-Ast, then north. The cold wind carried a tang of woodsmoke from the city, faintly hazing the air as the smoke billowed out to the plains. A few patches of clear, cold blue sky were showing through the clouds, and on the plains ahead of them, patterns of sunlight and shadow whirled and shifted. They began to follow the line of the river, following the willow-lined banks towards the mountains. After about an hour's riding, the river curled away before them in a broad curve and a pang of recognition shot through him. *That curve in the river, that slight rise a few hundred yards from the course of the river. We're nearing my old home.*

"Do you want to go and pay a visit?" Azariel asked. "I can see the high bank you're looking at. Do you want to go and tell your family what you're doing?"

He smiled, then shook his head. "We wouldn't if we were riding with other soldiers somewhere. I don't know; maybe I should tell them. We may never return alive – unless the Power protects us. Which, of course, He does. But then..." He broke off in a snort of laughter. "I remember only too well what my brother and sisters did to me when I tried to do something lethal, and they might do it again."

Her lips twitched back in a smile, baring her even white teeth. "What happened – and what were you doing?"

"Firalina, Anna and Yvain tied me to a tree when I told them I was going to ride an unbroken stallion. It's just as well they did, as that stallion, whatever his name was, was extremely vicious and Father had to kill him." He ran his hand through his hair and looked at the slope and spread of grass. One or two horses were grazing at the crest of the rise. "Of course I could tame the stallion if I saw it now, but my Gift hadn't fully developed back then."

She threw back her head and laughed. "They'd have a job catching you and tying you down now, my strong man. Do you want to stop in and see if they do?"

"Well, we're not on leave, so I'm not sure we ought to." Some of the horses on the slope raised their heads from the grass and looked down towards them. *We're so close and I might never have the chance again.* He clenched his hands around the reins, feeling the unfamiliar ring on his left hand dig into the calluses on his palm beneath his gloves. "What am I thinking?" he said aloud. "We'll be back. We'll be back. And even if we are killed on this adventure, then I'll see them again after death. This isn't the first risk I've taken and it won't be the last, unless we are killed. Come on, Stormwolf. Let's get up the river and we'll tell them about it after we've set the Stones in their places." He tapped Princess's sides with his heels and put her to a brisk trot.

The ghostly disk of the sun hidden behind the silver clouds swung to the zenith. He looked up at the mountains before them as they drew nearer the foothills. A light and bitterly cold breeze, heavy with the tang of snow, drifted past him, sliding icy fingers over his bare skin and into his ears. Clouds hung over the foothills and hid the peaks, an odd patchwork mass of soft yellow, grey, white and apricot. Beneath them, the barely visible upper slopes were patched brown and white with snow. "It looks like more snow will be coming to the hills," he said. "The clouds are heavy enough and it's growing colder."

"Snow as well as phantoms. Well, we knew this wasn't exactly going to be a pleasant ramble."

They followed the course of the braided river to the foothills. The ground rose beneath them and soon he heard Princess's snorts and huffs of breath as she climbed the slopes. The bare trees gradually thinned out and were replaced by the evergreens and wizened mountain plants. Rabbit burrows scarred the hills, and patches of dirty snow lurked in the small hollows hidden from the sun. He shifted his weight forwards to help the mare climb, the saddlehorn pressing into him. The creak of the tack and the slow steady beat of the horses' hooves filled the quiet mountain air as they worked steadily upwards. The rush of the river to their right faded as it dropped away to run through a deep-carved gorge. The cloud grew thicker and the air colder as they climbed through mountainthorns and tussock. Ahead, the cloud lowered to become clammy fog that hid the tussocky slopes in front of them. He reined Princess in and looked behind him. "We must be near the border. Take a last look at the Kingdom – if you can see it." The slopes dropped away to the greens and browns of the plains. A flock of birds circled a grey bare tree, descending one by one. Then the plains faded as mist spun around him. He shivered. "Now for the unknown."

She pushed the edge of her hood back from her face slightly. Her lips, purple with cold, were set in a grim line. "In the name of God Incarnate, then, we'll ride on." She tossed her head back, and laughed defiantly. "But not totally unknown. I've been here before, although everything looks the same in this fog. Come on." She thumped her heels lightly into Storm's sides and rode into the thick grey mass of cloud, with him following her.

The white patch that betrayed the sun shifted to the left, heading westwards as they climbed higher. Tiny beads of moisture silvered Princess's mane and the tips of her shaggy winter coat. The cold damp air swirled around him, feeling as if it had seeped into his bones. The black shape ahead of him resolved itself into Azariel on Storm again, and she held the gelding still. "Do you want to stop somewhere soon?" she asked as he climbed level with her. "I think we're at the top, but I'm not sure."

"Yes." He reined Princess in. "It's time for a halt anyway. She'll start sweating if I keep her going much longer without a break. I suppose Storm's in the same condition." He swung himself off the mare's back, jarring his feet on the hard-frozen ground as he landed. Azariel dismounted beside him and wrapped herself completely in her cloak.

He cautiously walked a little way ahead into the fog and felt the ground level out beneath him. As far as he could see in the fog, fifteen paces to the left and right, the crest of the hill ran away from the river gorge in a ridge. He walked about thirty paces on again and the hillside began to slope down. "We are at the summit," he called out. He paused a few moments, breathing in the mountain air. Faint sound filled his ears: the panting breath of the two horses, the gentle hiss of a light wind through the grass, the moan of wind in trees hidden somewhere down the slope below them and, fainter and further away still, the Illin-Ast. He drew a deep breath and let it out slowly, then walked back up the slope, using the sounds of the horses to guide him.

Azariel held out one hand to him as he returned, a smile in her lips and eyes. A breath of wind, soft and chilling, passed through the thorns and tussocks around them. He came closer and noticed a few flecks of white on the hood of her cloak. More appeared, then he felt something soft and cold fall on his bare forearm. "Snow," he said, brushing it off before taking her hand. "There must be another cloud above this one."

She said nothing, but opened her arms and pressed closely against him, catching the sides of his cloak and pulling it around both of them. He bent his head and felt under her hood with his lips for her forehead. "You're so cold, sweetheart," he murmured, wrapping his arms tightly around her and feeling the icy links of her chainmail under his hands. He kissed her mouth, feeling the chill on her lips, cheeks and nose. A snowflake caught on her eyelashes and he gently brushed it away.

A sweeping noise that sounded like a huge pair of wings hissed through the air overhead. One of the horses neighed and he started back, suddenly tense. Storm and Princess both stood with nostrils quivering and ears laid back as they stared up at the sky. A huge dark shape plummeted down from the cloud, growing steadily more distinct. He seized Princess's bridle and scrambled onto her back. *That's far too big to be an eagle, even a great-eagle. King of Heaven, not a dragon!* The big black shape wheeled again then dived towards them.

"Alphurrhn!" shouted Azariel. He turned his head and saw her mounted and fighting to control Storm. "Get down the slope as fast as we can gallop to cover," she ordered.

He reached for the bow hanging at his saddlehorn and fitted his hand around the familiar grip. "You can't run from them," he called after her as she swung Storm away down the north side of the ridge. "They're nearly as fast as we are – and they can fly. Stay and fight!"

The alphurrhn, a winged mountain bear, plunged down through the fog, huge bat-like wings threshing the air and whirling the flying snow. Princess reared, ears laid flat on her skull. The wind from the bear's wings buffeted his cloak. *No time to shoot. Even if I hit it, it'd kill me.* He gave Princess her head and the mare bolted. For an instant, he saw the open mouth with fangs bared and the big heavy forepaws raised to strike. Then he bent over Princess's neck and let her run, gripping the bow as well as the reins. He heard the snarl behind him, then a heavy thud as the rush and sweep of the bear's wings suddenly stopped.

He brought Princess around in a wide circle and looked back at the alphurrhn. It was lumbering towards him, massive shoulders rising and dipping as it ran, big black wings furled over its back. *The angle's no good for a heart-shot and I daren't aim for its eyes. The only way I can kill this beast is if I let it rise to attack me.* He fumbled for an arrow in the quiver at his belt, twitching it out of its metal clip. Holding Princess still by strength of will and his Gift, he fitted the arrow to the bowstring and watched as the winged bear approached. He began to draw, left shoulder straining back as his right arm pushed the bow forwards.

Ten paces from him, the alphurrhn reared onto its hind legs and roared, spreading its black wings like a sail. The small sight-notch on the belly of his bow aligned with the beast's chest. *There's no way I can miss at this distance,* he thought as the string slipped from his fingers and the arrow hissed through the air. He heard it strike flesh, and as he let Princess rear and spin away from the attacking alphurrhn, he saw the arrow break through behind the bear, landing quivering in the tussock and snow, bright blood spurting behind it.

The bear lumbered on, roaring. Breathing hard, he turned Princess around and watched it. *Not long now. That was a good shot, thank the Power!* Once again, the bear furled its wings and dropped to all fours surging like a small furry hill towards him. More blood spattered and spurted from the wound in the bear's chest. *It's not giving up. It's dying, but it wants to take me with it.* His mind and heart raced as he watched the bear draw closer. *What am I going to do now?*

Instinctively, his left hand reached for a second arrow and nocked it into place. "Round again, my lady," he whispered to the mare. "Maybe a second shot will finish if off quickly." Snorting, shivering, the mare wheeled around. He looked into the almost black eyes of the alphurrhn as it rose onto its hind legs for the attack, forepaws spread wide for the kill. The second arrow leaped from the string. For a second, he saw the bright red feathers against the brown bear's pelt, then the arrow buried itself in the bear with a sharp crack of metal against bone.

The bear lumbered forwards a few paces, wheezing and roaring. Princess backstepped, tugging at the reins and screaming as he removed the touch of his Gift. Slowly, the alphurrhn toppled forwards, bleeding heavily. It struggled to rise a few times, then slumped down, moaning. He lowered his bow and turned his head away, pity shooting through him. *I hate watching an animal die. I'm glad I shot it cleanly both times. My second arrow must be inside it still. Poor beast, it was probably only hungry, and I killed it.* He looked at the dying alphurrhn again. One massive forepaw sprawled across the tussocks, curved claws jutting out from the broad paw. *One blow from that would have killed Princess or me – or Azariel. It's better that it dies rather than us.*

The carcass lay still at last. He hung his bow back in its place and dismounted. He ran his hands over Princess's nose and hugged her neck, feeling the surge and race of his blood calming down. "There, my lady," he murmured. "You're safe now." He patted her one more time, then left her and went to retrieve his first arrow, using the beaten snow and the bloodtrail to guide him. He pulled the arrow out of the snow, cleaned it and fitted it back into the quiver. Shivering with cold and the aftermath of the attack, he walked back to the carcass, tugging off his gloves. *Now to get the second arrow out. My guess is that it struck the shoulderblade or one of the big bones near the wings.* He knelt by the warm corpse of the winged bear and looked at the wound on the beast's chest, mentally drawing a line through the body. He felt carefully along the area of the back between the wings where the line led. The smell of fresh blood stung his nostrils, mixed with the scent of the bear. The point of the arrow, barely above the skin, jabbed his fingers. *I'll have to borrow Azariel's dagger to get that out. Where is she? How are we going to find each other in this fog?*

CHAPTER FOUR

The valley dropped down below the covering of cloud, and the snowflakes whirled around Azariel as Storm cantered down the slope into a pine forest. Above the thunder of hooves, she heard nothing. She glanced back over her shoulder, shaking back the hair that whipped around her face. The fog covered the head of the hill and the fuzzy shape of the alphurrhn was hidden. She leaned back and hauled on the reins. "Enough!" she commanded the gelding. "It's not after us. Slow down!" She tugged at his mouth and slumped her weight backwards, but the gelding sped on. She cuffed him roughly round the neck and sawed at the reins. "Go back," she said. "I've got to help Farren." Ears laid back, Storm came to a half-rearing halt, clouds of breath steaming up in the cold air. "Thanks to you, I've lost my bearings, old fellow." She turned her head and looked back up the slope. A short climb above her, the pines began to fade to hazy dark grey shapes and beyond that hung the thick grey fog. The trees nearby, black and dripping, hissed slightly in the breaths of wind. *I think Storm ran straight down the slope, but with all the trees, I can't be sure.*

She cupped her hands to her mouth. "Farren!" she called. Her shout sounded hollow and dead. A light breeze stirred the pines and made them moan. More drips fell from the green-black needles of the pines. The wind wafted a foul smell into her nostrils, the smell of something long dead. *It's no good. He can't hear me down here.* She looked at the hoofprints gouging the muddy hillside between the tussocks and rocks nearby and sighed. *Storm must have changed course at least once by the looks of those prints and probably many more times on the way down. And he's got a big stride. I could lose the trail too easily in this fog if I tracked it by sight.* She drew a deep breath and looked at the ruts in the mud. *This needs a wolf's nose.*

She swung herself off the gelding's back and rummaged around in the saddlebags for a rope. She fastened it loosely around his neck, then tethered him to a tree. "You wait here," she told him, patting his neck. "I'll come back as soon as I've found the others."

She walked a short way back along the trails of slipping hoofprints, far enough for Storm to begin to look hazy when she glanced back over her shoulder. She drew a deep breath and closed her eyes, concentrating on the shape of her body. *Change,* she told herself. Her limbs swiftly shifted position, realigning themselves around her deepening chest and dwindling hips. Her balance-centre moved and she tottered forwards onto all fours, mind spinning with a wild mixture of animal desires and senses. The sharp green scent of the pines, the stench of death hanging in the air, the small earthy smells of the undergrowth all doubled and trebled in intensity. She smelt Storm's hot body behind her, sharp and rank, and the scent repeated beneath her. She waited a few seconds while her human will and intellect dominated the seething cauldron of instincts and desires, then opened her eyes to a monochrome world. *Not that black and white vision makes much difference here.* She looked down at the rain-beaded tussock and grass by her large shewolf's paws and snuffed at the crushed grasses where Storm had trodden. Then she lifted her muzzle and let a long mournful wolf-howl ring through the woods. *Farren, I'm coming!*

She bent her head to the trail, dog-trotting up the slope. She detected the sharp horse-scent of Storm coming from somewhere slightly to the left. She veered towards it, nose quivering as the scent grew stronger. She followed the track of waxing and waning scent, fur collecting moisture from the long tussocks as she ran. *Will Farren still be up there with the bear or will he have gone elsewhere?* She halted above a hoof-gouge in the mud and felt the thick ruff of hair down the back of her neck rise slightly. *Or is the bear up there standing over his body?* Fear and fury surged in her heart and she bounded up the slope, sides beginning to heave with the effort of her climb. *Farren, Farren, are you alive? Am I too late?*

She reached the first flecks and dapples of snow in the tussocks. More snow was flying around her, catching and settling in her long pelt. She shook it off. The scent of the trail was fresh and sharp in the bitingly cold air. She padded across the thin crust of snow, paws steadily crunching huge prints into it. The scent of horse and human drifted down the slopes on the wind, a new horse-scent. She pricked her ears. *Alive or dead?* She snuffed the air again. Faintly, she caught the smell of blood and bear. Closing her eyes and halting, she drew a deep draught of the scent. *Bear's blood. Thank the Power! He's alive.* Tail a joy-banner behind her, she ran on. She pricked her ears into the wind and heard the slow steady thud of hooves on earth. She bounded over a tussock, guided by sound and scent. She threw back her head and howled.

Ahead, she heard a horse snort, then saw a dark shape come out of the greyness. The scents were overpowering: Princess's lighter horse-smell, sweat, blood, leather and the heart-tugging musky sweetness of Farren. She pulled up and changed shape again. Abruptly, the scents faded and Farren's auburn hair and scarlet cloak above Princess's chestnut, and the white and gold of the snowy tussocks became a vivid shock of colour after the greys and whites of the wolf's world. She got to her feet, brushing snow off her gloves and shaking the hair back from her eyes.

A smile flashed across Farren's face and he checked the chestnut mare. He swung himself off Princess's back and came over to her, arms held out. She ran up the rest of the slope, flinging her arms around him and nuzzling against his cheek. His arms tightened about her chest and waist, almost crushing the breath out of her. Then his grip slackened and she drew a deep breath as the pressure on her ribs eased. "I'm glad to see you," she panted, looking into his face. "The alphurrhn didn't hurt you? Are you all right? I didn't smell your blood, but…"

"It didn't," he replied, dark eyes flashing proudly. "I killed it. And I'm glad to see you. I wasn't sure how I was going to find you with all the fog. But I know you're a good tracker."

"Thank you," she said, dropping her head down to rest on the shoulder of his cloak. The small silver star was cold against her cheek. "I used my Gift."

"I know – I heard the howls and I rode towards them." He chuckled and the corners of his mouth twitched into a wide smile. "What have you done with Storm? You haven't brought him along with you this time."

"I had to concentrate on the trail. And I'm going to have to do it again to lead you down to him."

His hands slid up to her shoulders and she noticed a trace of blood on his forearm. "That's a shame," he said. "I had hoped to have you riding pillion behind me. Warmer, for one thing, and I like being close to you. But never mind. Lead me and I'll follow." He squeezed her shoulders, fingers pressing against her cloak, chainmail and clothes. Then he let go of her and stood back, reaching towards Princess's bridle.

She drew a deep breath and let her body slide into shewolf shape again. The colours faded before her open eyes and her mind span with the red fog of instinct as she fell forward into the snow. A few snowflakes fell on her thick grey pelt and she shook herself before snuffing at the cold winter air. She smelt her own trail and Storm's beneath the sharper scents of Farren and Princess. She turned, slumping her head down to the snow. She padded back down the way she had come, listening to Princess's hoofbeats behind her. She stumbled slightly on the snow and slippery ground, righted herself and ran on.

Storm raised his head as they came towards him. She side-stepped out of Princess's path and shifted shape to walk towards him. She unhitched the black gelding from the tree, gloved fingers fumbling with the damp rope. *It's cold back in my normal shape without fur. But if Farren can put up with it, so can I.* She coiled the rope around her arm and stowed it back in the saddlebags. "Back on the march now, I suppose," she said. "Shall we follow the course of the river or pick a path through the hills?"

"I think we deserve something to eat first after all that excitement." He stretched his arms, then glanced uphill over his shoulder. "Besides, we're well past midday if the sun's anything to go by."

"What sun?" She looked around the foggy forest as the mist swirled through the trees and around them. "This valley hasn't seen the sun for days, by the looks of it."

"Never mind that. But before long, we should start looking for a campsite and hunt wood for a fire tonight. We don't want to get caught unprepared."

"By nightfall or by something worse?" A finger of mist reached coldly down the back of her neck and her hands tightened around Storm's bridle, knuckles whitening. The smell of death seemed to intensify for the space of a heartbeat. She looked around the dripping patch of trees again, seeking the white patch of fog hiding the sun amidst the black tops of the pines. Memory sent a shudder down the back of her neck, heightened by the chill of the mist. "The phantoms will come when daylight goes," she said quietly, trying to shake off the unease. "We have the rest of the afternoon – and it will pass too quickly."

"That's what I'm talking about," he said. "We'd better not stand around in the snow chattering. Ride on a bit, maybe, find a site, then light a fire and cook something to eat." He smiled and ran a gloved hand through his hair. "There's plenty of good eating on a bear and it's a crime to leave all that good meat on the top of the hill for the carrion birds. Can I borrow your dagger?"

"Can you find your way back to where it is and then back down again? Or do you want me and Storm to come too?" She tossed the reins over the gelding's neck and led him out from under the low-hanging branches of the pines.

"The trail's worn enough for me to follow now that Princess has come down it as well as you. I can get back to my kill. But we don't want to waste too much time. I've got to get my arrow out of the carcass as it is. That's not going to leave us much more travelling time if we want to find enough wood for a fire. And the horses are nearly done in for the day." He frowned. "Go to the river and find a campsite for us," he said after a pause. "I won't lose you if you're there, and if you light a fire, then I'll have the smoke to guide me as well."

"Very well then, Lieutenant Farren Blackarrow," she said, winking. She swung herself up onto Storm's back and leaned over to hand him the dagger. "I'll wait for you by the river. And if you can tell the difference between smoke and fog by sight, you're a better judge than I am."

Farren swung Princess around and headed her back up the trail beaten by hooves and paws into the mud and wet grass. *What is it in that valley? It reeks like several week-old carcasses!* Princess scrambled up the slippery tussock, neck lunging forwards as she pulled herself up. The mare halted at the top of the hill, sides heaving and breath steaming. He dismounted and led her along the ridge until he found the dead alphurrhn. The carcass had a thin crust of snow covering the shaggy brown pelt. A crow stood near it, regarding him with beady eyes. "Get away with you," he said, waving his arms at the bird. "There'll be plenty for you when I've finished."

He knelt in the snow beside the beast and pulled his gloves off. *It's easier to wash hands than gloves.* He stuffed them into the hood of his cloak and twisted the heavy wool broadcloth out of the way behind him. *I'll find my arrow first, then cut some meat.* He looked down at the damasked blue steel blade of the dagger as he settled the handle snugly into his left hand. *This long thin blade isn't ideal for this work, but it's better than my sword.* He felt between the beast's wings for the point of the arrow and found the small sharp tip. He drew a deep breath, then began to slit and strip the skin away to expose more of the broadhead. The strong smell of blood filled his nostrils. *I wish I had the time to take a good warm pelt like this one as well as the meat.*

He dug the point of the dagger around the arrowhead and widened the small gash, noticing that one of the blades of the broadhead was bent and blunted. *That will have happened when it struck bone, blast it.* He pressed the sharp metal to one side, seeing and hearing it move in the bear's flesh. *One day, I'll come back here and hunt a bear for its pelt.* With his right hand, he reached down for the shaft beneath the head of the arrow. *I'd like to give a warm thick pelt like this to Azariel.* He smiled as he pictured her lying on a soft fur rug, hair tumbled out around her head. *And I'd like to join her there.* He felt a small hairline of pressure on the pad of his forefinger, then drew his breath sharply as it began to throb and sting. *Cut myself – in all this blood, too. Damn. Serves me right for letting my fancies run away with me.* Through the pain, he felt the smooth round shaft. Gripping it between his thumb and forefinger, he lifted it slightly, then brought the dagger down beneath the broadhead to lever it up further. Slowly, the arrow dragged up, inch by inch as he tugged and twisted it from the bear's body. Bright blood welled up behind it, dripping from the fletchings onto the snow and tussocks. *What a bloody mess! It's a shame it didn't pass right through it this time.*

He drew a deep breath, then looked down at the small slash on his forefinger. Blood covered it, both his own and the alphurrhn's. Something itched on the tip of his nose and he fought the urge to scratch it. *Ignore it and it'll stop. I had better get on with my task. Azariel's waiting.* He stripped away a larger swathe of skin along the alphurrhn's spine and sliced a few rough fillets off the dead beast. He laid the meat carefully down on a clean patch of snow, steam rising from the still-warm flesh.

He cleaned the dagger and his hands as best he could and slipped the bloodied arrow into the quiver. Carefully holding the meat in one hand, he remounted Princess and rode down the slope, bearing right towards the rush and roar of the river. Princess passed through the thick ranks of pines and came to a more open place, a narrow strip of gravel and grass beside the green swirls of the river. The mist seemed lighter here, though the smell of decay was still strong. A plume of smoke rose behind a boulder and he heard Azariel's voice coughing.

He dismounted, boots crunching on gravel. Taking Princess's bridle, he led her towards the boulder. Azariel crouched behind it, bent over a small crackling fire of sticks and cones, carefully balancing a blackened metal billycan over it on some flattish stones. Smoke poured up from between the sticks, rising to mix with the mist overhead. Storm was drinking at the river behind her, unsaddled, unbridled and with his blanket rolled over his back. Azariel looked up as Farren approached her and smiled. "How much have you got?"

"Enough for a good meal. What are you going to do with it?" He let go of the mare's bridle and came over to her with the meat.

"How hungry are you?" She took the meat from him and laid it on a flat rock. "If you don't mind waiting a little longer, I'll hunt down some herbs and stew it. If you're in a hurry, then I'll skewer and roast it over the embers."

"Stew it," he said, unbuckling Princess's bridle. "That beast was excited, so the meat will be tough. And here's your dagger – thank you. One day, I'll remember to put my hunting knife on my uniform belt." He handed the bloodied dagger back to her, holding it carefully at the bottom of the blade. He turned back to unsaddling the mare and grimaced as his hands left dark smears of blood across the leather. "Make sure you don't get you herbs from near wherever that dead thing is. I thought we'd be away from that stench here by the river."

"You won't get away from it anywhere in this accursed valley," she said grimly, head bent over the meat as she cut it into cubes. "That's not something dead – not a cadaver. That's the phantoms you can smell."

"What?" He jerked up sharply, the back of his neck prickling as he scanned the black dripping pines as they faded into the grey haze. "Already? Was I that long?"

"They're not here yet, I don't think." Her eyes met his as she looked up and he saw lightning playing in the storm-grey depths of her gaze. "We've a few hours left to eat, drink and get ready."

He shrugged and clapped Princess on the withers. "I didn't think I took too long. Now, off you go, my lady," he told the horse. "I'm going to clean up properly."

He bent over the river and washed the arrow he had drawn out of the bear. *No good now, except in an emergency or for practice with that blunted blade. I could sharpen it, but...* He fitted it back into the quiver, then opened the pouch at his belt and found the small leather wallet that held his shaving kit. He opened it and took out the small cake of lavender-scented soap and began to wash his hands. The icy water gnawed at his knuckles as he plunged them in and he gritted his teeth as the painful cold lapped around his wrists and the soap stung the cut on his finger. He dried them on the corner of his cloak and knelt by the fire, rubbing life back into his hands beside the crackling yellow flames. A glow of warmth slowly seeped back into his hands and he murmured softly with pleasure.

Azariel laid one hand on his knee. "Now you're ready, will you mind the fire while I hunt out some more stuff to put in the pot."

"Certainly." He sat cross-legged by the fire, staring into the flames. "Be careful – and be quick. He listened as her footsteps faded, scrunching into the ground, then fixed his attention on the lapping and crackling of the fire. *A few hours until nightfall. A few hours until the phantoms come.* He picked up a handful of small sticks and broken pinecones and tossed them into the fire. *I must think of something – how to fight them. I haven't got long.* The flames danced and murmured and ideas played around in his mind. *I will have to ask Azariel to be sure of what to do. She knows more about it than I do – more than anyone else alive.*

The sound of her boots crunching over the gravel jerked him out of his reverie. "Mushrooms, spearmint, sorrel and some rosehips," she said, kneeling down and unwinding the bundle she had made with her cloak. "I don't know how all this will taste, but it will be edible."

"Anything will taste good, as long as it's hot," he said, carefully feeding some sticks into the fire underneath the simmering pot. "Stormwolf, what can the phantoms do? Can they fight us with fire?"

"They didn't try to blast me," she replied, looking up from the pile of foodstuffs she had found. "I think they were trying to catch me and Cloud bodily – trying to seize us. I don't know what they did to poor Cloud when they… after I left him." She drew a deep breath and let it out slowly. "I hope I don't find out. He was a good horse."

He got up and crouched beside her, one arm around her shoulder. "He was. No wonder you miss him," he said softly. "I know I'd be shattered if Princess was lost or killed. I'm sorry." She leaned her head against him and he pressed a kiss into her hair just above her ear. The tangy smell of smoke clung to her hair. "You said fear draws them. Do they sense it, do you think?"

"Probably." She rubbed her face against his, once, then bent back to slicing the mushrooms. "It saved my skin last time. But we can't run now. What are you thinking?"

"I'd rather pick where we're going to fight them than let them hound us."

"They'll come to us wherever we are. The horses will be half mad with panic the moment the phantoms appear. Unless you can take their fear away."

He whistled softly through his teeth and looked over at the two horses grazing and drinking at the river. Wind blew a stinging swirl of smoke into his eyes and mouth. Coughing and rubbing his eyes, he sat down again, reaching behind his head for his gloves and putting them on. "No," he said. "I can't take away the fear of two. Not totally. I can stop them running away, though. That's why I was thinking of using them as bait to draw the phantoms over to us. We won't ride them this time."

She dropped the knife and looked sharply at him, a lock of hair falling across one of her eyes. "That's cruel. I never thought you'd put your horse in danger, let alone use her fear to help us." She pushed the lock of hair back with one hand.

"Can you think of anything else? I'd rather not upset Princess either." He leaned his elbows on his knees and rested his chin on his clenched hands. His rings dug into the hard line of his jawbone and he twisted them inside his gloves so they moved away. "We could ride them, but then we've got to make sure we stay on their backs while we fight. I can hold them still, all right, but they still might buck a bit. If there's too many phantoms to deal with and I drop my concentration then one of them might bolt. We can't let them run mad while we're trying to fight."

"I suppose you're right. You had better tie them up, then, as well as using your Gift on them. There's hundreds of the phantoms, and I'll need as much of your help as you can give in fighting them."

"I feel sorry for both of them. I suppose it can't be helped." He looked around the valley. The mist had lifted slightly, revealing more of the spearhead shapes of the pines. Still the dead smell wafted through the air. "Here's as good a place as any, I suppose. We'll be able to see them coming. I'll tether the horses to the trees here."

She raised her head again, picking up the knife. "Then it's up to the Power – and us."

"There speaks my Stormwolf," he said, smiling. "I've never known you to run from a fight. I'll tether the horses now. They've drunk and there's enough grass under the trees."

He got up from the fire, leaving her throwing the odds and ends into the pot of stew. He took two ropes from out of the saddlebags and knotted a loose loop around each of the horses' necks. "There you go, my lady," he said as he tethered Princess to a tree with a wide reach of grass around it, tugging and testing each knot as he made it. "Wait there." He put his arms around her neck and let her rub her big head against his chainmail as he scratched around her ears. "Poor thing. I don't want you to be frightened, but I'll be looking after you. I only wish and hope you can understand me and remember that when the phantoms come." She whickered softly, nudging and huffing at his bare forearms. "That's my lady," he said. "Enjoy a rest while you can." He patted her on the rump, then turned to tether Storm to the tree next to hers.

He walked back to the fire, brushing horsehair off his hands. Sitting on a stone, he watched while Azariel stirred the stew with a stick, then pulled off his gloves and idly picked at the grime and blood encrusted beneath the nails. After what seemed like hours, Azariel lifted the billycan off the fire and set it on the stones. He stood up and came closer, catching the delicious smell that rose with the steam. "It's done," she said.

They shared the meal out of the billycan. He licked his burned fingers and savoured the odd medley of flavours in the stew. *Quite nice. Salt would improve it. And onions.* He leaned back against a boulder, contentedly watching the horses grazing under the young pines. The light was beginning to fade.

"Don't get too comfortable," she said, placing a few more sticks on the fire then crouching beside him with her hand resting lightly on his knee. "They'll be here soon. Get ready."

He shifted around so that he crouched ready beside her, glancing around the valley. *What do they look like? Where will they come from?* Birds shrilled somewhere in the forest, a last salute to the light. Then silence, apart from the rushing gurgle of the river behind them and the hiss of wind through the pines. One of the horses snorted. The embers of the campfire gleamed red-gold in the fading twilight. "How much longer?" he whispered.

"Any moment."

The sky darkened from pale silver to blue-grey. The shadows and the black trunks of the creaking pines grew darker, pools of darkness against the dewy grass that faintly showed in the little moonlight that penetrated the clouds masking the night sky. From a distance, carried clearly on the cold night air came the call of an owl. Then silence fell again.

A light wind crept softly through the pine trees, making them moan and shudder lightly. Azariel felt the breath lift a lock of her hair slightly and smelt the putrid smell of death and decay on it. The moaning of the trees died away into a small soft sound like a snicker of pale laughter. She listened intently to the sound as it faded to silence. *Was that the branches creaking? Or them?* Every muscle in her body had tensed, every sense grown sharp and alert. Again the nightwind sobbed in the black pines, followed by the same snicker, longer, louder and clearer than before. An icy finger of suspense passed down her backbone. She pressed nearer to Farren. "They're coming," she breathed.

More cackling sounds filled the air. Her eyes darted to and fro, watching the pines. A flicker of white caught the corner of her eye and her heart kicked in her chest. *They're here. Now, Master, help us fight!* She raised her gloved hand and pointed as a pale nebulous patch of light appeared and grew in intensity. Fire began to prickle in her shoulders, slowly travelling in a coruscating river down her arms. Tension and heat grew in her fingertips, and her heart thudded loud and steady in her ears. A second phosphorescent shape joined the first, a short distance to the left. The first had taken on a vaguely human form and it was slowly drifting like smoke towards them through the pines.

Princess lifted her head and neighed, and Azariel heard her hooves shuffle through the grass away from the drifting white shapes. Again the mare neighed, a long, terrified cry ending in a squeal. Storm scrambled to his feet from where he had been resting and she vaguely made out the dark shape of his body rear up, hooves flailing. He darted to one side then pulled up sharply as the rope jerked taut, humming. He squealed and reared again, tossing his head and fighting the rope.

More white shapes appeared and began to drift through the pines, heading towards the two frightened horses. The phantoms gleamed palely all over their humanlike forms, except for two empty spaces in their heads: sightless eyes. She got to her feet, drawing off her gloves. The bitterly cold air nipped at her hands except for the band of silver around her fingers, which pulsed with heat. Farren got to his feet beside her and she saw his eyes flash as her as he nodded. "You lead, arch *minyaster*," he whispered.

She raised her hand, fingers trembling with the pent-up fighting energy in her heart and hands. She stepped forwards, venting her wild wolfish warcry, tossing her hair back from her face. Turquoise flame burst from her hand. It seared through the night air and struck the leading phantom. The figure blazed with pale green-blue fire for a few heartbeats, then faded away to nothingness. The other phantoms paused and turned their empty eyes toward her for an instant. Then they closed back in towards the terrified horses, cackling laughter rising from them.

"They don't want us; they're after the horses." Farren's boots ground on the gravel as he started to run. "Come on, Stormwolf. This is the wrong place for us." He threw brilliant cobalt and yellow flames at the phantoms. "We'd better keep them back from the poor creatures."

She darted after him and spun sharply round short of where Storm tugged and strained at the tether. She smelt the rank sweat of fear on the black gelding and heard his laboured breathing. Blood thundered in her ears and fire prickled in her veins as she bared her teeth and looked into the black eyepits of the phantoms approaching them. Lightning crackled out of her fingertips, shining violet and crimson in the mist. From the corner of her eye, she saw Farren, golden fire flying off his hands and lighting up the sharp angles of his face. The phantoms ringed them, some blazing like torches, then fading. More phantoms drifted through the trunks of the pines, taking the places of the ones that had melted away.

She sidestepped, mouth dry and breath coming short and fast as Storm jerked at the rope beside her, half mad with fear. More fire burned out of her fingertips. *Poor horse. I wish I could stop and comfort him. But if I do, they'll get us all.* The air throbbed with the shrieking laughter of the phantoms and an almost solid wall of ghostly whiteness surrounded them. She drove back a section of the wall with many-coloured fires: leaf-green, silver and scarlet. A gap opened momentarily in the ring where her fire had struck. Then the gap filled with more of the white shapes and black eyes. More fire flooded through her, making her fingers tremble and the silver of her rings burn.

The night dragged on, and still the wall of phantoms surrounded them, shrieking and cackling. Her ears rang with their shrill cries and the frightened screams of the horses. Her arms, legs and shoulders ached and a heavy cloud of weariness filled her mind. *How much longer? How many phantoms are there in these accursed mountains? I can't keep this up for ever. God Incarnate, help me.* She looked over the army of white shapes. Some of them stretched ghostly hands that trailed mist behind them towards the horses, the pines almost visible through the clutching fingers. She burned the pallid hands away with red and blue fire, and squared her shoulder. *I won't stop fighting. I will not. I'll fight until I'm asleep on my feet or until I'm dead or both.*

She staggered backwards a few paces and ran into something soft and warm against her back. "Stormwolf?" Farren's voice said, pale with tiredness. "Stay there. I'll watch this side of the circle and you watch the other."

"I'll be glad to," she said. "I'll lean my back against yours and you can lean on me. Then neither of us will keel over backwards with exhaustion." She gritted her teeth and let a cobalt blue blaze of lightning sear through the darkness from her ring, leaving yellow after-images in the air. "At least here we're safe from being kicked by the horses."

She braced herself against him and forced her knees to stop trembling. *Still more phantoms! When will they stop coming?* Quivering, she let the fire fly from her hand. Time dragged on Numbly, hardly aware of what she was doing, she held herself upright and kept her hands raised and the fire flowing through her. Extreme tiredness tugged at her and made her head spin, intensified by the constant ululation of the phantoms. *How much longer? When will the daylight come?* Still the phantoms shrieked and reached for her and the horses, the noise seeming as if it had gone on forever and always would. *Stand steady,* she urged herself sleepily. *Otherwise, you're dead. Stand firm.*

Dizzily, she looked up at the sky, forcing her heavy, gritty eyelids to stay open. To the east above the river, a faint line of pale light spread across the sky. "Praise the Power," she whispered. "The dawn."

The wash of pale light spread across the sky and the phantoms wavered and hesitated. A gentle breeze blew through the pines, rustling and stirring the branches. The light swelled and spread, revealing the greens and russets of the pine valley, blackened in places where the fire had struck into them. The wind blew from the south again, and the phantoms seemed to boil and fade into it, swept into the mists and vanishing. Birds shrilled in the misty hills beyond the river and a fantail swooped and swirled above the river. Only the smell of the phantoms remained, the faint smell of decay mingling with the green smell of the pines.

Farren drew a deep breath and let it out slowly. The prickling energy in his arms faded, leaving his limbs heavy and weak as wet sand. *Thank you, Master. It's over and we're still all alive.* He lowered his hands, trembling and almost sick with lack of sleep. Azariel's back was warm against his for a few moments longer before she left him. He turned towards her, head heavy and eyes desperate to close. "Stormwolf," he mumbled. "Thank you for being with me through that."

"Thank you," she replied, yawning. "Now for a few hours' sleep before we have to march on again."

"Don't know how you can think of travelling now. But you're right." He stared blearily at the horses, who were still rolling their eyes and covered with a lather of fear-sweat. "And I've got something to do before I can sleep." He gathered the last shreds of strength together and walked towards his mare.

He held out his hand to Princess. "Come on, my lady," he murmured. "It's all right. They've gone. Nothing to hurt you now. Sleep, Princess, my lady. You're safe." The mare's ears pricked up. The white ring around her eyes still showing, she stepped cautiously forwards. He ran his hand over the shaggy winter coat of hair on her neck and combed his fingers through her wiry mane. "Easy, my lady," he said. Calm, warm energy flowed down his hand and he felt it spreading over the horse. An invisible cord of energy and love binding the mare to him tugged at his heart, the touch of his Gift. He leaned his head on her damp neck, warm haze flowing through him. He jerked up sharply, realising he was nearly asleep. The white rim around the mare's eye had gone and she turned her head around to nudge her velvety muzzle against his hand. "There," he said to her. "Rest while I calm your stable-mate."

He used his Gift to calm Storm, then left the black gelding grazing. He tottered forwards to a patch of pine-needles beneath an older pine and sank onto his knees to brush the wet layer of needles aside. A clean, earthy smell came from the drier needles underneath. Wearily, he tugged his cloak around him and lay down. Briefly, he twitched about to make himself comfortable, then swiftly sank into a deep sleep.

CHAPTER FIVE

Farren stirred and rolled over, half asleep. His neck felt stiff and his head throbbed. Irritably, he felt for his cloak and yanked it back over his body. The wool was damp with dew and pine-needles were sticking to it. A bird carolled and chirruped somewhere overhead, shrill and piercing against the small sounds of wind and water. He groaned and rubbed his eyes. *It's no good lying here,* he thought. *I'm going to have to get up if we don't want another night in this damn valley.* Rolling fully onto his front, he pushed himself to his knees, limbs sluggish and reluctant. He opened his eyes fully. The mist in the pine valley had lifted slightly and he could see clearly across the river to the steep slope on the other bank. He ran his fingers through his hair, then scratched at the bristle on his cheeks and chin, dislodging more pine-needles. He clambered to his feet and began to walk towards the river.

Out of the shelter of the pines, a very faint breeze blew across his cheeks and he caught the scent of woodsmoke. Curious, he turned his head and looked upwind. Azariel was kneeling by a small pyramid of sticks, which had a small plume of white smoke curling out from it. He took a step towards her, treading heavily on a twig, which snapped sharply. She looked up at him, hair falling over half her face. A smile parted her lips and she brushed her hair back from her eyes. "Good morning," she said. "I thought I'd get a fire going before I woke you, but you've woken already."

"How did you manage to wake up so early?" he said, rubbing at the stiff place on the back of his neck and trying to soothe the muscles through the chainmail. "Sorry. Didn't mean to sound so surly. I've got a headache. How are you?"

"Weak as a rag doll." The sticks in the fire beneath her snapped as yellow flames engulfed them and she bent to feed more fuel into the flames. "The cold water in the river works small miracles in restoring humanity."

He grinned and continued walking towards the river. "I'm sure it does," he mumbled. 'I'll come and kiss you properly when I've finished, sweetheart."

He trudged across the gravel and knelt by the water's edge. Bending his head, he splashed a shock of cold water over his face that shuddered and shivered across his skin. Twice more, he dashed the water over himself, feeling some of the sleepy haze clear from his mind. *That's better*, he thought, rubbing the water off his face again. His fingers met the coarse covering of stubble and in response, his other hand reached down to the pouch on his belt where he kept his shaving kit. *Whatever lies ahead, I'll face it barefaced.*

His hands were still weak with sleep and he cut himself in several places with his razor before he hand finished. He walked back to the campfire, skin tingling from the cold water, and the little gashes stinging in the chilly air. He sat down on a flat stone beside Azariel and she slid her arm around his waist. He put his arm around her shoulder and turned his head to kiss the soft skin of her cheek. "Good morning, Stormwolf," he said softly. "Sorry I didn't say it before."

She cocked her head at an angle to look at him, eyes sparkling in spite of the dark sleepless hollows beneath them. Her free hand reached for his hair and picked a small cluster of pine-needles out. "They're almost invisible in your hair, being the same colour," she said, tossing them into the small fire. "Have some breakfast." She leaned away from him for a moment, then straightened up again with some dried fruit, bread and cheese in her hands. "And there's cold stew if you want it."

"Thank the King of Heaven," he said and began to eat. *I had no idea I was so ravenous*, he thought.

Azariel got to her feet, a wizened apple in her hand, and wandered about in a small circle while she ate. She stopped short, swallowed and looked hard at him. "We'd better not sit around too long. The morning's half gone and we'll only have another night here with the phantoms if we don't leave soon."

"Aren't the phantoms all through these mountains?" He tore another mouthful off the bread and cheese.

She shrugged. "I don't know what's north of here. I don't think anybody does except the Power Himself. But all the same..."

"If we do nothing, we'll get nowhere." He hastily crammed the rest of his meal into his mouth and clambered to his feet. "Let's go," he said as soon as he was able.

They caught and saddled the horses, and headed them northwards along the river and out of the pine-filled valley. The hillside sloped up steeply, and as they climbed, the mist began to fall away behind them. The sky overhead was clear, apart from a few white clouds streaming in the fresh south wind. High above them, a bird of prey wheeled, a dark speck against the pale blue. A few minutes' more riding and the death-stench of the phantoms had gone, leaving only the green tang of the softly moaning pines.

They reached the top of the slope and paused for a few moments. Azariel looked ahead past Farren, feeling Storm's sides heaving with the exertion of the climb beneath her. The land lay in a long plateau above the river, covered with broadleaf evergreen scrub. A sweetish earthy smell came from the tangle of green and brown. A thin strip of grass bordered the bush, then a scree slope fell sharply down to green glass of the river two bowshots beneath them. She looked at Farren and caught his eye. "Well?" she said. "Do we work our way through the scrub or do we chance it on the edge of that?" She pointed at the thin strip of grass between the scrub and the scree.

"Four feet are more stable than two," he said thoughtfully. "But six feet are more stable than four. It's as wide as a trail and we can lead the horses along it. Come on." He swung himself off Princess's back and flicked the reins over the mare's head. "It would take too long to work our way through the bush. Look at all the creepers. It might be better further from the river but we don't want to lose our way."

She nodded and dismounted, heels squelching into the soft muddy ground. She took the reins under Storm's chin and gently tugged him on, following Farren and Princess along the narrow trail. A sleepy haze still lurked in the back of her mind, and from time to time, she shook her head to clear the fog away. Breathing the fresh cold air deeply, she raised her head and looked across the river to the opposite bank. There, the slopes stretched sharply up from the river to the cloud-mantled peaks. Her gaze travelled down again to the broad braids of the river and the scree slopes. Here and there, little rivulets of stone and sand slid down into the water.

Her foot caught in a tangle of stick and grass, and she stumbled forward, catching herself on Storm's reins. The big gelding snorted and laid back his ears. He jerked his head sideways, sending her to her hands and knees into the grass and mud. Her shins and knees had landed on the grass, but she felt nothing beneath her feet. "Storm!" she scolded. She pressed down with one knee, then felt and heard the ground and gravel give way beneath her. She clung to the reins and pulled hard as her legs slid back over the edge. More of the ground gave way and Storm's hooves began scoring gashes in the mud as he fought back from her. One hoof slid towards her and she felt the blood drain from her face. Desperately, she fought for a foothold on the scree. The roar of the river was loud, almost as loud as the thunder of her heart. Storm jerked and tossed his head, fighting her pull on the reins but slowly slipping inexorably forwards. Eyes rolling and ears flat on his skull, he reared, yanking the reins from her hands.

She grabbed at the grass that grew on the edge as she felt the gravel slide out from beneath her feet. "Hold on, Stormwolf!" Farren yelled. "I'm coming!" Storm staggered backwards, hind hooves skidding on the mud. The ground beneath him was caving in. One hind hoof slid out from underneath him and his black bulk lurched towards her. She twisted and arched her body out of the big gelding's way, striving to reach the top of the slope. The grass broke in her hands and she felt herself fall. Everything about her was noise and dust, gritty pain on her face and forearms, and the taste of gravel in her mouth. The roar of the river filled her ears, then cold water embraced her.

She opened her eyes, fighting to keep her feet as the strong current tugged at her. A large boulder untouched by the small avalanche of gravel jutted out from the river and she wrapped her arms around it. She hauled herself out of the river, water weighting her cloak and boots down. Above her, she saw Storm with two hooves on the firm ground and two on the scree slope. Another slip ground and poured down the slope, and the big gelding plunged down in a cloud of dust. He crashed into another of the boulders fringing the river with a squeal and she winced. The gelding staggered, then steadied himself on all fours, scattering gravel as she shook his mane.

"Stormwolf!" Faintly, she heard Farren's voice above the roar of the river and looked up to see him crouching at the edge of the incline. "Are you all right?"

She spat out a mouthful of grit and saliva. "I'm all right, apart from a few bruises and grazes," she called, surprised at the shakiness in her voice. "I think Storm is, too. Nobody's broken anything and we're both on our feet."

He shouted again, but the words were lost in the roar of the river. She pushed her hair back behind her ears and leaned forwards. "What? I can't hear you with the river."

"Can you get up again?"

"I could – just," she shouted. "But I don't think he can." She looked at Storm, then at the dark brown gouges in the gravel. "That's not stable enough."

He stood up and walked over to Princess for a few moments, then turned back to look down at her. "Catch!" The end of a rope snaked and coiled through the air, then slapped into her hand as she caught it. "Make it fast around his withers and we'll haul him up. There are a few big tree roots here where I am, and I think the ground's stable enough to hold us all."

She idly twisted the end of the rope and looked over at Storm. He was pawing at the debris and trying to scramble up the slope. Behind him, the water sparkled and glinted in the midday sunlight. "You're a big horse, Storm, and one rope won't hold you," she said softly, half to herself. "I don't want to break the rope. It suffered enough strain last night. Two will hold you, though, old fellow."

She waded her way through the slumped pile of debris, sinking nearly to the tops of her boots in gravel and grit. She reached Storm and took her own rope out of a saddlebag. "Easy, old fellow," she crooned to him, stroking his neck and withers, and brushing some of the grit out of his thick winter coat. She looked at him, then at the two ropes in her hand. *Rope cuts like metal if it's tight enough,* she thought, eyeing the thick muscles in the gelding's forequarters. *I don't want to hurt him more than I have to.* She dropped the ropes, unbuckled her cloak and draped it across his back. He snorted and tossed his head. "Don't fidget, old fellow. You'll be glad of this before long." Quickly, she knotted the ropes about him, nestling them into the folds of her cloak.

She checked the knots one last time to ensure they wouldn't slip, then turned to look back up the slope, pulling her gloves on. Farren's rope was pulled taut above the slope and he stood watching her, one hand fidgeting with his betrothal earring. "What have you done with your end?" she called.

"Tied it to a tree. Come up to me, sweetheart."

She took the free end of her rope in her teeth and took a firm grip of the rope he had thrown down. It gave a little in her hands, then pulled taut as she leaned back, pressing her feet into the gravel. She began to climb up the slope, feet gouging out more and more debris as she heaved herself up. The rope bit at her hands, sliding and working at the leather of her gloves as hand over hand she pulled herself up. Her heartbeat thudded in her ears and a sweat began to break out on her shoulders and forehead. Another area of mud and gravel slid out from under both her feet and she clung to the rope, dangling like a hooked fish for a few seconds. She brought one foot up and lodged it in the dirt, then heaved herself up again, scrabbling her way up the slope.

She reached the top and pitched forwards onto her hands and knees, spitting the rope from her mouth and drawing a deep, noisy breath. Farren helped her to her feet, then gathered her into a tight embrace. His lips pressed onto her forehead, then lightly travelled down to the small graze on her cheek. She flinched and he pulled back. "Sorry," he said. "Does it hurt much?"

She shrugged. "A little." She kissed him lightly on the mouth once, then wriggled out of his embrace. "Now to get Storm back up to the path. How strong are you feeling? He's a big horse."

Farren turned his head and looked down at the black gelding. Storm pricked his ears up at them, neighing and trying to scramble up the slope. *Poor old fellow,* he thought. "Princess can help us – if we get off the slippery ground." He caught the mare by the bridle and carefully turned her towards the scrub and bush.

He unbuckled his cloak and twitched it off his shoulders. "Do to her what you did to Storm," he said, handing it to her. He turned and unbuckled the saddle from the mare's back. Azariel's back pressed into his as he worked and her elbow knocked into him. He stood back and watched as she finished tying the ropes around Princess, one rope on each side of the mare like a harness. He ran his hands through his hair and looked down the slope, then up again. "Now, Stormwolf, I'll wager your arms still ache from your climb, so you'd better guide Princess. I'll pull with her."'

He walked cautiously to the edge of the slope and gripped the ropes. He glanced over his shoulder at Azariel, who stood by Princess's head at the edge of the undergrowth, her sword drawn. "I'm ready when you are," he said.

He heard the slash of her sword cutting through the undergrowth and her clicking her tongue to coax Princess forwards. He bent to the ropes and put himself, back, legs and arms, into pulling. He felt the sinews of his arms tighten and stand out, hard like iron as he hauled on the tight ropes. He gritted his teeth and groaned with exertion, sweat breaking from his forehead. He took one agonising step backwards, then another, almost slipping in the mud. The black gelding below him had risen a few yards higher above the river's edge. He paused, mouth dry and chest heaving. The slash of Azariel's sword through the undergrowth filled his ears again, mixing with the thud of pounding blood. *Come on,* he told himself. *Do it, even if it kills you.* Again he pulled, muscles screaming with the pain of effort and the ropes cutting the blood from his hands. *Even through the gloves. And it'll be hurting the horses more than it hurts me.* Storm slowly came up the slope then rose, ears pricked, above the edge. One hoof pawed at the grass and mud. Farren staggered backwards as the ropes suddenly slackened, and he fell heavily into the wet grass. Storm scrambled onto the narrow margin of turf with a small snort and promptly bent his head to tear up a few mouthfuls of grass.

"Stop," he gasped, hearing Azariel's sword hack and slash through the brush behind him again. He closed his eyes, inhaling the sharp smell of crushed grass and waited for his heartbeat and breathing to slow to normal.

Her footsteps rustled beside him and he opened his eyes to look up at her. She knelt down beside him, a leaf clinging to her long black hair. She caressed his cheek lightly, then ran her soft fingertip down his nose. "You're strong," she said, eyes shining.

"I don't feel it at the moment." He eased the leaf out of her hair, then held his hand up to her. "Help me up, Stormwolf. We'd better get back on the march. Midday has passed already, to judge by that sun in my eyes."

She pulled him to his feet. "My fault we've lost time. I'm sorry I was careless enough to send Storm and myself down."

"I'm glad you're safe, in spite of the time lost." He brushed a few flecks of mud off himself and turned towards the horses. "And to be fair, it could just as easily have been me going down."

They took the ropes from the horses and he re-saddled Princess. He took the mare by the bridle and they trudged on along the thin strip between the forest and the river. They marched over the flatter ground of the bush-covered plateau for at least another hour, then the hillside began to slope down again. He raised his head and looked ahead. A broad valley spread out below him with a stream running to join the Illin-Ast at its centre. Tussocks, grass and a tangle of mountainthorns covered the slopes. *That's odd,* he thought. *Why hasn't the forest grown down to cover the grass? Was there a fire here once, or was it inhabited?* The strip of grass beside the bush widened and he swung himself onto Princess's back and rode the rest of the way down the slope.

He dismounted by the stream and let Princess wander to drink from it. He yawned and stretched himself, then glanced up towards the sun as it hung above the mountains, slowly wheeling westwards. Fingers and hands of mist poured around the heads of the mountains from the south, reaching for the sun and covering it. A cold wind sobbed through the Illin-Ast gorge, raising the hairs on his arms and ruffling his hair. *It's going to be cold tonight. It did snow a bit yesterday. We'll need a good fire tonight for whoever's on watch.* "Stormwolf," he said aloud. "Do you know what lies further up the river?"

She shook her head. "The phantoms didn't drive me this far. Why do you ask?"

He sat down on a boulder beside the grazing horses and crossed his legs. "I'm thinking ahead to tonight."

"What, already?" She sank to the ground and looked up at him, hugging her knees to her chest. "It's only mid-afternoon at the latest."

"Well, we'll need to collect a lot of firewood for tonight, and there's not a lot here." He ran his gaze up and down the valley. "Apart from that, it would make a good campsite: flat ground, water, good grazing for the horses, and reasonable shelter from the wind. But there could be something better further up the river." He shrugged and toyed with his betrothal earring. "If we want to camp here, though, we'll have to spend the rest of the daylight hours hunting wood."

"Well, we can decide while we eat something." She uncoiled herself with a jerk and stood up. "I'm famished and I'll wager you are, too. If you want my advice, I'll quote an old proverb and say that the trout on your hook's worth five in the brook." She walked towards the horses, turning her head to look at him while she spoke. "Anyway, if there are any enemies in this valley, we want to be ready for them. If there aren't, then we could always do with some extra sleep after last night."

"Well, of course we'll stop for a meal. The horses need it." He got to his feet and joined her in unsaddling the horses.

They ate quickly, then began to set the campsite. Once the tent had been pitched, they began searching for dry wood among the mountainthorns and the few straggly birches in the valley. Bit by bit, armload by armload, the pile of thin, gnarled sticks grew. Azariel dumped down another armload onto the pile and stood beside it, picking out a thorn that had dug itself into her arm. Farren trudged up to the pile, hauling an old sunbleached branch of a long-dead tree. "Where did you find that?" she asked.

He dragged the old log up to the pile. "Half-way up that slope," he said, pointing to the southern face of the valley. "There's more like this one back there. I think I'm right about there having been a fire here once."

She looked down at the pile of brushwood then up the slope where the tussocks were tinged with gold in the late afternoon light. "I'll come with you to get more. This pile we've got already looks big but you know how quickly mountainthorn burns. Let's go and get some more of your big logs."

Together, they climbed up the slope to the remains of an old mountain beech tree several bowshots away from where the thick scrub covered the hills. She tucked a thickish branch under each arm and carried them back to camp beside him, their shadows slanting long and dark down the hillside in front of them. The heads of the hills were hidden in clouds and more wisps and tendrils of vapour rose from the river as birds shrilled their salute to the dying day.

She knelt down and built a small pyramid of sticks and dry grass in a ring of stones. *That mist from the river's odd with this wind,* she thought. *But it doesn't stink like the mist in that other valley. Maybe there won't be an attack tonight.* She looked up and a cold shiver travelled down her spine. *All the same, I don't like the look of it.* She took her tinderbox from her belt-pouch and struck sparks from it. One caught and the wad of soft frayed cotton around the flint took flame. She touched the hot yellow tongue of fire to the dry grass. A white plume of smoke rose to join the mist as the edges of the grasses blackened, a thin line of flame bordering the charring. The thorn twigs crackled as the fire engulfed them, and she place more on the small fire, eyes watering from the smoke, and the chilled skin on her face and bare forearms warming.

Farren sat down beside her. "Here's your supper," he said, handing her some slices of bread covered with cheese and dried beef, and an apple. "It's a shame I had no time to shoot something for us, but thank the King of Heaven anyway."

"So be it." She took the food from him and ate in silence for a while. Once the edge had been taken from her hunger by the bread, salty meat and cheese, she sat hugging her knees to her chest and nibbling at the apple. She looked into the fire, then up at Farren as he sat beside her idly feeding sticks into the fire. Yellow-orange firelight played over the sharp, angular lines of his jaw and cheekbones, and struck a rich colour from his red hair. *He's a good-looking man. Every time I look at him, I'm amazed and thankful that he chose someone like me. My love, how I long to be free to run my hands and lips over every inch of you!* He yawned, then leaned forwards to collect more twigs. He sat back and caught her eye, winking and briefly flashing his teeth in a smile. She reached out and rested her hand on his knee. "You're tired, beloved, and so am I," she said. "Time to turn in for the night. Who'll take first watch?"

"I will, if you'll let me. You fell down that slope and probably feel a bit sore still."

"You old fox." She prodded him in the ribs, digging her forefinger into the links of his chainmail. "You know I don't like being pampered. Anyway, you worked harder to get Storm back up the slope, so you ought to be the one to sleep first."

His hand went to the pouch at his belt. "We'll toss a coin for it. Loser takes watch. Now, Stormwolf, do you choose King or Kingdom?"

"King."

He flicked the gold coin into the air and caught it as it fell. He slapped it onto the back of his right hand, covering it with his left. She leaned over as he took his hand away. The shield emblem with its crown and stars winked on the gold in the firelight and he chuckled. "I win and I get the cold blankets." He reached over to the store of wood and broke off a stick the length of his arm. "Set light to the end of that, and when it's burnt to the other end, wake me."

"Go and enjoy your sleep." She shuffled closer to him and leaned her head on his shoulder, breathing in the smells that hung around him: horses, woodsmoke, grass and sweetish masculine sweat. "I'll wake you when it's your turn – or if any enemy appears."

He put his arm around her shoulder, warm and heavy. His other hand brushed over her cheek, then cupped under her chin. She tilted her head up as he bent down to kiss her warmly. "Goodnight, Stormwolf, my sweetheart," he said softly. "See you when you wake me to watch." He smiled at her, dark eyes dancing. "And make sure you do. I want you to have your fair share of sleep."

"I'll wake you. Don't worry about that!" She nuzzled his cheek, then drew back as he stood up, his fingers lightly resting in her hair. "Goodnight and sleep well, beloved."

"Goodnight." He turned and ducked inside the tent, pulling the flap closed behind him.

She pushed one end of the timing stick into the embers, then settled herself comfortably on the grass beside the fire. She pulled her cloak about herself, trapping a wealth of warmth to her body against the cold air. The small sounds of the night drifted to her as she stared into the fire: the almost musical rush of the river, the horses cropping grass, distant birds and animals calling, and the gentle snap and murmur of the fire. Her mind began to roam as the flames leaped and danced in front of her. Her head felt heavy and her eyes fell closed. She pinched herself sharply and shook her head. *I must be careful not to fall asleep.* She threw back her cloak from her bare arms and let the night air chill her, raising the tiny hairs on her forearms. Slowly, the timing stick burn down, the end charring and burning, then turning to ash and collapsing into the fire. Bit by bit, she nudged it along until it had burnt to the end.

CHAPTER SIX

Azariel yawned and stood up, stretching her cramped muscles. The rippling sound of the creek called to her, and she walked towards it and knelt down at the water's edge. The water was bitingly cold, drawing a line of ice down to her stomach as she drank. Thirst quenched, she got to her feet and turned back to the golden-red glow of her campfire. *And now to sleep,* she thought.

A flicker of movement caught her eye from somewhere beyond the campfire. *The horses?* She peered through the gloom. Again, the soft sound of something hard on soil came, and something indistinct moved. Behind her, she heard the breaths of the two horses. *What is that?*

She strode to the pile of brushwood and seized a handful of dry broom. Plunging one end into the fire, she lit it as a torch and held it over her head to see into the darkness. A long-drawn-out scream filled her ears and a sickening quicksilver line of fear plunged through her body. Higher up the valley, lit by the flickering torchlight, stood five creatures: living human-shaped skeletons with the heads and necks of herons. Red eyes glittered at her from above the long pointed beaks and the creatures lifted their long bony arms, displaying sickle-like claws in place of fingers. One opened its beak and screamed again, sending fresh ripples of fear down her spine and into her belly.

Heart thumping and mouth dry, she raised her left hand, fingers splayed. *Master, help me.* She cleared her throat. "Go away," she commanded. "Leave us in peace."

The five creatures hesitated for a moment, shuffling their feet. Then they stepped towards her, movements jerky and stiff as puppets. *We're in for a fight.* She leaped back, blood pumping through her veins and fire beginning to pulse in her fingertips. She rammed her torch into the campfire then kicked more fuel into the heap. A blaze sprang to life from the embers. "Farren!" she shouted as loud as she could as the creatures screamed again.

She let red fire fly from her hand as the creatures rushed at her. Behind her, she heard noises coming from the tent and the neighing of horses. Her bolt of fire flew wide of the creature she had aimed at as its snaky neck jerked to one side. They surged all around her, swarming through the campfire unharmed, and she scrambled backwards. Her shoulder knocked into something hard and she half-turned, hair in her eyes and heart in her mouth. Her hand was up, ready to strike. "Stormwolf, it's me," said Farren's voice, and she lowered her hand, blood rushing tingling into her face as she turned back towards the creatures. His hand clutched at her shoulder. "Oh, hellfire!" he said. "What are they? We'd better get to the horses – quickly."

She leaped over the tent ropes and began running towards the river. Behind her, she heard their feet pursuing her. She turned and aimed her opal ring at them, a pulse of fire surging out from the stone. The bolt took the creature in the arm and she saw the white bones blacken as the creature hesitated and stumbled. Then her foot struck something and she went sprawling into the dewy grass.

She rolled and twisted to and fro, dodging and ducking as the things swarmed around her, claws hissing through the air. Fire burst from her fingertips, blackening one and missing another. The claws of one caught her on the elbow, scraping across the chainmail then gashing her with a rush of hot pain. Instinctively, she rolled into a crouch and drew her sword, slashing and striking up at the creature that had wounded her.

The blow struck the creature on its bony pelvis with a sharp crack. A surge of elation filled her as she saw the bones separate and tumble disordered to the ground. She leaped to her feet and backed away, tossing her hair back out of her eyes, ring and sword both at the ready. She shot a bolt of lightning from her ring at the creatures and in the blue glare, she saw the bones on the ground twitching once or twice. Blood trickled down her arm from the gash and her heart kicked double-time in her chest. She saw the silhouettes of the other four creatures against the red glow of the fire; they stood still.

The bones at her feet, dim pales shapes in the dark, moved again. Then they grew, making soft clicking noises as prong after prong sprang from each bone. Slowly, they took shape. A silver shiver of cold ran down her spine as she saw more of the bird-headed skeletal shapes rise from the ground. She clenched her left fist more tightly, her nails digging into her palms. The metal of her rings pressed hot against her hands and she fought the numbing fear that rose to cloud her mind. With a shout, she let the fire blaze from her ring at the new-grown creatures. Dimly, she noticed one or two fire-blackened bones lying still on the ground. Then she turned and ran towards the sound of the river, hearing the swish of feet through the grass behind her.

A shape rose up out of the darkness with the thunder of hooves. "Stormwolf?" Farren's voice said. "Are you all right?"

"Yes, but there's more of those things now."

"More? But where...how?"

"I haven't time to explain." She glanced backwards at the creatures. They were striding towards her and Farren, taking long, slow, steady strides. "Just fight." She wheeled and stood beside Princess's shoulder. The mare's breaths came fast and sharp. "Where's Storm?" she asked.

"Hobbled. I can't control two alone."

She tossed the hair from her eyes, a sting of shame beginning to rise inside her. *I ran like a frightened hare.* She clenched her teeth. *I am the Stormwolf. I have no need to flee anything. And, Master, help me remember that!* She re-sheathed her sword and tightened both fists. Pent-up fire surged and prickled in her knuckles. The creatures, dim shapes against the fire-haze, drew within striking range.

Her hands rose to the attack and fire flew out, green and silver. It crackled through the air alongside Farren's yellow and blue lightning to strike the creatures. Some bones blackened and one creature toppled to the ground, totally burned. Then they swarmed all around her and Farren, screeching and long beaks stabbing. She dodged and ducked around them, knocking into bones, feeling and hearing claws scrape and scratch across her armour. Fire burned through the darkness, picking out nightmare shapes in lurid colours. All the time, her ears rang with the steady creaking of bones, the occasional scream from the creatures and the steady pulse of her heartbeat.

After what seemed like hours of confusion, she found herself standing with one foot in the river grappling with one of the horrors. One of her hands held a bony wrist, struggling to keep the claws away from her body while her other hand clenched around the feathery throat as the beak strove to drive at her face. Its other claw was meshed in her cloak and she heard the woollen material slowly tearing. The monster screamed shrilly, setting her eardrums ringing painfully. Her palms were damp with sweat, and she felt the hard bone turn and loosen in her grasp. An acrid smell rose form the creature's burnt ribs. She kicked her leg to one side, wrapping her foot around the bony leg behind the knee in a wrestler's move. *Hellfire,* she thought as she heard the phantasmal sinews crack. *Now there'll be even more of them.* She twisted and lunged, hurling the creature into the water. The claw tore loose from her cloak and she staggered away from it.

A pale golden glow hung over the water above where the creature had fallen. Thousands of tiny bubbles rose to the surface, hissing as they erupted. The bird-head reared from the water and the beak opened in a silent cry before it sank. It dissolved like salt in the ripples of the current. Then blackness.

Thank the Power! thought Farren as he shifted his seat slightly on Princess's back and watched the bones dissolve. *It seemed as if those things were unkillable.* He touched the mare lightly on the neck and pressed her firmly on the flank with one leg, turning her. "Come on, my lady," he said softly. "Herd them like cattle if you can."

He edged the mare around the group of creatures, striking a bolt of fire into the centre of the group. For an instant, he saw Azariel, eyes flashing with wild triumph, on the bank of the river, holding one of the horrors by the beak. "Go into the river, Stormwolf," he called. "I'll drive them in." He punched Princess's flanks with his heels, cantering her in a tight circle around the melee.

"Right." Her voice had a hard edge to it and she ended with a wild wolfish yell. He heard a splash as something fell into the river, and the pale golden light glowed over the surface of the river again.

He urged Princess on. The mare reared slightly and he felt her mane spill across his hands as she tossed her head. *On, my lady,* he willed her, using his Gift. The mare surged forwards, snorting. Fire flashed from his ring and in the one brief moment of light, he saw Azariel lunging for one of the creatures, one hand held across her face and the other reaching out. Princess stopped suddenly, jerking him forwards. She neighed and reared, and he grabbed at the mare with arms and thighs to stay on her back. One of the creatures screamed in front of him and he punched fire at it from his emerald ring.

The creature jerked its neck to one side as the fire seared through the air towards it. The others came on slowly. Azariel was grappling with one of them, her hair flying in dark whips across her face. "Go back," she commanded as she pushed it towards the river. "*Drasasei!*" she repeated, using the Old Tongue. Lightning flashed from her free hand and he joined it with his own.

He looked ahead through the maze of snaky necks that wove to and fro around the coloured shafts of lightning that sizzled out of his hands. Here and there, the close-set feathers on the necks gleamed with iridescent colour. With a penetrating screech, one lunged towards his right. The hard bone of one claw caught him on the knee and slid off the leather into Princess's shoulder. The mare squealed and shied to one side, trampling one to her left as she landed. He slid his feet from the stirrups and launched himself off her back at the one that had struck her, seizing it by its neck and one upper arm.

He landed on top of it, the underside of the long beak pressing against the top of his head. Sliding his grip up against the grain of the soft feathers and feeling the muscles squirm and quiver beneath him, he shifted his grip to the beak. Something slammed across his back and he heard his cloak tearing. Yelling, he straightened up, heaving the one he held with him. Energy coursed through his arms and legs, half powered by alarm. Using the creature he held as a shield, he pushed through the group around him. The bones and beak in his grip twisted and writhed, abrading the skin on his palms, and the claws clicked over the links in his chainmail as it raked at his waist. *Can't let go. It could gouge my eye out with one thrust.* Its legs and feet tangled with his and he lurched forwards. It fell beneath him onto a rock with a sickening splinter of bone, and as he staggered to his feet again, he saw a dark crack in the upper bone of an arm that hung uselessly.

His boots ground on the loose stones and gravel by the river. One more step, then the chilly water spilled in and soaked his feet. Groaning with effort, he flung the creature forward. A plume of water rose behind it, faintly illuminated as the creature dissolved into golden haze. He shook the water from his face and dipped his burning palms into the river before turning to face the creatures again.

Slowly, they drove and dragged the creatures back into the river. One slashed at his leg, catching at his boot and nearly dragging it from his foot as he thrust the creature into the river. Sweat was dripping down his back, chilling him in the night air in spite of his cloak. The mist was almost bright with the golden haze from the river as the creatures melted. Finally, the last one melted into bubbles, then blackness returned.

He wiped the beads of sweat off his forehead. He heard Azariel's fast, heavy breathing somewhere in the darkness beside him and he held out one hand towards her. "Sweetheart?" he said.

"Here." Her hand touched his bare arm, then his hand found hers and their fingers intertwined. Her rings still felt warm, like his. His other hand wrapped around her and pulled close with a grating of metal on metal as their chainmail tunics rubbed together. He held her tightly, feeling her chest rise and fall against his. The fire in his arms faded to trembling as the fighting touch of the Power vanished and his breathing and heartbeats returned to normal. "Are you hurt, Stormwolf, my love?" he asked.

"They got me on the arm, but it's stopped bleeding already, I think. Where's Storm? Is he all right?"

He whistled and listened for the gelding's answering neigh. "He's safe," he said. "I'll see to him soon. First, you need to take your turn sleeping. That stick should have burnt down by now."

"It had," she said, half-yawning as she spoke. "I was about to wake you anyway."

"And what a waking!" he chuckled. He looked about him and picked out the lingering glow of the fire. "I'll come back with you and build up the fire before I do anything else, though."

He fell into step beside her and walked back towards the tent with her. The campfire had become a heap of dull red embers. He put a few bundles of brushwood onto the fire, then knelt to blow them into light and life. He felt her hand on the back of his head above the edge of his chainmail, then she knelt beside him. Gently, he took her in his arms and kissed her, catching the tang of smoke in her hair. "Good night, sweetheart," he said softly as he drew his head back. "Sleep well. You deserve it."

***

Dawn came to the valley, pale morning light picking out the scrubby leopard-spot patterns of the mountainthorns against the tussock. A strong, cold wind was blowing from the south up the river gorge, and heavy cloud hung over the mountains to the south. The mist still lingered in the valley but it was quickly blown away. Farren stirred from his place by the dying fire, rubbing life into his chilled arms. Hunger gnawed at his stomach and he glanced over his shoulder at the tent. *Shall I wake her now for breakfast?* He stood up and stretched the cramped muscles in his thighs and buttocks. *I'll let her sleep a while longer. She's had a hard night.* He strolled to the saddlebags and fetched out the end of a loaf and a complete circle of soft cheese. He cut some for himself and set out more on a rock for Azariel as he ate. Hunger satisfied, he went to the river to drink and shave.

He shivered and rubbed the bare skin on his arms as he returned to the tent. *We'll be lucky if it doesn't snow today,* he thought, looking at the heavy clouds to the south. *I hope we can cross the next range of hills safely.* He paused by the tent door. "Azariel?" he called.

Something rustled inside the tent. "What?" she mumbled sleepily. Then she hissed between her teeth. "Are they back?" she asked sharply.

"No, but the sun's back. Well, day's back. Time to get on the march, if you can drag yourself out of the warmth into this cold wind."

He waited by the door of the tent as she came out, dark circles under her eyes and her hair hanging dishevelled about her face. He caught her hand and dropped flamboyantly to one knee before pressing a kiss onto her hand. "My lady awakes; the sun has arisen!" he exclaimed, mischief simmering inside him.

She laughed and tossed back the black snakes of her hair back. "Get up, you ridiculous redhead. I know perfectly well 'my lady' is what you call your horse, so stop quoting hackneyed ballads." She tugged him to his feet. "Good morning, my beloved."

He circled his arms around her, savouring the sleepy warmth of her body. "Good morning, sweetheart," he replied, kissing her. "I've already eaten, so you can have what I've left out for you while I strike camp and get the horses ready."

"Thank you." She returned his kiss quickly, then wriggled out of his embrace, pulling her cloak about her shoulders.

He walked to the river and chirruped to the horses. They came to him, warm and whickering. He gave Storm a quick pat, then ran his hand through Princess's wiry mane. "Come with me, friends," he murmured. "Let's get you both ready for the day's march." He grasped Princess's mane, then reached up to take Storm by the forelock. The black gelding bent his head and plodded beside him to where the tack lay piled. A light sheen of dew covered the saddles, and he wiped the moisture off before slinging the blankets and saddles over the horses' backs and tightening the girths. "There you both are," he said, sliding the tongue of Storm's girth buckle into place. "Now wait here for us while we load you up."

He turned towards the tent, ready to pull it down and fold it up to slip into the saddlebag, but saw Azariel already busy with the green canvas. He shook the biggest of the bags open and helped her fold and bundle the tent into it.

He swung himself onto Princess's back while she strapped the tent-bag behind Storm's saddle. He watched as she put her toe into the stirrup and mounted the big black gelding. "Ready?" he asked as she settled herself into the saddle with a squeak of leather. She tossed her hair back from her face and nodded.

He turned Princess upstream and looked ahead at the hills. The steep tussock and mountainthorn-covered slopes stretched upwards until they were hidden in low dark cloud. "How much of that do we have to ride through?" he wondered aloud. "It must be snowing on the heads."

"We'll be lucky if it doesn't snow in the valleys and the gorge by the looks of the black clouds behind us. Can't you smell the snow on the wind?" She turned her head to look southwards, a flurry of black hair billowing across her face.

He shook his head. "I haven't got your sharp nose, Stormwolf." He faced north and looked along the gorge, scalp cold as the chill south wind blew over him. The hillside sloped gently up from the river, grassy and dotted with pines. "The course of the river looks easiest to follow," he said, after a pause. "Let's ride along there and we might escape the worst of the weather."

They headed along the river course, weaving through the pines and boulders studding the river bank. Above them, the gently sloping hill gave way to a steepish face, scarred with bare rock and a few small tenacious plants. Above that, the heavy cloud hid the ranges and peaks. Cold hissing wind blew on his back and pushed the hood of his cloak up against the back of his neck. He let Princess choose her own path, lightly holding the reins in one hand as he trapped the warmth against himself with his cloak. Another gust of wind ruffled his hair, and with it came a bitingly cold drop of something. He shivered. "The snow's coming," he said, reaching around to wipe the wetness form his hair and pull his hood up.

Her storm-grey eyes darted up towards the heavy blanket of cloud. "We'd better cover all the ground we can, then, and find shelter," she said. "If the first heavy snowfall of the season comes, then it will be natural forces that kill us, not supernatural."

"I wish we'd waited for warmer weather," he muttered. He bent his back before the wind, hunching over against the cold, and rode on.

Another hour passed. The toe slopes and foothills of the ranges began to open out into broad river flats. A small spur running east to west lay in front of them and the Illin-Ast arched around it in a wide sweep. The southwest wind howled in his ears and swept through the grass and tussock around them. He turned his head and screwed up his eyes into the wind. It swirled and whirled across him, biting and exhilaratingly cold and leaving the skin on his face tingling as the hot blood beat inside his chest and upper arms in defiance. Thick, dark, soft cloud hid the south, and the hills they had just come from were smothered in dark grey. Another stronger gust of wind struck him in the face and with it came the snow, gritty powder snow that stung his eyes and cheeks.

"Quick," he said. "Get to that spur ahead of us. We've got to find shelter." He put heels to Princess and headed her towards the finger of land ahead of them. *I think I can risk a faster pace. She won't sweat over a small distance in this cold.* The mare glided into a smooth canter and he rocked with her stride. Above the scream of wind in his ears, he heard the triple-beat of Storm cantering beside him, keeping pace with Princess.

They rounded the end of the spur. A jagged line of tall rocks stood below an old landslide at the end of the slope. Snow already lay pushed up against the big grey boulders and against a small spinney of gnarled mountain beech trees at the end of the boulders. On the north face of the rocks and trees, the tussocks and gravel lay bare of snow. *Thank the Power!* He turned Princess around the trees out of the worst of the screaming wind and the driving powder snow.

He checked the mare and swung himself off her back. "This will do," he said. "There's shelter enough for us and the horses.

Can you see to them, Stormwolf? I'll put the tent up for us. We can't go any further until this snowstorm blows itself out."

He ducked beneath her as she dismounted and unbuckled the big leather bag holding the tent. He lugged the heavy bag beside the trees to where the gravel and rock gave way to grass and soil. He shook out the green canvas and began to join the wooden rods together to make the first tentpole. He pushed in the pegs to anchor the tent, worming them through the stony soil. Tree roots and rock blocked the path of the pegs. He pushed them until his hands ached, but they remained half-exposed. *No good. They'll have to do, and I hope they'll hold!*

Carrying the long pole, he pushed his way through the opening in the canvas, breathing in its grassy smell as he fought his way to the end. He put the pole in place, then struggled back out into the wind again. The small spinney of wizened black trees hissed and shuddered in the strong wind, but no snow penetrated the coarse foliage. He flung the door of the tent wide and knelt down, feeling in the bag for the rods to make up the second pole.

A mighty gust of wind whined around the boulders and he saw the canvas billow like a flag, then fill like a sail. A guyrope flailed in the wind, peg dangling useless from the end. The walls of the tent bulged, then began to move. "No!" he cried, and lunged to catch the whipping ropes. He caught hold of the edge of the canvas and struggled to hold the coarse material. "Azariel!" he called. "Help me hold it!" He heard her footsteps above the howl of the wind, coming closer as he fought the wind for the tent. Then the tent began to slip from his hands, breaking one of his fingernails as it pulled free. He clutched at it, but his fingers closed on empty air.

The tent flew up like a child's kite, scattering pegs on the ground. He got to his feet and ran out of the shelter of the rocks and bushes. *Maybe I can catch it when it drops again.* The wind struck his back like a flooding river and he leaned back into it to brace himself against it. The tent dropped to the ground and scurried like an animal across the open ground. Desperately, he ran after it, wind propelling him. It zigzagged around bushes and boulders, tantalizingly close. He leaped at it, striving to stamp on one of the guyropes. The tent danced and rolled away. *Damn!* The tent almost dived into the river and was tugged and whirled away by the current, slowly sinking.

He groaned and clutched at his forehead. *I'm not going in after it. We've lost it.* He turned on his heel into the wind and began to walk back to the shelter of the rocks. His heart sank as he squinted at the spur's end at least three bowshots away. *Did I really run that far?* He bent his head into the wind and began to slog back. Snow stung his eyes and cheeks, blinding him, chilling his head and arms. He clutched at his cloak and pulled the hood over his head, but the wind snatched it back. Step by step, he staggered on, shivering and his throat gripped in the icy stranglehold of chilled steel armour. He stumbled, landing heavily on his hands and knees. Snow bit painfully around his fingers. *Where are my gloves?* he asked himself numbly. *Haven't seen them since those things last night. Oh, damn, damn, damn it all!* He struggled to his feet again, freezing wind screaming in his ears. The wind buffeted him again, and the snow seemed to find every tiny gap in his chainmail, soaking and enveloping him in cold.

He staggered and stumbled forwards as he reached the shelter of the bushes and rocks, eyes streaming with the cold. Azariel was waiting for him, sitting with her back against one of the rocks. She wrapped her arms around him and felt for the laces at the back of his neck. "Take your armour off so I can warm you," she said softly. "My poor beloved, you're soaked and shivering." She peeled the armour off him, then threw a blanket around his shoulders and pulled him to herself, her leather-clad chest against his.

She cupped her hands around his head, feeling the cold melted snow under her fingers. His head slumped heavily onto her shoulder, then all his weight pressed down onto her. She closed her arms around him tightly. She closed her arms around him tightly and ran her hands up and down the line of his spine, trying to stroke warmth into him. Her fingers brushed the stiff leather seam at the top of his trousers and jerked away as she grew suddenly conscious of the heavy warm sensuality of his body and the firm, taut flesh beneath the clothing.

A strange heat crept up from her loins, spreading fiery fingers through her lower body. She drew her breath in sharply, desire beginning to run hot in her veins. *No,* she told herself. *Not now. I'm trying to keep him warm, not seduce him. I can't have him yet.* The urge to yield her defences quivered through her and she fought it, stiffening herself against the storm of desire.

He convulsed in her arms, seizing her tightly about the waist and chest. Breath sobbed out of her, fast, hot and sharp. He raised his head and looked into her eyes. His pale skin was flushed, his lips were parted and the pupils of his dark eyes were dilated. She saw him swallow and the tip of his tongue running around the inside of his lips. *No!* her will screamed at the storm of longing inside her.

She writhed in his embrace, desperate to free herself from the maelstrom of dark fire that began to engulf her. *I've fallen into deep water now. He's burning as well. May the Power be my witness I didn't mean to start this! I love him but if I need to, I'll strike him to save the two of us from this.* She swallowed. *Or you could let him do as he pleases and enjoy it,* a small voice whispered at the back of her mind. *You know you want to.* His eyes bored into hers and she saw battle raging in the deep brown. *I will not dishonour him or myself. I am the Stormwolf, and I will not break the laws of the Master I swore to serve.* "Farren," she said softly.

He bared his teeth and flung back his head as if he had slain an enemy. "No," he groaned, and let go of her. He rolled to one side, relieving her of his tantalising weight. He clutched at the blanket as an eddy of the wind caught it. "I won't. I can't. Not yet. Stormwolf, no, my sweetheart."

She bowed her head, hair covering her face. "Thank you for releasing me," she said quietly. "I was about to ask you to stop."

He hunched himself into the blanket and looked at her over the edge of it. "I wouldn't have ravished you. If you didn't want it, your resistance would have knocked some sense into me. Literally, knowing you." His mouth twisted into a wry smile.

"Don't be too sure of that." She looked at him and swung around to sit clasping her knees, hair still draped across her face. "I don't know what I would have done. I was prepared to slap you, although I would hate to hurt you. And my blood's as red as yours, my beloved. I don't want to think about what might have happened." She smiled, her eyes meeting his. "You were enticing me almost unbearably. You're irresistible."

"And so are you." He shivered, pulling the blanket about himself again. *My sweetheart, your body was so warm,* he thought. *Too warm, too soft, too feminine. I've got something to look forward to.* He saw that the bare skin on her forearms was covered in little bumps where the hairs grew, and her lips were turning bluish-pale with cold. "Oh, hellfire! Now you're growing chilled. What are we to do? We need warmth to survive this snowstorm. If we keep apart, we'll freeze. And if we snuggle together, we'll... burn. If only the tent hadn't blown into the river!"

She hugged herself and looked up at him, the eddies of wind stirring the hair hanging about her face. "Too late to lament that now," she said, teeth chattering. "Wishes won't keep us warm. The horses are up against each other, but I don't know how we can fit in with them."

He went to throw the corner of the blanket about her, then stopped. "We might have to find some way of huddling up to them until the storm stops."

"How? They're awkward to lean forwards over, although you can lean back over them. Or you could hug a horse's neck. Dogs would be better." She looked over at the horses, then suddenly turned to him, eyes flashing. "Of course!" Her hands reached for the buckle of her cloak and unclasped it.

"What are you doing? You'll freeze without your cloak. I won't let you freeze yourself and give it to me. Stormwolf, don't be a fool." He pushed back the thick black wool cloth she offered him.

"I won't freeze in a wolfskin," she replied, tossing the cloak over him. She edged closer to him so that their knees touched side by side. Her hands rested on the grit and withered grass in front of her. "When I'm a wolf, I have a wolf's tastes. I enjoy raw meat – blood, hair and all. I don't feel any sexual desire for you when I'm in that shape. Fond of you, yes. Aware that you're extremely good-looking, yes. But anything sexual, no. I'd be in the wrong body for that." She chuckled. "I do stay human enough not to go on heat like a bitch, but not human enough to long for you. And I won't arouse you. Put the cloak on."

He buckled the black wool cloak about him, catching the faint scent of rosemary and the smell of her hair and body in the material. A faint line of silver light flashed down her body as she shifted shape. Huge paws appeared where her hands had been. The thick grey fur lying heavily about her neck and shoulders softened her outline, looking warm and appealing. He picked up the blanket and carried it to the horses, smiling. He squeezed between the two horses and the rock wall, and lay down on the bare ground under their necks. "Easy now, friends," he said. "Let me get out of the wind in front of you. Stormwolf?"

The beast she had become swung around and flopped heavily down in his lap, large head pressing against his chest. One golden eye winked at him. He hugged the shewolf, burying his face in the thick warm pelt and drawing the cloaks and blankets around them both. "It's strange to think that you're in there somewhere,

Stormwolf," he murmured in the wolf's pricked ear. "I love you, my sweetheart. Even when you're in this shape instead of your own." He shuffled around on the rocks and lay back. "I'm sorry I got over-excited before. I wouldn't want to spoil things between us by taking your maidenhood here in the dirt and rocks in lust. I want to wait for you. I will wait for you. I promise."

The shewolf whined, and a cold nose and a warm wet tongue passed across his chin. Instinctively, he recoiled in distaste, then chuckled and held her closer. The wind howled around the rock, and snow billowed overhead. Warmth enveloped him and he felt the tiredness from the last two nights' broken sleep catch up with him. He grew drowsy and slowly drifted off to sleep, the shewolf's soft fur tickling his arms and cheeks.

CHAPTER SEVEN

Azariel slumped her head against Farren's chest as he slept, the rise and fall of his breathing beneath her. Small eddied of wind that reached behind the end of the spur stirred the ruff of fur about her neck. She glanced at the horses, lying close beside them with their backs to the wind and their manes streaming forward about their necks. The wind howled and moaned around the boulders and through the small spinney of trees, driving flurries of snow across the river flat. A mix of smells carried on the wind, vivid and sharp to her wolf's nose: the clear scent of snow; the scents of forest, grass and hills; and human and equine bodies. She closed her eyes, dozing lightly.

Gradually, the snow and wind eased and the thick black snowbearing clouds moved northwards across the mountains ahead of them. Overhead, the cloud thinned, leaving patches of pale sky. Haze still hung over the arch of the river and the hills above her. The disk of the sun showed palely through the haze, wheeling towards the west and beginning to sink.

She squirmed back and up, breaking out of Farren's embrace slightly and putting her forepaws on his shoulders. He stirred slightly and the regular rhythm of his breathing broke for the space of a few heartbeats. *Wake up, my beloved. The storm's stopped and we can go on.* She nuzzled at him, his musky smell flooding her wolf's senses and almost making her sneeze. She whined and nudged at his cheeks with her nose.

He's a sound sleeper. I'll shift shape and try. She closed her eyes and concentrated, feeling herself slide back into her own woman's body. She opened her eyes, savouring the brilliant red of his cloak and the rich pine-needle chestnut of his hair. Her hair tumbled about her face as she looked down at him, and the ends brushed his face and shoulders. For a fleeting instant, she remembered the magnetic power of his passionate embrace, then shook the memory away. *Not now. That's to enjoy later.* "Wake up, Farren," she said, running and tickling her fingers up his chin and lightly tugging on his ear just above his betrothal earring. She bent her head and kissed him hard on the lips.

He groaned and his eyes opened, small slits at first, then wide, revealing the warm dark brown depths. She sat upright, shifting her body to one side of him and pushing the blanket and cloaks back. He yawned and scratched the back of his head. "What's up, Stormwolf?" Then he frowned. "How long have you been on top of me in your own shape?"

She shook her head. "Not long. I've only just changed back to wake you. The storm's blown on and it's only the middle of the afternoon. We can move on, if you want to." She got to her feet and helped him up. She flexed and tensed the cramped muscles in her arms, neck and shoulders, and shook her hair back from her face. "I hope you slept well."

"I did." He unbuckled her cloak and handed it back to her before bending to pick up and fold the blanket. "Do you think it's worth moving on? There's shelter here and it's going to be a cold night – with no tent."

"We'll reach more shelter in a few hours' travel," she said, pulling her armour over her head. She wrestled her arms through the sleeves, then fumbled with the laces behind her head. "Look ahead at where we've got to go. There's only these river flats to cross, and then we're bound to find somewhere in the hills beyond."

The wide white expanse of the river flat sprawled away to the rolling foothills and forested mountains to the northeast. Wild cattle moved across it, distant black specks on the snow. To the north, above the curving course of the river white mist hid the landscape. The wind hissed through the scrubby trees beside them, and beyond that, the soft rush of the river. A deeper note than the rushing of wind and water caught her ear; a sound like faint and constant thunder. She drew her breath in sharply. "Do you hear that?" she asked in a whisper.

"What?" His head worked its way through the neck of his armour and he turned to look about. "I haven't got your keen senses, Stormwolf."

"The sound of a waterfall in the mist ahead. We've nearly reached our journey's end."

He finished lacing up the neck of his armour and turned. "Well then, Stormwolf, shall we ride on and reach the waterfall tonight, or do we wait until the morning?" He ran his hand through his hair and his shoulders rose and fell several times as he breathed deeply. "If you want my advice, arch *minyaster*, I'd say: press on."

She picked up Storm's bridle from the bundle of tack. The leather was damp and the metal buckle felt like ice. *Poor Storm, having to put this cold iron bit in his mouth.* "And should we do more, if we can?" She stared at the thick pall of grey-white ahead and shivered. *That mist must be more than vapour driven up by Moonlady Falls. It's unnatural. It reminds me of the mist in the phantom's valley.* A feeling of vague dread crept over her. *What is waiting for us?* She went to Storm and slipped the bridle over his ears, eyes flicking back to the mists as she saddled him.

"Well, we're rested enough," he replied, leaning on Princess's saddle as he tightened the girths. "We could. We'll probably have to fight at some stage, unless there's some other way of getting the Stones back. But we may not get the choice. She may know we're coming already." He fidgeted with his betrothal earring and grimaced. "The Power will show us. But whatever we do, I'd like to have something to eat first."

She pulled the girths tight around Storm's belly, leather squeaking as the buckle slid into place. "Let's ride to the river and we'll drink, too. I'm more thirsty than hungry."

She swung herself onto Storm's back and rode out of the shelter of the rocks into the cold south wind. The gelding's hooves crunched over the crisp new snow and his black mane was pushed forwards by the wind. Farren and Princess were beside her, brilliant splashes of red and chestnut against the snow-covered river flats. He pulled his hood over his head and turned to smile at her as they rode. "Are you planning to take a drink from the source of the Illin-Ast? You once mentioned some old Zenifi tradition or story to do with it."

She twisted one strand of hair between her fingers. *I can almost see old Granny Marhya telling her tales. Who was the hero of her favourite one?* Pictures swarmed into her mind, the old imaginings of the tales. *It's so different here from how I imagined it.* "There was a story about a chieftain's son who searched for it and found it. According to the story, Moonlady Falls – or the source of the waterfall, depending on who's doing the telling – is a fountain of youth. Those who drink from it never grow old or die except in battle. Another tale claimed it was a spring of healing and the hero had to bring a dying king a drink of water from the fountain to win the hand of the princess and become the new ruler of the kingdom." She gazed along the curve of the river and the mists hiding the distance as she swayed easily with Storm's walk. "I don't know whether to believe them or not. They can't both be true. We never studied the Zenifi or Wayasti myths when we were acolytes, did we?" She shrugged and shook her head. "But they were good stories."

"Well, shall we try it anyway?" His eyes were sparkling with fun. "You never know, and we are the first people to come with far since whenever the phantoms and those queer skeleton things came. At the very least, it'll be refreshing."

She tossed her head back, letting her hood fall off as she laughed. "Why not?" The cold wind wormed its chilly way into her ears painfully and she pulled her hood back up over her head. "We need to drink something soon anyway. We've got nothing to lose, even if it is only ordinary water." She smiled at him and settled into the rhythm of riding along the riverbank.

The horses crunched slowly through the snow, following the curve of the river west then north. Mist wrapped around them, white, clammy and carrying the hint of an unfamiliar aromatic scent. Somewhere to her left, a bull bellowed. She looked ahead and saw the dark bulk of a single mountain shadowing the white haze. A thin line of white light shone through the shifting shadows of the mist, travelling down the length of the mountain. She followed it with her eyes down from the heights to the river. She caught her breath sharply and her heart leaped. *That line of light – it's the Falls themselves!* The river sped past them, alight with a faint golden sheen on the choppy foaming water. The golden light sparkled, played and swirled in and around the depth-blue water, revealing the dappled stones and gravel of the riverbed with startling clarity. *No wonder water this clear, shining and pure has gathered legends.* Deliberately keeping her breath from racing, she rode on, damp fingers of mist reaching softly under her hood to her face and groping her bare arms. *Crajaval will be there.*

A shape came into sight through the mist and resolved itself into the gnarled and craggy lines of trees. She rode closer and recognised them as a small stand of crabapples, branches still heavy with brilliant red fruits and fluttering brown and yellow leaves. The wind had blown fruit onto the snow beneath the tree and the scarlet fruits lay like drops of blood. Storm tugged the reins form her hands and bent his head to feed on them. "You wanted something to eat, Farren," she said over her shoulder. "Here's something we didn't expect. Something fresh, for a change." She reached out and plucked a handful of the small fruits. "Thank the Power. Catch." She tossed one of the fruits to him.

"So be it." He dropped Princess' reins and caught at the fruit. "If we crushed and bottled them and left them for long enough, we'd get a good drink, too. These crabapples are rather sharp, but they'd make excellent cider."

"We don't have that long to wait under the apple trees." She nibbled tentatively at one of the fruits, expecting sharp, mouthpuckering acidity. To her surprise, the bright red fruit was slightly sweet along with the sharp. She ate the small apple, then reached out to gather more.

She ate her fill of the small blood-red apples, then let Storm graze until Farren had finished. She hauled Storm's head up and nudged him on. The black gelding tore a mouthful of apples off the trees before walking on through the soft cold mist. She ducked beneath the heavily laden bough of one of the trees, snow falling from the apples onto the black wool of her cloak. She brushed it off, bare fingers flinching from the ice, and looked ahead past the twisted branches of the small stand of apple trees.

Two rough columns of granite stood ahead of them, snow piled around the bases. The river roared loudly beside them and the golden sheen from the water shone off the white mists. The waterfall thundered from her left and a slight wind from it stirred the faintly scented haze. "We must be nearly there," she called above the roar of the river. Storm walked close by the fingers of stone and she looked at them. Carvings had been worked in the rough stone slabs, weathered figures of circular labyrinths, stylised women carrying sheaves of grain and an antler-crowned man leading a stag with a rack as magnificently multi-pointed as his own. Above the carvings of the people and the maze were two crescent moons, one waxing and one waning. She shivered as a cold line ran down her back. *Icons of the Moon Lady. This is her sacred ground.* She turned both her rings straight then clenched her fists. *Even so, we'll enter, and the Power will come with us.* Her rings grew warm, driving the clammy chill of the mists from her hands.

Her heart thudded heavily as she looked between and beyond the pillars.

A bridge spanned the river, a row of planks suspended from chains fastened to the two pillars with another pair of chains running above them as a handhold. The chains were rusty, but he planks nearest her looked sound. Princess pushed beside her, squeezing her leg between the horses' flanks. Farren touched her hand and she looked up at him. "Well," he said, "here's our road. Shall I cross first or do you want to?"

She looked at the bridge. "I don't want to see you drown but I know you wouldn't want to see me drown either. However, that bridge looks sound enough to carry us." She wormed her leg out from between the two horses and dismounted awkwardly. She went to the bridge and ran her bare fingers over the rusty metal, flakes of cold red-brown iron jabbing her fingers. She prodded and yanked at the chains, listening to the grate and rattle of links along the length of the bridge. She let go, leaving the bridge swaying gently, and turned back to him. "It's sound enough." She ran her eyes over the planks. "The wood looks hardly weathered. It must have been treated with something. We'd better lead the horses, though, in case we overbalance."

He swung off Princess and crunched down into the snow. "I'll go first," he said. "Then I can summon Storm if he balks at the bridge." He took his chestnut mare by the bridle and led her onto the bridge of planks. Azariel followed slowly, leading Storm. The planks swayed and bucked as she stepped gingerly onto them, one hand on the hand-chain. The black gelding pulled back, ears slanted, but then walked forwards after her. The boards and chains creaked, whined and groaned as they crossed, undulating like water but holding. One or two planks were missing and she stepped over the gaps, catching sight of the deep, bright water swirling strongly beneath her. A cold thrill spread up from the soles of her feet and she passed on hurriedly. *I hope it holds, I hope it holds,* she repeated silently as she walked.

She stepped onto the steady ground at the end and clapped Storm on the neck. "Well done, Storm, old fellow," she said. "Brave horse." Droplets of water left by the mist on his thick winter coat collected on her hand and she shook them off. Farren was waiting for her and he leaned over to squeeze her hand, teeth bared in a wide smile. The mist seemed thicker as the light began to fade. *The afternoon's passed more quickly than I thought. It won't be long until nightfall.* In the wasting light, the light of the river shone more brightly, lighting up every droplet of water that swirled past her face.

She shook her hair back from her face and threaded the fingers of her left hand through Farren's right. They walked along the edge of the river, the horses plodding behind them. The water grew choppy and small tufts of foam danced on the shimmering surface. The wind of the waterfall blew stronger on her face and she blinked out the moisture that swirled into her eyes. They stood almost on the edge of a round pool and she could see the foaming base of the waterfall. The tussocks at her feet were beaded with silver droplets and her clothes were beginning to feel damp. It looked like any other cataract, apart from the preternatural clarity of the water and the golden glow.

She gazed around at the rocks, tussocks and water, feeling almost disappointed. *No sign of Crajaval, no palace, no portal or anything other than an ordinary mountain, apart from how the water shines. And certainly no signs of the Stones of Protection.* She twisted a lock of hair in her hands. "Well, we're here," she said. "What do we do now?"

Farren led his mare to the edge of the river to let her drink, well back from the foaming pool beneath the waterfall. "We look for where we could find Crajaval or those Stones. I wonder if we have to wait for night-time or the right phase of the moon or anything like that. Shayim only appeared during the Blood Moon in autumn."

"She's supposed to be actually here somewhere. Shayim was only a wraith," she replied. She let Storm wander to the edge of the river to drink beside Princess. "We could wait until nightfall. Or we could try to find some way into the mountainside."

He looked up. "I hope we are looking in the right place and we don't have to climb up there." He gestured with one hand to the head of the waterfall as it plunged down a sheer cliff face from a cuplike cirque formed by the three peaks of the mountain, barely visible through the haze of mist.

"If that's where we need to look for the Stones, we'll have to come back in summertime with climbing equipment. And people who know how to scale cliffs." She stared at the shining white line of water as it flowed over the top in a thin smooth plunge then spun itself out into droplets and rivulets cascading from rock outcrop to outcrop until it plummeted into the pool in a rush of foam and spray. The late afternoon sun reached through the mist to catch the droplets from one angle and make them flash fire.

Princess began to wander away from the river and search for grass and he walked with the mare. "If we ride around the waterfall and these cliffs, we might find a way up to the top or a way into the mountain, or maybe one of those stone circles." He ran his hand over Princess's shoulder as she cropped the tough tussocks. "We'll need to find shelter for the night before much longer as well."

She tore her gaze away from the almost hypnotic interplay of light and water. Something else to her right reflected the pale gold light of the falls and she turned her head to look at it. A large copper gong scarred with age and verdigris hung on a dead tree by the riverbank with a hide-headed hammer lying beneath it, almost hidden by the tussocks. She turned away from the pool and slipped her hand into Farren's again, leading Storm with the other. "What's that?"

"A gong, of course. What does it look like?" He stepped towards it, gently tugging her along with him. Two figures, a nude antler-crowned man and a dying stag, were worked in the centre of the copper disk. *Shayim.* Skin crawling on her shoulderblades and spine, she looked away from the blunt, stylised features of the horned man to the rim of the circle. It bore a border of crescent and full moons at the very edge and below the moons ran the curved lines of runes. Farren let go of her hand and stepped between her and the gong as she tried to make out the letters.

He raised a finger to the image of the full moon at the top and slowly began to work his way sunwise around the circle of runes. *"Darrinase ea eil atrevyasa, sihraybastin y charreder-daw,"* he read aloud. *"Ahuase domaster, mar azul y duhn. Sanastin, talithain, lavannin, ro ash van ro urri. Darrinase ea eil atrevyasa, van carrase carr."* He paused, a slight frown on his face. "Strike me who dares, lover of the bright – silver – white lady..." he began translating.

"I've heard something like this verse before," she interrupted. "When I was younger. Some of my kinsmen worship Crajaval and I often heard them singing their songs as the moon rose." She closed her eyes remembering and the hauntingly beautiful melody came back to her mind. "I never asked them why they sang it, but I heard it often enough to learn the words. This verse was only part of it. Mother was furious when she heard me singing it and said she'd leather me if she caught me singing it again. But the tune was so beautiful..." She swallowed down the lump of embarrassment in her throat and her shoulders bowed slightly. He chuckled and winked at her, then lightly tugged at lock of her hair. She shook her head and cleared her throat. "I'll sing it for you now, though. This verse, anyway." She drew a deep breath and closed her eyes before softly singing the lilting melody.

> *Strike me who dares, White Lady's lover,*
>
> *Summon the Queen, the earth's dark mother.*
>
> *Hunter, priest, victim, for grain and for cattle*
>
> *Strike me who dares, and fight the battle.*

"Summon the Queen… Strike me who dares and fight the battle," he repeated. "Very well then, I will. Get ready, Stormwolf."

"Are you sure?" She glanced at him then back at what she could see of the waterfall.

"Can you think of anything else? There doesn't seem to be anything else here – any other way of finding her." He reached for the hide-headed hammer in the tussocks beside the gong and raised it. "In the name of God Incarnate." He shook his cloak back from his shoulders and swung the hammer. It struck the centre of the gong, making the copper boom and echo. The sound rang off the mist-hidden mountain and off the rocks that gleamed in the light of the waterfall. Again he struck it as the first sound was dying, then a third time.

A single voice rang out through the mists, cold, clear and piercingly sweet. It sang words in a language she did not recognise, although it sounded kin to the Old Tongue. She started, feeling Farren's arms stiffen under her hand at the same time. Fire began to prickle in her veins and her rings were hot circles about her fingers. The singing continued, more exquisite voices joining the first. "On the horses," he hissed, letting go of her. "We'd better be ready for them."

The mists parted, clearing from the pool of churning, shining water at the base of the huge cataract that crashed and foamed between the rocks that glistened with moisture and the light of the pool. Graceful white deer with gilded antlers walked towards them with stately paces, almost floating over the ground near the brink of the deep pale-blue pool. Behind and among them walked cats, half black and half white with curling rams' horns growing from their heads. A large horned cat stepped forwards, tail arched over its back and brilliant amber eyes fixing them. "Who are you?" it asked in a sweet voice. "You who come for the sacrifice, what are your names, O priestess and victim?"

Ice clutched at her in sudden horror. *What have I done, singing like that? I never guessed the song and the fruit were part of a ritual sacrifice.* Fire flooded through her and burned the ice away. Her hand tightened around Storm's bridle and she swung herself up onto the gelding's back. She whipped the hair back from her face and swept her cloak behind her as she locked eyes with the horned cat. It had the shape of a crescent moon with the horns pointing upwards in red on its forehead. Her eyes narrowed and she bared her teeth. "I am Azariel Stormwolf, arch *minyaster* of the Kingdom. You'll find neither priestess nor victim here!"

The cat arched its back and screamed shrilly. The other cats bristled and bared their long needle-teeth. The white deer reared up onto their hind legs and shifted shape from deer to male and female human forms, winged, fanged and cloaked with the gilded antlers still jutting from their heads. A hot musky stink emanated from them. In a group, they closed in howling.

She punched green fire from her opal ring at the leading cat. The bolt struck it between the eyes and she saw the amber light fade. She smiled, grimly triumphant, expecting to see the cat fall dead. It kept stalking towards her, pupils malevolent slits. In the light of the golden water, she saw its muscles rippling under the sleek fur. It leaped at her, claws bared. Another bolt of lightning burst from her rings and struck the cat. This time, she saw it drop lifeless, then wither into empty air. Other creatures were all around her, keening and striking. She threw bolt after bolt of flame at them, ducking low under the stag-people as they took to the air and flew at her, wings stirring the mists. She heard the stamps and snorts of Princess to her right, mixed with the sputtering crackle of Farren's lightning bolts. She stood in the stirrups and shouted a wolfish battlecry, fire flying from her hands.

Storm charged, then shied as a cat clawed at his leg, butting at his breast with its ram's horns. He reared beneath her and she seized the reins with one hand, fighting to control him. *No, Storm! Don't run, even though you're not used to this kind of enemy!* Fire blasted from the fingertips of her free hand at the cats. The black gelding tossed his head and laid his ears back flat on his skull. "Come on, old fellow," she urged him. One of the stag-people swooped down at her, long fingernails crooked and ready to rake. She dodged to one side as the white hand struck down. It brushed past her arm and lashed into Storm's shoulder, tearing red lines into him. The black gelding screamed and bucked, lashing out at the cats and stag-people around him. One stag-woman fell beneath his hooves with a crack of breaking bone. Feet firm on the stirrup-bar, Azariel gripped him between her thighs and knees, fighting to keep her seat. He pitched forwards and the high saddlehorn jabbed her in the stomach. Gasping for breath, she buckled her hand into a fist and struck at the flying stag-man. Red and black fire burst from her ring as her knuckles cracked into his back, killing him.

She pivoted, fighting for balance and control of the pain-maddened gelding. Her hair lashed around her face, blinding her momentarily with black. She heard the sounds of the fight around her: the yowls and keening of the creatures, the hiss of wings, the snorts and neighs of the horses and, above all, the roar of Moonlady Falls. She shook her hair back from her face and put all her effort into pulling Storm under control. *If we can't work together, we're both dead.* Rearing and sidestepping, he fought her but stopped bucking. A cat, all claws and bristling fur, leaped at them, making the gelding shy. It landed on his neck and bunched itself up ready to spring again. The acrid stink of cat filled her nostrils, mixing with the smell of her own sweat. She bared her teeth and thrust her hand at it, fingers splayed and white flame bursting out to consume the cat.

Two of the flying stag-people came at her, one on each side. She dropped the reins and punched fire at them from both rings, feeling the wild rush flood down her arms and burst, golden, green and deep blue, from the stones. Storm back-stepped, reared and turned, ready to bolt. Her muscles ached with the effort of controlling him. The stag-people flinched at the touch of the flame, then pressed closer, fingers crooked and horned heads lowered to gore. She twisted in the saddle to meet them, hair filling her dry mouth. The black gelding wheeled around, colliding with the one on the right as blue flame burst from her lapis lazuli ring at the other. Storm bucked and kicked out wildly behind him, then jerking her forwards as he trampled the stag-man. Then he began to run.

He struck into Princess's shoulder. Her eyes met Farren's as he looked around, teeth bared and hand poised to burst with flame. "Sorry," she panted. "It's all I can do to stay on his back sometimes, let alone fight. He's not used to these kinds of enemies."

"Protect me for a few seconds," he replied, dark eyes flicking towards the remaining cats and stag-people. "I'll quieten his fear and put him under some control."

She swivelled in the saddle to face the beasts. *Thank the Power for his Gift – and mine.* Fresh fire blazed down her arms and burst in crackling golden lightning from her fingertips. She saw Storm's ears prick forwards and his fierce pulling on the reins stopped. "There," said Farren. "I can't do much while I'm fighting, but that should give him enough courage to beat down the rest of these things."

"Thanks, beloved," she said, wheeling the gelding around into the fight again.

Fire sprayed from her hand, withering and annihilating the beasts when it struck them, blackening the rocks when it flew wide. Her heartbeat pounded in her ears and her throat and mouth were dry. *They're nearly all dead. A few more blasts and we'll have won. And then for a drink!* She shifted the balls of her feet back properly onto the bars of the stirrups and stood, both hands raised. "*Yshyr y Tahelods tar vitasad van minyator, khrista-ar mar darr dam-vidai!*" she barked. Fire blazed from her hands, while from the corner of her eye, she saw matching fire flare from Farren. The coloured lights consumed the few remaining cats and stag-people, withering them to empty air.

She tossed her hair back from her eyes and drew a deep breath. Prickling fire still coursed through her veins and tingled at her fingertips. The mists began to creep back over Moonlady Falls, completely hiding the bright pool and the foaming water. "Now what?" she said to him.

He opened his mouth to answer, but a loud baying interrupted him. Out of the mists burst a pack of about twenty hounds. Blue flames spurted from the hounds' long muzzles, illuminating their brilliant red ears and white fur, and casting swirls of blue light on the gravel beneath them as they bounded towards her. "Hellhounds!" she hissed under her breath as she gathered up the reins. Right hand held high for the attack, she punched her heels into Storm's flank to urge him on.

The hellhounds surged around the two horses, biting and snarling. Storm reared, lashing out with his hooves. He crashed down, felling one of the dogs as flame burst from her hand. "Go, Storm!" she yelled. "Charge!" She raised her hand, energy coursing down her veins, coruscating through her wrists and burning out. The beam of scarlet light seared the white hairs of one of the hounds to black. The other hounds leaped at the horse and she saw one close its burning jaws over his leg. She shot flame at another and two fell back out of the path of the lightning. Storm jerked up screaming, mane flying in her face. The hellhound released the gelding's leg and flew backwards, a hoof in its ribs. She gathered up the reins, the leather slippery with foam and sweat. Storm pitched and tossed, throwing her wildly back and forth, nearly shaking her from her seat. She felt hard, bruising teeth catch her ankle and press down. Then another burning mouth caught her arm. She gripped the saddlehorn desperately to keep herself from being dragged off. Storm was screaming, bucking, twisting and lashing out at the hellhounds surrounding him. Her heart races and she felt sick. Desperately she looked through the curtain of her hair at Farren as he rode Princess, burning down the hellhounds right and left. "Farren!" she called, half screaming herself. "Please! Help me control Storm before he has me off!"

He swung around sharply at her, eyes and mouth furious and frustrated. "Can't you ride better than that?" he snapped. "I'm doing all I can!"

A clear voice called out from behind the mists. The hellhounds fell back from them, growling softly. For a second time, the mists parted, revealing the shining waterfall. A small gap had opened in the rocks beside the pool. A hellhound the size of a horse came out and on its back rode a shining white woman. Braids of cornsilk-pale hair coiled like serpents about her head and a silver crown set with moonstones flashed on her brows. She was exquisitely beautiful: figure voluptuous and flawless, lips brilliant blood-red against her glowing snow-white skin, eyes clear crystalline blue. She raised her dazzling white arms, letting the shimmering white samite draping her fall apart, baring her perfect full-moon breasts.

Farren felt his jaw drop and his bones turn to water inside him as he looked at the dazzling white lady. *Crajaval the Moon Goddess. No wonder men have lost their minds, lives and souls to her. She's beautiful!* He swallowed and lowered his hand from the attack, warmth and longing beginning to stir inside him.

Then he gritted his teeth, iron will re-asserting its control over his body. "Idiot," he muttered to himself, turning his eyes away. "What would I want her for? I've got my Stormwolf." He turned to look at Azariel as she fought her bucking, foaming horse. He sent out a wave of calm over Storm and saw the gelding stand still. Azariel's hair and cloak whirled about her like shadow and he caught a glimpse of her bared teeth.

He heard the paws of the hellhounds click and grate on the stones and he darted his glance up. *Have you forgotten one of the first rules of fighting, Blackarrow? Never take your eyes off your enemy.* He fixed his eyes on Crajaval. Again his gaze wandered down to her breasts and his untamed male instincts began to beat in his blood again. He hesitated, wavering between looking at her and looking away. *I'll have to look at her. I'll have to ignore the fact she's so damn beautiful.*

Crajaval's hellhound strode closer. He gritted his teeth as an almost palpable wave of musky-sweet perfume rolled out from the white woman. She was beside him, looking across at him from her mount, close enough to touch. Princess's ears flattened back onto her skull and the mare shied away from the hellhound. *No, my lady. Stand still.* He sent warm calming energy down through his hands into the mare, feeling the invisible cord of love that bound her to him tighten. Dimly, he was aware of the thinner cord binding and almost-calming Storm, but he ignored it and focussed on Princess. His strong left hand tightened into a fist.

Crajaval laughed softly and caught his eye. She reached out an exquisite white hand and brushed it over Princess's muzzle. The mare reared, squealing and kicking wildly. He pivoted in the saddle, fighting to keep his seat and re-assert his hold over the chestnut horse. The white goddess smiled and touched the mare again. Something cold seemed to well up from the horse, pushing back the warm, calming energy he sent into her and quenching it. The mare leaped and twisted like a hooked salmon and he felt himself sliding to one side. *I'm off! Curse that white devil's magic.* He fell, striking heavily into the rocks below and twisting to one side as the mare crashed down. She reared, eyes rolling, teeth bared and withers covered with foam, then whirled and bolted into the night.

Crajaval stooped down from her mount over him. Behind, he heard Azariel cry out and a clatter of hooves. He staggered to his feet, bruised and winded from the fall. His hand went to his right hip and drew his sword. He looked at Crajaval, ready to stab. *Damn her, damn her, damn her for being so beautiful! I can hardly bear to strike at something as perfect as her.* His sword wavered in his grip. Crajaval raised one hand, palm out.

His right wrist flew in front of his face, ready to block the white woman's fire. Blood pulsed in his ears. A flicker of white caught the corner of his eye. Her hand smote the side of his face, icy and stinging. Then he staggered forwards and everything went black.

Azariel saw the pale lady strike him and savagely wrestled Storm under control, pulling the reins painfully tight. Then she saw Farren fall to the stones for the second time and her strength faltered. "No," she whispered, a terrible cloud of fear, rage and dismay covering her mind. "Farren. My love." She let the reins drop.

Shaking with horror and disbelief, she watched as Crajaval dismounted from her huge hellhound and lift the fallen man up. His body lay limply in her arms like a carcass. Crajaval bent her head over him and kissed him on the mouth. The traces of colour on Farren's cheeks faded to a deathly white. The shining white woman raised her head and smiled coldly and triumphantly at her.

A mere minute had passed since Crajaval had appeared. Storm tugged the reins from her trembling hands and wheeled around. He plunged into a gallop, unfettered by Farren's calming touch. Instinctively, she clung to him with her thighs, her hands, with everything, hair whipping around her face and half blinded with grief, shock and cold fury. She heard the bay of the hellhounds behind her and Storm screamed in response. He was running wild, and she did not try to check him.

CHAPTER EIGHT

The bridge lurched and swayed beneath her, pitching her and Storm back and forth wildly as he galloped over it. Behind her, the hellhounds bayed, nearly drowning the thunder of the river. Storm leaped onto the far bank and landed on firm ground. She bent low over his neck and felt a lather of sweat on his withers under her hands. His heavy hooves thudded and crunched over the blurred white snow beneath her, and she faintly caught the soft padding of the hellhounds behind her. *I can't stop Storm and I can't turn him to fight. I'll have to let him run, poor fellow, until his strength gives out. And he's already weary.*

She shook her hair back from her eyes and scanned her surroundings as best she could. Storm raced out from the shadow of the mists along the river flat, heading westwards into the hills. The stars showed between the patches of broken cloud above her, pale light glimmering off the virgin snow. Another light shone behind her, and she turned her head as it flickered in the corner of her eye. The hellhounds ran behind her, blue flame dripping like slaver from their muzzles.

Storm plunged on into the night, the hellhounds following. She screwed up her eyes against the bitterly cold air that stung her eyes and chilled her skin. *How much longer will Storm be able to run from them? Those beasts are supernatural – they'll run him to death.* She glanced behind her again through the whipping veil of her hair. Ten hellhounds were pursuing her, neither falling back nor gaining. Their red eyes glowed in the blue flame of their mouths and she caught a glimpse of their bared teeth behind the flame. *They're waiting for him to collapse. And then...* She pictured what would happen; the hard teeth closing on the gelding's neck, hocks and belly; fangs catching her from the saddle and tearing her apart. She shuddered. *King of Heaven, what now? There's no way I can check and turn Storm to fight. Show me what to do and help me do it.*

An answer came out of the darkness, ringing through her head almost as if it had been spoken aloud. *They want you, not him. Even if he were to drop, they would not touch him. They have been sent to kill you.* She closed her eyes and flowed her movements into the quick rock of the bolting gelding's gallop. His mane lashed her hands, strong-smelling foam whipping up with it. All she could hear above the scream of the cold wind in her ears was the heavy thunder of Storm's hooves. *If I was to leave Storm, then I could turn and fight. But not yet. Maybe I can put more distance between them and me.*

Storm crashed into a tangle of trees, a mixture of birch and pine as she guessed from the bittersweet scent. She bent low over his neck, eyes narrowed against the stinging air. Branches caught and clawed at her hair and cloak, and snow slid from them and dashed into her face. Twigs and thin branches snapped around her as Storm ran. Something hard struck her on the shoulder and neck, knocking her off balance. *Thank the Power that didn't break my neck!* She clung to the gelding, striving to keep her seat, pulling on the tall saddlehorn. Storm swerved suddenly and she felt her body lurch past the point of recovery and slid her feet from the stirrups. She rolled and crashed onto the forest floor, thorns raking her arm as she fell. Storm fled without her, snapping and smashing his way through the darkness.

Quickly, she bounded to her feet and looked at the hellhounds. The rough line of blue muzzles wove through the trees towards her. Once again, she saw Farren falling in front of Crajaval's huge hellhound, the memory fresh and vivid. She clenched her fists, ready to fight, when something gave way within her. *I can't stand alone against this many. And I've lost Farren.* Tears suddenly blurred the flickering blue flames. *Maybe I should surrender and let them kill me.*

Never! She clenched her jaw. *I'll outrun them and then I'll return to avenge him.* The hellhounds had approached to ten paces away and the leader opened his mouth and bayed, revealing huge fangs. She wheeled and dived away from them, shifting shape as she flung herself forwards and down. Abruptly, the cold air of the night left her bare skin as the night world of sight, sound and smell sharpened. She galloped through the undergrowth, long wolf-legs eating up the distance.

She jinked and dodged around the trees, the noisy breath and thudding paws of the hounds following. She hurdled a fallen log and squeezed through a dense spinney of young beeches. She twisted her head around to glance over her shoulder. The hellhounds were hidden behind the screen of bushes. Here and there, flickers of flame showed, and she heard the drumming of their running. *They're gaze-hounds by the looks of them, not scent-hounds. I might be able to hide and throw them off.* A huge black beech loomed above her and she glanced up. *No good. That lowest branch is too high for me to climb.* She dodged around it and pushed her way through a thornbush. A sharp needle dug into the pad of her right forepaw. Gritting her fangs against the nagging pain, she ran on. Still the hellhounds followed, just out of sight. An enormous log lay ahead of her, hollowed by age and insects. *Help me hide, King of Heaven,* she prayed, loping towards the log. *Stop them scenting or seeing me in here.*

he squeezed into the log and crouched down, trying to hush her panting breath. The padding of the hellhounds came closer, then she spied the pack through a thin crack in the log. *At least I've got my flanks protected if it does come to a fight.* Silver fear played in the pit of her stomach, and her breath stayed trapped behind her teeth. They came closer to the log, running straight as arrows towards it. She tensed. The leader of the white pack came within a pace of her hiding place, then leaped. It hurdled the log and ran on, the other nine leaping after it.

Relief poured over her like water as she heard the rush of their bodies through the air above her. She waited, crouching with ears pricked as the crash and swish of their path through the forest died away into the distance. Shaking, she dropped her head down onto her paws and closed her eyes. The log smelt bitter and she heard the little scrabblings of insects inside the log. *Thank the Power. They're gone.* She stopped panting and closed her mouth. Grief, shock and exhaustion overtook her limbs and weighted her head. She wriggled around, seeking a comfortable position inside the hollowed tree trunk and fell asleep.

She woke to the sound of birds calling and shrilling. She pricked her ears and opened her eyes. Sunlight shone through the canopy of the woods, casting dappled shadows onto the leafmould and the ground smelt damp. She crawled out from the log, shaking scraps of decayed wood and beetle fragments out of her fur. Something itched halfway down her flank and she turned her head to scratch at the itch with her fangs. Two places on her legs stung and throbbed from the bites and scratches she had suffered during the fight. Hungrily, she lifted her head, looking and sniffing about her.

The sun had reached the peak of its late autumn arch and was shining strongly. *I have slept late. No wonder I'm famished.* The wind had shifted to the northeast quarter and the snow around her had melted to slush and pools of dirty water. The mountains, free from the strange mist and mantled in fresh snow, shone dazzlingly against the almost-clear sky. A few broad fingers of cloud stretched from the northeast towards the southern horizon. Willow trees surrounded her, the mass of dead leaves beneath them smelling nutty-sweet and damp. Behind them, she heard the gentle chatter of a stream and smelt fresh water. Thirsty, she trotted towards it.

She pressed through the bare trailing streamers of the weeping willows and came to the stream. She bent her head and saw her shewolf's reflection looking back at her from the water below as she drank. Thirst quenched, she looked up. A finger of cloud had taken hold of one of the mountains ahead of her, and beyond that, she saw the mist over the Illin-Ast gorge. *That's where I've come from. But where am I to go? I've lost my horse and I've lost...* She interrupted her thoughts with a whine. *Farren, I've lost you!*

She lifted her head and howled the wolf's lament for a lost mate, repeating it over and over until her throat was sanded with thirst. She returned to her own shape, unsure why she did. For a few heartbeats, she struggled to hold back the hot tears that prickled behind her eyelids. *Oh, what does it matter if anyone sees me cry, if there is anyone to see? My Farren is – was – worth it.* Covering her face with her hands and hair, and with her head bowed, she wept. Eventually, even her tears failed her and she knelt on the small patch of gravel by the stream, spent. *I've lost him and I'm lost without him,* she thought, staring blankly at the grey stones and bare willows. *I never knew I needed him so much. Some tasks are easier to do when you have a friend. And I loved him.*

A small dark flame sparked into life in her heart. *I must go back and fight. This time, Crajaval must die. For taking the Stones and for killing Farren. And if she kills me, then so be it. Then I'll be with him again.* She clenched her fists and stood up, tossing her hair back across her shoulder. Her face still felt swollen and the salt of her tears stung the half-healed graze on her cheek from where she had fallen down the scree. A dead golden willow leaf had caught in her hair and she combed it out. *But how? I must kill her. I must take the Stones back, but how am I to do it – alone and unhorsed?*

She turned and looked back into the small forest behind her. *I could always go and look for Storm. His trail will be easy enough to follow by sight or scent.* Thoughtfully, she ran her eyes over the mixture of evergreen leaves and bare branches in the woods. Then she shook her head. *No. He's terrified of supernatural enemies, bold as he is against other cavalry. I'd never control him without Farren to help me. Facing Crajaval will be bad enough without that.* She looked down at her hands, studying the flickers of colour in the heart of the fire opal. *King of Heaven, what should I do?*

A pang of hunger shot through her stomach. *First of all, I'd better find something to eat, otherwise I'll have no strength to do anything.* She chuckled softly. *Thank the Power for my shapeshifting gift.* She closed her eyes and made her body change into a wolf's once more. Her mind seethed in a cauldron of instincts and desires as the wolf-brain fought with her human will and intellect for dominance. Her willpower slid into control and she opened her eyes again. Hunger still gnawed at her stomach and she snuffed at the air and ground for the scent of prey.

She picked up the scent of a goat in some short grass near the stream's banks. She followed it out of the trees and onto a small tussocky knoll with broom and thistles punctuating the golden grasses. She jog-trotted up the slope, pressing low to the ground as she reached the crest. She peered over, expecting to see the goat on the other side of the little hill. The small valley between where she was standing and the rise beyond lay empty. She loped down into the valley, head bent low over the scent trail.

A hare darted out from behind a thistle as she passed. She started and swerved towards it, accelerating with the full force of her wolf's legs. She fixed her eyes on the scurrying shape in the tussock, waiting for the moment when the hare would double back or zigzag. It swung sharply to one side, black-tipped ears pricked. The fierce thrill of the chase surged in her as she swung towards it, gaining ground. Again the hare swerved abruptly. She could hear its paws on the earth amidst the whisper of the tussocks. She leaped over a diminutive broom bush, glancing down. *Not hiding. Good.*

She closed in on it, jaws wide and ready. Two paces lay between them. One. She pounced, forepaws stiff and the smell of the hare's fear strong in her nostrils. It struggled and squealed under her pinioning paws. For half a heartbeat, she saw its sides heaving and its whiskers quivering. Then hunger swallowed the moment of pity and her jaws snapped shut, all the force of her fangs shearing and crunching though the hairy, bony resistance. The struggles beneath her paws and between her lips stopped and she tasted the warm salt of blood. She bolted the hare down, then trotted back across the hills to drink again.

She shifted shape again and wiped the water away from her mouth. A sharp, bloody taste lingered in her mouth and she scooped up a handful of water, grimacing. *I didn't wait long enough after eating to shift shape or drink enough to wash the blood away.* She rolled the water around her mouth, then spat it out. *Well, Master, thank you for my breakfast – or should I say my luncheon? But now, do I return straight away to Moonlady Falls or shall I return to the capital for reinforcements?*

She waited for an answer, gazing at the greens and olives of the rolling land around her and listening to the tiny sounds of wood, wind and water. Birds swooped and fluttered over the small wood nearby and a falcon soared and circled over a long ridge. Her gaze drifted down from the slopes to the stream. A large chestnut leaf twirled down the course of the water, spinning in eddies and dancing over the small rapids among the rocks. She caught the leaf up and stared at the fine veins and traceries in the golden-red. *His hair was this colour,* she thought, choking and blinking back the fresh tears that sprang to her eyes. *I wish she had left his body alone. What does she want with him – it? When I go to fight her, I'll not only take the Stones back but I'll lay him to rest with the honour he deserves.* She gritted her teeth in spite of the tears, watching the drops fall from her cheeks into the stream where they made little ripples in the stiller patch of water by the bank. *Or I'll die fighting and join him!*

She set the leaf on the water and watched it dance its way east as the stream flowed towards the gorge. She drew a deep breath and brushed the tears off her face. *It's gone to the Illin-Ast, and I must follow it. Whether I'm to go to the capital or to Moonlady Falls, I've got to reach the river.* "God Incarnate," she added aloud, "show me which way to turn when I reach the end of the stream."

She got to her feet, brushing her cloak behind her, and began to walk along the course of the stream. Her riding boots crunched over the gravel, then thudded on the water-softened dirt beside the stream in strong, steady strides. She raised her head and looked about her. Most of the hills and mountains were tinted in bright colours in the early afternoon sunshine, but the peak slightly to the left of where she was headed was cloaked in mist. *That's where I'm bound, sooner or later.* She trudged on. A solitary drone, outcast from the hive for the colder weather, buzzed beside her, a bass note to the treble of the stream's constant chatter.

A cloud covered the sun and the heat left her. She looked up and saw massive cumulus clouds drifting through the pale blue sky. One or two curled clusters of white stayed more or less in place above the mountains, huge cauliflowers and fleeces tinged with grey around the edges. *Stormclouds,* she thought, stepping over a large boulder and half stumbling in a patch of mud on the other side. *I'll have to seek shelter when it breaks. And I'm going to enjoy watching it.* She walked on, glancing up at the clouds from time to time. A flock of starlings shrilled an alarm ahead of her and took to the air. *It's odd,* she thought as she watched the high sweep of the thunderhead begin to form. *I didn't think the winds were right or the air hot enough to bring on a thunderstorm. It's not storm season.* She shrugged. *But I'm no weather-prophetess. Perhaps I'm wrong.*

The stormcloud grew and the sky darkened. A second stream had joined the first and the two ran as one through a gently sloping valley. She scrambled through the tussocks, muscles starting to tire with the effort of long walking, and the sweat dampening her back and the hollows behind her knees. Her mouth grew dry and she halted to drink from the stream. She quenched her thirst and dabbed a little water on her face. *Not too much. I don't want to chill myself if the storm catches me in the open.*

She sat down on the damp ground with her back against a large cluster of tussock and blissfully took the weight off her legs as she rested. The smell of mud and grass wafted around her, a clean outdoor smell. Somewhere upwind of her, wild thyme was growing and the almost bitter aromatic scent sent a ripple of refreshment down her spine. She thought wistfully of the cheeses in Storm's saddlebags, then shook the thought away. *That would go nicely with that thyme I can smell.* The sky to the east had grown thick with cloud and the hills beneath it looked unnaturally bright against the dark blue-grey background as the sun shone on them. A pair of hawks hovered and wheeled on the wings of the wind, bright pinpoints of gold in the leaden sky. A gust of wind lifted the hair back from her neck and cheeks and she caught the grumble of distant thunder. A shiver of pleasure and anticipation shot down the length of her body. *It's coming, it's coming.*

Another roll of thunder came from the dark clouds ahead of her. The wind grew stronger and she felt a few small spits of rain strike her. White fire split the darkness for the space of a heartbeat, then the heavens roared again. She stood up, cloak and hair swept behind her by the wind. Rain began to drive down over her, then stinging hail battered down, smarting on her bare arms and face. She gave a small shout of laughter and shifted shape, turning her wolf's head into the storm and ignoring the flying pellets of ice on her face.

Something fell with the rain and hail, catching the corner of her eye. She turned her head, detecting a foul smell. A small creature, human-shaped but with a large froglike belly and pointed ears, sat cross-legged on a tussock looking at her. It grinned and squeaked at her, showing a mouth of little pointy teeth. A second fell from the sky and picked itself up. The two imps sprouted claws from their long bony fingers and began to strut towards her.

Storm demons. I should have known the storm wasn't natural. She bared her teeth and felt the hair rise on her hackles. *Go away!* A deep bubbling growl rose in her throat. The imps squeaked and glanced at each other, grinning maliciously. A third joined them, then a fourth, the foul smell growing stronger as they increased. She growled at them again, ending with a snap of her teeth. She lunged at them, jaws wide, and they leaped backwards, tumbling over each other into the mud and laughing in high squeals. *Oh, blast the little pests!* She shifted shape again and got to her feet, heat beginning to prickle in her fingertips. Rain and hail stung her eyes and cheeks. "Go away and leave me alone!" she shouted at them.

Their insane laughter stopped abruptly and the imps darted back, squealing like half-starved piglets spying a meal. She waved her arms at them as if she was driving chickens. "Go away!" she shouted again. "Or do I have to blast you?"

The squeaking and mad laughter began again, then was drowned in another roar of thunder. The wind and rain lashed at her as she watched the imps, irritation building. The four imps turned their heads to the sky and whistled shrilly. The sound set her teeth on edge and a cold shiver prickled down her spine. Fire surged in her heart in response. More storm demons fell to the earth, larger ones that stood as high as she did. She stepped back from them, raising her hands to strike. Fire burst from her hands into one of the larger ones and she saw it evaporate in a cloud of acrid steam. More large demons appeared. She gritted her teeth. "All of you! Leave me in peace!"

All of them cackled in laughter as more of them fell. She heard a rustle in the grass behind her above the battering of rain and the howl of the wind. She glanced back. Another demon, taller still, stood behind her, claws unsheathed and ready. *There's too many of them to fight with my back unprotected.* She shifted shape and darted around the giant demon, loping and bounding over the tussocks into the hills.

She heard them skittering and swishing through the grass behind her, shrieking with glee. The stench emanating from them made her stomach churn with nausea. Through the rain, she saw the small wood where she had started out from in the distance. *I'll stand at bay under a tree and there I'll fight. And may the Power help me then!* She opened her wolf's mouth, drawing in deep breaths of air to her labouring lungs. The roof of her mouth felt dry and her tongue hung out as she panted, hot and exhausted. The tussocks and grasses passed away beneath her in a blur. She scented and half-saw her own footprints facing the other way in the gravel. *I've returned more quickly than I've come. I should have travelled as a wolf.* A large boulder stood in front of her. She gathered herself to spring and leaped onto it. Her paws met hailstones on top of the rock, fresh and still solid. One paw slipped on the little round balls of ice and she scrabbled madly with the three others.

One of the demons screamed with laughter and she felt hot claws rake into her hind legs. She half howled with the pain as she pulled herself onto the rock. Willing herself to ignore the pain, and blood, she leaped off the boulder onto the gravel. The wound burned and throbbed as if acid or salt had touched it. *There's poison in their claws. Master, I need your help!*

She staggered into the small wood, her leg throbbing. A tall oak stood in front of her, craggy branches reaching black to the thunderclouds. Its trunk looked thick and sturdy. She reached and whirled around, shifting shape and drawing herself up to her full height. Her hair whipped around her face with the wind and she shook it back. "Go away," she commanded the demons, raising her hands. "You cannot defeat me. I am the Stormwolf, arch *minyaster* and the servant of the Power."

The demons halted in a semicircle around her, retreating out of her range. Squinting through the driving rain, she watched them, running her eyes around the semicircle. One of the giant demons lifted a long-nailed finger and pointed towards her. She clenched her fists, ready to block enemy fire with her heavy silver armbands. The demon's bony finger lowered, fireless, but she felt a tingling grow around her legs. She looked down and saw nothing. The prickling grew higher and she felt her hair lift on her scalp and heard it crackle softly as if she were combing it with a horn comb in hot dry weather. An arrow of fear shot through her as she smelt a strange white smell in the air. *Lightning!*

She dived away from the tree as white fire broke overhead, rolling and scrambling for shelter, covering her head with her hands. For an instant, the tree was a black skeleton blazing purple-white flame. Then as the thunder rolled, it exploded. She fell to her knees, shielding herself from the scalding, bruising pieces of the flying wood and bark, screaming as boiling sap struck her bare skin. She opened her eyes as the debris stopped hitting her. The oak had caught fire and the demons were closing in on her.

She ran deeper into the little wood, stumbling over branches and with tree limbs catching at her hair and cloak. She jerked a tangle of hair free from a branch, wincing as she heard and felt hairs pull out from her head. A small group of elder trees stood in front of her, too thick to run through and too wide to run around without losing ground to the demons. *At least they're too small to draw lightning.* She wheeled, holding her hands ready to strike. Fire ran in her veins and tingled at her fingertips. It burst out at the wall of brown demons, sending two of them to steam.

They pressed in all around her, scratching and biting with hot, poisoned teeth and claws. Dizzy, weary and hungry, she sent fire at them again and again, dodging the claws as best she could as they reached for her hair and cloak. Her forearms were a mass of pain and one hot scratch ran down her cheek across the scalding from the burning oak. She saw another demon vanish in steam as a bolt of green fire struck it in the chest, but another took its place beside her. "God Incarnate," she called, chest heaving and fighting for breath, "help me. Somehow. Please."

Her hair hung across her eyes, stuck to her cheek by blood. Sweat and rain poured down her face, stinging in the burns and scratches. Trembling with pain and shock, and her vision blurring with bloodloss, she raised her arms to strike. More fire flew from her hands, the effort making her head reel. *And I can't call up a shield against this sort of enemy. This is where I die. Master, I'm in your hands.*

She braced herself, ready for a last effort. Behind her, she heard a snapping of twigs and something heavy striking the ground rhythmically. Her heart sank. *What now?* She drew a deep breath, savouring every small scent and taste in it: the scents of blood, sweat, bruised elderberries and leaves, the reek of the demons. *Last deep breath. Now I'll end it all.*

Something white crashed out of the trees. Silver lightning burst from it and blasted several demons to steam. A wail of terror went up from the brown demons, and they turned and fled. Giddy, she staggered backwards, her back against the thin trunks and branches of the elder trees. "Thank the Power," she whispered, slumping backwards. Stars swam before her eyes, then everything turned black.

CHAPTER NINE

Farren woke. Every muscle in his body ached and something in his mouth tasted sour. *Well, I'm not dead anyway. What's happened to me?* Water dripped somewhere nearby and the air smelt of smoke and filth. He tried to move but his arms and legs felt cramped and numb, as if he had been lying down for a long time. Something was jabbing and tickling at his bare arms. He opened his eyes and saw a rock floor in front of his eyes. Dim reddish light burned somewhere to his right, casting dancing black shadows onto the stone. He raised himself up onto his elbows, groaning as his muscles unstiffened, and found he was lying on a thin straw pallet. His cheeks itched and he scratched at them, wincing as he pressed his fingertips into bruises. He felt several days' growth of stubble beneath his fingers. *How long have I been out cold? She must have put me into some dungeon somewhere.*

He rolled over and looked about himself. He was lying in a bare rock cave that opened into a corridor. A torch in an iron bracket burned on the corridor wall opposite the cave mouth. Water was seeping down the wall nearest him and collecting in a little pool. Dimly in the distance, he could hear a faint, steady murmur somewhere inside the rock. *Crajaval must have put me behind the waterfall.*

Something rustled in the corner and he looked around. "Azariel?" he said.

"My name's not Azariel." A man shuffled forwards out of the corner, picking repetitively at his long grey-brown beard or at the colourless rags of his clothes. He would have been a tall man standing erect, but he kept his head down and his shoulders bowed.

"There's nobody here," the man said again. "Nobody human. There's only Her and her nymphs."

"Her?"

"You know who I mean. Crajaval. The Moon Lady. The White Goddess. Who did you think I meant?" A trace of a wry grin flickered across his face. "I suppose you're allowed to be a bit hazy. You've been lying there out to it for more than a whole day."

Farren stared down at the floor. "No. Don't tell me Azariel's dead."

"If this Azariel you're talking about is dead, they're lucky. I wish I was. I don't know how long I've been in here and I don't know how long I will be. There's no way out of here. No way out. I wish I could kill myself. I wish she would kill me. No other way out."

"Who are you?" Farren asked. "How did she catch you?"

"My name – when people called me anything – was Tristan. I was a hunter, I think. The phantoms caught me in the mountains. They didn't let me keep my knife. I know what I'd do if I still had it. I'd cut my own throat. I wish I was dead. I wish she'd kill me. Even if she starved me to death or tortured me or burned me alive or anything. I'll take anything, as long as it leaves me dead and gets me out of here. There's no way out. No way out. I want to die."

After a time, Farren closed his ears to Tristan's endless wishes for death. He sat cross-legged on his straw pallet and stared at his broken, grimy nails. Idly, he picked the dirt out from underneath them. *I hope Azariel isn't dead. Maybe she escaped.* The memory of her on Storm as the black gelding pitched and tossed burned into his mind and again he heard her calling him for help. *I should have gone to help her instead of staring like a dead fish at Crajaval. Then we might have been able to win the fight, or at least been able to escape together.* A flash of salt sparkled in the corners of his eyes.

My Stormwolf, I've failed you badly. I hope I get the chance to see you again and say I'm sorry. If only I could have...

He stopped himself. *It won't do me any good to think like that.* He stood up and stretched, feeling the stiffness in his legs, back and arms slowly disappear. A flash of torchlight on something metallic near the ceiling caught his eye and he looked up. His belt, complete with sword, pouch, dagger and quiver, was dangling from the ceiling too high for him to reach. The top vanished into the shadow, hiding what held it to the roof. *How did that get up there?* He looked towards the doorway, feeling his neck muscles twinge as he turned his head. "Tristan," he said, "where does this corridor lead to?"

"What?" The other man looked up. "Oh, nowhere much. Only to an iron gateway at one end and solid rock at the other. There are a few other caves down here, but they're all empty. The cave next to this one's the latrine, by the way. I don't know why I bother. It's hell in here, but I guess there's no point in making things worse. The nymphs come once a day to feed me. I wish she'd starve me. I want to die. But she won't." He stopped and cocked his head on one side. "But maybe she will now that she's got you. She'll have finished with me well and truly. She wants new blood."

"What do you mean?"

"I won't spoil it all by telling you about it. I almost envy you coming to it new. But she'll tire of you as she tired of me. You'll wish you were dead, too, before long. I know I do. If only I could find some way of killing myself. Then I'd be free. I wish I was dead. I wish..."

Farren ignored him and wandered out into the corridor. More torches burned in brackets on the wall and the roof of the corridor was stained black with soot. He shrugged and strolled back into the cave and sat down on his straw pallet, hearing one of the straws snap as he sat on it. The rock dug into his legs and buttocks through it, and he shifted around to find the most comfortable seat.

A noise like fluttering flags drifted in from the doorway and he looked up towards the archway. It grew louder, then two of the stag-people, females with moons embroidered in silver on their white robes, came in. "Come," one said, placing a long pallid hand on his bare forearm. "The Moon Lady wishes to see you now you have woken."

"I'm not going," he said, pulling his arm away and pushing himself to his feet.

"Yes, you are," the two said in chorus. "Come." They grabbed him by the arms, softly but strongly as steel. He struggled, then relaxed and allowed them to lead him into the corridor. *I may as well go along. I might find out more about this place, about what happened to Azariel and even about the Stones.*

A stag-man was waiting for the two others by the iron gate, holding it open. The two females led him through, then the gate clanged shut behind him. They led him up the staircase step after step to a dark landing. The red light from the torches in the lowest level had dimmed and he could hardly make out the shapes and outlines around him. Hands groped at his arms in the dark and led him on. To his left, he felt his elbow brush lightly against a solid metal surface, then across a crack, stirring a heavy ring that clanked and creaked. The stag-people pulled him around in a half-circle, then he stumbled as he knocked his shin against a stone step. Again, he followed them up a flight of stairs. Green light shone down from above him and the dead, still air carried the faint scent of some sweetish incense. He fidgeted uncomfortably. *The air feels as thick and dirty as if I'm being stifled in a blanket. Does a breeze ever blow through here?* The legs and body of one of the stag-people brushed against him and he shrank away, feeling oddly vulnerable. *Is it just my belt or am I missing something else?*

The pale green light grew stronger as they climbed and he could make out the embroidery on the robes of the creatures leading him. He blinked as they reached a second landing, this one lit by four torches, each burning with a green, smokeless flame. The incense smell grew sickly sweet and he felt his temples and the bridge of his nose begin to throb with the heavy scent. The two stag-women fell back and the male led him around into a brilliantly lit corridor that seemed, at first glance, to be made of ice. More pale green torches burned along the length of the hallway and the light sparkled off thousands of crystals set in the rocks and picked out shadows in fine, curved carvings which lined the walls. They led him to a pillared archway and thrust him through it.

A round bed lavishly spread with cushions, furs, deerskins and silk dominated the room, and in the centre of the bed on her side lay Crajaval. She wore a spiderweb-fine chemise that draped around her curving breasts and thighs, revealing and suggesting much more than it hid. She was crowned with a tiara that sparkled with moonstones, amethysts, pearls and diamonds whose inner star-fires were echoed by many others ringing the room on a rock lintel. She sat up and smiled as the stag-people pushed him forwards, and she drew the tiara off her head, letting her pale gold hair cascade down across the side of her face. A wave of perfume, musky and rich, rolled out from her body towards him. Blood heated his cheeks and he swallowed at the lump in his throat. "Welcome," she purred. "I have been waiting for you, Farren Blackarrow."

He backed away from her and felt something smooth and hard behind his back. Glancing over his shoulder, he saw nothing but felt a wall there, an invisible wall of air blocking his escape from the room. "What do you want?" he demanded, putting his hands on his hips and feeling almost naked without his sword hilt to grasp and draw. His eyes darted around the room, noting a jewelled tub filled with steaming scented water in one corner, but little else save Crajaval and her bed.

"Don't you know?" She smiled and winked at him from behind the curtain of her hair, then tossed it back behind her shoulder. The movement reminded him sharply of Azariel, and a pang of loss and longing shot through his heart. "I am the Goddess and I take lovers."

"Shayim?" he asked. "Is this what all this is about? Are you going to kill me for cheating him of his King Elk?"

She laughed, her voice rippling down the scale. "Oh, Shayim is my consort, but I take my lovers as I will. Mortal men. They used to bring them to me, you know, long ago. Men with hair like blood and fire, like yours. Men to enjoy, then send beyond the stars to immortality. Men with quickened souls as sorcerers – yes, and *minyastini*, too." She inched towards him and took hold of his arms. Her face came within a foot from his, and her breath tickled the skin on his cheeks. "And you're perfect. More than two centuries is far too long. Lie with me."

He stared at her numbly. *I'm dreaming. I know I'm dreaming. A perfect, exquisite beauty wanting to make love to me.* Blood and desire surged through his veins and he leaned forwards with a small sigh. A sharp cramp shot up his leg and he straightened with a gasp. *This is no dream. I'm awake, and that's the goddess of the Wayasti trying to seduce me.* Some of Tristan's words coursed through his memory and he pulled away out of her grasp. "I'll not let you steal my soul by bonding with my body. Let me go!" A wave of nausea churned in his stomach as the full realisation of what he had been about to do came over him. *She's not even human! I'd rather not give in to either of the seductresses that have locked hands onto me, but of the two, I'd prefer Stessa the Nightraven.* "Do you really think I want to end up like Tristan?"

Her fingertips traced his cheek, delicately running along the line of his jaw. "Oh, you would not end like him, Farren Blackarrow. Not one with a sorcerer's or a *minyastin's* soul." he arched her back, making the light glance on her full breasts.

Unbidden, his manhood rose and howled for her, but he willed it quiet. He glanced down at his hands and noticed how dirty and broken the nails had become, and abruptly became aware of the dirt and stains of travel on his clothes and body. *As if she really finds me attractive and irresistible when I'm all filthy like this. It's a trap.* "No. I will not. I won't lie with you."

"I can give you pleasure like you will never know with any mortal woman. More than what that scrawny virgin of a werewolf can give you."

"Don't speak about my Azariel like that." Anger mixed with hope. *Azariel – maybe she's not dead after all.*

"You forget that I am a goddess," she replied, voice low and icy. "Do you dare deny me?"

He stared at Crajaval. *She believes it? She really believes she is truly a goddess?* "You are not," he said, clenching his fists. His stomach churned and his pulse throbbed in his ears. "You're no goddess. You know you're a mere weakling beside the Most High God, my Master – and yours! Who are you to set yourself up against him?"

She shivered. "You are strong in the fibre, Farren Blackarrow, strong as steel." Her voice rang clear, cold and menacing, and the sweetness had almost left it. "Stronger than I expected. I have had other *minyastini* before now, you know. Jamin Bluecloak was like you, even down to your red hair, and he was mine. If you come to me and join with me, you won't be the first."

"And you corrupted Jamin into a thief, a murderer and a traitor. You won't do that with me. Do your worst, or let me go."

She tossed her head and began winding and braiding her hair up in coiled snakes. "My worst? As you wish. You refuse to satisfy my desire." She got to her feet and wrapped a white fur mantle around herself, hiding her figure in swathes of fur. "I won't kill you, in spite of that. You have other uses. I shall use you as bait to draw her back to me."

"Her?" He looked up, heart beginning to pound inside his chest. *If she means my Stormwolf, then she must be still alive. Thank the Power!* "Azariel?"

"Yes. Azariel Stormwolf. The werewolf. The only werewolf, the only skinchanger of any kind that doesn't serve and worship me." She clenched her fists and her exquisite lips twisted into a thin narrow circle of fury. "She has escaped me so far and I want her: dead or mine! She will escape no longer. I'll use you, the man she desires, to draw her here and then I have her!" She threw back her head and laughed one of her lovely rippling laughs.

He gritted his teeth. "If you think I'm going to betray the woman I love, you're wrong. I won't do it. Anyway, she probably thinks I'm dead. She won't come back for me."

"Maybe she does think that." Crajaval rubbed her long white hands together, staring past him. "But she won't if you do as I tell you." Her eyes fixed on him again and held his gaze as she spoke sweetly. "And she'll come. She will. Don't you want her to?"

He turned his head away. *I won't do it. I won't betray her. If I had helped her in the first place, I wouldn't be in this trouble. If only I had gone and helped her with Storm! We could have escaped or at least we would have died fighting together.* A heavy weight of guilt crashed down onto him and he bowed his head, tears starting to sting his eyes. *I'm starting to sound like Tristan already.*

"Well?" said Crajaval, cutting into his thoughts. "Will you?" She strode towards him, eyes boring into him.

"Even if I did, you'd never break her or bend her to your will, any more than you did with me. She's the arch *minyaster*, and I know she's as true as steel to the Power our Master."

Again Crajaval winced. "Speak about him again and I will kill you as slowly and painfully as I know how. And I know many ways!" Her voice hissed in a thin whisper. "Will you do as I command, or won't you? She'll bend." Her voice rose again, soft and melodious, as she paced about the room. "I'll make her. I know how. But will you do as I say?"

He pressed his back up against the invisible wall. The sickly sweet smell of the incense made his head throb and he was nearly shaking from the bubbling cauldron of fear, hope, anger and guilt boiling inside him. Suddenly, he felt reckless and the traces of fear left him. *I'm going to die slowly now, but I don't care any more. Even torture won't last forever. I'll die for Azariel and the Power.* "I will not!" he shouted. "Do as you please; flay me, burn me over a slow fire, anything you like. But I won't betray her, even to save myself. Do your worst, she-devil!"

She strode across the room, full lips pursed to a narrow line. She seized him by the shoulders and threw him down onto the floor, bruising his knees. One hand clutching him chokingly around the neck and the other arm steel around his waist, she lifted him and carried him out of the room and down the corridor, past the row of green torches. *What's she going to do to me? Hurl me from the top of the Falls, or is she dragging me to a torture chamber?*

They reached the end of the corridor and she strode down the steps to the second level. She dropped him, then thrust out a hand at the iron door. It flew wide open and she thrust him backwards into the darkness. He fell heavily, wincing as he landed on his bruises, gasping for breath. In the dark of the corridor, he could see only Crajaval shining faintly in the doorway. He heard something in the passageway behind him and turned, drawing himself up on his hands and knees. Blue flames were approaching him, and as they drew nearer to him, he recognised the hellhounds. They ringed him, jaws dripping saliva and flame from between their long fangs. Red eyes fixed on him, hungry, vicious.

He turned his head towards the figure of the woman standing at the entrance to the corridor. She nodded her head once, then rested her hands on her hips. The paws of the hellhounds clicked over the stone floor and he heard them growling softly. A ring of teeth faced him, closing in. He knelt up, staring into the eyes of one and sending a warm strong wave of energy towards it. The touch of his Gift was thrown back at him as if he had rammed a stick against a stone wall. They moved in a blur of blue, white and red around him then leaped on him, pushing him down, their bodies smelling more of incense than dog. He clenched his fists, expecting to feel the rush and tingle of fire flooding down his arms. Nothing. Something was stopping the fire: a heavy mass of dirty fog. *So that's what was missing. King of Heaven, no!* He struck out with his hands, trying to beat them off with his fists. He felt a mouth close around his thigh. *This is how I die. Eaten alive by her hellhounds. There could be worse ways.* Twin points of pressure, two above and two below, tightened, crushing and bruising. He groaned hoarsely. *Once they've torn the veins in my upper thigh, I'll bleed to death quickly enough. Master, I'm coming.*

The hellhounds swarmed all over his body in a frenzy of biting. He watched one clamp down on his arm and shake its head. *No blood, anywhere! They're just trying to hurt me, not tear me.* One seized him by the shoulder and jerked him backwards onto the hard stones. He heard the crack as his head struck the floor of the corridor and for a few moments, everything was confusion, blackness, pain and noise. Then he regained his senses. Another dog was standing on his chest, thrusting its flaming muzzle towards him. Its breath and the flame smelt of burning wax. He caught his breath as the hellhound bit down on his throat. Pressure sang in his ears and stars swam in front of his eyes. Then the jaws relaxed. He fought for breath, the horrible choking pressure gone from his larynx and windpipe. *The last time I ever want a dog's jaws on my throat.* Another one lunged at him and he wrested an arm free, feeling a dog's teeth rake down on it and draw blood. He thrust his arm in front of his face as the flaming jaws closed. Then the world exploded in blinding, visceral pain as jaws closed over his groin. He heard himself screaming and he vomited.

After a while, he felt as if there had never been a time when they were not biting him. He was dizzy and confused, punch-drunk. *What's all the pain of the past to this?* he thought as yet another set of teeth tore an explosion of pain from his groin for at least the fifth time. The stones of the floor came up to meet him again and again. His face was pressed against the cold hard stone and the dogs gnawed him everywhere: at his arms, his legs, his back, his neck, his buttocks, clawing and trampling on his spine. The blue, red and white shapes swam in front of his eyes. *Can't take much more. I'm going to pass out. Thank the Power for that!*

"Enough!" Crajaval's voice cut through the chaos of growls and his own cries of pain. The hellhounds left him panting, sobbing, retching and groaning on the floor. She strode over to him and rolled him over to look at his face. He stared back. A fierce smile parted her lips. "Think carefully before you defy me again, Farren Blackarrow. You will help me. If not, I will throw you to my pets again. And I will never let them kill you or even let you pass out." She straightened up and clapped her hands. Two of the stag-people appeared in the corridor from the air. "Take him back to his prison and feed him," she commanded. "I will send for him again tomorrow."

CHAPTER TEN

Azariel came to and felt a presence hanging over her. Sleepily, she opened one eye. The rain had stopped falling but drops still fell from the trees around her and onto her. A pearly white horse shape stood over her. She opened her other eye and brushed a lock of hair back off her face, arm shaking and stiff with her injuries. The white horse, delicate and fine-boned as a highly-bred royal mount, looked at her with large dark eyes. A waterfall of pure silky white mane and tail hung down, its tail brushing the ground and the mane halfway down its face. From its forehead, a tall spiralling horn rose, silver and shining. The unicorn bent its head over her and she smelt a faint aroma of violets coming from its horn. She reached out a hand and touched its warm velvety muzzle. "Unicorn," she whispered. "If I had been married to Farren, then I would be dead now."

"Thou hast heard that old legend?" The unicorn spoke, voice like falling water. "I would have come to thee, whether thou wert virgin, wife or widow."

"I have heard the stories about your kind, unicorn," she said, running her hand through the silk of the unicorn's white forelock. "Only virgins can see or touch unicorns. Isn't it true, then?"

The unicorn shook its head, mane gliding through her hands and giving off a stronger scent of violets. "True in part only. Not only virgins: the chaste, be they celibate or constant." It bent its head to her again, nudging at her breast with its muzzle. "Thou art wounded, *minyaster*. I must take thee with me and heal thee. What is thy name?"

"Azariel Stormwolf, arch *minyaster* of the Kingdom," she replied. "Thank you, unicorn, for saving my life."

The unicorn huffed out a deep breath. "I could not stand idle while the fiends of the storm stole thy life from thee. The Master sent me. But come. Ride on my back, Azariel Stormwolf."

She got to her feet, leaning on the warm silver of the unicorn's horn. Groaning with effort and the excruciating pain in her arms, legs and face, she heaved herself astride the unicorn. She slumped forwards across its neck, burying her head in its mane. *I only hope I don't fall off.* "I'm ready – I think," she said. "Please don't throw me, unicorn."

"I shall keep thee on my back," the unicorn said, turning its head to fix her with one large, dark eye. "Cling to my mane if the strength of thy legs fail thee. And I shall tell thee my name: I am Menkalinan."

Menkalinan galloped westward through the trees. Azariel slumped down low over his neck and clung to his back, her hands knotted through the living silk of his mane. The scalds and scratches on her arms and legs throbbed and burned, and she saw a small trail of blood fall from her arm across the shining white coat of the unicorn. The unicorn raised his head and parted the trailing branches with his horn. The twigs and dead leaves flickered past, whipping at her face and almost raw arms. "Menkalinan," she mumbled. "Where are we going?"

"To the Ulfskin-Aza forest," replied the unicorn, turning his head slightly, checking his arrow-swift pace. "Cling to me. We shall come ere the night falleth."

"That's a day's march from the Illin-Ast at least." His mane whipped into her mouth as she bent low beneath a thick branch, feeling the leaves brush over her hair. "Why are you taking me there, away from Moonlady Falls? I have a task to complete there."

"No matter. Thou must be healed."

"Oh." She closed her eyes, breathing in the faint scent that hung about his head, and blended her motions with his. His bare back swayed and rocked between her wounded thighs and the veins in his neck pulsed under her hands.

The hills, valleys and woodlands passed by in a blur. The stormclouds dispersed and a blood-red sunset remained, tingeing the snow-dusted landscape with scarlet. She caught the faint cold scent of pines from the black trees around her and shivered in the icy air. The unicorn plunged on, his hooves beating a swift tireless rhythm over the snow and tussock. Little balls and puffs of snow flicked up into the air from the unicorn's hooves and her eyes stung with the cold. Ahead, she saw a black mass of trees on the slopes under the mountains that sprawled to the horizon. The shadow of a mountain fell across them, cutting off the brilliant golds and reds of the sunset. Menkalinan ran on, heading for the huge forest.

She had half fallen asleep on the unicorn's back when she realised he had halted. His shining white sides were heaving and the smell of roses clung strongly and hotly about him. She slid off his back and steadied herself with her arm around his neck. "Come," said the unicorn. "Thou art weary and wounded, and I need to heal the worst of thy wounds ere thou sleepest."

He turned his head and nudged her, slowly stepping forwards. Exhausted, she walked with him to an oak tree. He pressed her down with his muzzle on her shoulder. "Sit with thy back against the tree. This one will not burst into flame." She sank down, eyes closed and conscious only of the pain and the heavy cloud of exhaustion. *To think that this time yesterday Farren was alive.* She felt the hot sparks behind her closed eyelids and willed them away. *I don't want Menkalinan to see me weep. It's humiliating enough to have him save my life. I don't want him to think me weak.*

She felt a soft warm touch on her bare arm. She hissed between her teeth as the thing brushed over the burns and gouges. Then the pain dissolved into the warmth. She opened one eye and looked down. The unicorn was touching her arm with the point of his horn. It travelled along her arm and behind it, the fierce burning pain stopped. The deepest gash on her arm oozed with half-clotted blood and a clear yellowish viscous fluid. As Menkalinan's horn brushed over it, the bleeding stopped and the yellow fluid bubbled and steamed up from her skin. She closed her eyes and relaxed as the soothing warmth of the unicorn's horn passed up and down her arms and washed across her face. Then she felt the soft muzzle and warm breath of the unicorn press against her cheek. "Sleep now," said the unicorn in a whiskery whisper. "I have stopped the bleeding in the worst of the wounds and taken the poison from the cuts. In the morrow, I shall do more."

"Shall I sleep here?" she asked sleepily. Her forehead felt clammy and hot as she brushed her hair back from where it had fallen across her eyes, but she shivered. "I'll sleep as a wolf, then."

Menkalinan nudged at her with his nose then put his horn gently under her armpit and lifted her to her feet. "Thou shalt sleep in greater ease than that," he said, carrying her forwards. Ahead, the thick forest and vines closed in around the clearing, except for one hump of mossy rock and soil. A small opening as high as her waist led into the hillside, in the twilight and the faint translucent light from the unicorn, she saw a pile of leaves on the floor of the little cave. "Rest thee here," he said. "I bid thee good night."

She tumbled onto the pile of leaves and lay staring into the darkness. Her head pounded and she hugged her cloak to herself against the chill inside her, feeling sweat coat her forehead. Her tunic and trousers rasped against her skin, which felt twice as sensitive as usual in spite of the lack of pain in the tears and burns. She fell into a restless sleep filled with confused dreams. She woke once with a hideous dry taste in her mouth to see Menkalinan's head reaching through the opening into the cave and felt his horn brush over her body again, the gentle warmth and scent taking the chills from her body.

The sound of birdsong woke her and she listlessly opened one eye. Daylight shone through the opening, showing her the greens and browns of the clearing. *Dreaming still?* she asked herself. Then the memories returned. *I must have taken a fever from the poison in those demons' claws. And he healed that as well.* The thought seemed to exhaust her and she closed her eyes, breathing in the nutty scent of the leaves beneath her. Warmth and weakness overtook her and she fell asleep again.

When she woke, her neck felt excruciatingly stiff and her right hand and arm prickled with pins and needles. She groaned and rubbed the muscles and twisted her head to one side. *If I'm going to sleep here again, I'll have to sleep in wolf-form or else find more bedding.* She stretched her arms and sat up, feeling the tension slowly relax from her muscles as warmth and blood flowed back into them.

A rustle of dead leaves caught her ear from outside the small cave. She turned her head and saw Menkalinan grazing in the small clearing where they had slept, brushing the leaves aside with one silver hoof. He looked up at her. "Good morrow to thee," he said in his musical voice. "Hast thou slept well?"

She nodded, stretching her arms and relishing the lack of pain. "Did I sleep all day and night? No wonder my neck was sore. But I'm feeling better now, than you." Then she looked down at her arms and stopped in shock. Huge patches of raw redness dappled her skin. Tentatively, she touched her cheek and found it was sticky to the touch as well. She prodded at one of the raw patches with one finger. "It doesn't hurt," she whispered. "Why? What have you done to me?"

"I dulled the pain for thee when I took the poison and fever from thy wounds. As for the rest, thou shalt be healed, but for that, I shall need help." Menkalinan lowered his delicate white head back to the short grass he had exposed. "Break thy fast at thy leisure," he said. "When thou art ready, I shall take thee to where I can find the help that I shall need." He shook his long flowing mane back from his eyes and glided over to the oak tree in the centre of the clearing. "I have prepared these for thee. Will it suffice?" He prodded at something at the foot of the trunk with one hoof.

She walked over to where Menkalinan had indicated and saw a small pile of nuts, crabapples, berries and mushrooms resting on large leaves. Her stomach tightened hungrily. "Thank you," she said. "That's plenty." She dropped to her knees and scooped up the red and black berries in one hand. "Thank the King of Heaven, too." She ate the berries one by one, alternating the tangy rowan berries with the full sweetness of the blackberries and raspberries. *It must be days since I've eaten properly. I remember that hare yesterday morning – no, the morning before – but nothing since then.* A drop of juice fell onto one of the open wounds left by the burns and she gritted her teeth, expecting to feel it sting. She felt nothing. *He's numbed it. I'd be in agony otherwise, by the looks of it, so I'm grateful. I'll have to take care that I don't damage my injuries further.*

She finished eating the berries and began on the mushrooms. "Menkalinan," she said in between mouthfuls. "Thank you for this. But I don't want to be more of a burden on you than I have to be. I can forage for myself, and I'd like to make that cave a bit more comfortable to sleep in if I have to stay here until I'm fully healed."

"By all means," replied the unicorn with his mouth full of grass. "Do so at thy leisure. But tax not thyself overmuch. When I take thee to my helpers to heal thee, it will take all thy strength."

She leaned her head back against the tree trunk as she ate, watching a sparrow as it fluttered, sang and perched on the branches above her. Once she had finished the mushrooms, she cracked the walnuts Menkalinan had provided for her and slipped the insides into her belt pouch. Walking to the edge of the clearing, she found a few silvery-brown circles of fungi scattered in a rough ring under the eaves of the forest. She knelt down to pick one and inspect it. *True mushrooms,* she though as she turned it over and ran her eyes over the dark brown gills. *Thank the Power it's autumn. If there's a good time to be forced to forage, it's now, what with these, nuts and apples. And stags easy to track by their roaring.* She brushed the dirt off the end of the stalk and bit into the mushroom. Eagerly, she ate it and reached for more. *But I won't hunt today. I'll leave that for tomorrow, whatever shape I hunt in.*

She harvested all the mushrooms she could find in the clearing, using the skirt of her cloak as a basket as well as her hood. Then she returned to the cave where she had passed the night and stacked them neatly in a dry corner at the back. Her hands were stained brown from the mushroom spores and she brushed the dirt off on a patch of damp leaves. *There won't be any more mushrooms for a few days. I had better enjoy these while I can.*

The sparrow she had watched while eating flew away suddenly, taking its song with it. She listened carefully and heard a rushing, chattering liquid sound coming from the forest to the northwest of the clearing. Suddenly, she became aware of her thirst and got to her feet. She pushed her way through the undergrowth, keeping the sound of the stream in front of her. Before long, she found it, a small, swirling watercourse that cascaded over mossy rocks and around gnarled tree roots. She knelt on a patch of moss on the bank and drank deeply.

As she walked back to the clearing, bracken clutched at her legs and dry twigs snapped beneath her feet. She stopped and looked down at it, smiling. *This will do to sleep on.* She drew her dagger and hacked off several large armfuls to carry back to her cave, where she spread them into a rough bed.

Leaves rustled behind her and she turned. Menkalinan walked towards her, head held high. His flared nostrils twitched and his ears were pricked forwards. She ducked out of the cave and paused as her head span giddily. Stretching one hand out to the damp moss on the rock above the cave, she steadied herself and sat down. He sat down beside her, bending his legs beneath himself. "Azariel Stormwolf," he said, lowering his head so that his delicately scented horn was almost horizontal and level with her chest. "Art thou ready and willing to come with me to where thou canst find healing?"

She put out her hand and touched the warm, firm horn of the unicorn. Slowly, her head cleared. "Of course I am," she said, looking down at her arms. "I won't be able to go back to Moonlady Falls and face Crajaval like this."

The unicorn whickered softly. "Thou shalt complete thy task, but not yet." His dark eyes stared into hers. "I wish to complete mine and heal thee fully. But I cannot do it unaided."

She caressed the unicorn's horn again. "Do you want me to help you? I'll do whatever you want. I owe you that much."

"Nay, nay. Thou need'st do naught. I shall seek aid from the Stallion, the Wolf, the Falcon and the Cat."

"The Zenifi tribal branches? Of course I've met members of all those. And it's called the Horse tribe, not the Stallion." She twirled a lock of her hair in her free hand. "My tribe is the Wolf tribe, half-blood as I am."

"I speak not of the tribes, but the spirits of the four winds that blow across the Kingdom, Wayast, Helmn and Elend. There was a time once when all the *minyasti* knew them and spoke with them to learn the news of the land. Come with me to the Hill of the Four Winds. There I shall call them and they shall aid me."

She folded her arms across her chest and leaned back against the knotty trunk of the oak. *I should have known it was too good to be true. All this must have been some plan of Crajaval's to get me to become a sorceress and call up spirits. I'm no fool.* "You will not call up spirits. I am a servant of the Power, and I will have nothing to do with this." Her eyes narrowed as she looked at the unicorn. Suddenly its shining white body reminded her of Crajaval's white limbs. "Who sent you?" she growled.

The unicorn shook his head and neighed. "Thou art wise to be wary. But I am a servant of the King of Heaven, God Incarnate and the Power even as thou art. This is no sorcery that I shall show you. Is it sorcery to bid thy comrades to aid thee or to visit thee? Once, all the *minyasti* knew and spoke with the spirits of the wind."

She bowed her head and closed her eyes. *Master? Is that true? It makes sense.* She opened her eyes and cocked her head sharply at the unicorn, studying the waves and curves of his tumbling mane. One dark eye stared at her through the white waves and she saw her reflection in the depths. She smiled at him.

He got to his feet and turned his head towards the north of the clearing. "Come. Let us go."

"I'm coming." She got to her feet, ducking beneath a branch. Dew fell from the bare twigs and brown leaves, spattering her hair and face. "Is it far to travel?"

"It standeth beyond the forest. Ride on my back."

The unicorn halted and she vaulted and swung herself onto his back. *I'll never ride a mount like this again. This must be what Farren experiences – experienced – when he rode Princess without any tack. I wish I could tell him about this.* She sighed and felt the tears well up in her eyes again. *I will one day when I see him in Heaven.*

The unicorn turned his head again and brushed her leg with his horn. "Art thou ready? Then I shall gallop."

She braced herself on his back, knotting her fingers through his mane. The unicorn surged forwards into a swift, smooth gallop through the forest. Branches whipped in her face and tugged at her hair, blurred with speed as she rocked with his rhythm. Ahead, she saw small animals scurrying into the undergrowth as the unicorn crashed along a narrow trail, and heard birds taking to the air with shrill cries of alarm. The woody, earthy scent of the forest was all around her, blurring the aromatic scent of the unicorn.

The ground began to slope upwards and the tree types began to change from the thick-trunked and deciduous to thinner evergreens. A new smell caught her attention, the sharp smells of tea tree and pine, and the sickly smell of something dead. Sharp memories of the phantoms forced her alert and she looked around, searching for the telltale mists through the trees. The trees ahead opened into a long wide clearing filled with grass and half-dead hemlock. She shrugged. *I'm worrying about nothing. It's natural to smell dead animals in the forest where things live and die.*

The unicorn cantered up the slope and broke through the treeline onto an open tussock ridge that led up to a high smooth knoll. His bony spine dug into her as she clung to him and her legs ached with effort. *I had forgotten how uncomfortable it is to ride bareback in a thinly built horse. I'm going to have a mass of bruises between my thighs at the end of this ride. And I had no idea I was so weak!* The mountains, every valley highlighted by a fresh dusting of snow, stood ahead of them. A fresh southwest wind was blowing, billowing her hair around her face from behind. It smelt cold and clean with the scents of the forest. She shook her hair to one side of her head and looked about herself as Menkalinan picked his way up the steep slope towards the knoll, passing wind-warped mountainthorns and a jumble of limestone rocks halfway up the slop. One of the rocks lay apart from the others and for half a moment, a rounded lump with two points looked like a mountain lion crouching, and she looked at it a second time, half expecting to see it move. Far in the east, she glimpsed a patch of grey cloud between the snow-capped mountains, roughly where she guessed the Illin-Ast gorge was. *There's Moonlady Falls. That's where he died. Farren, Farren, I loved you so much.* A sharp pang of longing shot through her, fiercely shaking her. She fought back the sobs that welled up inside her. *Not here, not now with Menkalinan looking on. What will he think? And what will these windspirits think?* She won her battle and held them back.

Menkalinan halted and she slithered off his back and sank into the tussock. *Those demons took a lot out of me.* Again, she looked at the raw flesh on her arms. *It's so hard to remember I'm like this when it doesn't hurt. And I guess the rest of me is just as bad.*

The unicorn shook his mane, then turned and rubbed his horn against his flank. "We are come to the Hill," he snorted. "When I have regained enough breath, I shall call the windspirits and present thee to them." He stood, head lowered, puffing slightly for a few seconds. "Did I tell thee why we have travelled here to the Hill of the Four Winds?"

She idly twisted a strand of her hair and looked into the fresh south wind. "You said that you would call the windspirits. Is there any other reason?" The huge dark tangle of the Ulfskin-Aza forest spread out beneath her, covering many of the foothills like a blanket. *The Watchtower of the North is somewhere at the southern edge of the forest, maybe twenty or thirty miles from here. Arruran Silverhand will be there, and neither he nor any of the other* minyasti *knows I'm here. Or what's happened to my beloved Farren.* Again, she blinked back the hot salt brimming behind her eyelids. Eyes clear, she looked back into the wind. The plains of the Kingdom beyond the forest were swallowed up by the blue hazy distance at the horizon, a thin line of grey cloud covering the place where the sky came down to meet the earth.

"No," he said at last. "But I have not told thee this: that only here may the spirits of all four winds be summoned at any time. Elsewhere, thou mayest summon only the spirit of the wind that walketh the heavens: the Stallion of the Northwest when the northwester bloweth, and thus forth." He whinnied a laugh. "Imagine how it would fall about if all four were summoned elsewhere! Either no wind would blow or all four at once. The land would perish with wild weather. But no. Here is the place. And I shall call them."

The unicorn paused and his sides heaved once under her hand, making his finely sprung ribs stand out for a moment. Then he raised his head and shook his mane before bowing his horn to the earth. "I Menkalinan salute the windspirits." He raised his horn again and whinnied loudly and musically. "Stallion of the Northwest, come and help thy fellow-servants."

A strong wind struck her on the back, driving back the cold southerly. Her hair whipped about wildly and she caught a wild hot smell of freshly cut hay mingled with sweet, sweaty scents. Anticipation prickled down her spine and on the back of her head. She turned, looking northwest. The fierce wind was warm and she shielded her eyes against the dust that flew in a golden, swirling cloud towards her. She blinked. The wind dropped and the wild smell vanished. A huge chestnut stallion twenty hands high stood in front of them on the smooth knoll. Muscles bulged beneath his glossy coat down the length of his thick neck and powerful quarters.

He stepped forwards and bent his head to touch noses with the unicorn, who seemed frail and tiny beside the massive stallion. "Greetings, Menkalinan," said the Stallion. His voice was deep and breathy, raw around the edges. He raised his head and looked at her with his dark brown eyes. "And greetings to you, arch *minyaster*. It is a long time since I've spoken with a human, though I have wild horses enough that work for me."

"And to you." She bowed her head formally to the Stallion

His large chestnut ears slanted back slightly. "Your arms and face – what happened to you?"

"She hath fallen foul of the storm demons," Menkalinan replied. "That is why I have called thee, Stallion. I need thy help in healing her."

"So there's something that pretty horn of yours can't do, unicorn." The Stallion's nostrils flared in a small snort. "Well, arch *minyaster*, you'll want to lie down for this. And maybe take your clothes off. If the rest of your skin's anything like this, you'll need to."

She looked down at her leather-clad legs. Although a few scuffs and white lines marred the black, her trousers looked sound and sturdy. *They haven't got me through those or through my armour but did they get me as a wolf?* She sighed and unclasped her belt. *Better safe than sorry, but I'm going to be cold lying on the hillside in just my skin.*

She stripped all her gear off and piled them roughly beside the tussock. Shivering and hugging warmth to herself, she looked down at her pale legs, angling her body slightly away from the unicorn and the Stallion. *I'm not usually body-shy around horses but with them... And they're both male.* She shook off the feelings of awkwardness and embarrassment and inspected her bare legs. A deep purple line ran down the outside of one thigh, and other tears and gashes criss-crossed her skin. *They did get me. I'm glad Menkalinan took care of the poison in that one.* She eased herself down into the tussock and lay back against the touch, springy grass, feeling the shorter stems brush across her hand and hearing the wind hiss through them. The two horse-faces, one huge and chestnut and the other delicate, white and horned, looked down at her. "Do what you must," she said. "I'm ready."

The Stallion shook his mane as he looked down at her, then turned his head to look side-on at her with one of his dark eyes. "You got to her just in time, unicorn," he said. "Look at what they've done. She's lucky to be alive. And you're not going to need just me. You'll need all four of us to get her back to normal."

"Thinkest thou so?"

"Well, you don't want to leave her all scarred, do you? It's not fair to a woman her age. She'd be all scars, and I know what those humans like in a mate. I've seen them."

She closed her eyes as she felt tears welling up. *I can't cry here, but that hurt. Why did I ever think that anyone would look twice at me even before this happened? Only Farren's ever looked and he's dead. And now, even he would turn from me.* She bit her lip hard and fought the tears before opening her eyes again.

"I feared it would be so," replied Menkalinan. "I shall call the other three winds. He shifted around to face the northeast, bent his horn, then raised it.

"Excuse me," she interrupted, getting to her feet and groping for her clothes and armour. "Why the ritual? Why do you bow to them before you call them?" A cold hand of suspicion gripped her heart. "They don't demand worshipping, do they?"

"Thou art too wary, arch *minyaster!*" Menkalinan snorted above the loud neigh of the Stallion, which sounded like a laugh. "Hast thou never saluted thy superiors? Dost thou not bow the knee to thy king?" He shook his mane and snorted again. "Falcon of the Northeast wind, come, for we need thy aid."

She braced herself and looked towards the northeast, waiting for the touch of the new wind. It came, cool, fresh and brisk, sharp with the scents of jasmine and freshly crushed pennyroyal. She breathed the scent in and a small sigh of pleasure escaped her. A faint touch of light rain pattered onto her cheek for a second. A cold shadow fell across her and she looked up. A falcon with the smoky grey and black barred plumage of the large swift *issenym* falcons but more massive than a great-eagle wheeled above them, then stooped sharply. It landed on the grass of the knoll, talons clutching at the ground as it landed. The Falcon flexed wide wings, showing the mottled markings of a female bird.

The Falcon folded her wings and turned her head to fix Azariel with one dark brown eye. "Hail," she said in a clear, cold voice. "Both Menkalinan and Azariel Stormwolf." Both huge glittering eyes locked onto her, dark, intense and piercing.

Azariel bowed her head. *Now I know how a pigeon feels when the falcon stoops on it.*

"You may summon me, Azariel Stormwolf," the Falcon said, cold voice slicing through her thoughts, "if you need me when my wind blows across the Kingdom." Azariel raised her head again and looked into the windspirit's dark eyes again for an instant. The Falcon flexed her wings again, the broad black and grey primary feathers standing out, then bent her head so that her beak, terrifyingly warm and smooth, brushed over Azariel's hand. "Call the other two, Menkalinan. Let us do this swiftly."

Menkalinan faced into the wind and lowered and raised his horn a third time. "Wolf of the Southwest wind, come."

The wind blew more strongly in her face and she narrowed her eyes to slits, expecting to see the sky darken with clouds and feel the bite of snow. She shivered and clutched her cloak, the fine hairs standing up on her arms with the cold. From somewhere, there was a distant growl of thunder. Her lips parted, drawing in the icy air, and fierce heat rose from inside her to greet it. She toyed with the idea of shifting shape and howling back at the wind, but thrust the thought aside. Bitter green and grey scents of pine, rock and thyme stabbed into her nose, mouth and lungs. She screwed her eyes shut, blinking out the water that rose against the cold. When she opened them again, a huge wolf the size of a large horse stood on the hillside beside the unicorn. He nodded to Menkalinan then turned his head towards her.

Burning amber eyes fixed her. *If I were in my wolf shape, I'd be grovelling with my belly and throat up before this wolf.* She lowered her eyes, staring at the huge pads and nails of the Wolf's paws. Then she clenched her fists and raised her head again to look the Wolf in the eyes. "It is a pleasure to meet you, Stormwolf," the great Wolf said. "I know who you are, woman of the tribe I lent my name to." He took a step towards her and touched his nose to her cheek. "I trust we shall meet again, run together even. If you need my help when I cross the Kingdom with the snow in my teeth, call me and I'll come."

Memories of the past spring flashed through her mind: the forced march through the blizzard to shelter, the whitened slopes above Falcon Pass, and the avalanche that had brought victory to the Kingdom. She looked keenly at the Wolf, then smiled. "I think you've already helped the Kingdom, thank you," she said.

"I was obeying my orders," said the Wolf, a hint of laughter in his husky voice. "As you were. The Most High God cares for his people, after all." He bent his head and licked her forehead, breath warm and sweet-scented, not the rancid breath of a dog.

The wind struck her from another quarter, softly scented with lavender and the wet forest smell of moss and ferns. *I didn't hear Menkalinan call whoever pilots the southeaster. I guess it will be the Cat.* She brushed her hair back from where it had wandered across her face and looked to the southeast. Mist wafted up the slope, billowed and spun by the soft, damp wind. The mist enveloped the knoll, then parted, revealing a sleek white and tabby cat larger than a mountain lion but with the more rounded face and large green eyes of a domestic cat. The Cat stepped daintily across the tussocks then sat down and curled a black-barred tail around her forepaws and stared intently at the unicorn. "Greetings, Menkalinan," the Cat said, then shifted her gaze to Azariel. "Greetings to you, too, Azariel. I am the Cat of the Southeast wind. It is seldom that my wind is set to blow across the Kingdom." The tip of the Cat's tail twitched as if it had a will of its own. "But if you need my help when I am sent here, I will come. " She turned to Menkalinan and the other three windspirits. "We are all here; let us begin. Lie down again, arch *minyaster*."

Azariel shook out her cloak and smoothed it flat before lying down again. The wind swirled through the tussocks and around her, lifting the tips of her hair. Menkalinan stepped forwards and stood with his forelegs at each side of her shoulders, close enough so she could smell the faint floral smell from the unicorn's skin. The four creatures stood facing Menkalinan across her. "I must warn thee, arch *minyaster*," the unicorn said. "This shall tax thy strength gravely."

"I'm glad you told me," she said. She rubbed the tip of one finger down the length of the scar that reached from collarbone to breastbone, feeling the hardened line of skin ache in the cold. "And if this is anything like the healers do, it will hurt."

"It won't," said the Stallion. "Now be quiet and still."

"First, we need to destroy the dead flesh in her body," the Wolf said. He padded forwards until he was standing with his forepaws outside her knees so his long pelt brushed her skin. He reached out his head so the tip of his dark nose almost touched Menkalinan's muzzle above her. "King of Heaven, let it be so."

The two heads met above her, silhouetted against the grey sky overhead. Her heart thudded slowly and steadily in her chest as she watched them. Both heads held completely still as if they had been painted on a grey roof. Very faintly, she heard a sound like bells, some high and bright and others deep and echoing. The bell-sound continued for ten heartbeats, then died away.

The two heads pulled apart and the Wolf's fur swept down across her leg as he drew back. Menkalinan lowered his head so that his horn pointed at her heart. She set her teeth, waiting. Light blazed out from the point of the unicorn's horn, soft-edged as a sunbeam, but in swirls and rivers of deep purple, blue-grey and icy white. The light hit her chest with a shock of cold that spread across her body, raising her skin in little bumps. She fought to keep still and not wrap her arms around herself, but she felt her lips and teeth tremble in the cold.

The cold dissipated and she felt something pull at her arms and face. Glancing down, she saw the open wounds on her arms had widened, exposing slick muscle and sinew, though no blood flowed. *And I don't want to know what my face looks like right now. My imagination's grisly enough.*

She looked away as the light above her was cut off and something brushed her knees again. The Stallion turned his head to look down at her through his tumbled forelock. "Now for the flesh to be restored," he said before touching his muzzle to Menkalinan's. "King of Heaven, let it be."

She drew a slow breath of the cold grass-scented air and let it out again. Counting her breaths, she waited, watching the two horse heads above her and listening for the bell-sound to ring. A musical note, a deep, warm, violin-like chord, caught her ear and she steeled herself. The heads drew apart and the spiral of the unicorn's horn angled down at her. *Here comes the cold again.*

The unicorn's horn gleamed as gold, khaki and scarlet light flowed out from it. Warmth struck her chest and washed over her, pleasant at first like sunwarmed stone, but increasing until it felt like metal left on a roof in the midsummer noon. Her breath hissed out of her and she gritted her teeth. Energy prickled and burned at the raw places on her arms, making them sting. Hunger suddenly churned in her stomach and she felt the muscles of her leg quiver as if she had been running hard. *New flesh can't be built from nothing,* she thought, one tooth raking at her lip.

The painful heat faded and she shivered as the cold air blew over the hill. "How goes it with thee?" Menkalinan asked, bending his head over her so that the tips of his long mane tickled her bare shoulder.

"I feel as though I've just put myself through a punishing sword-drill," she replied, lifting one hand then lowering it as she felt it trembling. "What else do you need to do?"

"Rebuild sinew, hair, blood vessels and the like," croaked the Falcon as she stepped forward and spread broad wings over Azariel in a canopy and leaned forwards so the tip of her raptor's beak touched Menkalinan's horn. The large primary feathers, black and mottled grey, stirred faintly in the air just above where Azariel lay. "King of Heaven, let it be," the Falcon continued.

Nine, ten, eleven, twelve. She counted breaths again while the two figures stood motionless above her and listened carefully for the musical sound. *What will it sound like this time?* The sound of a trumpet rippled up in a high fanfare, faint and clear as an echo. She braced herself, feeling her muscles ache and shake again.

Menkalinan's horn lowered as the Falcon's wings and head withdrew. Zigzags of lemon yellow, green and light blue sparkled from the tip. The light struck, neither hot nor cold but hard like a rock wall or tightly meshed chainmail. The hardness pressed her all over and her eyes sagged closed as she felt energy and strength draining out of her again, mixed with something tingling and prickling on her arms and face. The sensation passed over her, but the dizziness and shaking remained.

Vaguely, she felt a presence beside and above her. "May there be no scarring and the skin be restored to how it was before the touch of the demons," said a soft purr. "King of Heaven, let it be so."

She heard only the hiss of breath, hers and Menkalinan's, and the beating of her heart. Then the faint music began, a series of cascading arpeggios played by flutes. She peered through half-open eyes to see the colours of light as the music faded, struggling to hold them open. Plumes of smoky grey, lavender and sage blue fell from the unicorn's horn and brushed softly over her chest. The velvety sensation slid and caressed her arms and face, then passed on to the rest of her body. Tiny coloured stars swam in the darkness behind her eyelids as more strength was sapped from her.

Someone lifted her, pushing and pulling at her limbs. She groped for her clothing and armour and managed to drag them onto her weary body, leaving the neck of her chainmail tunic hanging open. She staggered once or twice as her vision swam with a galaxy of shimmering lights against the blackness, but warm fur and feathers caught her and steadied her. Finally, she pulled her swordbelt tight about her waist and buckled it firmly. The strong scent of rose and violet filled her nose as something warm and soft touched her hands and legs. The Falcon's claw curled around her and lifted her onto the unicorn's back. "You had better take care of her," one of the voices said. "Don't let her fall off."

"She shall not fall," replied Menkalinan's voice beneath her. She slumped her head against the soft scented hair in front of her and gripped a tuft of mane. The unicorn lurched forwards and, by instinct, her legs tightened around his middle. Dimly, she heard and felt trees and bushes whipping past and around her as she moved in and out of consciousness. Finally, the movement stopped and she felt herself falling. Something hard and smelling of dead leaves and bracken broke her fall, cool and dry. She rolled onto it and let the darkness take her completely.

CHAPTER ELEVEN

Farren lay on his side on his straw pallet in one corner of the cell nursing his bruises. Crajaval had sent for him daily since the first day of his imprisonment. Each time, she had demanded his help in baiting Azariel to Moonlady Falls and when he had refused, she had thrown him to the hounds to be mauled again. Tristan was muttering and whimpering to himself in another corner, a broken lute with one string. Farren ignored him and ran his fingers over the blackish-purple bruises, wincing as he lightly jabbed a place where the hounds' teeth had broken his skin. *Will I have to endure this every day for the rest of my life? How long will the rest of my life be? King of Heaven, help me! When will you get me out of here, either by taking me home or sending someone to get me out?*

He looked up at the ceiling and walls of rock as the shadows cast by the red flames flickered across them. *I wonder what's going on in the world outside these rocks.* He shrugged and lay on his back, letting his arms rest heavily by his side. *The latrine cave has a crack in one wall wide enough to see if it's day or night. If I could stand it, I'd be there with one eye to the crack and watch the sky and wind or whatever passes. But I can't stand the stench for longer than I have to.* He rolled onto his side again, then sat up gingerly, groaning as more bruises pressed into the stone floor through the thin pallet. *But it's no good. There's no way out of here, and it could be years until there is one. How long? Or will I never get out?* He buried his head in his hands, a thick cloud of mind-numbing despair descending on him. *Will I never get out?*

Tristan's broken muttering rose to a faint wail. "Anything, anything, any way to get me out of this hell of a life. I wish she'd kill me, even starve me! But nothing, nothing, nothing, nothing!"

He raised his head and looked at the other man who sat clawing at his ragged hair and beard. *I'll start to sound like him if I'm not careful. I don't want to be broken and wailing for death like that poor fellow. There's hardly a rag of humanity left in him.* He looked down at his nails. Most of them had become broken and ragged; all of them were grimy. He busied himself cleaning them and felt the black cloud lift from his mind. *Boredom's my worst enemy. Boredom and despair. I must keep myself busy if I'm to keep my sanity. Maybe that's what she's trying to do: break my mind and make me easy meat. Well, I won't let her!* He set his teeth and got to his feet. *No good trying to talk to Tristan again. All I hear from him is his wish for death. So what can I do?*

He paced around the room twice then his eyes fell on the heap of pallid rounds of dough the stag-people had given them to eat. He knelt beside them and picked one up, eating it slowly. It tasted almost flavourless, bland white flour mixed with water and half-baked. He nibbled the flabby cake into shapes, remembering and imagining delicious meals he had eaten.

He finished the cake and drank from the rusty iron bucket of water that stood beside it, washing the sticky, clammy paste from his mouth and savouring the metallic taste of the rust in the water. *Here I am drinking water from the source of the Illin-Ast. This is a long way from what the legends said would happen.* He shuddered. *I wouldn't want eternal youth and life in here if it was offered to me, although a healing spring would be welcome.* He sat in the archway, leaning his back against one rough rock face and his feet against the other. He looked into the flickering red flames of the torch in the corridor and escaped into the warm darkness of his mind. He replayed the events of the war six months ago and several of his best hunting expeditions. He recited as much as he could remember of the Holy Book. He thought of the illuminated copy of it he was making and planned several pages of it, lovingly working out the details of calligraphy and artwork. *Please, King of Heaven, may I be able to finish it one day. I wanted to have it done as a wedding gift for*

Azariel. My beautiful Azariel. He laid his head down on his knees and closed his eyes, daydreaming of her.

His neck grew stiff and he raised his head again, rubbing the cramped muscles. He stood up and slowly unlaced his chainmail tunic, massaged the muscle again as he arched his head back to ease the tension, then put the armour back on again. *I miss having my belt about me. If I had it on, maybe I wouldn't get so badly hurt when the hellhounds go at me. It's a thick belt and it hangs low. The buckle might even protect my groin. Might. And I wish it could! They've probably done lasting damage to me already.* He turned his head and looked up at where his belt with his sword and quiver dangled from the ceiling from an iron hook, tantalisingly out of reach. *Well, there's nothing to lose by trying to fetch it down. And a lot to gain if I succeed.*

He strode to the place where the belt hung, and leaped. Again and again, he tried to reach it. He kept trying, running up before leaping, yet never managing to seize the belt. Once or twice, his fingertips brushed the tip of the sheath. He stood beneath it, disappointed and panting, looking up. The Kingdom arms etched on the big polished buckle winked in the torchlight. *It's too high. If I were taller, I might be able to get it down.* He looked over at Tristan's hunched form and heard the insane mutterings again. A glimmer of an idea flashed in his mind. "Tristan," he said, "can you do something for me?"

The other man looked up with hollow eyes. "What the hell can I do? There's no hope, no hope! I started out like you, trying to keep myself busy after she had tired of me. But it's no good. There's no way out. You'll end like I am. No way out. Ever."

"Well, right now, I'm trying to get my belt down. If you help me, I can. Will you?"

Tristan tugged on the grizzled hair around his mouth. "All right. Won't hurt. Might help. What do you want me to do?"

Farren knelt on the stone floor beneath the swordbelt, bracing himself. "Get on my shoulders and I'll lift you up. Then you can fetch it down."

A faint flicker went through the other man's hollow eyes and he uncurled himself from his hunched posture. He scrambled to his feet and walked over to him. Farren gritted his teeth as the other man climbed onto him. He felt legs come down astride his neck and a hand clinging to his hair. "Hold on tight and balance if you can," he said. "I'm going to stand up." The grip tightened on his hair. "Not like that! Hold onto my shoulders or my cloak."

The hands left his hair and he stood up slowly, the weight of the other man pressing cruelly down on him. *At least he's half-starved after eating nothing but those tasteless pancakes. He would be much heavier in full health.* He stood straight and planted his legs wide for balance, feeling Tristan sway and totter on top of him. The bruises on his shoulders screamed unmercifully as the weight pressed on them. "Can you reach it?" he groaned, voice creaky with effort.

He heard a faint clink. "Got it! I've got it at last!" Tristan croaked excitedly. "I've got your belt – and your sword!" He scrambled down off his back and stood holding Farren's belt. "A good sharp blade."

Tristan drew the sword and looked at it, belt dangling from his other hand and eyes wild. Farren looked at the other man in bewilderment for an instant. "It's only my army sword, and it's not even what I wanted the belt for. Why are you...?"

He broke off in horror as Tristan dragged one of his wrists across the blade. Blood flowed down onto the floor. "At last!" shouted Tristan, fey animation shaking him. "I'm free!"

"Hellfire!" shouted Farren. "Don't do that!" He lunged forwards, reaching for the sword. Tristan thrust one arm out, jabbing it into his face and spattering him with blood. Farren staggered back, wiping it off. The other man raised the blade and thrust it, teeth bared and lips trembling with frenzy into his own throat. Farren's stomach turn over as bile rose in his throat. He dashed to the latrine cave and vomited.

He was shaking as he came back and a foul taste lingered in his mouth. *I've seen bloodier deaths than that in battle, but to watch someone die by their own hand!* He shuddered, then spat onto the floor before he walked back into the dormitory cave. Tristan's body lay on the floor, the obscene wound in his throat rimmed with bubbling blood. The man's eyes stared at nothing and the sword lay beside him on the floor. Farren clenched his fist and lightly punched the doorsill, hissing as his knuckles jabbed the rock. "You're a fool, Farren Blackarrow," he told himself. "You shouldn't have let a man like that touch a blade. I should have thought beyond the end of my own nose. And now what am I going to do with him?"

He stooped and picked up his sword. He looked at the blood on the blade and winced. "You've done it now, haven't you, old friend?" he said to it. "Let's clean you off." He reached behind him for the corner of his cloak, then stopped. *The Power knows when I'll get out of here and be able to clean my cloak. I'd better not bloody it.* He looked around, then knelt and cleaned the sword on the dead man's clothes. He buckled on the belt and sheathed the sword, then leaned over Tristan's body. *Poor fellow,* he thought as he closed the dead man's staring eyes. *May the King of Heaven keep me from that depth of despair!*

He heaved the heavy corpse over his shoulder and staggered to his feet. Where am I going to put him? I don't like the idea of throwing him into the latrine cave, but I can't leave him in the room with me while he... while he returns to dust and earth. He lugged the body into the corridor and lurched to the end farthest from the iron gate. He let the body down, sweat beginning to break out on his forehead and across his shoulders. He arranged his limbs, crossing the arms across the chest and attempting to cover the rip in the throat with the man's frayed and faded collar. "He's yours now, Master," he whispered. "I don't want to think about where he's gone to. Have mercy on him."

He stood up and walked back to the main cave, wiping the sweat off his forehead. He poured a little of the water in the bucket onto his hands and washed the blood from them. He shook the drips off and got to his feet. He drew a deep breath and let it out slowly, leaning back against the hard wall. A single drip splashed onto his head and he raised his hand to wipe the small patch of water away as he looked at the bleak rock of the cave. *I wish this water would drip onto that blood on the floor and wash it away.* Blankly, he fidgeted with his betrothal earring while the sickening sight of Tristan's suicide replayed itself in his mind. He shook the thoughts away. His eyes roved over the jagged rocks of the walls and down onto Tristan's straw pallet. He grinned wryly. Well, that's a small comfort. He picked it up and stacked it on top of his. Then he lay down on his back, hands behind his head. A few ends of straw prickled the back of his head and he wriggled slightly to push them aside. He closed his eyes and escaped into his mind again.

He heard a noise from the corridor and started. The skin on his forearms felt chilled and his hands had grown numb from the pressure of his head. *I've been sleeping. What's that noise? Have they come for me already? Or...* He felt the hair on the back of his neck prickle and rise slightly. The smell of smoke and filth seemed to sharpen in his sudden dread. *Has Tristan returned from the dead to some horror of existence? It can't be! Things like that don't happen – or do they?*

He got to his feet and walked to the entrance to look out into the corridor, one hand on his sword hilt. Two stag-men were gliding towards him. A wave almost of relief washed over him. *That's all it is. Did I sleep that long?* He sighed and set his shoulders, resigning himself to the inevitable mauling ahead. *At least this time they won't get at my groin as easily. And I've got my sword, too.*

He readjusted his belt down to his hips and held out his wrists to the stag-men. The white hands seized his arms and wrenched them behind his back as they led him along the corridor and through the iron gate. He drew a deep breath as they climbed the stairs to the second level, expecting to see Crajaval standing by the gate. The gate stood shut and the landing was empty. His heart pounded with relief that mingled with bewilderment. The stag-people led him up the second flight of stairs to Crajaval's corridor where the sickly-sweet green incense-torches burned.

They brought him to a room on the right-hand side of the passageway that he had not noticed when Crajaval had brought him to her bedchamber. Crajaval stood in the doorway, white fur wrapping her from her slender throat to her ankles and bare feet. Behind her, the room was lit with dim red flame. She put her hand, soft and heavy, on his shoulder and drew him to the doorway. In the centre of the chamber, a copper cauldron winked in the red light from the middle of a white pentagram on the floor. A lance lay on the one side of the circled star and a sword on the other. He hissed between his teeth as he saw them and his heart kicked at his breastbone. *I don't know much about sorcery, but I can recognise it.*

"You may leave us," Crajaval said to the stag-men. Her hand tightened on his shoulder and guided him completely in through the archway. She whispered something and he felt a cold shiver of energy go up the back of his spine. He glanced back and saw the archway, empty and ordinary-looking, but a cold knot began to tie itself in his stomach. *She's blocked the doorway with her magic. Now I can't get out of here. What is she going to do to me now?* He ran the tip of his tongue around the edge of his dry lips and flicked his eyes to and fro. The cauldron, the pentagram, the lance and the sword filled the room, apart from a single torch burning above the doorway. A haze of smoke hung in the air near the smooth stone ceiling three feet above his head, natural, woody smoke. He breathed it in, grateful not to smell the sickly-sweet incense. Crajaval pushed him towards the cauldron. He shoved backwards with his feet, resisting her at first, but then he let himself be forced on. *She can't be going to boil me. There's no fire under it – yet.*

"Well, Farren Blackarrow," she said, voice soft and sweet. "I have found her. Will you help me draw her?"

He looked around at her, staring into her blue eyes. "No," he said. "I won't."

She laughed. "Stubborn still. You'll bend one day. But watch this." She bent down and picked up the lance and the sword, holding one in each hand. The pentagram at his feet flared suddenly and he started backwards as hot white flames flickered and danced along the lines painted on the rock underneath the cauldron. Gingerly, he inched forwards again, getting as close as he could bear to the heat of the flames so he could rest his hands on the cold metal of the cauldron rim. Crajaval leaned over the cauldron and breathed, little ripples spreading out across the surface. In the wake of the ripples, the face of the water changed. Blurred, cloudy shapes appeared, green, black, brown and white. The shapes sharpened and cleared as if coming closer through fog. A woman with long dark hair sat beneath a tree and beside her stood a unicorn, its graceful head bending over the woman as her hand caressed its horn. *It's a legend come to life*, he thought.

The picture grew clearer and closer as if he and Crajaval were walking closer to the woman and the unicorn. A sharp arrow of longing and recognition stabbed him. "Azariel, sweetheart!" he gasped.

"Yes," said Crajaval. "Azariel Stormwolf, the only werewolf, the only shapeshifter of any kind who has escaped me. But she will be mine one day soon."

You'll never control her and I'll never betray her. He bent over the water again and watched, holding the rim of the cauldron. He saw her mouth moving as she spoke to the unicorn, then got to her feet and stretched her long limbs. She walked to the side of a small clearing among the forest trees. The light was fading slowly, and he saw her yawn and brush her hair back from her face. *I can almost hear her doing it. My Stormwolf, my sweetheart.* He watched her creep inside a small cave in a mossy hillock which was carpeted thickly with bracken and a few smallish animal furs. Footmarks pockmarked the beaten grass and mud beside the shelter, and a small store of nuts, wild fruits and mushrooms lay piled to one side of the cave. She took a few handfuls from her store and ate them, then wrapped her black cloak around her body as she curled up tightly in the bracken. He felt a fresh wave of longing surge in his heart and his arms ached to hold her. "Goodnight, sweetheart," he whispered. "I wish I could kiss you before you sleep, even if I can't hold you through the night." He smiled and shook his head. *One day I will. One day, Master, please.*

"I'm sure you want her," breathed Crajaval. He jerked up, slewing his head around sharply towards her. "But you'll never have her again unless you draw her," she went on. "Then, maybe, I'll let her have you, if she behaves herself. If she still wants you once she's mine. And she will be. Watch and listen."

She lightly touched the water with the tip of her sword. The image changed from a view of a forest clearing to show only Azariel's face as she slept, a strand of hair lightly rising and falling with her breath. A murmur of longing escaped his lips and his mind melted as he studied the details of her face: her red recurve-bow lips, the straight line of her nose, the first marks of nearly twenty-five years' experience and outdoor living delicately etched in the fine skin under her eyes, her long lashes and the shapeshifter's heavy black brows that sent out fine hairs that met above the bridge of her nose.

Steam began to coil from the surface of the water, white curls and twists that reached towards the red light of the torch. It thickened and coiled, almost obscuring the image. He inhaled a small wisp of steam and sneezed, nose and throat irritated and burned by a strong camphoric smell. It wreathed and billowed around Crajaval's face, forming itself into four columns. "Mistress," hissed a soft voice from the steam. "Command us. What shall we say?"

Crajaval smiled and half closed her eyes to languorous slits. "I have watched her long and I know the crack where I can drive my wedge in to bring her toppling to me. Oh yes. Her weakness. She doubts herself, doesn't she, Farren? Doesn't she?"

He looked Crajaval in the eyes, jaw set firmly and the first traces of anger beginning to thicken at his temples. *She does. May the Power help her, she does, in spite of all I've told her.* He gripped the edges of the cauldron until the blood was squeezed from his knuckles, leaning forward over the cauldron to shield Azariel's image from her. "As if I'm going to tell you anything of the sort," he growled.

Her hand clamped over his right arm and she lowered her face to within an inch of his. "Answer me." He continued to stare at her eyes, feeling his breathing and heartbeat quicken and mingle with the pulse of anger in his temples. Her lips narrowed and she jerked her hand away sharply from his arm, pulling and plucking. White-hot pain exploded down his arm with a small tearing sound and he drew breath sharply with the agony. He clamped his hand over the place on his arm and held it, panting. Then he glanced back at her. She held a tuft of chestnut hair in her white fingertips, maggot-like white roots dangling on the end. He looked back down at his arm, moving his left hand away. *I can't believe she didn't flay me. That's what it felt like.* A white line ran down his arm, smooth and vulnerable as an infant's skin. He shuddered and looked down at the water again.

"Well?" she said. "Will you keep silent still? There is much hair on a man's body that can be plucked. I won't hurry the task. I certainly won't hurry over your chest or around your manhood." She reached out and tore a second line bare down his arm, catching some of the broken skin along with the hair, then a third. "Maybe

I'll start stripping off your skin after that. Just a little here and there." His eyes watered involuntarily and his hands trembled on the rim of the cauldron. "Don't think I'll ever kill you, either. You're too useful for that." She dropped the tufts of hair to the ground and he heard them sizzle in the white fire. Her hand seized his arm for a fourth time, fingertips pinching up the hairs. "Which will it be? Will you speak, or shall I strip you smooth? She doubts herself, doesn't she?"

His stomach and spine became a cold mass of fury and fear. The skin on the centre of his chest began to itch and prickle in sudden awareness and the rim of the cauldron dug into a bruise on his hip. The stripped and outraged lines of skin on his arm still stung. He looked down at the face in the cauldron. "You seem to know already," he growled. "What's the point of threatening me?" He hung his head, staring down into the water, furious at himself. *Should I have said that? Or should I have kept silent?* Then he clenched his teeth and looked up again.

The four columns of steam wrapped around Crajaval again as she drew away. "What shall we say?" hissed the voice again.

"Come in and see," said Crajaval. She inhaled the steam, eyes closed ecstatically and her ruby lips parted. Then the steam hissed out of her mouth and stood again in four columns around the cauldron. Crajaval looked at him and chuckled softly and musically. "You are not going to like this. Are you sure you want to hold out against me?"

He held her gaze for a few moments, his stomach churning. *What's she going to do to her?*

The steam formed itself into four figures. He watched them, recognising three of the four wraiths. *Stessa of the Nightravens, Azariel's mother Zorayha, that officer Azariel pointed out as the old dragon she had as her first cadet trainer, and a man I don't know.* The four wraiths bent over the cauldron, trailing little clouds of steam across the calm surface of the water.

"Who do you think you are, Azariel?" whispered the first wraith, the one mimicking the cadet sergeant, raising a ghostly hand that held a whip of shadow. "You're no good. You never will be. Who do you think you are, girl? I'll teach you to get cocky with your betters, Zenifi slut. You think you're someone special with your fancy rings and armbands? You're not and you never will be." The figure touched the water lightly with the shadow-whip. "Let that wipe that pert look off your dirty face. Who do you think you are? I'll break you. I'll make you crawl as you should."

He saw Azariel flinch and grimace in her sleep. She twisted on the bracken and one hand jerked. His blood thundered, loud and steady in his ears. *She can hear them in her dreams. Azariel, Azariel, did she really say those things to you once? Or is it all Crajaval's lies?*

Stessa's wraith stooped over the cauldron. "Look at me then look at yourself." The figure produced knives from each of its sleeves, then spun them away through the air. "I've got skills that you'll never dream of mastering. Don't you wish you were like me, the Weapons Mistress?" The wraith drew a sword from her side and began a complex series of guards, lunges and slashes. "You're not. You never will be. You know how clumsy you are when you fight. You're lucky that you haven't been killed yet." Then the sword vanished and the wraith put one hand on its hips while the other loosened the plunging neckline of its tunic. "Look at me then look at yourself." It began to gyrate its hips seductively and pulled the neckline low to reveal most of a full bosom. A sharp kick of memory plunged through Farren's stomach and he fixed his eyes firmly on the image of Azariel's face. A frown furrowed the smooth ivory of her brow. The wraith's voice went on. "Heads turn when I walk in. They'll never turn for you. You're as scrawny as a spear and your breasts are pathetic. Why do you bother pretending you're worth your place in the army? You may be hanging around for Farren's sake, but you know deep down that he must have been blind or mad to choose a useless besom like you over me."

A hot coal of anger burned in his chest and he felt his head begin to throb at his temples. "Shut up! Don't listen to them Azariel!" He let go of the edge of the cauldron, fists tightening. "It's not true, do you hear? Don't listen to them!"

The male wraith bent over the cauldron. "You're only good for one thing, aren't you, you little slut?" The face sniggered and the tip of its tongue ran around its lips. "And even then you wouldn't be much good. You'd be no good at all. A man would get more fun by—"

Farren lashed out with his fists at the wraith as it spewed obscene abuse at her. "Don't you say that again, mongrel!" he yelled. His fists met the air, the steam coiling about them, moist and warm. The ugly voice drawled on. He clutched at the edge of the cauldron, angry and frustrated tears spilling out of his eyes. They stung the grazes on his cheeks and fell into the water, making rings on the surface. "Don't listen, Stormwolf. Don't listen. Oh, Stormwolf, if only I could tell you what is true." He gritted his teeth and snarled at the wraith. "Curse you! Damn you and your lies to the pits of hell!"

A hard cold hand slapped him in the face, making white sparks dance in front of his eyes. "Silence," said Crajaval softly. "She can't hear you anyway. Not unless I let you speak, which will be when you say what I command you to say." She turned her head to the fourth wraith. "Continue," she said.

The four wraiths stood still for a few moments. Farren looked down into the water, breathing hard and eyes filled with hot salt. *What now? I can't bear hearing them do this to her. I wish that white bitch had contented herself with throwing me to the dogs. What have I done?* He swallowed as the fourth wraith, the one in the image of Azariel's mother, leaned forwards in front of him, long locks of hair falling down on each side of the wrinkled face. "What do you expect if you turn to the *dawni* and their ways? What do you expect if you follow their God? They don't want you. They don't appreciate who you really are. They hate you. Who are you, my daughter?" The wrinkled face smiled. "You are a werewolf. You are one of the Zenifi, born and bred. Come back to us. Come back to the old ways and the Old Religion. Return to your own kind. It's the fault of the *dawni* and their God that you feel so wretched and worthless. But we want you. Come back to the Goddess to whom you belong. She can give you what you crave."

Azariel twisted and her lips twitched. Her eyes snapped open and her breasts rose and fell in fast, sharp breaths. He saw her lips frame a single short word and she shook her head before her eyes closed again and she slumped back into the bracken.

The first wraith was bending over the water again, whip raised in its hand. He watched it then drew on a reserve of courage and energy deep inside him that he hardly knew he had left. "No!" he shouted, ripping his sword from its sheath. He whirled it through the wraiths, aiming for the heads. "In the name of the Power, leave her alone!" With a groan of effort, he leaped onto the cauldron, balancing one foot on each rim above the steaming water, brandishing his sword. The wraiths drew back from the water and Crajaval staggered backwards. With a cry half of triumph, half of desperation, he plunged his sword into the water, shattering the image into a thousand shimmering shards. Then the water turned black and the steam melted away.

Crajaval strode forwards. "You've won – for now. Get off my cauldron." She seized him by the shoulder and pulled him down. A jolt of pain jarred his leg as he landed awkwardly. "But I'll speak to her again. And you'll watch. If you won't bend with what I do to you, you'll bend when you listen to what I say to her." She clapped her hands and four stag-people materialised. "Take him away until I send for him again."

Slender, cold white hands grabbed him by the wrists and arms. He struggled to bring his sword free, but his arms were wrenched behind his back. Something hard and bony jabbed him in the small of his back, forcing him into the passageway. *Here it comes,* he thought as he was thrust down the stone steps. *And I can't use my sword when they're holding me like this. At least the belt and buckle will help.* The gate to the second level gleamed dully in the red torchlight and cold dread filled his stomach. *I'll probably get a worse mauling than I've had before after what I did with her cauldron. If worse is possible.* He closed his eyes and waited for the inevitable grating as the door opened and the dogs' growls.

The sounds never came. The stag-people forced and dragged him across the landing. He saw the solid black metal gate over the shoulder of one of the stag-men. His knees buckled beneath him with relief and he let them push and pull him down to his cave. They shoved him forwards through the cave mouth and he fell on his knees on the rough stone floor. He stayed there, listening to the sound of their footsteps dying away down the corridor, followed by the clang of the door as it closed.

***

He collapsed onto the straw pallets with a groan. His arms and legs, still wet and slimy in places from the hellhounds' mouths, throbbed and pulsed with deep dull pain. He lay face down, burying his face in his hands and weeping with pain and despair. Then he lay breathing heavily, a straw tickling his cheeks. *This can't go on,* he thought. *Neither for me nor for Azariel. King of Heaven, the mauling's bad enough, but I can't stand seeing and hearing those things tearing her apart with words any longer. It's gone on for days! It can't go on!* He clenched his fist and raised it, ready to pound and smash it against the floor. Then he checked himself, clutching at one of the pallets. *I won't do that again.* He looked at the knuckles of his left hand and grimaced as he saw the crushed skin and bruising from where he had smashed it into the wall in frustration several days before. *That was a fool's thing to do, Blackarrow. You're lucky you didn't break your hand.*

He rolled onto his back and scratched at his chin where the straw had been tickling him. His thumb rasped over the growth along his jawline and he gave a small snort of disgust. *How long have I been here? Seven – no, eight times I've seen Azariel through the cauldron. And some days before that. Too long.* His belt-pouch dug into his back and he tried to shuffle it out of the way. He sat up with a jerk and unclasped the buckle. *I may as well take all the gear off the belt for all the good it does me. The belt helps, but everything else is useless. If only I could use the sword!* His right hand went to the red welts on his left wrist. *I wish she wouldn't tie my hands so tightly. I'd love to stir the images in her cauldron again and protect my Azariel.*

He folded his belt neatly and laid it beside the pallets. Almost ritually, he pulled each arrow out of its clip in the quiver and sharpened both cutting blades on each head with the whetstone taken from his belt-pouch. After the soothing ritual of sharpening the arrows, he replaced each one, then began methodically sharpening his razor and his sword. The bright edge of his sword gleamed as he lifted it into the red light of the torch. *I've sharpened this so many times over the last week or whatever it is that it could probably cut through silk with a single light stroke.* For a moment, he toyed with the idea of slashing at Crajaval's silk robes and watching her fall. He sighed, passed the whetstone over the blade a few times, then re-sheathed it. Then he tucked the whetstone and razor back into the pouch and pulled out his thin cake of lavender-scented soap. Closing his eyes, he breathed in the tangy scent of the lavender for a few heartbeats before replacing it in the pouch.

After the ritual of sharpening blades and enjoying the aroma of the soap, he replaced everything neatly in one pile, sighed and started to lie back down. *I may as well see what they've done to me this time,* he thought as he felt for the lacings at the back of his armour. He stripped off his cloak, armour and clothing and looked down at the mass of bruising on his legs. Here and there, the hounds' teeth had punctured him and the wounds itched and throbbed when he pressed them gingerly. *How much longer can I stand up to this? How long?*

He wrapped himself in his cloak and lay down again. The straw scratched and tickled all over his skin. Disgusted, he got to his feet and pulled his clothing back on. Breathing hard with irritation, he lay down again. *I wish I could be free of the stink of that filth. And the dark. And these thin, itchy straw pallets.* He tossed and turned, ending lying on his back staring at the flickering torchlight on the ceiling and the irregularities of colour and texture in the rock. *This can't go on. I wish she'd see that I'm not going to help her and either let me go or kill me outright. Then at least she'd leave Azariel alone.*

Something snapped inside him and he got up and paced from the door of the cave to the wall then back again. "Master, King of Heaven, God Incarnate, Most High God, where are you?" he asked aloud. "We need you, both of us. You know how they're pouring poison into Azariel's ears every night. You know how that will hurt her. And I don't want to rot here forever! Where are you? Why did you send us here? You're all-powerful, but why don't you work through me to kill that white devil? You know I've tried to! Where are you? What are you going to do?"

He knelt in the doorway and a buried his head in his hands. Tears welled up in his eyes. "Have you abandoned us?" he choked. "What did we, what did I do? I know I was angry with Azariel and left her when she needed me. I'm sorry. I am. Please forgive me. Please make them leave her alone. And please get me out of here." He leaned his head against the cold rough stone of the archway and wept silently.

They will leave her alone and you will go free. But you must call her when you are next summoned to the cauldron.

He looked up as the voice shivered through his mind like an arrow in a target. "Master?" he said aloud. *Was that him or a cheat?* "Did you tell me to call her through that thing?"

The emerald on his right hand flashed with sudden fire, sending brilliant green pulses of light onto the stone. The shield of wariness left his mind and his heart raced with sudden exhilaration. *I cannot let either her or you be tested beyond what you can bear,* the Voice said. *She been healed and has found the weapons she needs for the fight. When you are brought to the cauldron, summon her to Moonlady Falls.*

He looked up and around, one eyebrow twisting, perplexed. "The cauldron, King of Heaven? Must I use that? I can't! I won't touch sorcery."

The harm will fall on Crajaval's head and not on yours, Farren Blackarrow. It will delude her and make her sure of victory. But victory she will not have. Do it. Call Azariel tomorrow night.

"I will, Master." He got to his feet and smiled. "I will. And thank you!" He wrapped his cloak about himself and lay down on the pallets, hardly noticing the bruises. *I'm going to see her again, face to face,* he thought delightedly. *I'm going to see her soon.* He sighed happily and closed his eyes, thinking of her before the river of slumber swept him away.

CHAPTER TWELVE

Azariel woke up and yawned. *That's the third night in a row that I've had that nightmare where Sergeant Karissa, Stessa and Edwin Feller are sneering at me. And my mother telling me to embrace the Old Religion.* She rolled over and stretched, then idly played with some squirrel skins she had used to line the cave, running her fingers through the soft chestnut. *My mother would never suggest that, but Karissa said the things she was saying in my dream.* She shook her head and winced, the memory of old pain prickling on her back, face and neck. *Will I ever be free of what Karissa said and did to me?* She laid her head on the chestnut squirrel fur for a few heartbeats, inhaling the slightly acrid smell of the rawhide.

She lay on her back looking up at the cracks and fissures in the rock ceiling above her as she combed tangles out of her hair with her fingers. *I had better think of something else to take my mind off those dreams, if I can.* Her fingers tugged at another snag in her hair and yanked it loose with a sharp jerk. *What will I do today? I was good for nothing the first day after Menkalinan brought me back from the Hill of the Four Winds and since then, I've only just had enough energy to walk about to drink, collect more nuts and set squirrel snares.* She smiled to herself and let the lock of hair she had been working on fall back across her shoulder. *I never thought I'd be homesick for searching through all those old books. Menkalinan's been good to me, keeping me amused with his talk of stars and herbs and improving my use of the Old Tongue, but it would be good to have something to read while I'm recovering.*

She sat up and glanced down at the small pile of nuts and dried mushrooms lying in the corner of the cave. She stretched her arms. *I feel like eating something else today.* Meat. Her stomach clenched and growled. *I might go and hunt for my breakfast in wolf-*

shape for a change. Closing her eyes, she concentrated and slipped into wolf-form. She stretched her hind and forelegs, feeling the muscles strain and relax, then ran her tongue around the dry inside of her mouth. *I think I feel well enough to hunt further afield than the squirrel snares today. I'll drink first, though.* She trotted out of the cave and into the woods, following the well-worn path to the stream nearby.

A rich mixture of scents near the stream filled her sharp shewolf's nostrils as she quenched her thirst: scents of animals, birds, fruits, old wood and leaves. She raised her head from the water and inhaled the medley of smells again. She worked over the ground and the wind, nostrils quivering, probing the earth on both banks. She caught the scent of a wild pig and her mouth began to water. *Yes. That's what I'll hunt. They'll be moving from the mountains down to the lower forests at this time of year. I'll find a small one – one that will not put up much of a fight – and it'll provide meat for a few days.* She trotted along the trail, eagerness rising in her wolf's blood, mixing with her hunger and sharpening it as the two mixed. *I'd better make sure I don't kill a piglet still with its dam. I'd rather not face the rage of the mother. A yearling will do.*

She followed the scent-trail into a rutted track through the undergrowth where little tunnels had been worked by tough skins under thorns. The scent she was following blurred with others and the trail became heavy with signs: dung, spoor, and marks of teeth and tusks rooting beneath trees. Eagerly, she loped down the twisting trail, head bent to the scent, mind intent on the rich odour beneath her nose and revelling in the regained strength of her muscles. The smell grew sharp and vivid, and her hunger rose higher to meet it. More scent wafted through the air between the trees. Eager for the kill, mouth dripping, she rounded a large tree-trunk.

A deep snort and the sound of grinding brought her up sharply, sliding to a standstill. A large black and grey boar stood staring at her with small angry eyes. *Idiot! I'm in for a hard fight now.*

Why on earth didn't I take more care? She backed up with hackles rising, growling between her fangs. The boar, his back a forest of thick bristle and his tusks jutting like daggers above his snout, snorted again. He lowered his head and charged like a battering ram.

She stood her ground, watching for a place to seize the boar as it charged. It moved startlingly swiftly for its bulk and it rushed almost on top of her before her heart could kick. She leaped and rolled to the right, the full stink of pig overpowering her, bristles brushing her fur. It struck her as she leaped, hot and hairy. She heard its laboured breathing for a moment before agonising white-hot pain slashed into her left shoulder. She howled in pain as the boar ripped its tusk up through her, feeling her own blood spatter over her pelt and hearing it drip onto the forest floor. The smell of the blood, hot and salt, stank in her nostrils. The boar freed its tusk as she writhed in pain on the ground, gasping and fighting for breath. Its small round eyes flashed and it lowered its head for the deathstroke.

She shifted shape as the boar's blow thudded into her stomach, knocking the breath from her. The steel of her chainmail took the blow, grating on the bony tusks. The boar snorted and started back in surprise. She staggered upright, kneeling and feeling at her side for her dagger, chest heaving like a landed fish. The wound, now on her left shoulderblade, throbbed and screamed as she held the knife ready for the next attack of the boar. The red piggy eyes rolled as the boar lowered his head again, grinding his tusks against his upper teeth before the charge.

She rolled out of the way of the boar's charge, twisting her legs out of reach of the tusks. Its rump was turned towards her for an instant, within reach. She grabbed its short bristly tail and let the impetus of the animal's rush jerk her to her feet. The pig squealed and twisted, bristles cutting at her grip. Sweat made the palm of her hand greasy. The boar's tail began to slip from her grasp. Her cloak whipped behind her, catching on branches and holding her back as she strained to keep pace with the boar. She ran as the boar wheeled around, struggling to reach her. Her wound screamed at her and hair was plastered to her face with sweat.

The tail slid out of her hand and she threw herself forwards. She landed astride the boar, bruising herself on its spine. The enraged pig shrieked at her and bucked, thrashing its head to and fro in an effort to get at her. Her knees thumped against the ground as she tried to lock her legs around the pig's back. *This is no horse, you fool. You're going to get yourself killed.* She plunged the dagger back into the sheath and leaned forwards, grabbing the boar under the neck. *I can't haul this beast's head up to slit its throat easily and I can't reach the hollow behind the foreleg without nearly slicing my own leg. There's only one way.*

She lowered her head so that her chin reached just above the pig's ear, the coarse bristles rasping at her. Two heartbeats to change her shape, then she bit. The boar stank overpoweringly and the skin tasted salt as she locked her jaws' grip on its ear. The boar squealed again and shook its head, jerking, leaping, twisting to swing its head round at her. She growled softly through her locked teeth as she bounced with the thrashing of the boar. One tusk, the left tusk nearest her, was stained reddish-brown. Her sides heaved and her shoulder screamed with pain. *The leg. I've got to change shape and grab its back leg. I can't tire it – I'll give out before it does.* She pivoted around, swinging her hindquarters around almost within reach of the boar's mouth, shifting her teeth to higher up the ear.

She saw its hind leg and stretched her paw across the brushlike back, dewclaws scraping through the bristle. *I've got one chance. Hopefully the surprise of fighting as a shapeshifter will buy me the time I need to grab it.* She drew a deep breath, cold air whistling in through across her bared fangs and tensed herself ready for the simultaneous change and spring. *In the name of God Incarnate, go!*

She lunged towards the back end of the boar, releasing her locked bite on the ear and shifting shape. Her right hand met the leg beneath the hock, closing around the bristle and bone. A hideous taste filled her dry mouth and her feet found the wet leaves and mud of the forest floor, firm and solid. She gripped the boar's leg with both hands and stood up, shouting with effort as she tipped the boar over to its side. With her left hand, she plucked her dagger from its sheath and drove the thin, narrow point in behind the boar's left shoulder, sinking it to the hilt as the boar squealed. A wash of hot foam and bright scarlet followed the knife as it withdrew and the hot stink of blood rose. Again she stabbed behind the shoulder, the handle of the dagger growing slippery with blood. The boar collapsed beneath her, a shuddering, twitching mass of bristle, bone and muscle. She released it and her legs buckled beneath her. She fell, shaking and in pain, onto the churned and muddied leaves.

The boar lay dead and its death-throes had stopped. She lay on the forest flood, pressing her right hand over what she could reach of her wounded shoulderblade. Her woollen undershirt felt warm and sticky against her back beneath her armour. She stared at the patchwork of dead leaves and bare branches against the partly cloudy sky above her, the fierce pain of the tusk-slash throbbing and pulsing. *And I'd only just finished healing. What a fool I am!*

She drew a deep breath and ran her tongue around her dry mouth, longing for something to wash the bitter animal taste of the boar's ear away. *I can't lie here forever, bleeding myself to exhaustion or to death. I've been a big enough fool for one morning, not looking and listening ahead and blundering into that boar. A stupid, stupid, witless fool! This slash across my back is all I deserve.* She rolled onto her right side, groaning with effort as she twisted. She clamped her hand back onto what she could of the wound. *And what am I going to do now? I can't cart or even drag that boar back to camp with my shoulder like this. And I don't want to leave it for the scavengers after all my efforts.* She sat up and eased her hand off her shoulder, tacky red staining her fingers. She picked up the dagger from where it lay between her and the dead boar. *Well, I'll gut it here and eat a bit as a wolf. Then I'll come back and get the rest when the wound's clotted over enough.*

She got to her feet, stars whirling in front of her eyes and her head spinning. She staggered to the carcass and unbuckled her cloak. Bundling the wool well away from her, she bent over the dead pig, then rolled it belly up. For a few seconds, she considered shifting shape and devouring the offal as a wolf. Then she shook her head. *No. I know I'd like the taste well enough when I'm a wolf, but when I shift back, the taste remains. The ear was bad enough.* She grimaced and swallowed down the nausea that rose in her throat. *I had better do this properly.*

She carefully slid the knife into the beast's belly and began the long, tricky, filthy job of opening the pig and removing the entrails. She was halfway through the business when she heard the sound of hooves behind her. She looked up and saw the unicorn canter around the bend in the pig-path. He halted, mane tossing and horn erect. "I heard the sounds of strife, so I am come to help thee. What hath passed? Art thou wounded?"

"I've got a bad slash on my left shoulder, Menkalinan." She looked at the gore coating her arms to the elbows and her nose wrinkled in disgust. *I'm so filthy and he's such an exquisite creature. What does he think of me?* "If you're wondering how it got me up there, it got me while I was in wolf shape." She bent back to her work, the boar's blood making the handle of the knife slippery.

"Then thou must let me heal thee with my horn," the unicorn said, lowering his head so that his horn pointed towards her. He stepped gracefully towards her and stopped an arm's length from her. She looked up from the boar's body and into the unicorn's dark eyes.

She nodded and laid her knife down on the leaves. She stripped off her armour, tunic and underclothes, gritting her teeth as the cloth rubbed across the open wound. She let out a long, slow breath as the light breeze brushed across her bare skin. *I'm a mess,* she thought as she saw the blotch of blood staining her side. *I need to wash my clothes and I need to scrub that blood off me.* She leant forwards, resting her elbows on her bent knees as the warm horn of the unicorn brushed over the tear in her shoulder. A faint scent of violets wafted around her. *I'm going to have another big scar now. Not that I'm much of a beauty anyway with this scrawny, lanky body. Poor Farren; I wouldn't have been much for him to look at even if he had lived to marry me. My Farren. I did love him. Now there's nobody else who will ever want me again.* She fought back the tears that welled up under her eyelids. *King of Heaven, I miss him so much! Why did he have to die? Why didn't I go and save him instead of staring like a halfwit and nearly falling off my horse? I doubt if I could have done much, but at least we could have died together. If only I could make the sands of time run backwards! But I can't, so there's an end to it.*

"There," said the unicorn's musical voice, cutting into her thoughts. "Little remaineth. Thou canst finish thy task and haul thy prey back to thy store." He broke off with a soft whicker that sounded like a laugh. "But then thou shalt rest and let this new wound of thine heal fully. Thou art too eager for action, arch *minyaster.*"

"I'm sorry. I've asked a lot of you already and I shouldn't have made a mess of myself as soon as I had come right again." She reached for her clothing and pulled it on, letting it hang loose and unlaced from her shoulders. "I'll need to wash my gear in the creek – and myself. I don't want to stink of blood." She put on her belt, picked up her dagger and bent over the boar again as Menkalinan turned, the sound of his hooves fading down the path.

She finished gutting the boar and stood up. She looked down at the carcass, then at her cloak and back to the carcass again. *I can't carry both and I can't wear my cloak while I'm carrying the boar. Now what?* She stared at the two black things, running her fingers through her hair then pulling and teasing as her fingers met a matted tangle of hair. She knelt down to buckle the cloak about the boar's neck, then burst out laughing as the fat jowls and piggy snout nestling almost humanly in the folds of the cowl. "Hail, arch *minyastin* Pig!" she said, dropping to one knee and drawing her sword in a flamboyant salute. She glanced back along the pig-path. *I hope Menkalinan's not watching.* She sheathed her sword, then heaved the pig onto her shoulders, holding it by the front legs and its head behind hers. She drew a deep breath then lunged and staggered with the pig back to the clearing.

Quickly, she gathered wood and lit a fire. Once it was going well, she set the back steaks from the boar to spit-roast and walked to the creek. She stripped and plunged her leather and woollen clothes into the stream, apart from her cloak, then knelt in the cold water. She shivered as it lapped around her knees and thighs, and felt the small hairs on her arms standing up in hundreds of little bumps. Working briskly to keep the blood flowing warm in her limbs, she scoured the dried blood off herself, feeling a slight stiffness and a cold ache across her shoulder where the boar had slashed her. She pounded the clothing in the flowing water, staining the stream brown-red with blood. She scrambled onto the bank, wringing the water out of her hair as her shoulders shook with cold. She threw her cloak around herself, the rough wool prickling her bare skin. She twisted the cold stream water out of her clothing and carried them back to the clearing.

She spread them on a clump of young lemonwood near the fire then looked around. Menkalinan was watching her. She lowered her head and drew her cloak around her cold nakedness. *I am a barbarian, running almost naked in the woods with my hair matted like a stray dog's.* Shame heated her. Holding herself as proudly as she could, she sat beside the campfire. "It's a pity I can't share the meat with you," she said aloud.

"No matter," said the unicorn. "Thou canst share it with the crows and ravens if so thou wishest."

"Are you going to tell me something I didn't know about ravens and crows, Menkalinan?" she chuckled, leaning forward to put another stick onto the fire and hearing drips fall from her hair and hiss on the hot stones surrounding the fire.

"Wantest thou that I should?"

"Very well then." She drew her cloak tighter around herself. "I'm listening."

***

Cold rain spattered onto her face, shocking her awake. Ten days had passed since she had come to the clearing with Menkalinan. She wiped the water off her face and inched away from the mouth of the cave. Another gust of wind whined in, flicking some of the raindrops onto the dry stone and leaves. *I'm glad to be free of that dream, but what a way to waken!* She pulling her cloak back around herself. *I'd rather be soaked, though, than stay asleep to dream about Karissa giving me the cutting edge of her tongue and whip, or about Stessa sneering at me.* She sat up against the back wall of the cave and began picking broken bracken out of her hair. *I've had no other dreams except those – and the dreams of Edwin Feller's lascivious talk and my mother persuading me to become a sorceress. Why those dreams?* She let her hand fall idle in her lap and stared at the rain-slick grass outside her shelter. *Am I going mad? Or merely facing the truth about myself now that I'm alone to think about these things?* She shrugged and crawled out into the clearing. *One thing's certain: my mother would never really say what she does in my dreams. The other things, I'm not so sure about.*

She followed the path to the stream and found her favourite crabapple tree. After plucking a handful of fruits and eating them, she kept strolling to the stream still crunching the sour little apples. She returned to the clearing, wiping the water from around her wet mouth. The water from the rain-swollen stream left a gritty, muddy taste in her mouth. She looked around for the unicorn but the clearing stood empty. She shrugged and crawled back into her shelter, pulling her hood over her head and wrapping her cloak around herself as she hunched up hugging her knees to her chest and resting her head on them. She closed her eyes and listened to the rain pattering and dripping a complex rhythm around her, mixed with the gentle rustle of wind in the trees. The leafy, earthy scent of the bush grew sharper in the rain, and the wet wool of her cloak smelt mildly acidic. *Master, how much longer will I have to wait? When and how will I kill Crajaval? Will I be able to do it at all, or are you preparing me to come to you? How will I know when the time is right for me to return? Menkalinan has told me nothing of that.*

Heavy warmth wrapped around her, relaxing every muscle in her body. Her eyelids felt heavy and she became aware that she could not stir her limbs or head even if she wanted to. Darkness and warmth spun around her head then vivid pictures welled up in her mind's eye.

She was standing on a tussock-covered hillside, a free wind blowing in her hair. Huge limestone boulders carved by wind and water stood in front of her, bracken growing around the bases. She stepped towards the boulders and walked around them. Twigs snapped as her boots moved through the bracken. She scrambled around the rocks to a smooth limestone face in the hillside above her. A cave opened in the hillside, a black pit in the tussock and bracken. She pushed her way through the mountainthorns and small spiky mountain plants growing around the entrance. All was black inside except for three points of light: one blood-red, one deep blue and one white. A brilliant flash of white light flared around the cave, then she stood outside the cave with three gems in her hands. "Take your weapons, Azariel Stormwolf," said a deep voice from the empty sky above her.

Half a heartbeat later, she had left the hillside and looked down at it from high in the air. Slightly to the southeast of the hillside lay the dark mass of the Ulfskin-Aza, while the white peaks of the Seranyai-Cheli mountain range ran in a line to the north. Further to the east lay the Illin-Ast. A cold wind blew around her and whipped her hair about her face.

"Azariel?" A soft musical voice jerked her back into the cold air and the sound of the rain. She opened her eyes and saw the unicorn's head stretching into her shelter.

She raised her head, a cramped muscle in her neck aching as she moved. "You've woken me from the first pleasant dream I've had for at least a week," she said. "If it was a dream. I didn't think I was tired. It was vivid, too." She let go of her knees and straightened her back, running over the details in her mind. Something tingled at the base of her skull and passed down her spine. *That was no dream. That was Vision, full-blooded and strong.* "I had better tell you what I saw." She waited while the unicorn sat down beside her shelter and turned his head towards her, fixing her with his dark jewel eyes. She laid her hand on his horn, breathing in the perfume of rose and violet as she told him what she had seen and heard.

Menkalinan blinked his large eyes a few times. "Weapons," he repeated. "And thou art healed. The time draweth nigh for thee to return." His nostrils flared, revealing the pinkish flesh inside them. "Thou wouldst be a prophetess if thou wert not a skinchanger. Thy inner sight is clear. Yet still, thou must beware. Weapons are not victory."

"A prophetess?" She chuckled and ran her hand through the silk of his mane. "I don't know if I'm cut out for years of solitude in the wilderness and a life of wandering – even if that's what I'm doing now! But I am cut out as a fighter." Suddenly the prospect of facing Crajaval again swelled in her mind, almost tangible. She swallowed. "Perhaps I was cut out to kill Crajaval and die fighting her," she said, voice a little above a whisper. For a moment, she felt cold inside before a spark of warmth leaped into life. "Perhaps. But I might win and live." She clenched her fists and set her jaw grimly, then relaxed. "No prophesies about this, I'm afraid. But I can't just sit here. I need to find these weapons. Do you know where that cave is, Menkalinan?"

The unicorn raised his head and looked around the clearing, then polished his horn against his flank thoughtfully. "No," he replied. "I seldom venture forth from the forest, save to the Hill of the Four Winds. But thy vision showeth this: that the cave lieth above the treeline where the land's bones are limestone and somewhere between the forest and the river." Again he rubbed his horn in slow circles against his flank. "The rock beneath the soil of the Hill of the Four Winds is limestone, I can tell thee that at the least. And it likewise standeth to the east of the forest."

"Then the Hill will be a place to begin searching, anyway." She stood up and flicked her hair back from her face with a toss of her head. "And I must start searching soon. If I am to face Crajaval, I'd rather face her soon and get it done with. Winter's approaching fast. If you think I'm ready."

"Thou art ready, I judge. But thou must wait until a sign is given. Go not too fast."

She stooped over her store of food and filled her belt pouch until it bulged with nuts and crabapples. One of the little fruits had turned rotten and her finger pierced the skin into the pulp. "Will you come with me, Menkalinan?" She straightened up and threw the rotten crabapple into the undergrowth.

"I will," he replied, turning his head from his flank and nuzzling at her, warm and soft on her hand. "This time I will come with thee. When thou goest to Moonlady Falls, thou must walk alone."

She closed the pouch tightly and looked keenly at the white animal. *Returning alone, unhorsed. Maybe I am going there to die. The hellhounds alone could pull me down.* She drew a deep breath and let it out slowly. *So be it, then. So be it.* "Let's go now," she said aloud.

The unicorn turned to present his flank to her. A long strand of his silky mane covered his eyes. She swung herself onto his bare back and settled herself astride him. He set off at a smooth canter along the deer-trails through the forest. The rain fell through the roof of bare branches and lingering evergreen leaves. The damp smell of the bush rose around them, fresher than usual in the rain. His hooves plashed through small puddles in the paths, splattering mud over his creamy sides. She ducked beneath the branch of an evergreen tree, the wide, rain-sodden leaves brushing over the top of her head and drenching her hair. The ground began to slant up beneath them and she leaned forwards to balance the unicorn, gripping his mane as she slid slightly backwards.

Menkalinan pushed through the last few trees and scrubby mountainthorn bushes onto the tussocky hillside. A low sweep of grey cloud poured and crept over the head of the hill above them, heavy with rain. She shivered as they left the shelter of the forest and the rain beat down on her. The mountains to the north were hidden behind the silvery sheets of rain. She pulled her cloak about her with one hand, still gripping the unicorn's mane with the other. She leaned further forwards as he climbed the slope, pressing herself closer to the warmth of his sweetly scented body. The cold southerly winds hissed through the tussocks and howled in her ears. *And well it may howl, being the wind of the wolf.* She glanced up at the thick grey clouds overhead, half expecting to see the great Southwest Wolf loping through the skies.

The unicorn halted on the top of the Hill of the Four Winds. "We have arrived," he panted. "Now to search for thy cave of limestone."

She slid off his back and wandered about the knoll. Her hood slipped back from her head and the wind blew achingly cold in her ears. She pulled the hood back up and wandered to the boulder that looked like a mountain lion, and sat on it, one hand idly caressing the weather-formed simulacrum's head and ears. She scanned the surrounding hillsides, searching for expanses of bare rock amid the tussock and mountain plants.

"Rememberest thou more from thy vision?" asked the unicorn. "Saw thou how high is the hill of the cave?"

She closed her eyes. "The hill wasn't massive, but it wasn't a little knoll like this one, either. It's quite steep and the cave opens into a rock face behind the boulders. The cluster of rocks has a lot of bracken around it." She hesitated. "I don't think the rocks and the cave are at the top, but there's a small shelf – it's grassy – where the boulders are resting. I don't know if that helps much, though."

"The hill must be a foothill then," he replied. "On my back again, Azariel Stormwolf, and we will search for it."

She put her hands on his wet withers and vaulted onto his back again. She leaned slightly forwards as she settled herself into the right place, restraining the urge to nudge his sides with her heels. *This mount needs no spurring! I'll never ride another like him, and my time with him is nearly done. I've learned a lot. It's been worth it.*

The unicorn headed down the slope, heading westwards. Gingerly, she slumped her weight backwards, feeling her leather trousers slip on his wet back and leaving her almost astride his neck. *For this terrain, a saddle would be ideal. But I'd never dare to ask to saddle him, even if I had one. I wonder what happened to Storm – and to Princess.*

They travelled along the undulating line of the foothills in the rain. Her eyes roamed over the slopes, studying the cairns and crags of yellow-grey rock on the hillsides. The day wore on slowly, and the clouds began to break up from around the heads of the mountains. Far to the south, beyond the black tangle of the forest and over the plains, patches of blue sky appeared in the rainclouds. The rain eased, then stopped and she threw her hood back from her head. The southerly wind still whined in her left ear, keen and icy. She shook her hair back from where the wind let it wander around her face and looked at the slope of the hill above them. Like many of the others they had passed, it was knobbed and studded with grey-yellow weathered boulders. *Another heap of limestone rocks. Are these the right ones?* She ran her eyes over them, comparing what she saw to the shapes in her vision for the hundredth time.

She picked out the lines and shapes of the rocks. The lowest one in the cluster was carved by the rain into the shape of a clenched fist. Behind it was another, a small hollow worn on the top. Bracken and mountainthorn grew around the boulders and on the rabbit-hole-pitted slope above the boulders. Recognition sent a silver arrow through her heart, leaving it pounding. "Stop," she called. "This is the place."

The unicorn halted, sides heaving. "Now thou must seek the cave where the jewels are," he panted. "Suffer me to rest; I am weary."

She swung off his back and walked towards the group of limestone boulders, slipping slightly on the wet grass and shortest tussocks. She zigzagged up the slope towards them and approached the boulders from the south. She walked between them, hands brushing over the weathered rock. An insect flew up from the small rock face above the loose boulders, buzzing loudly above her head. *It should be here, behind this rock, facing almost west,* she thought as she pushed through the dripping, crackling bracken. The westering sun reached through a rent in the clouds and pointed a finger of golden light across the yellow-grey stones. A black shadow appeared in the rock face and she strode forwards eagerly, a small mountainthorn catching at her cloak. Her heart thudded with excitement. *Here's the cave. Now for the jewels.*

She ducked her head beneath the low roof of the limestone cave and stepped in, expecting to see the tiny pinpoints of coloured light she had seen in her vision. The inside grew dark as her shadow cut the light from the hollow in the rock. A cobweb stuck to her forehead and she brushed it away. She waited for her eyes to adjust to the gloom, but saw nothing but dim shapes and shadows marking the walls and roof of the cave. She ran her hands over one of the walls, feeling the rock. *How am I to tell the jewels by touch? I'm not Taramaritan to know a gem by its hardness.* She gave an angry pant of failure and stepped back out of the cave again, stumbling over the bracken at the mouth. More spiders' webs clung to her face and she rubbed them off impatiently.

"Hast thou found them?" Menkalinan's voice came from behind her.

"No," she replied, turning to look at the unicorn. "I can't see well enough in the dark. Perhaps you could look, with your unicorn's eyes. I would shift shape, but I can't see colour as a wolf. I couldn't tell a garnet from a dark pebble."

"Thou couldst make fire to illuminate the darkness." The unicorn pawed with one silver hoof at the bracken. "Some of this is yet dry and would make thee a good torch."

She knelt and felt around in the bracken to the dead and dry parts beneath the rain-sodden fronds. One or two sticks were comparatively untouched by the rain. She probed around all the bracken nearby and plucked up enough dry twigs, holding them in a tight bunch. Placing it on a rock with one hand, she felt in her pouch for her tinderbox with the other. She struck spark after spark from the steel and flint, and finally coaxed a small flame onto the dead bracken. She waited, listening to the soft crackle of burning while the flames spread, then carried the burning bundle into the cave.

She ducked beneath the roof of the cave again, lowering her torch. Thick white smoke rose from it, making her eyes water and irritating her nose and the back of her mouth. She coughed, then held her breath against the sting of the smoke while she peered around the cave through a haze of tears. After a few seconds, her breath rushed out then she inhaled again, drawing in a lungful of stale, smoky air. Racked with coughing, she backed out. "That was no good," she said as soon as she had driven the smoke from her lungs and throat. "Too much smoke and the cave is too small. I couldn't see a thing."

She stubbed the torch out on a small patch of rock, grinding the charred branches to black smuts with the heel of her boot. Drawing a deep breath and savouring the clean smell of earth and grass in the air, she looked over at the unicorn. The sun sank lower and shone over his ivory back, making each hair stand out like a thread of gold. His shadow fell towards half the mouth of the cave, striking one part of the floor. Pale gold sunlight struck the back of the cave and she caught a glimmer of red. She drew breath sharply and spun around, staring at the cave wall. She crouched beneath the point of colour, keeping her shadow below it. Something unmistakeably red glittered in the stone and above it, two more points of colour winked, one deep blue, and one white. "There they are," she said over her shoulder and pointing. "Thank the Power."

Crouching beneath the stones still, she inched forwards and touched the lowest one. It was the opaque, blood-red garnet, gnarled and hard. She held what she could of it with a finger each side of it and pulled, then with two fingers to one side. She tugged and dug into the rock until her fingers hurt. *Come on; come out of the rock. I've got to take you before the sunlight leaves the cave. I haven't got long.* She scrabbled at the rock, breaking her untrimmed fingernails on the limestone. "Now what?" she asked. "How am I going to get that out? Not with my sword or dagger, surely."

"How tookest thou them in thy vision?"

"I didn't. I only saw a flash of white light, and then they were in my hand. I did nothing."

"A flash of light? Then let the Power flow through thee and blast the jewels from the rock. How else could light flare within the depths of the earth?"

"It's not that deep in the earth!" she snorted. She looked down at her rings and twisted the lapis lazuli and the opal to sit straight on her fingers. *Master, if this is how I am to take these jewels, help me do it. Flow through me.* She watched in silence, watching the rings and holding herself ready for the familiar coursing of energy through her veins. Her chest rose and fell as her breath flowed smoothly in and out. The rings stayed dark, apart from the usual red and green glints in the opal. She lowered her hands. "I don't think that's the way to get them," she said, shaking her head. Hair wandered into her eyes. "Maybe Taramaritan can use fire to take stones, but I can't do that any more than she can change into a wolf."

"Mayhap I can." The unicorn stepped forwards, horn pointed at the garnet. "Wait thou down at my hooves to catch the gem as it falleth."

She pressed between the unicorn's legs as he came into the cave. The bright beam of sunlight was cut off from the back of the cave, but she kept her eyes locked onto the gems were, two little dark points and one white in the grey. She waited, hands cupped beneath where the garnet sat in the wall. The unicorn's horn pressed against it, glowing faintly. A flash of white light burst from the point, dazzling her. After-images danced green behind her eyelids and something small, smooth and warm fell into the palm of her hand. She opened her eyes and looked down, catching a brief glimpse of something red before bright light exploded above her again. Something else fell into her hands. She kept her eyes closed and a third pulse of light flared, turning the black behind her eyelids red for an instant. A third thing fell into her hands. The unicorn snorted softly, then she felt and heard him back away.

She opened her eyes and looked down at the jewels in her hand. One was quartz, one sapphire and the garnet the largest of the three. She studied them as they lay in her palm, turning them so that the golden rays of the setting sun caught the natural facets of the quartz and made it turn to white fire in her hand. She cleared her throat and opened her mouth to thank Menkalinan.

A brilliant flash of light from the stones cut her short. It flared around the cave, lighting up every wind-smoothed knob in the limestone. Fire pulsed in her veins once and the stones in her hand glittered with inner light and grew warm. Energy tingled in her palm beneath the gems, prickling into her veins and fading. "Thank the Power," she whispered as the light faded. She straightened up and closed her hands around the three jewels. "And thank you, Menkalinan."

She came out of the cave and shook her hair back to fly free in the wind. The southwest wind was blowing, tugging her hair northeast towards the Illin-Ast gorge and Moonlady Falls. *Not the sign I'm waiting for but true enough.* She looked at the remaining banks of cloud hiding the mountains northeast of her, then down at her hand closed around the jewels. She clenched it hard, hearing the stones grate on each other. *I have weapons. When I am told to go, then the fight will come.*

CHAPTER THIRTEEN

Farren bent over the steaming cauldron, the flames beneath it hot on his legs. Steam lapped and curled around his face, moist and smelling faintly bitter. His heart pounded and his mouth felt dry in spite of the steam. *I hope I was right about what I heard last night. I hope that really was the Power's voice.* His stomach churned. *It sounded like Him. Please, Master! Don't let a foolish mistake lure Azariel to her death. I love her.* He shifted as Crajaval stirred the water with the lance and sword, and it changed colour. He drew a deep breath and wiped the condensed steam off his face, watching and waiting for the familiar image of Azariel sleeping in the forest to appear. *I'm glad I've got the use of my hands. I must have managed to act beaten enough for her not to tie me up again.* He started slightly as he saw an open hillside appear. He stared at it, then saw Azariel among gnarled rocks and bracken. *Where is she now?*

She was sitting with her back against a big weathered boulder, hugging her knees to her chest. The fading light in the west lit up her pale skin and a light breeze from the south stirred a wisp of her black hair across her face. The first winter stars showed in the gaps between the ragged clouds above her, silver points on patched velvet. She was awake, her eyes flicking to and fro around the hillside. He gazed at her with a small murmur of pleasure. *My love, my lady.*

He rested one hand on the edge of the cauldron. In the water beneath him, Azariel tilted her head up, lips parted, then bowed it, staring towards the ground in front of her. One hand went to her cheek as if she was brushing something away. Then she pressed her thumb and finger onto her closed eyelids. She sat like that for a few heartbeats, lips curling inwards almost fiercely before she covered her face with her hands and hair as her shoulders shook. *She's crying,* he thought, arms and chest starting to ache with the longing to hold her close. *Why? I've never seen her weep like that. She'd hardly cry more if she'd lost someone she loved.*   He knelt and leant his head on his arm as it lay along the rim of the cauldron, watching her. Then it hit him almost physically. *She has! She thinks I'm dead. Oh, Azariel, Azariel, don't cry. I'm here, I'm alive.*

He heard Crajaval's sandaled feet shifting on the stone floor and looked around. She had a smile twisting her full lips as she looked at the water and she seemed to be chuckling softly. He rose and stood between Crajaval and the cauldron. *Azariel never lets herself weep in sight of anyone except me, and even then hardly ever.* He felt his neck and cheeks heating in shame on her behalf and swallowed. *Crajaval shouldn't be able to see her like this. I know Azariel would be furious if she knew. Damn pretending to be beaten now.* "Well?" he said aloud, almost insolently. He rested one hand on his sword hilt.

"Will you defy me yet again?" she asked, smile vanishing. She strode towards him so that the silk draping her breasts almost brushed his face. Ice crawled in his stomach at the touch. "The hounds are waiting below – or shall I put you to something fiercer?" Her hand touched his face, nails pinching at the bristle on his cheeks.

He held the gaze of her blue eyes, then looked to the cauldron again. Azariel had raised her head and was wiping her eyes with her long hair. *At least I stopped Crajaval seeing some of that.* "What do you want me to do?" he asked sullenly. *At least that's no lie. I'm not going to say I'm defeated or even act it any more than I have to.*

"Call her." Crajaval smiled again and her voice had a note of triumph. "Speak into the cauldron."

"She's awake; she won't hear me," he replied, swiftly glancing at the shining white woman, then back down. *If we – if I have to wait for her to sleep, I'll have all this time to sit and look at her.*

"Call her now," came the reply. "She will both hear and see you."

I don't like this sorcery at all. He turned and bent over the cauldron again, gripping the rims. *Here goes, and I hope I'm right about what I heard.* "Azariel," he said softly.

He saw her startle up out of her relaxed position and look towards him. For a moment, a flash of joy blazed in her eyes, then her eyes narrowed and her teeth were bared. She leaped to her feet, hands tightening into fists as she raised them, rings outwards. "Who and what are you? How dare you take on his shape?" she demanded.

"It is me, Stormwolf," he replied, bending over the water. "I'm alive. I'm not on the mountain with you, though. I don't know what you can see of me."

"Tell me where you are, then, if you're alive." Her tense poise relaxed and her face softened, but the opal and the lapis lazuli winked at him, fires burning in the heart of the stones.

"Crajaval has me imprisoned – behind Moonlady Falls, I think, sweetheart. And I don't blame you for thinking I'm a ghost or something. I'm speaking to you through her cauldron."

"What?" Her heavy eyebrows cocked quizzically. "What cauldron?"

"Do not trouble to tell her," said Crajaval's voice above him. "Call her here. Get on with it, now that she knows you're alive."

"I can't tell you now," he said, nearly overbalancing into the water as he leaned further over. *Oh, sweetheart! I want so much to hold you.* "But I'm here. I'm alive." He tried to swallow down the hard lump from his throat but his mouth was dry. *Please, Master, may I not be making a hideous mistake.* "Please, Azariel, come back to me. Come and fight her and get me out of here. And may the Power fight through you when you do!" He tore his glance away from her and up at Crajaval, who was grimacing and gasping as if

220

she were in pain. He gripped the sides of the cauldron fiercely so that the felt the blood squeeze from his knuckles. *Now. Now's my chance to expose what Crajaval's been doing to her.* "Stormwolf, stand firm. Don't let anyone, not even in your dreams, tell you…"

A hand of cold steel clamped over his mouth. The hand pressed him down and he snatched a breath of air an instant before the hot bitter water closed around his head. After a while, the breath rushed out of him and he struggled desperately as his lungs fought to breathe again. The hand yanked him up by the hair and he came up, spluttering and gasping in the sweet air. The image of Azariel still showed on the water. She was staring wildly around. "Farren? Farren!" she called. "Where are you? Come back, beloved!" He leaned back over the water to speak, but Crajaval seized him by the shoulder. She flung him down to the floor. He gasped with pain as he landed heavily on his bruises. Crajaval took the lance and the sword and plunged them into the water; the pale flames from the pentagon by his face died.

He drew himself up onto one elbow, shielding his face as she kicked at him. "So," she said. "Even now you defy me. But it is done. She will come." She rubbed her hands together and smiled. "And she will be mine."

He looked up at her, heart thundering. *That's what you think, demon!*

***

Azariel stared into the twilight, searching for the misty image of Farren's face that had hung in the air. "Farren," she called again, feeling hot sparks flaring behind her eyes again. "Farren." Tears trickled down her cheeks, then she bit the rest back. *Where did he go? What did she do to him?* Then she smiled. *He's alive. He's alive! Thank the Power.*

She walked a few paces to the northeast, letting the evening breeze play with her hair. *Was that really him speaking? Was that the summons I've been waiting for? Or was it a cheat? I know I want him.* She clenched her fists by her sides and closed her eyes. Her heart beat strongly and warmly. *No. That really was him, somehow. I would have sensed if it was some evil wraith. I may be hopeless at a lot of things, but that's one thing I'm sure of.* Her hand went to the belt pouch where she had stored her jewels. *I will go back to Moonlady Falls tomorrow as soon as it's light.* She turned back from the northeast, flicking her hair out of her face. Somewhere, an owl called. *Sleep first, though. I'll need it. If only those dreams will stay away!*

She awoke in the cave the next morning, excitement crawling in her stomach, mixed with nerves and hunger. The unicorn lay at the mouth of the cave, sunlight shining over the rock onto him and turning his horn to fire. She yawned and his dark eyes turned towards her. "Good morning, arch *minyaster*," he said. "Art thou ready to ride back to the forest? We need not wait on the hilltop until a sign comes to thee that thou shouldst return."

She sat up, unwinding her cloak from around herself and setting it straight on her shoulders. "The summons came last night, Menkalinan," she said slowly. "I will go to Moonlady Falls today. Will you take me?"

The unicorn shook his head. "I may not go that far from my forest. These hills are almost too far from my permitted range. And thou needest me no more."

"But what am I going to do? I can't walk there on my own two feet – or four feet." She ran her fingers through her hair, tugging and yanking out a few tangles. "Well, I can if I must, but I'd rather face Crajaval when I'm at full strength, not exhausted from a long march."

"Thou knowest all thou needest to know," said the unicorn with the ghost of a chuckle burring the edges of his words. "Break thy fast, Azariel. Then maybe thou canst use the knowledge I have given thee."

The unicorn stood up and left the cave. She got to her feet, stretching her arms and legs as she walked after him. Her clothes felt clammy and unclean, but she shrugged the discomfort off. *It doesn't matter. Before long, I'll be where I can get clean clothes on my body again, or else I won't be in my body at all.* She stepped outside and screwed her eyes up as the brilliant morning sunshine struck her in the face. Birds trilled and chirruped, and one or two flew overhead. A warm wind blew around her and a broad blanket of high blue-grey cloud spanned the sky from one horizon to the other, but arching to the northwest to reveal the blue vault above. Beyond that, dark wind-smudged cloud hid the furthest peaks and ranges. *Northwester,* she thought, striding out of the shelter of the rocks into the full fierce strength of the warm autumn wind, the wind's energy making her heart rise.

She walked about the hillside breathing in the fresh grassy smell on the wind as she searched for food. She found a cluster of wild rosebushes hung with little vermilion rosehips. She nibbled at them, filling her mouth with the tangy flesh, then spitting out the bristle-covered pips at the heart. She left the bush after eating most of the hips, little plant-hairs tickling the inside of her mouth. *I'll have to go down to a stream in one of the valleys to get water to wash all this bristle out of my mouth. After breakfast, though.* She bent over one of the bracken bushes and searched among the fronds for the young tender shoots. She found a few, then plucked and ate them.

She straightened up from the clumps of bracken and looked towards the northeast. Blue sky beneath the far end of the northwest arch stood over the mountains, but the head of the Illin-Ast gorge was hidden in cloud, pale rather than the darker grey cloud that covered the most distant mountains. *That's it,* she thought, nibbling at the last young bracken shoot. *Moonlady Falls. Somehow, I've got to get there, then fight Crajaval and her hounds at the end of it – alone.* She glanced down. A small broken frond of bracken clung to the black broadcloth of her cloak. She picked it off and crumbled the metallic dry leaf into small pieces. *Can I do it after a tiring march across the mountains on foot? Alone? I know the Power will be there, but can I do it? We didn't do it last time. But I must.* She began to trudge down the hillside towards a small stream in a valley, thoughts spinning inside her head.

She drank deeply, then splashed the cool water over her face, driving away the sleepy heaviness that lingered. Menkalinan was waiting by the rocks for her, looking down with the northwest wind billowing and spinning out the fine silk of his mane and tail. "Hail and farewell, Azariel Stormwolf, arch *minyaster*," he said, tossing his head and sending a river of white mane around his silver horn. "The time had come for me to leave thee and return to my forest, and for thee to journey to Moonlady Falls. If the One who is Maker and Master of us both hath woven it into the pattern of his tapestry, then we shall meet again. And if not, then some other adventure awaiteth us." The unicorn trotted down the slope and pressed his muzzle against her chest, his perfumed horn touching her face. "May the Power protect thee, God Incarnate watch over thee and the King of Heaven grant thee long life," he said, his musical voice dropping almost to a whinnied whisper.

She laid her hands on the unicorn's horn. "And you also," she replied. She turned her head and kissed the smooth scented ivory. Menkalinan gave a short, warm whicker, then pulled free from their embrace. He reared, silver hooves pawing the air and glittering in the morning sunlight. Then he turned and galloped down the slope, heading southeast towards the black tangle of the Ulfskin-Aza forest. She stood on the side of the hill, northwest wind streaming about her as she watched the brilliant white shape travel across the gold tussocks, dwindle, then vanish.

She sighed as he passed out of sight, then turned back towards the northeast. She squared her shoulders and stretched out a slightly cramped muscle in her calf. *It's going to be a long walk.* Her ankles ached as she picked a path that followed the contour of the land around the hill, pushing through the clumps of tussocks. The fresh scent of dew mixed with the softer smell of older grass blown on the wind. An eagle soared and swooped on the currents of air above the hillside, spiralling up then angling away with the sunlight catching the browns of its wings.

She walked all morning, pausing briefly to drink from a small steam that trickled along the bottom of a narrow valley between two of the foothills. The sun rose higher and the wind blew stronger. She sat down on a tussock briefly to rest, then stood up again quickly as the lingering damp hidden in the grass soaked into her trousers. *It's hard going, even though I'm not going completely head on into this strong wind.*

She pulled up, throwing her head back and looking up at the slatey sky. *The wind.* She smiled and scrambled up to the rocks. *I need a horse and the northwester is galloping. But will he come if I ask him?* She stood beside the rocks, bracing herself against the strong wind. It blew in her face, leaving her skin feeling dry and taut. The smell of dry grass and earth flew with the wind, fresh and clear, a golden-olive smell. She cleared her throat and closed her eyes against the strength of the wind.

She drew a deep breath, inhaling the fresh smell of the wind again. Her hands tightened into fists. "God Incarnate, give me the authority I need to call him," she whispered. Words sprang into flame in her mind, the Old Tongue, honed and trained from the unicorn's teaching. She tossed her head back and looked up, hair and cloak whirling back behind her. "Stallion," she said loudly, *"Ahinahin magnan y ahira yan-bar, ea, Arrurer-y-Dharva, rhuakaso dea ilnas."*

She waited as her words were whirled away on the wind. The black wind-whipped clouds to the north darkened and seemed to grow closer, almost overhead although she still felt the sunlight on her back. The wind doubled and trebled in ferocity, almost driving her backwards. She leaned into it, still looking up at the black sky as knives of white lightning stabbed through the heavens. A thrill passed down her back, hot and icy at once, and she felt herself trembling with the charge. She raised her hands and white fire crackled from her fingertips in answer. Thunder roared rhythmically like giant hooves echoing on a huge wooden bridge. More lightning split the sky, red-gold and brilliant scarlet against the black.

A blinding flash of light seared the air in front of her and she covered her eyes with her hands. She felt the wind drop around her and smelt a faint hint of musk mixed with the grass-scent. A prickling wave of fresh fire coursed down her spine. She lowered her hands and opened her eyes. In front of her, the huge Stallion of the Northwest wind stood, dark eyes fixed on her through a tousled chestnut forelock. She smiled, reminded of Farren for an instant, then bowed her head to the Stallion. "Hail, Stallion," she said. "Thank you for coming to me."

The big horse tossed his head and stamped a hind hoof. "Of course I came," he snorted. His voice was rough, warm and husky. "It's a while since a human called me. Now, Azariel, what can I do for you? Why have you called me? Just for fun, or do you have a reason?"

"I wouldn't call you for fun," she said. "I wouldn't play around like that. I've called you to take me back to Moonlady Falls."

"Why do you want to go there? Don't you know about Crajaval? Take you back?"

She tossed her hair back and clenched her fists. "I know about her," she said slowly, looking beyond the Stallion to the Illin-Ast gorge. "I'm going there to fight her and set my beloved free." She breathed deeply, then realised her teeth were bared as excitement and her fighting mood began to build inside her. "And take the Stones back to the Kingdom." *I had half forgotten that in my excitement about Farren.*

The Stallion's ears pricked forwards and his wide nostrils quivered. "Bravo! It's time somebody gave her what she deserves. Mount and ride, Azariel Stormwolf, and I'll take you there. Then, well, may the Power be in your sword and hands."

She climbed onto the rocks and mounted the Stallion's broad high back. She clung to him as he wheeled, half-rearing. She felt the huge muscles beneath her move, then she and the Stallion were in the air. The foothills, the forest, the mountains dropped away beneath them. The Stallion passed over the jagged snow-capped lines of the mountain ranges and travelled north, moving in slow strides through the air. "Where are you going?" she asked. "This isn't the way to Moonlady Falls."

"It is if you can only gallop from the northwest quarter. Trust me, comrade. I know the way and I'll take you there."

She saw the land spread out beneath her like a huge map: plains, hills, forest and mountains seeming small and delicate from the height she looked down. North of the mountains lay a thin line of bush-covered land bordered by a long coastline. *What country is that? Or isn't it one?* Beyond the land lay nothing but water strewed with a few islands, vast, deep green and blue.

The Stallion halted, tossing his head. Slowly, he turned to face the landmass again. She felt him tense up ready to charge with his head held high, and she braced herself astride him. His ears pricked forwards and his reared, half-screaming in a high, passionate fighting neigh. He surged forwards, striding through the air swifter than the swiftest mortal horse. Hot wind swirled around her and banks of cloud swept aside before them. She leaned forwards, his mane hissing and whipping in her face. Her heart thundered and fire began to burn in her veins. The air screamed in her ears as the Stallion galloped faster and faster. Ahead, through the haze of water torn from her eyes by the fierce speed, she saw the tall mist-draped mountain with shining water pouring endlessly down one side. Exhilaration shook her and she threw back her head in a fierce laugh, almost echoing the stallion's neigh. Above the mountain, the Stallion neighed and curvetted, wheeling as he halted. Then they stood beside the falls on the brink of the pool where the shining gold water raged itself to white foam.

She slid off the Stallion's back, mouth dry and heart beating a marching beat in her ears. She hugged the Stallion hard around the neck, pressing her forehead into his wiry mane. The huge horse tossed his head, then nuzzled her in the back as she let go. "The Power be with you, comrade," he said.

So be it, she thought as she turned and walked away from him. She turned towards the waterfall. It shone with its own golden light as well as the gold of the westering sun. Her shadow streamed before her to the pool of water. The northwest arch of cloud caught the sunlight and the underside of it shone with gold against the streaks of slate and cream. She drew a deep breath and took another step towards the pool. *Master, I'm ready. Help me,* she prayed silently.

Fierce energy struck her, almost physically, dizzying for a few moments in its intensity. The familiar prickling flame of the Power burned in her veins, stronger than before. Her arms shook and her rings heated to scorching. The lightning-energy crackled up and down her spine and she half felt, half imagined it continuing along the length of her hair as it whipped around her face. *I'm ready as I can be. Much more fire inside me, I'd black out.* She walked to the south of the pool and threw back her head, tossing her hair back into the wind. "Crajaval!" she called. "Come out! Azariel Stormwolf is here!"

The mists parted around the waterfall, revealing the face of the mountain. Crajaval stood between the rocks beside the pool, tall and proud, clad in a white robe that rose in a collar like a lily behind the braids of white-gold hair coiled like serpents on her head. She raised one hand, glittering like a star, and a smile parted her perfect red lips. "Welcome, Azariel Stormwolf," she purred. "I am so glad you have come. Put your hand in mine, lady of the werewolves. Join with me and learn what you were born for."

Azariel felt laughter welling up inside her. *Fool! White fool! I'm here to kill her!* She threw back her head and let the shout of laughter out, the pent-up energy making her arms tremble. A flurry of wind sent her hair flying across her face. Her hand tightened around the hilt of her sword, ready to draw it. The energy seemed to leap into her mind, drowning the laughter. In her mind's eye, she saw Menkalinan again, seated underneath his favourite tree as he talked to her *Words are weapons,* she heard him say in her memory. *Fight fire with fire, steel with steel and words with words.* A flood of words poured into her mind: rhythms, images, rhymes straining like a pent-up dam to flow free. Her eye met Crajaval's and she released the floodgates of her voice.

> *Ahira-ran tar minyator.*
> *The shadows sleep, the moon is young,*
> *The bright clouds on the sunset flung,*
> *The wind I ride, the wind I call,*
> *Thus came I to this waterfall.*
> *I lift my sword against all Hell*
> *With might the bloodstained hosts to quell;*
> *A blow struck in the holy war.*
> *Ahira-ran tar minyator.*

She drew her sword and brandished it as she chanted the words. The blue steel flashed golden fire in the late rays of the sun. Her hands quivered with pent-up energy, making the point tremble. She flicked her wandering hair back from her face again, breathing hard. *What now?*

Crajaval's smile vanished into a cold thin line. "You fool. You turn down your own good," she whispered menacingly. "Do you really hope to fight against me?" She lowered her hand and clenched it into a fist before spreading it out in front of her, palm down.

Listen, proud Azariel,
What powers have you against my spell?
What shield have you against my hate?
Come bow your neck, accept your fate
And in your flesh I'll set a fire
Of power, strength and fierce desire
(My werewolf queen, my priceless pawn)
Or perish vanquished and forlorn.

Azariel held the tall shining woman's gaze, keeping her face in a grim mask. *So this has become a war of words. I can't afford any carelessness. I'm only human, after all, and she's immortal. But I'll never go over to her!* Thirst sanded the back of her throat. She tried to swallow it away, but her saliva had grown sticky. A pinch of fear seasoned the cauldron of flame inside her. She lowered her sword so that the point touched the stones and raised her left hand, palm outwards. More words poured through her mind and out of her mouth.

I am the Stormwolf, fearless, valiant;
I do not waver, do not bend.
I am loyal, changeless, adamant;
I have come to make an end.
By the raging, purging water,
By the Falcon's keening cry,
By the Power, foul demon-daughter,
Stumble, perish, falter, die.

She flung fire at the other woman and a bolt of lightning swirled and shimmered through the air in shades of blue, green and dark brown. It broke like a wave around Crajaval, but she brushed it calmly away, a sneer crossing her beautiful pale face as she looked up.

You cannot fight me with your song.
You rebel, come where you belong.
You want him, don't you? Burning hot

> *To feel him loose your virgin-knot.*
> *You're mine, I tell you! Come to me*
> *Or taste full-strength my cruelty.*
> *By red-hot lust, bow to my name*
> *Or suffer in remorseless pain.*

Crajaval made as small twisting gesture with one hand. Azariel jerked her hands up across her chest and face protectively, peering around her forearm, watching for an answering bolt of fire. None came. Cautiously, she lowered her hands and flicked her eyes back and forth, always returning to Crajaval. Five figures appeared in the mist and she drew breath sharply, poised and ready to defend herself. The figures came closer and she saw them clearly. All were male, all were completely naked and all looked exactly like Farren. Light from some unknown source touched them in shades of gold, highlighting each line of muscle, bone and sinew of their well-formed bodies. The figures danced and twisted, beckoning to her with dark flashing eyes and inviting parted lips. Something seemed to be trying to clamp her gaze in one place to look at every part of the naked male figures, whispering promises of sweet secret pleasure.

She shook her head angrily as her blood stirred and heated inside her belly. *No. It's a cheat. That's not really Farren, and he's who I want. And I can't enjoy him sexually yet, anyway.* She looked through the figures at Crajaval. Her eyes narrowed and her teeth bared. *You won't catch me like that. But was what I saw last night a cheat too? Maybe I shouldn't have come. I'm doomed.* A hard knot tied itself in her throat and stomach. *But if that's so, I'll die fighting.* She shook her hair back from her face and tightened her grip around her sword, more words kindling in her mind and burning away the inner voice of temptation.

> *I'll yield no place to lust or lechery;*
> *My desire stands curbed and still.*
> *Against him, I'll not wreak such treachery;*
> *Never can you break my will.*

> *I am the Stormwolf, fearless, valiant.*
> *I do not waver, do not bend.*
> *I am steadfast, changeless, adamant;*
> *I have come to make an end.*
> *By the earth, the firm foundation,*
> *By the Stallion's mighty neigh,*
> *By the Power, you vile damnation,*
> *Vanish, wither, fade away.*

She raised her hand, flashing black and gold fire from her fingertips. It sliced through the nude figures, withering them back to mist. Crajaval beat the flames down, lips parted and teeth bared. Azariel waited every sinew taut and ready, blood throbbing and hammering at her wrists and temples. The white woman's large eyes narrowed and she spoke again.

> *Try me not too far, false jade.*
> *You, not I, are doomed to fade*
> *Unless you yield beneath my hand.*
> *See how your fire-temper's fanned!*
> *Each whip of wrath, each goad of fury,*
> *Draws you closer, closer to me.*
> *By vicious anger's wounding spite,*
> *I draw you to my endless light.*

The white woman threw out one hand. Azariel flinched, ready to guard herself against flame. Instead of flame, something struck her like a wave, painless but palpable. It shook her, leaving a wake of white-hot wrath behind it. She stepped forwards, hands clenched, sword angled to attack and a snarling scream of rage beginning to tighten the muscles in her throat. *It's a trap. It's a trap.* The thought cut coldly through the hot angry turmoil. *Don't let rage blind you. Don't drop your guard. You're only human and you could so easily get this wrong.* She clenched her fists tighter, the blood squeezing from her knuckles on her right hand around her sword as her rings dug hot metal into the calluses on her palms. She drew a deep breath and let it out slowly. Again the fire of words blazed in her mind.

> *I spurn the sharp-barbed hook you've baited.*
> *Do you strive to break me still?*
> *Each move you make I have check-mated*
> *And naught can daunt my strength of will.*
> *I am the Stormwolf, fearless, valiant;*
> *I do not waver, do not bend.*
> *I am constant, changeless, adamant;*
> *I have come to make an end.*
> *By the winds, the breaths of heaven,*
> *By the Wolf, the silver shade,*
> *By the Power, damned devil-leman,*
> *Vanish, die, end, wither, fade.*

Her right hand tightened around the hilt of her sword and she slashed it up before her face, almost to the salute. A fresh wave of prickling energy pulsed down her arm and silver grey snakes of lightning leaped from her fingers and wrapped around her sword, turning it into a tongue of flame. She drove it towards Crajaval and let the fire crackle through the air. A strange white smell lingered in the air in the wake of the fire. The flame struck Crajaval in the shoulder, wrapping around her head. The white material of her high collar darkened slightly before she brushed it away.

Yes! thought Azariel, striding forwards restlessly, her sword humming with energy. *That burned her. Now to finish this.* She raised her sword again, breath coming fast and sharp. Fire flew from Crajaval's hand. She whirled the sword in front of her, blocking the blue flame. The sword sang and quivered, stinging her fingers. The fire died around her sword, leaving it ordinary damasked blue steel. Teeth bared, she raised her left arm to guard as she lowered her sword.

Crajaval stood still for an instant, fists clenched by her sides and her face twitching. Then she relaxed and laughed a low, soft laugh in her sweet voice. "Azariel!" she said. "You fail to understand what I am offering. Why do you fight?"

You think I seek to bend and break you?
Not so. Through wisdom's path I'll take you
If you will yield. Pluck fruit from this tree;
Taste and savour my deep Mystery.
Taste it, Stormwolf! Or beware;
If shunned, I'll not forgive, I swear.
I'll see you as you writhe and scream
In pain-wracked hope you merely dream.

The mists thickened about Azariel again and more images appeared in succession. A white stag pranced through a thicket of thirteen sacred trees. Blue-robed priestesses and saffron-clad sorcerers danced in spirals between two fires burning in a circle of stones. A woman held a sheaf of wheat to her chest with one hand pressing her fingers to her lips with the other. Moonlight glistened on the blood of an antelope as it was poured over the head of a naked initiate. A voice whispered at her. *Don't you want to come inside? Cross the threshold. Learn the secrets and the rites that will speed you on the path to being a goddess. Be one of the sacred initiates, one of the few. Choose this and come. Know what real power is!*

She ignored the voice and its chatter as she watched the images pass in front of her eyes. For an instant, something tugged at her insides towards them, but then a small snort of laughter rose and she stifled it before it burst from her. *Secret rites to become a goddess! That old trap still? As if we don't have our own rites and rituals in The Way! I remember my own initiation by water well enough.* She let out a slow breath, dispelling the laughter as the visions faded and the mists lightened to leave only the mist-damp rocks and white water of the falls and river. She tossed her head and shuffled her feet impulsively. *Why should I turn sorceress only to burn at the end of it? I wish she'd stop all this tomfoolery and fight fire to fire!* Then she laughed aloud and the torrent of words flooded out on her laughter.

The tang of that dark fruit is ashen;
Poison strong to sap the will.
I'll brave the full force of your passion.
So wreak your worst! I shun you still.
I am the Stormwolf, fearless, valiant;
I do not waver, do not bend.
I am true-heart, changeless, adamant;
I have come to make an end.
By the fire's bright hand of scarlet,
By the Lion's roaring blast,
By the Power, you demon-harlot
Finish, end and breathe your last.

Fresh fire, black, gold, red and silver burst from her fingertips and roared through the air at Crajaval, leaving her arms and jaw trembling and her head dizzy. Crajaval crossed her wrists in front of her and blocked the fire, stepping backwards a few paces. She recovered, smoothing her white robes. "You can't defeat me, Azariel," she said softly, a serpent spitting poison. "You never will. Who do you think you are to defy me? You can't win. Don't even try. You can't do it. You're not strong or clever enough. Who do you think you are?"

Who do you think you are...? The words echoed in Azariel's mind, wrenching the door off the dungeon where she had pushed her nightmares. The three figures, Stessa, Karissa and Edwin Feller, all began to jabber at her in her mind. Then she started back, dread coursing ice-water down her back. The three figures were in the mists in front of her, all looking at her with sneering mouths and hard eyes. The Karissa shape loomed over her, riding whip in hand, and she stepped back. Her heart sank and she lowered her sword. *I'm no good. I should never have come here. I'll never be better than her and I might as well die now.* She looked beyond the mist-figures at Crajaval through the locks of hair covering her face, heart thundering.

Crajaval's dark eyes bored into her, cool, confident, eyes. She dropped her head. *She's more than a match for someone as useless as me.* The white woman's scarlet lips moved as she spoke, a shade above a whisper.

Does God really love you, Azariel, Azariel?
After you have failed him, will he take you back again?
Are you really someone special in his eyes, Azariel?
Are you hoping, watching, dreaming, fighting all in vain?
Does he think you're worthy, Azariel, Azariel?
You with all your foibles and all your stubborn pride?
Aren't you just a nobody in his eyes, Azariel?
And because of all your weakness, won't he cast you down aside?

The quiet words pierced her ears and plunged deep into her heart. She stared down at the shining white water, then at the gravel at her feet. Her chest heaved as the nightmare figures within and without whispered at her. She gripped her sword for support and looked up again. Crajaval threw back her head, lips parted ecstatically. *Trapped,* she thought as she saw the other woman's look of victory. *She's caught me. I fell for the bait. How did she know my weakness so well? Now dying is all I deserve for being so stupid.* She swallowed at the knot in her throat and looked up at Crajaval.

"What is your so-called Power to mine?" said the woman. "Don't you see that now? But even now it is not too late to choose to join with me. Come. Be mine." She opened her hands in welcome. "Put your hands in mine."

"No," she whispered, bowing her head. "Even if you kill me. I won't. Even if the Power has left me..." She choked on the words, realising that the tingling in her arms and hands had almost faded. "Even if He has, I won't leave Him. Never. Never."

"I won't kill you," snarled Crajaval. "I'll see that you don't die. However much you wish for it. Until you yield, there'll be no end to this!" Flame burst from the woman's fingertips and seared through the air. Instinctively she raised her armband of protection into the fire, blocking it. The garnets set in the silver glowed brilliant blood-red, scalding hot. The metal burst into a hundred bright shards, jangling onto the stones around her. More fire flashed at her and split into wreaths and vines of white flame that licked across her face and hands. Agony stabbed her like white-hot knives from all sides and she screamed. Her sword slipped from her grip and fell with a clatter onto the stones, the sound almost lost in the roar of the flames.

She dropped to her knees, moaning thinly as the remorseless pain continued. She looked down at her hands and arms; they were unmarked in spite of the flames that licked around them. She bit back another cry as it rose in her throat. *Master, please! Don't let her do this!* White fire wrapped around her head, filling her world with white light and searing pain. "God Incarnate, help me," she whispered between her bared teeth.

The fire continued to rage in a column around her, but the pain began to ebb away. She raised her head, dizzy stars spinning in front of her eyes. *Come on,* she told herself. *One last effort. For the King of Heaven, for the Kingdom, for Farren.* A picture flashed into her mind's eye of Farren in the darkness behind the rocks. Then the picture was swallowed up by another cave hewn from rock, a massive boulder to one side of it and light blazing from inside. Her heart kicked in her chest and wildfire ran in her veins again. She got to her feet and raised her sword. Crimson flames blossomed around the blade. *Who do you think you are?* rang a voice in her head, strong and warm. *You know who you are and you know who I am. Tell her who I am!*

Every fibre in her arms, back and legs was tingling. Her left hand went to the pouch at her belt, fumbled the laces open and felt for the three jewels. They sat snugly in the palm of her hand as she tightened her fist around them inside the pouch. She raised her sword and slashed at the column of flame surrounding her. Dark crimson warred with white and beat it down. Crajaval was standing with her hands clenched and her eyes open wide.

Azariel's heart thundered quick dull beats in her ears and slow, white-hot anger rose in her. *Your time is finished, Moon Lady! You won't keep my Farren trapped any longer.* She stepped forwards, burning sword in her hand and fresh words on her tongue.

> *I remember that He made me.*
> *In that alone, I'll place my pride.*
> *I know that He once died to save me;*
> *I see the spear stabbed in his side,*
> *The thorns, the scourge-stripes on His shoulder,*
> *His blood poured out, His humbled might.*
> *These firm-fixed facts have made me bolder*
> *And I'll not turn back from this fight.*
> *I am the Stormwolf, fearless, valiant;*
> *I'll not forsake this King I've found.*
> *I am loyal, changeless, adamant;*
> *My feet stand firm on holy ground.*
> *By the stones, quartz, sapphire, garnet,*
> *I know the Power still works through me,*
> *And in the name of God Incarnate,*
> *I charge you, hell-spawn: set him free!*

Crajaval stepped backwards into the rocks behind her, fear stamped across her face. Azariel pulled out one jewel, the sapphire, and hurled it, spinning it as if she was skimming it over water. It flashed fire the colour of the night sky as it caught the other woman on the arm. Crajaval screamed and clutched at her arm, eyes wild. The quartz flashed in the air like a star, then burned a hole in the white garments around her. Azariel raised the garnet and threw it, shouting her wolf-howl battle cry. The red stone struck Crajaval full in the face and her head snapped back.

Azariel tightened her grip on her sword, still blazing with crimson flames, and ran at the white figure as she reeled. Crajaval raised one white hand and spurted fire at her. She flashed her sword in the path of the flame and whirled it aside. A sickly sweet-smell of incense rose from the white woman's robes as Azariel halted, raising her sword diagonally, ready to spring into any move. "In the name of God Incarnate," she panted, "In the name of Yeshua." She lunged and thrust, stabbing the burning point of the sword between Crajaval's breasts. She felt the resistance of the blade easing home between the ribs, ripping the white silk and the skin beyond. Her enemy's body shuddered, blood spurting through ruby lips, then withered around the sword, spinning into soft white mist that writhed and coiled away to join the mist about the falls.

A gust of the northwest wind blew, swirling the mist and sweeping it away. Moonlady Falls stood naked under the twilight sky, shining in its own golden light and the outdoor silver of the half-moon, clean from the strange white mist and beautiful. She looked up at it, chest heaving, hands trembling with exhilaration and exertion, and a shout of triumph bursting from deep inside her.

Then the trembling fire faded from her hands and arms and everything went black with a roaring noise in her ears.

CHAPTER FOURTEEN

Azariel's eyes opened on moonlight glittering off the wet stones and dancing in swirls and ribbons of silver beneath the waterfall. Water slicked her hair and her bare forearms were chilled. She got to her feet, then stooped for her sword, blood roaring in her ears and sparks flying in front of her eyes. She sheathed her sword and drew herself up straight again. The moonlight cast soft shadows over the spray-dampened rocks and gravel at the edge of the pool. She looked up at the stars and the moon, watching a scrap of cloud stream on the northwest wind across the half-disk. Her eyes travelled down from the night sky to the mountain, only the snow showing a ghostly silver in the light. The waterfall fell in a long golden line to the pool, faintly illuminating the cliff face beside it. *Farren's in there somewhere,* she thought, staring at the black bulk of earth and rock that towered over her and listening to the roar and rush of the water. *But how do I get to him? Where's the door?* She brushed the fine wet sheen of spray off her face and arms, then ran her hands through her hair. *There must be a way. Crajaval could materialise through the rock, being a spirit, but Farren's solid flesh and blood.* Briefly, the obscene wraiths Crajaval had conjured up flickered in her memory but she shook them out of her mind. *I don't want to think about those; I want to think about him. Those things weren't real. Back to the task.*

She scrambled onto the rocks beside the pool and looked across the churning white water. The copper gong stood on the other side of the river, metal shining faintly in the soft golds and silvers cast by the moon, water and stars. *That's where the door's most likely to be, but I won't leave this side until I've searched.* She ran her eyes over the rock face in front of her, studying each crack and cranny in the rocks. She slid down off the rocks and went to the cliff face, feeling at the cold wet stone with her fingertips. Nothing yielded. She felt the rock and pressed her ears against it. The roar of the waterfall came through the rock, deeper and more like thunder. *How can I tell if there's a cave behind here?*

She moved from one edge of the narrow cliff face towards Moonlady Falls themselves. She paused, the rush of wind generated by the falling water and the spray pushing her back and nearly blinding her. Squinting and rubbing water off her face with her free hand, she looked at the curtain of water. *Is the door behind the waterfall? I've heard you can walk behind them.* She looked down at the foaming cauldron of water in the pool beneath and shuddered. Cold, numbing dread of deep water spread out from the pit of her stomach. *Master, keep me safe as I pass behind it. I don't want to slip and fall into there in full armour.*

She twisted her cloak into a coil and wrapped it about one shoulder, tucking the end in through the neck. *If that gets sodden with water, it'll drag me in.* She drew a deep breath and walked forwards, screwing up her eyes against the fine stinging spray and the wind of the water. She gripped a fissure in the stone, made sure one foot had a secure hold, then slipped into the side of the shining cataract.

For a second, she felt the weight of the water press down on her head and shoulders. Then she broke through, pressing against the wet rocks with the deafening roar of water around her. Clinging to a water-smoothed projection in the wall of the cliff, she inched her way along, feeling with her fingers for the fissures in the slippery rocks. She paused, feeling with one toe for the next foothold. The end of her cloak began to worm and slide out from where she had tucked it in over her shoulder. *No! And I can't stop it falling, either.* She stepped to the next smooth place in the rocks, then felt the cloak fall behind her. The heavy water caught the wool and hauled at it, dragging her backwards by the throat. She gasped and bit her fingers into the rock as hard as she could, nails scraping against the rocks and blood squeezing out of her knuckles with the effort. Her heart pounded in her ears and her skin crawled. She inched to her right, still moving along her path behind the waterfall.

The golden light shone on a dark recess in the rocks ahead. *At last! I've found it.* Staggering, slipping, stumbling, she made her way to it and fell forwards onto her knees. She stayed on all fours recovering her breath and waited for her heartbeat to quieten. She stood up and peered around the recess. The pale gold light shone on three walls and the roof of a small hollow, damp and empty. She gave a small sigh of disappointment, then began to work her way around the cave, prodding and prying. She caught a faint smell in the air, not the smell of wet rock and mud but the unpleasant earthy stink of a privy. *Where's that coming from?* she thought, a surge of excitement pounding in her heart. She scanned the rocks for any signs of a doorway or a hidden catch. Nothing yielded to her probing fingers. She gently sucked the chafed skin on her fingertips and looked up and down the grey-gold stone. *Well, at least air can get through the rock. There's nothing in this hollow to make that smell.* She slowly felt and prodded her way around the small cavern and back to the waterfall again.

She moved along the wall of the small cave out to the narrow gap between the water and the rock. Head and shoulders drenched and hands aching from clutching the rock, she moved along. At one place, just as she passed through the curtain of water, she saw a crack in the rock that opened into darkness. Ignoring the battering of water on her cloak and scrabbling for a foothold, she wedged her fingers in the crack and heaved until her arms and hands cried out with the pain of effort. The stench was strong, emanating from the fissure. The rock face did not budge. Panting, she scrambled off the wet rocks beneath the falls and stood upright on the gravel. She wrung the water out of her hair and listened to the sound of her own heartbeat. After a few moments, she continued along the cliff face.

The foul smell vanished, leaving only the clean, outdoor smells. She frowned and her heart sank. "Where is it?" she said aloud, stooping for a stone then hurling it into the pool in frustration. "King of Heaven, do I have to ask you to split the mountain open?"

She stared at the moonlit rock, expecting to see a way open in the rock, or at least a crack. Nothing happened. A gust of wind blew, stirring the spray churned up by the falls. Behind her, above the roar of falling water, she heard a soft sound on the gravel. She spun around, groping at the hilt of her sword. In the darkness, she saw the shape of a huge horse, twenty hands high, standing beyond the copper gong. She relaxed and let go of her sword. "Stallion," she said. "I'm glad to see you. Do you know the way into here?"

The Stallion of the Northwest stepped towards her, mane and tail flicking and streaming about him as he walked. "I do," he said in his breathy voice. He walked to the stretch of rock beside her. He reared and snorted, striking out with his huge hooves at the rock. One hoof struck the rock face. A grating, creaking noise came from the rock and slowly, a fissure in the rock widened until a door stood open into the belly of the mountain. The Stallion landed, then whirled around. "There you go." He reared again, then leaped to the air and vanished.

She stepped towards the gap in the rock. A cold wind, heavy and ghastly with the foul smells of decay and filth blew into her face. Something lay on the threshold of the cave, moonlight palely illuminating it. The stench of death struck her in the face. She glanced down at it and her stomach turned over. The dead body of a man, hideous with decay, lay at her feet. Her head spun for a few moments. *Farren? No!* Fighting the trembling in her knees, she looked down at the corpse. The man's hair and beard were long and his clothing was tattered, but the rags looked sound enough to recognise as civilian clothing rather than the Kingdom uniform. She sighed and looked up. *It's not him, thank the Power. Farren hasn't been here long enough for his hair to grow that long, or for his clothing to be that tattered. And by the looks of…things, this fellow has been dead for several days.* She took another glance at the bearded face. Even with the heavy growth of hair, there was no way that its broad curves could be mistaken for Farren's sharp angles.

She held her breath and stepped over the body into the cavern. A red glow dimly lit a corridor, coming from a torch burning in a bracket on the wall. The dull flicker spread a pool of light into the corridor, but beyond that lay darkness. Then blue flame and two points of burning red appeared in the blackness beyond the torch and began to come closer.

The giant hellhound stalked down the corridor towards her, growling softly between slavering fangs. Streams of blue flame dripped like fluid from its muzzle. The white hairs along its hackles stood out like stiff spikes, and the reek of burning wax rolled out from its body. Its nails scraped and tapped along the stone floor, echoing around the walls, pace after pace.

Farren crept out of the room on the third level where Crajaval's stag-people and the great hellhound had been guarding him. He had heard a scream coming through the rock shortly before the stag-people vanished, but the dog had stayed. Then a deep boom had echoed from the lower levels, followed by a noise of grating stone. He stalked after the hound, following it quietly down the stairs. Warm, fresh wind wafted up from the lower levels and his heart pounded with wild hope. He reached the top of the last flight of stairs and looked down past the huge white dog walking through the light beneath the red torch. Beyond it, a doorway opened to an indigo sky studded with stars. A slim silhouette stood in the gap, long hair flicking in the wind and a glittering sword in its hand. *Azariel!* His heart raced and he swallowed down the lump that rose in his throat. *She doesn't know the strength of what she's facing. That hellhound overpowered me many times. And it wasn't trying to kill me, either.* His hand went to the sword at his side and a flame began to burn inside him. *I'm not going to stand by and let her be torn in pieces.*

A fierce bubbling howl broke from the throat of the hellhound and it leaped forwards. He ran down the stone staircase after it, yelling. He heard the snap of fangs and the impact of flesh striking flesh. He sprinted down the corridor, legs working as hard as he could. Azariel's sword clattered onto the rock floor, the metal of the blade dulled. Then the huge beast reared onto its hind legs and it lunged down, seizing her by the shoulder. He heard her cry out as it forced her down to her knees and onto her back. Its head drew back, blue flames reflected in the links of metal guarding her throat.

He leaped at the beast, slashing for its chest. The blade bit into its shoulder, turning aside as it struck the shoulder blade. The beast howled with fury and wheeled around to face him, jaws wide and flaming. He hauled his sword free and drove it at the hellhound's throat. The blow went wild, then he felt the heavy, hot, hairy body crash into him. He stabbed at it, rolling over under its weight. He wrenched his sword free from where it had caught the hound's shoulder a second time and stabbed again. *Too close quarters to use a sword. Why haven't I got a dagger when I need one?* He dropped the sword and struck at the beast with his fists, feeling its teeth gash his forearm and smelling its rancid breath. He struck out again, dimly conscious of Azariel somewhere behind the hellhound. His knuckles drove into the beast's fangs and he heard the small snick of ivory striking the stone and metal of his emerald ring. *I wish I could use that against the brute, but I know I can't. She kept blocking off the full strength of the Power from me somehow.* He raised his arm across his throat as the fangs crashed into him, knocking the breath from him. He heard blows thudding into the hellhound's back and felt its hot blood dripping across him.

But Crajaval's power's broken now! His wildly pounding heart kicked afresh in his chest with hope. The heavy, dirty feeling in the air had gone. He wrenched his right hand free from where it was grapped between his body and the hellhound's as the beast turned its head towards Azariel. His clenched fist reached beneath the hellhound's chin. *King of Heaven, help me.* Energy seared down his hands and arms, full strength and vehement. He punched at the beast with both fists, exhilarated. Fire burned out of his ring, brilliant green searing the white dog's fur black. The hellhound reared back from him. He scrambled to his feet, hearing and half-seeing Azariel stagger backwards into the wall. He raised his ring. "In name of the Power, hellhound, die!" he shouted. Sweet fire blazed down his arms afresh, doubly sweet after being kept away from it. Green and black lightning crackled from both his rings, blazing around the beast. It whined, the blue fire around its muzzle dying. Its body slumped to the floor and twitched a few times, then lay still.

He staggered forward, bloody, heart thundering, chest heaving for breath. Dizzy, he held out his hands weakly to Azariel. Her arms wrapped around him and tightened. He bowed his head, slumping it onto her shoulder. He felt the weight of her head on his shoulder as he coiled his arms around her slender waist and felt the softness of her hair against his cheek, blurred slightly by the heavy growth of bristle on his face. He waited for his breath to return to normal, feeling the rise and fall of her breasts against his chest, inhaling the sweet female scent of her sweat.

He raised his head, half-aware that tears were streaming down his cheeks. "Azariel, Azariel, sweetheart," he said, pressing closer against her, crushing her to his chest. "You're here. You're real." He pressed his lips against hers and tasted wet salt. He drew back and saw her cheeks glistening. "You're crying, my Stormwolf."

"I'm so glad to see you alive again," she said softly, raising one hand to brush the tears from her cheek, then lightly wiping his own away with one fingertip, soft and caressing. "I thought you were dead. And..." She broke off, voice shaky. "You're alive. You're alive. Farren, Farren, my beloved." A wide smile parted her lips, teeth gleaming in the torchlight and her arms tightened around his middle, nearly crushing the breath from him. Her lips pressed into his, kissing him fiercely.

Reluctantly, he drew his head back from hers, desire beginning to throb in every vein in his body. "We'd better take care or else we'll lose our heads and do something stupid," he whispered. A strand of her hair was trapped by the growth on his chin. He laughed and let go of her to free her hair. "I'm sorry. I'm a mess, with nearly two weeks growth of beard on me, not to mention the blood and filth from that dog."

She touched his arms lightly and he flinched as her fingers brushed the places where the hellhound had torn him. She looked down at his arm. "There's blood all over your arm. How badly bitten are you?"

He looked down at his arms. "I can't see clearly, but these cuts don't feel very deep. Come into the light." He caught her by the hand and led her under the torch in the wall. He looked down at his mauled arm, hissing through his teeth as he ran his fingers across the gashes. "Not serious," he said after a few moments. "I'll see how it looks in the morning – by the light of day, thank the Power!"

Her hand rested lightly on his forearm, just above his silver armband. "How much did that hellhound bite you? There are bruises all over your arm. He must have caught and worried at you like a bone! How did you manage to get your arm free to kill him?"

He looked down at the blotches on his arms, ranging from dark bluish-purple to yellow. In three places, the hairs on his arm grew finer, giving him an odd skewbald appearance. "Some of those are old," he said grimly. "This wasn't the first time I've been bitten and hurt while I've been here. Not by any means."

"What?" She cupped her hands around his face and pulled him slightly down to look at her. "Did she torture you?"

He nodded. "She set the hellhounds on me. Never to kill, never to draw blood. Just to hurt me and – oh, hellfire!" He swallowed at the lump in his throat. "I don't want to think about it. Please." He caught her hands and drew them down to his chest. The torchlight fell and flickered across the soft pale skin on her cheeks and put red highlights in her shadowy hair. *I'd much rather think about you, my beauty.* He bent his head and kissed her lightly on the cheek, then ran one finger along the dark circles under her eyes. "You look tired. Come and we'll find somewhere comfortable and you can rest – after you've told me how you defeated her."

"I'll talk you to sleep and all through the night. But it'll be good to have some decent shelter tonight, even on hard stone. How have you managed it, sleeping on rock?"

He turned, sliding one arm around her shoulder and looking into the dark room where he had spent his time behind Moonlady Falls. *It doesn't seem so bad now that she's here and the door's open to the outside.* He glanced along the corridor to the stairs, the iron gates at the foot of them standing wide open. "I didn't sleep on rock, but I can find something even softer than what I had to sleep on. Come with me."

He led her to the stairs and began to climb them. "Crajaval had a soft couch up here on the third level. Her stag-people vanished when you killed her, I suppose, so we'll be safe. You sleep there, and I'll find a rug or something and sleep curled up on the floor." He paused with a shudder as they came to the second level where the iron door to the hellhounds stood closed. He almost leaped up onto the next flight of stairs and she ran to catch up with him.

"What did she want with a bed?" She twisted her head to one side to look at him through a fall of hair. "Does a spirit sleep?"

"I don't know. But she certainly had one for the mortal men she brought up here. And I mean men, not humans in general. Do I need to say more?"

The green light of the torches on the third level fell onto her face from above as they neared the top of the stairs. "You mean she bedded them?" Her eyes narrowed and she caught him hard by the shoulder. "How do you know this?" she asked fiercely. "You didn't…" The fierce look faded from her face and her eyes lowered to the floor. "She was so beautiful. She was a love-goddess."

He chuckled. "I've got more sense than that, Stormwolf. She was mindsnatchingly beautiful, but knowing what she was – well!" He shuddered. "Even Stessa had more real allure for me than she did." He saw her head turn away from him and her shoulders slump. *You've put your fool's foot in your big mouth now, Blackarrow. After all the things that Crajaval – or Stessa herself – said.* "And as for you," he said, putting his arm beneath her wet cloak and around her waist, "there's only one woman I want to make love to, and that's you. I'm looking forward to that very much." He drew a deep breath and let it out slowly as they walked on, her hand in his. He stopped by the arch into the white crystal chamber. "Here we are."

She let go of his shoulder and walked ahead of him into the white room. She went to the round bed and ran her hand over the silks and skins. Her face twisted and he saw her throat bulge as she swallowed. "I'm not sleeping on this bed," she said. "I can feel the taint of her evil in it still. And I don't want to make you sleep hard while I wallow in luxury."

He ran his hand over the ivory rim of the bed. "Let's strip off the coverings, then go back downstairs. I'm sorry it stinks down there, but I can't help it. At least the door's open to the fresh air now." He hauled off several deerskins, a large silken pillow and a swathe of white fur. "Come on. Let's go."

He rolled up the bundle of bedding and looked over the top of it as Azariel tugged the rest off the bed. The sickly-sweet smell of the green torches made his sinuses throb and it jarred with the heady, musky scent in the bedding he carried. His head was beginning to feel heavy with tiredness and his arms still throbbed where the dog had bitten him. She looked back at him, a strand of her long black hair falling across her face. She nodded, then he led her down the stairs again.

"Farren," she asked after they had gone part way down in silence, "who was that dead man at the end of the corridor?"

"Him? That was Tristan. I don't know how long he was shut up here, so don't ask. He killed himself using my sword. He never told me much about himself. I want to hear what you've been doing since I saw you last, if you're not too tired to talk."

"Don't worry about me," she said. "I'll talk you to sleep, if you like." She shrugged the bundle of bedding fully back up into her arms, then trudged down the stairs to the ground level. She walked on a little way, then paused outside one dark opening. "Do we go in here? It smells foul."

"Not that one. That's the latrine cave. The next one along is where I've been." He walked ahead of her and dumped the bedding onto the stone floor of the familiar cave. He bent down and heaved up one of the straw-filled pallets and lugged it off the other one. "Take this. It's not much but it's much better than bare rock. Make yourself comfortable for the night. I'm sorry I've eaten all there was to eat, tasteless as it was. There's water, though."

"Thanks." She dumped down her load of furs, skins and silks onto the pallet and took a long drink from the iron bucket. "Will you be able to sleep on only one with all those bruises on you?"

"I've been doing it for days." He smoothed one of the thick white furs over the pallet and kicked his boots off. He lay down and stretched his limbs, rubbing his face against the luscious softness of the perfumed fur. He lugged the rest of the coverings over himself, tucking another fur under his chin. "This is the first time I'll be able to fall asleep watching you in your proper shape."

She kneaded one of the cushions into shape. "I hope you're not thinking of doing anything you'll regret. You know that you could sweep me away if you tried." She knelt beside the spread-out bedding and looked sidelong at him, her dark blue eyes glinting through her hair. "And if I tried, I could seduce you. But I won't do that – yet."

Azariel, you wouldn't have to try hard, he thought as he ran his eyes over her long black-clad body. "I wouldn't dream of defiling you like that," he said aloud. "Why spoil the pleasures of waiting? That would be as foolish as spoiling my appetite for a royal banquet with those disgusting flabby cakes that Crajaval's been feeding me." He pushed back the covers and sat up, fumbling at his side for his sword. "I'm going to do something archaic as a token that I'll wait for it." He drew the blade out of the sheath and put it on the rock between them. "Until our wedding night, if we have to sleep like this, that sword will be staying out of its sheath, and I'll..." A snigger cut him off. "I'll stop that thought right there before it gets vulgar. Never mind. You look exhausted, Stormwolf. Don't tire yourself out with talking." He yawned. "Sleep well."

He lay back down, pulled the covers up to his chin and closed his eyes, listening to the sounds of her moving around on the silk and fur. He heard the rasp of a sword being drawn, then a small ring of metal from the ground beside his head. "These can lie together, even though we can't," she said.

Silence fell, and his mind began to wander. He heard the sound of her breathing and the occasional metallic scraping as the links of her chainmail rubbed together. He shifted around once or twice, moving his belt and the quiver around to a more comfortable place. *I wonder if I should tell her about what the hellhounds did to me. I don't want to, but maybe she should know.* One of his arrows dug into a bruise on his side and he yanked at his belt to move it. *She should know. She's got a right to, especially with the damage they've done to me.* He rolled over and looked over at her. She was sitting with her knees pulled up to her chest, looking at him. The circles under her eyes had darkened and she shook her head as if shaking sleep out of it. Her sword lay beside his on the stone floor. He swallowed. "Azariel," he said at last. He paused and drew a deep breath. He fumbled for words. "If you want to have children, don't marry me." The words came out of him with a wrench and he shook his head. He looked at her as if she was an enemy standing over him with a sword in her hand as he lay bound and stripped.

Her head tilted to one side. "Why? I want to marry you for yourself. You're not a stud stallion. It doesn't matter to me – much. But why?" She suddenly got to her feet, her eyes flicking away from his face to further down his body. "What has she done to you?" Her voice grew fierce. "If I had known this, I would have killed her a lot more slowly than I did."

He laughed, relief flooding over him. "Don't worry, Stormwolf. I'm a stallion, not a gelding. But her hellhounds hurt me." The laughter died. "They bit me everywhere, and it hurt like nothing else." He broke off, overwhelmed with the fear and horror that welled back up inside him. "Damn," he said, rolling onto his back and throwing back the covers. "When I want to hold you and cry on your shoulder, I can't touch you."

"Stand up," she said gently, leaning over him and offering him her hand. "That's safe enough. Tell me about it. It'll help you get over the pain."

He got to his feet and wrapped his arms around her waist. He buried his head in the folds of her cloak and the hair that lay tumbled over her shoulder. "There isn't much more to tell," he said into her cloak. "She made them bite me all over when I refused to call you here. She never let it go on until I fainted. Not her! I'm so ashamed of myself, thinking of how I had to lie there in front of her, hating her, hating them, hating myself, screaming and vomiting with the pain of it. Stormwolf, even you would have despised me then." He felt the hot salt sting behind his eyelids

Her hands ran through his hair, soothing and warm. "No," she said. "I wouldn't have. But it's over now, my beloved." He tightened his grip around her and let himself weep into her cloak. Her hands rubbed down onto his neck, finding the gap at the top of his chainmail

Eventually, he raised his head from her shoulder and rubbed his hand over his face. Her lips brushed his cheek, and he smiled. "I've been thinking a lot about that sort of thing – about you and me, and all we've wanted – over the last while. I've had plenty of time to think." He kissed her lightly on the cheek, then let her go. "I'm going back to my bed and you should too. You look like you haven't slept for a week." He went back to his pallet and took his belt off before lying down on the furs again. "You shouldn't have let me talk to you so much."

"It's not too much." She sat down on her pallet again, knees bent and her chin resting on top of them. "Tell me more about what you've been thinking. It's so good to hear your voice again. What about you? Were you looking on me as a broodmare? I know that Janna Greyhawk and the General have been beside themselves with glee at the thought that we two are to be man and wife. They'll be as sick as poisoned pigs now! You know that the *minyast* ability runs in the bloodline and the Kingdom needs more fighter *minyasti*. Confess, Farren Blackarrow."

He grinned sheepishly, then sighed. "Well, I've had a lot of time to think, as I said. I thought about our children: what they might have been like, how many, their names. It's pointless now."

She yawned. "Tell me. What did you call them?"

"Two girls – Flyrrin and Allana – and two boys – Yvain and Valerian. Don't laugh at a prisoner's fancies!" He put his hands behind his head and stared up at the ceiling. *Why does she want to keep talking? Anybody with half an eye can see that she's ready to drop with exhaustion.* He yawned.

"You forgot Yhriva," she said, chuckling. "I'm keeping you awake, beloved. Don't worry about me. I won't be sleeping, but don't let me keep you from it."

I'm not the only one left with lasting damage. Damn that white bitch and damn all those wraiths that came from her cauldron! He rolled onto his right side, looking at her. "Why won't you sleep?"

"For the last week, I've had nightmares. The same ones, every night." Her mouth hardened into a grim line. "I'm sick of them. I'd rather stay awake, even if it half kills me, than sleep and have them sneering at me again."

"They won't come again," he said softly. The fur brushed his cheek and sent out a fresh wave of its perfume.

"How would you know?" she said bitterly. "You haven't had Sergeant Karissa standing over you with a whip every time you sleep, or Stessa sneering at you, or Edwin Feller..." Her face twisted and she looked about to be sick.

He raked his fingers across the hot itch of the growth on his cheeks. "Was that his name? I wondered who he was." He suppressed a small smile as her head jerked up, dark eyebrows raised. "I know what's been in your dreams. Crajaval sent them."

Her breath hissed sharply out between her teeth. "So that's how she knew about those nightmare figures. They came when I was fighting her. Curse her! She planned that! I nearly lost against her, Farren, because of them and what they were saying." She bit her lip hard as she frowned.

"I don't blame you. I heard them – she made me listen." He sat up and began to reach for her, stopping as his shadow fell on the two drawn swords. "Sweetheart, let me say that being made to hear all those things said to you hurt me more than anything her hellhounds could do to me. I tried to warn you, too. I had to speak to you through the same cauldron that those wraiths did. I'll show you tomorrow. But you can sleep in peace. Those things won't trouble your dreams again."

"Are you sure?" She let go of her knees and rested her hands on the floor. The light from the torch caught the opal on her right hand, picking out red, gold and green points of fire.

"Certain. She's dead and the cauldron's standing unused."

She sighed deeply, changing to a yawn at the end. "Thank the Power for that." She smiled and unclasped her belt. "Sleep well, beloved. I will, too." She yanked her boots off and tossed them to the end of her pallet before lying down and bundling herself up in the furs and silks. Her hair spilled across one of the silken pillows and she looked across at him with half-closed eyes. "Goodnight," she said.

He slid his hand under his cheek, palm upwards. "Goodnight," he said softly. He lay watching her until sleep took him.

***

Azariel woke, stiff and with something jabbing her cheek. Unfamiliar and unpleasant smells filled her nostrils and her stomach growled with hunger. She opened her eyes and saw rock lit by flickering red light. *Where am I?* she thought sleepily. She rolled over and found the silks and skins pushed to one side and straws poking through the sacking of the pallets. Farren lay asleep a few paces from her on the other side of their swords, cheeks dark with bristle and his arm stained with dried blood. Memory flooded back to her. She sat up, rubbing the stiffness out of her neck before stretching the sleep out of her arms and legs. She yawned loudly and brushed the hair back from her eyes. *That was the best sleep I've had for a long time. He was right: I didn't have Karissa and company nagging at me in my sleep*

She heard a slight catch in Farren's breathing and looked around to see him stirring. She smiled as she watched him stretch and yawn. His eyelids opened in small slits. He lay on his back, staring at the ceiling for a few moments, then rolled over and looked at her. "Good morning, Stormwolf," he said. "You don't know how glad I am to wake up and see you here."

"You'll have another year and a half to wait until you see me every morning," she replied, reaching out and picking up her sword. She ran her eyes over the damasked patterns on the Elendi-forged steel before sliding it smoothly home into the sheath and buckling her belt back on.

"I don't mean just that, sweetheart." He sat up and reached for his own sword and belt. "I mean finding you really here and not just a dream. Any company at all would be welcome after at least ten days alone in the darkness, but when the company is you, it's heaven." He yawned again and scratched at his cheeks. "Come on, Stormwolf; let's get out of here. I've had enough of this rock and dark, and I'm thirsting for light and fresh air. And I'm hungry. Let's go and find something to eat – and drink."

She got to her feet and tugged him up with her. Hands still clasped, they walked down the stone corridor. Sunlight shone through the rent in the rock, drowning the red torchlight and making each chink and fissure in the rock stand out. She bit back her breath against the stench as she stepped over the dead body by the doorway, then breathed freely again in the fresh air. Farren let go of her hand and stepped forwards, blinking and shielding his eyes as if the light hurt him. Then he stretched, eyes slowly opening. His chest heaved and a wide smile broke across his face. "Yes!" he yelled, punching the air triumphantly. "I'm free!" The sun gleamed in his hair and she suddenly noticed streaky grey stains of soot and grime around his eyes and nose, and the matted tangles in his hair at the back. *Poor Farren! And he does like to be well-groomed!* She ran her hand up his back and around his shoulders, leaning her head against him. "Welcome back to the light," she murmured in his ear. "Enjoy it, beloved."

His arm coiled around her waist and his fingers dug the links of chainmail into her side. She felt his head move beside hers, then he gave a small murmur of surprise. "How did you get to the Falls? I was expecting to see the horses, or at least Storm, but they're not here."

"I've got quite a tale to tell you," she replied. "But it can wait until after breakfast." She slipped her arm down from his shoulders and went to the rocks beside the waterfall. The light blazed like white gold in the sunlight and the fine droplets of water flung up by the force of the cataract glittered. She knelt by the water, her hair tumbling down and the ends sweeping the water. Her own reflection, fractured and bizarre in the dancing water stared back at her. She shot a glance at him through the curtain of her hair. "Drinking from the source of the Illin-Ast," she said. "I wonder what really does happen."

He strode towards her, boots crunching over the gravel. His hands rested on her shoulders, then he knelt beside her. "We'll drink it together," he said. "Even if it's nothing out of the ordinary, we're thirsty."

She scooped up a handful of the bright water in her hands. For the space of a heartbeat, she looked at it. In the morning sunlight, the water cast hundreds of little waves of light across the metal of her rings, and the calluses and fine lines of her palms. *Whatever it does, I'm grateful for it. Thank the Power for water!* She closed her eyes and bent her head as she raised her cupped hands to her lips. It washed around her mouth as she drank it in, then coursed down her throat, cool and almost painfully refreshing as it travelled deep inside her. A silver arrow of energy passed down her back. She opened her eyes and was almost dazzled by the brilliance of the water. *It's as if I've never opened my eyes before now.* She raised her head, realising that she was trembling.

She glanced over at Farren to see how he was looking. His dark eyes shone with burning clarity; the whites, the dark brown iris and the black centre looked almost as lustrous as a bull's. His chest rose and fell as if he had been running and his hands dripped liquid sunlight. Suddenly she noticed that the bite marks on his arm had faded to scars and some of the bruises had vanished. She looked down at her own arm and saw that the burn-mark on her wrist where Crajaval had shattered her armband had turned to a reddish line. She glanced at Farren again and their eyes met. "Do you feel different?" he asked. "I do."

"I feel ready to fight Crajaval and her hellhound all over again," she replied, tossing her hair back from her face.

"So which of the legends is true? Would you wager that it's spring of eternal youth or a healing spring?"

She paused for a moment. "A healing spring." She paused and ran one finger over the red mark on her arm. "I don't think that springs of eternal youth really exist, or at least I hope they don't. Everybody would be coming here to drink and live forever and another war would start over it."

"It could start again anyway for a healing spring." He stared at the shining water and a frown furrowed his brow. "I can imagine an unscrupulous general taking risks with the soldiers if he or she knew that any wounded could be restored to full health to fight again."

"I see what you mean. Perhaps we'd better keep this a secret for as long as we can." She sighed. "Word may get out eventually, but for now, we'd best keep it quiet. Unless the Power tells us otherwise."

He nodded. "I can imagine what would happen if every spoilt rich person travelled up here to cure every single toothache and splinter." He scratched his chin. "It's a pity that this water won't shave me as well. I'll have to clean up the usual way. If you'll give me a few minutes, I'll clean myself up. It's been a long time." He drew a deep breath, then ran one hand through his forelock, ruffling it up from where the spray of the falls had flattened it and darkened the auburn to copper. "Can you find us some breakfast, Stormwolf? I've passed from being ravenous to cavernous, as the saying goes."

"There are plenty of apples across the bridge. I'll leave you to it." She tilted back her head to kiss him once again, then let him go.

CHAPTER FIFTEEN

Farren tossed the core of the sharp-tasting little apple aside, aiming it at a tuft of tussock that grew between the crabapple trees where they sat and the bridge leading back to the waterfall. The tang of the juice lingered in his mouth and a small trace of it trickled onto his chin, stinging as it touched a small nick. He licked his lips and leaned back against the tree trunk. *Sunlight. Fresh air. Food with flavour. Thank the Power!* He put his left arm around Azariel's shoulder and tugged her towards him. Her head slumped against his, her hair smelling of smoke and other outdoor smells. "Well, Stormwolf," he said, "time to get back to work. We may have – or rather you have – killed Crajaval or sent her to the underworld or whatever happens, but we haven't got the Stones we came for. We'd better go and look for them."

"Didn't you see them when you were brought to Crajaval?" Her hand caressed his knee gently.

"I didn't have the chance," he replied. "I didn't see much more than what you did last night, apart from the place where she kept her... her hellhounds and the cauldron room. The Stones weren't there." He looked down at her hand. The opal ring sat crooked, so he gently nudged it straight before laying his hand on top of hers. "She did say that Jamin Bluecloak had come to her – and slept with her, too, the idiot of a traitor."

Her hand tightened around his knee, then her fingers beat out a rhythm on the leather of his trouser leg. "Don't tell me they're not here after all! We've killed her, yes, but is that what we came here to do? I hope we haven't wasted all this time and taken all these risks for nothing."

He threw back his head and laughed. "You can't call killing her nothing. That alone would put you into the ranks of the greatest of the *minyasti*." He turned his head and kissed her on the temple. "Don't laugh at me; I'm not joking. I'm proud of you. But even so, I never said the Stones weren't there. There's at least one flight of stairs that I haven't been up." He patted her hand then uncrossed his legs. "Come on. Let's go back and find them."

She caught hold of his hand as he stood up, and he hauled her to her feet. "We ought to destroy all her paraphernalia," she said. "Now that her power is broken, the phantoms will have left the hills. Hunters will come up here – and Yellow Claws. And even if we keep quiet, it won't be long until others find out about the healing spring. If a hunter gets hold of any of her gear, that's bad enough. But if it got into the hands of a Yellow Claw sorcerer..." Her fingers tightened around his.

"Even the Nightravens couldn't hide us from their eyes if they got hold of the cauldron, and we *minyasti* would be worked off our feet." He stepped onto the bridge, pivoting and buckling at the knees to keep his balance as the bridge swayed. "I'd love to smash it to bits if I can." He stepped off the bridge and onto the firm ground again.

"Well, I suppose we start on the bottom level and work our way up. Shall we burn everything where it is or drag it out?" She knocked into him as she stepped around the copper gong. Reflected sunlight off the gong flashed over her face. "And what are we going to do about that dead man – Tristan?"

"Poor old Tristan," he said. "If he hadn't killed himself, he would be free now, too." He sighed and ran his right hand over the hilt of his sword. The metal knob at the end felt cold. "We drag him out here and pile all the stuff around him as a pyre." He looked ahead at the large dark crack in the rock and a cold dull sensation stirred in his stomach. *I hope I'm not going to be sick doing this.* "Ugh. Let's get it over with. We'll use that bedding to carry him in."

They wrapped and carried the body outside. He tried to shut off his sense of smell and looked down at the decaying corpse as little as possible. Then he returned to the brink of the pool and washed his hands, rubbing and scraping at them with a handful of fine gravel until they hurt. Behind him Azariel was retching, then she knelt beside him to wash and drink. He put one arm around her shoulder, then helped her to her feet. "Are you all right?" he said, glancing at her face. "You're pale."

She nodded. "Talk about something else so I can forget what we've had to see and smell." Her arm slid through his and they began to walk back. "Up to the second level now, I suppose. What's in there?"

"The hellhounds." He squared his shoulders and stepped into the cold air inside the mountain. "They're possibly still alive. The big one didn't vanish when she died." The darkness overwhelmed his sight for a few moments, then his eyes adjusted to the dull red-orange of the torchlight. The stairs leading up seemed like a black mouth.

They reached the landing by the iron gate and separated. He drew his sword and strode towards the door, reaching with his right hand for the ring that opened the tunnel to the hellhounds. Behind him, he heard her drawing her sword. His fingers touched the cold metal and the cold seemed to spread up his hand to his heart. Too many memories of what lay behind the door rose in his mind: sharp teeth, pain, hard rock and the stink of burning wax as a dog's jaws closed on his throat. His arm shook and he lowered his hand, fear prickling up and down the back of his neck. "Sorry," he said, staring at the floor by the toes of her boots. "I can't do this. I've suffered too much."

"Are you afraid of them, Farren?" She spoke softly, but with a sharp edge of challenge around the softness.

Suddenly his anger flared up, burning the cold fear back. "Damn it, I am!" he snarled, looking her full in the face. "I haven't got the sheer guts to open that door and go in and fight. Hellfire, I'm ashamed of myself." She stepped towards him, her empty hand reaching for his arm. He stepped back, catching her round the wrist. "No, I'm not going to break down and bawl this time. I've done enough of that and I'm sick of it. I hate letting these animals turning me into a bloody puddle. But, damn it, I'm still afraid."

She broke her wrist free from his grip and shook her hair back from her face, eyes flashing lightning. "Who killed the great hound?" she said fiercely, raising her sword so that the point almost brushed the metal around his chest. He stepped back, left hand instinctively raising his sword in reply. "And how? You've got your sword; you've got the Power running through you. Fight them – and win. You're blazing now, so use it!" Her expression softened and her sword lowered. "Do you want me to open the door? You don't have to do that if it makes it worse for you."

He swept his cloak back from his arms and laid his hand on the iron ring. "I'll do it," he said. He drew a deep breath, exhaling some of his anger. His mouth felt dry and his heart thudded in his ears. *King of Heaven, help me do this.* A faint prickling of fire began in the corners of his shoulders and began to travel down his arms. *Come on, Blackarrow,* he told himself. *Face your fears or live forever a coward.* He gripped the ring and began to turn it, each grate of metal on metal screeching through his skull. The emerald on his hand, a point of green fire, reflected dully from the iron nearest his hand. He threw the door wide with a clang and looked down the corridor, breathing hard.

Bodies shuffled at the end of the corridor. He raised his right hand, ring pointing outwards, as his left lifted his sword across his body at the ready. He waited, braced and waiting for the sound of running paws over stone, then the impact of heavy bodies crashing into him. Red eyes and blue flames flickered, then the hellhounds charged. Azariel's wild battle-yell echoed around the stone and was answered by growls. Two leaped at him. He gritted his teeth together to stop them trembling, fighting back the fear and stabbed at the foremost dog. The blade sank deep into its chest and the dog died snarling in his face. The second tugged at his left arm, teeth locked onto the chainmail. Flame burst out from his left, blue and yellow. The brief slash of light died, but he glimpsed all but four of the dogs at the end of the corridor, cringing and hackles up. His heart leaped, and his ring grew scorching hot around his fingers. Shouting, he punched the flame at the hellhound that had him by the arm. Green fire spurted up and the white body dropped.

Yes! he thought triumphantly. *I can kill them after all. They don't have to beat me.* He charged them, sword scything out and right hand flashing fire. He lunged and stabbed, heart beating a wild rhythm in his ears, his arms and hands columns of tingling fire. His muscles ached as he swung the sword at a beast's flank, relishing the effort of his muscles and the freedom to fight. One blow swung wild and his sword crashed into the stone walls, jarring his arm. He dodged and whirled around, back against the wall, chest heaving for breath. One hellhound caught him by the wrist, teeth slipping on and off his armband. His heart leaped into his mouth. *If that tears me, it'll open the big blood vessels and I'll bleed to death.*

The dog yelped and released his wrist abruptly. Azariel had the hellhound by the scruff of the neck and was holding it up so that its back paws hardly touched the ground. It arched its neck back, baying and snarling, forepaws scrabbling at the air. Green and purple flame flickered around the dog , making each stiff white hair on its back stand out like a spear. Then it slumped down, red fire in its eyes dying and the blue flames at its mouth flickering and fading to blackness. She let the dog drop. In the near darkness, her face and arms were all he could make out, pale shapes marked with black in the dark. "Any more of them?" he asked, looking around the cavern for any points of blue fire.

Her shoulder grated against his. "No. You've killed them all," she said, voice low and warm. "Well done. I'll wager that's the bravest thing you've done."

He bent to wipe his sword clean on one of the dead dogs. *I wish I could see how clean I'm getting it. I'll do it properly later.* "No need to talk about that now," he said, surprised to hear how heavily he was breathing. He sheathed his sword. "Let's get these bodies out of here." He inhaled deeply, trying to slow his quick, heavy breathing. "I'm out of condition," he said. "I tried to keep myself up to strength, but there's only so much you can do in a dungeon. You'll have to spar with me a lot, Stormwolf, to get me back up to full fighting strength."

"You won't have lost much in this short a time." Her hand felt for his, warm and firm. "But you'll get a chance to use your muscles now. We've got to get the great hound outside for burning, too."

***

The green light of the third level shone across the stone walls as they reached the landing and rounded the corner into it. Azariel's chest heaved beneath her chainmail after the exertion of hauling the hellhounds outside followed by the climb. A sharp tang of the incense coming from the green flames filled her lungs, tickling the back of her nose and mouth. She sneezed and coughed slightly. "What makes these torches burn and smell like that?" she asked, brushing away the tears stung from her eyes.

"You may not like the answer, Stormwolf." Farren's mouth twisted into a wry grin. "I hate that smell. I hope we can get everything out quickly. It makes me sick."

She threaded her fingers through his and walked behind him into the first chamber on the left of the corridor, the one they had taken the bedding from. Two of the green torches burned beside the doorway and the light glittered off the multitude of crystals about the stripped bed. "Where are our saddlebags now that we need them?" she said grimly. "Those pretty rocks will be hard to carry down and worse to burn."

"Oh, hurl them down the stairs. We'll throw them in the pool under the waterfall. They'll look pretty in that sparkling water." He turned away from her, looking at the nails on his right hand. She watched him, studying the small tufts of hair that brushed the tip of his ear. *I'd wager that the first thing he'll do when we get back to the capital is visit the barber's.* He looked round at her and she winked at him. "And we don't need to make twelve or twenty journeys up and down these stairs," he said. "If we turn that bed upside down and load it up with stuff, then we can toboggan the whole lot down at once."

She let go of his hand. "Good idea." She stepped to one side of the bed and took hold of the carved ivory foot. *What fine carving! I've never seen the like. It's a shame it has to be burned.* For the space of half a heartbeat, she felt slime beneath her fingers and clammy hands seemed to paw at her back, scalp and stomach. *But I can still feel her.* She hissed and shook the feeling out of her mind. "Ready?" she said, glancing over at him as he stood at the head. He nodded and she heaved and twisted at the bed, overturning it onto the stone with a heavy thud. She joined him at the head of the bed and together they shoved it through the doorway and to the landing.

She straightened up and kneaded her fingers at the small of her back, uselessly trying to massage her muscles through her chainmail. She gave it up and turned to go back into the bedchamber. "Not yet, Stormwolf," Farren's voice called. "We'd be best to put the cauldron on next. It's rather large. This way."

She turned towards him and followed him into a darker chamber on the other side of the corridor. She crossed the threshold and cold unease washed around her shoulders and in the pit of her stomach. Her eyes accustomed themselves to the gloom and she made out the bloated belly of a cauldron above a white pentagram painted on the floor. The green light that fell through the doorway played on swirling patterns worked on the copper and gleamed off a naked sword and the head of a lance lying beside it. She hissed through her bared teeth and a cold thrill went down her spine. "This is the cauldron," she said. "What did it – does it do?"

His shoulder brushed against hers. "She used it to spy on you, then conjured up wraiths from steam and sent them to talk to you." His hand gripped hers, the metal of their rings grating together. "I had to watch and listen, and I hated it!"

"Smash and burn them all," she said grimly. She let go of his hand and slid her sword from the sheath.

His hand touched her forearm gently. "Put your sword away, Stormwolf. You're more likely to shatter it than the cauldron."

"Then tell me: how are we going to break that pot?"

"Use hers." He stooped and picked up the sword from the floor. He twisted it around in his hand a few times, staring at the cauldron, then passed the sword from his left hand to his right then back again. He turned towards the copper cauldron. "If this doesn't break the cauldron, it'll break the sword instead."

He raised the sword and smashed it down on the metal and the great belly of the cauldron rang. His teeth bared with effort and the tendons in his arms stood out. He struck a second time, then a third. She clamped her hands over her ears to block out the brazen waves of sound that echoed and re-echoed off the walls and roof, the pressure from the noise closing her eyes. The sound died away and she opened her eyes, hearing him panting angrily. "Damn it," he said. "It's hardly dented and I haven't notched the sword either. What hellfire tempered that metal?" He wheeled around, the sword still in his hand, and dashed it into the stone walls with a groan of effort.

She ducked as a splinter of dull metal flew towards her. She heard it ring as it bounced onto the floor and Farren hissed. She looked up. He was rubbing his left wrist as the sword dangled from his hand. A large shard had snapped from one edge and lay glittering on the floor. "Sorry," he said. "I didn't think what would happen. However, I've paid for my folly." He kneaded his thumb into his wrist, then worked his way up his bare forearm. "That hurt. We're going to need fire to melt all these things after all." He tossed the sword away, sending it with a slap and splash into the cauldron. "It's going to take at least three days to make enough charcoal to get a blaze to melt metal. And longer still to get enough dry wood here to make the charcoal with. We're going to have to spend the winter here!"

She stared at the cauldron, twisting a strand of her hair to and fro. *Fire to melt something forged by hellfire,* she mused. She looked at the cauldron again, eyes following the spiralling flow of the decorations. Then she chuckled and set the opal and the lapis lazuli rings straight on her fingers. "Fight fire with fire," she quoted and tossed her hair over her shoulder. She raised her hands, fingers spread and crooked as if she was about to catch something, ready to strike. She drew a deep breath, praying softly as she breathed it out. Lightning seared down her arms and trembled in her fingers before bursting out, brilliant scarlet and green. *"Varraserad!"* she commanded the cauldron in the Old Tongue. Her arms shook and the inside of her mouth felt like paper as she panted with the fire that burned inside her. More lightning cascaded and crackled out of her hands at the copper.

The bolts of lightning struck the cauldron. For a fast heartbeat, she saw the coloured fire wrap and coil through the spiral patterns. Then a white sheet of flame exploded with a roar, throwing her back against the wall. She cried out as the back of her head cracked into rock and her hands flew up to shield her face. The burning died away, and she lowered her forearms and opened her eyes, heart hammering. "Farren," she said, fighting to master the shakiness in her voice. Her eyes were still dazzled by the light and she peered around the dark chamber, straining to see him. "Are you all right?"

He picked himself up off the floor. "I'm unhurt, I think," he replied. He dusted himself off and ran his hands through his hair before coming over to her and putting his arm around her waist. "What about the cauldron?"

She looked towards where the cauldron had stood. It lay in two halves like a split apple and a rancid smelling liquid that glistened like molten fat on water spread and lapped over the floor. Two twisted hunks of metal on the floor showed where the sword and lance had been, and the pentagram had vanished. "There," she said, leaning her head against his shoulder. "That's done, and I hope I never see the like of those things again."

They took the broken and melted metal out of the chamber and piled it on the upturned bed on the landing. Together, they turned and walked up the stairs to the fourth level, shoulder to shoulder, footsteps echoing off the stone.

Farren raised his head and looked up at the landing above them. Warm yellow light fell on the grey rocks. *Normal light for once, instead of that hideous green.* He quickened his pace up the stairs and heard Azariel falling into step beside him. His head began to throb from the sickly sweet smell emanating from the third level and he pinched the bridge of his nose, trying to rub away the ache. He reached the landing and turned left towards the source of the yellow light.

The light came from many candles that nearly ringed the wall of a single cave in the rock from the left-hand side to halfway down the right. Pictures of people hung on the walls, one above each candle, and the air shimmered with heat in front of each one. *It's a wonder they aren't blackened by smoke with those candles in front of them.* He looked again at the candles. Each looked as tall and smooth as if just lit for the first time, but the flames burned tall and steady. *More sorcery,* he thought, and stepped forwards to look more closely at the pictures. He felt Azariel's hand on his wrist and paused for a moment to take her hand in his. "Who are they?" he wondered aloud.

He looked at the one on the leftmost end, looking past the warm golden glow of the candle. The picture showed a man: a young, handsome, red-haired man who was dressed in the fashions of a long-gone era. "Looks like someone from a picture in one of those history books back in the monastery," he said. He ran his eyes over the canvas, humming with appreciation. "Look how well painted it is, though. It's so detailed; you'd hardly believe it was a painting." He pointed to the upraised hand on the man's hand. "That diamond ring on his finger looks almost as fiery as a real one."

"Well, we know he was a *minyastin* or a sorcerer." She touched the mother-of-pearl frame and ran her fingers along some curling runes in a brass plaque set in the white nacre. "Lakaitin Greenlake. That's all we'll know about him, I suppose. Who are the others?"

The next picture showed another man, one with a short red beard and the robes and ring of a sorcerer. Candlelight glittered off the brass name-plaque. Memories of hunters' houses surfaced: the rows of heads and horns, each with a small plaque underneath. He glanced along at the next picture, another redheaded man with a ring on his right hand and golden armbands about his wrists. *Displayed on the wall in a place of honour, like the head of the King Elk in my bedroom.* "This room's a trophy gallery," he said aloud.

She wandered on to the picture of the man with the golden armbands. "Trophies of what? These men are all either *minyastini* or sorcerers. Trophies of battles won, do you think?"

He shook his head grimly and looked around the ring of pictures. The last frame in the ring hung empty and a cold hand of horror raised the hairs on the back of his neck. "I don't think so," he said softly. "They're all men. They're all redheads. She said something once about how they used to come to her – or be brought to her alive as sacrifices – as her lovers and victims. This must be them." He shuddered and swallowed. "There's an empty frame at the end. It must have been meant... for me."

Her hand tightened around his for a heartbeat, warm and reassuring. "You're safe, my beloved," she said. She shook her hair back from her face and looked around the circle again. "Jamin Bluecloak must be here somewhere. If only I'd been better at the history they taught us, I'd know what style of clothing he would have worn."

"He's probably the prize trophy," he said. "If we look at these plaques, we'll find him."

He silently read the inscriptions on the trophy as they wandered around the ring. In the centre of the wall facing the cave mouth, he found the name he was looking for. "Here he is," he said. He gazed at the picture, studying the man's eyes and face before moving on to the clothing. Jamin Bluecloak had jaw-length auburn hair and wore lizard mail, links of metal stitched onto red and black leather. A faded blue cloak draped over his shoulder and in his raised hand, he held a blue globe wrapped in silver that matched the ring on his finger.

Azariel let go of his hand and laid both hands on the picture frame. "So he's the traitor," she whispered. She lifted the picture from the wall and held it high over her head, then cracked it down hard across her knee, wincing as it struck. The frame splintered, cracked and shattered in her hands like dry firewood, then she cast it aside. She blew on her hands and rubbed them together. He caught a brief glimpse of reddened skin on her palms. She smiled wryly at him. "I don't think we'll break all of them. Just carry them down and burn them."

They carried the pictures in piles down to the upturned bed and the other paraphernalia. He dumped his load with a clatter and a clang against the remains of the cauldron. "We've nearly filled this up now, Stormwolf," he said. He grinned and looked down the long flight of steps. *Why just push it down? It'd be fun to ride.* "Let's get it all outside."

She sighed and ran her hand over her forehead. "Fresh air at last," she said. "My head's thudding as if the barracks drummer's practising on it."

He gripped the legs at the foot of the bed. "Climb on," he said. "And brace yourself." A laugh was building up inside him and he could hardly keep it out of his voice.

She winked back at him, eyes sparkling as she knelt on the bed. "Ready," she said, flicking back a lock of her hair and glancing round at him.

"Then here we go!" he whooped. He pushed the bed until it teetered on the edge of the stairs, then flung himself beside her. The impetus of his leap thrust the ivory bed forwards, slithering and careering down the slope. It bounced on the steps, rattling the crystals in the cauldron. She laughed and grabbed him around his shoulders as they rode. The bed halted at the landing and they scrambled off to push it down again, throwing themselves lengthways onto it as it bounced and slid down again. Finally they reached the ground floor. She leaned her head against one of the legs and looked over at him as he sprawled on the upturned bed. "Shall we take it back upstairs and do it all again?" she asked. "That was fun."

"Rascal," he said, scrambling to his feet and catching her around the shoulders and thighs. He scooped her up and spun her around until he was panting, half with laughter. Then he pulled her close to him and pressed a hard kiss onto her open mouth. He drew back, kissed her again, then lightly nuzzled her cheek. "I'd better not lose my head through high spirits. Let's get all this outside and breathe freely for a few minutes before going up again."

After they had hauled the odds and ends outside to the pile they had made around Tristan's body, they went back into the caves.   Azariel felt her back aching slightly across her shoulderblades and the back of her mouth had grown dry with thirst. She trudged up the three flights of stairs and onto the fourth, her hand nestled comfortably inside Farren's as they walked shoulder to shoulder. A pale blue glow shone at the top, faintly illuminating the stone steps. Halfway up the stairs was a small landing like a single broad step, but perfectly circular. Two things shone palely on the step, one beside each wall. She strained her eyes through the darkness. *What now?*

They climbed a few more stairs and she saw the pale things more clearly. Two mother-of-pearl statues of dragons stood on the steps, their wings furled across their backs and their muzzles raised as they perched on crescent moons. The pale blue light picked out a small iridescent sheen on the mother-of-pearl, shifting and varying hue subtly as she came closer. A cold smell like camphor wafted from the statues, burying the sickly sweet green incense smell. She loosened her hand from Farren's. "You throw the one on the left down and I'll deal with the other." She let go of his hand and stepped onto the large round step.

The faint rainbows on the statues twisted and swirled suddenly. With a quicksilver shock that plunged into the pit of her stomach, she saw the statue move. Tiny pale green lights flickered in the dragon's eyes and its lips writhed back from its teeth. Instinctively, she raised her forearm and stepped backwards as she heard the gasp and hiss of breath. White smoke billowed from the small dragon and the camphor smell trebled in strength. A blast of icy air struck her forearm, setting the hairs erect and covering them with hoarfrost. She head Farren shouting behind her. The metal of her armband felt like a block of ice, painfully cold on her bare skin. She looked around at him and saw that a ring of pale fire burned in a circle around the perimeter of the landing. Farren leaped across them towards her half a heartbeat before the blue-white flames grew to breast height, trapping them on the step.

Steam rolled and coiled in the centre of the circular step, tangy with the smell of camphor. It twisted and thickened in a single column and took on form as the head and hood of a serpent that reached the roof. Ice-green eyes stared at them above a black pit of a mouth where a forked tongue flickered in and out between two needle-fangs. "None save the Moon Lady may come here," it hissed in a dry voice. "To come here is death!" Then it lunged forwards with a hiss like a cat.

A dark liquid sprayed through the air towards her from the serpent's mouth. She leaped to one side, towards the dragon-statue, raising her armband. The liquid struck the metal with a hiss and a small spurt of bitter-smelling steam. The silver grew hot for an instant, then bitterly cold again as the dragon breathed on her again. Shivering, she whirled towards the serpent. Farren had dropped to his hands and knees, fists clenched and pointing at the serpent. It lunged at him, but fire crackled out from his rings, scarlet and purple, wrapping around the snake. It hissed and spat, spurting more poison at her. It struck her armband, then the snake's head punched into her. The long curved fangs caught in her cloak and she felt a blistering hot liquid seep through the cloth onto her shoulder.

Then Farren stood beside her, hacking at the serpent below the hood with his sword. The blade passed through its body and came out bloodless. The snake disentangled its fangs from her shoulder and threw its coils towards Farren. He ducked and rolled out of its path, falling dangerously near the flames. A white sheen covered him as the ice-dragon belched out more steam. Shaking, muscles stiff and aching with the cold, she lurched forwards, raising her rings towards it. The metal grew hot, enabling her cold-crabbed fingers to uncurl more. Black fire streamed out at the snake, meeting bolts of blue and gold from Farren in the centre of the snake's hood. The ice-green eyes widened as the smoky shape dropped, withering to steam once more. Only the eyes remained, two circles of green in the midst of the blue fire, the steam and the cold.

She hugged her cloak about herself, noticing a small sheen of ice on the material. Her feet and lips had turned numb and she clapped at her arms to warm herself. "Got to kill those dragons before they freeze us," she stammered through chattering teeth. "King of Heaven, please." Another hiss of breath came from the dragons and she saw the strands of her hair beside her eyes glisten and turn white with frost. A familiar prickling and warmth spread down her arms, hot and painful in contrast to the killing cold. She moaned with pleasure and exhilaration, feeling fire flow through her veins. The hoarfrost on her arms melted into trickles of water. Closing her eyes with the ecstasy of warmth, she let the fire burn out of her fingertips. *Idiot! Keep your eyes on your enemy.* She opened her eyes again and watched the fire. Red lighting wrapped around the mother-of-pearl, faint mad rainbows shimmering over the scales and wings of the dragon as it writhed. Its muzzle twisted up to the sky and began to drip white oily drops that poured and trickled down the length of its body to the floor. The camphor smell grew overpowering as the dragon melted slowly, drip by drip, until it was all gone.

The tingling and trembling died away and she let out a long, slow breath. Comfortable warmth lingered in her limbs after the extreme cold and heat. She glanced over at Farren through the curtain of her hair. Traces of frost still remained in her hair and also glinted on his. The blue light turned his red hair an odd shade of grey. He turned towards her, eyes flicking up and down her with a faint light of concern in them. "That's two things we won't have to lug down," he said, panting slightly. She felt his hand brush over hers, searching, and she twined her fingers through his. "Come on. Fifth level, and I hope it's the last."

She flicked her damp hair back from her face and looked ahead. The ring of fire had faded, leaving a thin black line on the circular step. Beyond it, the stairs climbed a little way higher. She counted five steps to the corridor where the blue light shone, then looked beyond the passage, expecting to see the black mouth of the stairs leading on into the heart of the mountain. Instead, blue light shone on smooth grey rock. A wave of weariness and relief flooded down her back. "It is the last," she sighed. They trudged up the five steps then turned down the last corridor.

Blue light dazzled her eyes, burning out from something that shone like a small blue sun in the depths of the earth. Squinting and raising one hand with her fingers splayed to mask the bright light, she looked down the corridor. She breathed in sharply, then let the breath gasp slowly out of her mouth. A blue globe stood on a white column at the far end of the wide corridor, its light illuminating the smooth stone. Thin lines of tracery and filigree made fine black patterns across the brilliant cobalt. She took a small step closer, tightening her fingers around Farren's. "The Stone of Water," she whispered, a thrill of awe stirring her heartbeat.

"Just the one Stone?" He pressed closer against her, metal grating on metal as their chainmail touched. "Only one after all we've gone through to get it?"

"It's the only one we can see." She leaned her head against his shoulder, burying her face in the dirty-smelling wool of his cloak and closed her eyes. "That portrait," she said, opening them again and looking at the glistening jewel. "Jamin Bluecloak. It showed him with only one Stone – this one."

"So where are the others?"

She shrugged, a mixture of exasperation, elation, disappointment and relief swirling through her. "Oh, I don't know!" she half laughed. "The Power does. For now, let's take this one and let's go home." She squeezed his hand and looked up at him. "We'll worry about the rest later."

She tugged on his hand and he fell into step beside her as they walked down the short corridor to the Stone. Her heart was thumping slow and loud in her ears. As they reached the pillar where the Stone stood, she slipped her hand out of his and moved to one side. She ran her hand over the surface of the blue jewel. It felt as warm as if it had been lying in the summer sun for a day and as smooth as ice. Looking carefully at the network of tracery over it, she saw that it was made of damasked silver, spotted here and there with black tarnish. Then her fingers brushed over Farren's in the middle of the Stone and she raised her eyes to meet his. A smile was on his lips and his dark eyes looked black in the bluish light. "Are you going to take it?" he asked.

"You take it," she said. "You suffered the most to get it."

He leaned over the Stone, one hand on her right cheek as he kissed her. His fingers brushed around her ear, just above the top of her armour as he withdrew. She drew back slowly. His hands cupped around the stone, blocking off the light from the lower half. Cracks of light shone out here and there between his fingers as he lifted it from the plinth and raised it above his head. One beam of blue light fell onto his face, picking out the sharp lines of his jaw, nose and cheeks. *"Coloasti ast!"* he shouted in the Old Tongue, head thrown back proudly.

Yes, she thought as she smiled at him, an arrow of longing shooting through her as she looked at his face. *We have it.*

CHAPTER SIXTEEN

Farren stood in the early afternoon sunlight beside the heaps of odds and ends from behind the waterfall. The Stone of Water in his hood knocked softly against his shoulders with every movement he made. One of the green torches he held sputtered and he bit his breath back as a fresh wave of its overpoweringly sweet aroma rolled up. His temples and the bridge of his nose throbbed. *This must be just about the last of these damned stinking things. Every time I smell them, I expect to see Crajaval coming up behind me.* He heard the sound of footsteps to one side and turned as Azariel came out of the cavern carrying one green torch and the red one from the lowest level. She came to him, walking around the others that stood where they had loosely driven them upright into the gravel nearby. "Is that the last?" he asked. Her blue-grey eyes flicked at him and she nodded. "Finally! Let's get rid of them."

She laughed and hurled the torch into the centre of the pile. He tossed his after hers and watched the green flames lick and spread across the edge of a deerskin. Yellow flames began to override the green and the sickly smell was replaced by black, acrid smoke and the smell of burning hair. He stooped for more of the torches, hurling them one after another into the heap, then stood back. The heat from the fire smote his face and he watched the smoke and shimmering air above the blaze. *It's over,* he thought as he watched the blaze, curling his arms around Azariel from behind and resting his head against hers. The fire licked around one of the hellhounds' bodies. "I don't want to watch all this lot burn," he said, wrinkling his nose as the acrid smoke swirled towards him on the wind, stinging his eyes. "Let's go and sit by the river. We've got to throw those crystals away."

She eased out from his embrace and bent down to the pile they had made of the crystals. "Put them in my cloak," she said, catching the hem of her cloak in one hand and gathering it up. He helped her put the shiny rocks into the folds of her cloak and walked behind her to the edge of the pool. She dumped the crystals with a flash and a clatter onto the edge of the churning pool at the foot of the waterfall. He went to sit down with his back to one of the large rocks near the edge of the pool. A white stain was spattered on one of them, a mark like faint dried white ink. He ran his finger over it and noticed a blackened scorch mark beside it. "Stormwolf?" he asked, turning towards her, "What's this? Is this where you… she..?"

"Yes," she said. "That's where I killed her." She stood still, one of the crystals in her hand, glittering like a star.

He looked at the stain, then at Azariel. The sunlight played her hair, striking blue highlights in the black. "Well done, Azariel," he said softly, hardly able to hear himself above the roar of the waterfall. He turned and sat down, his back to the rock. He scraped a handful of the crystals towards him and began to toss them into the pool, sending them flashing like fire in the air and plummeting into the bright water to sink beneath the blue. The sunshine ran warm golden hands over his chest and arms, and dampness from the gravel began to seep through from his trousers. *We've got one of the missing Stones of Protection and we're both alive. As for the rest, the Power knows where they are, and we'll hunt for them later.* He reached for another crystal, the last, and saw the amethyst flicker white and rich violet before vanishing, the splash of its entry lost in the foaming, churning chaos of the pool. *Now all we've got to do is go home to the capital and whichever Watchtower this Stone belongs to – the South, I think – to put it back where it was meant to be.* He sighed and his other hand fidgeted with his betrothal earring. *It's a long way to walk, and winter's two week's closer than it was when we set out.* He stared at the shining water and the blue depths below the waterfall. *Where are the horses? Where's Princess now – and my bow? I'm going to miss both her and it.*

"What's wrong?" Azariel asked. "You sighed."

He looked at her, studying the soft curves and lines of her face and her smooth pale skin. Her eyes were flickering with the white and gold light from the waterfall in the sunlight and, as always, lightning seemed to play in the depths of the deep blue-grey. "How did you hear me above all the roaring of the waterfall?" he said. "I was thinking about the horses, Stormwolf. What happened to them?"

"I haven't seen them since the night of the battle," she said. "Princess bolted after you fell and I haven't seen her since you have. And Storm – I was knocked off by a branch, then he disappeared. The hellhounds were after us and he didn't stop when I was thrown like he usually does."

"Did they," he nodded towards the burning hellhound carcasses, "kill him?"

She shook her head. "I doubt it. They were hunting me, not him. I had a hard run to shake them off."

He bowed his head, a dull, sad ache inside him. "Poor Princess," he said softly. "Where are you now, my lady? I hope they didn't pursue her, too. Even if they did, she'll still have her saddle on and chafing her." He studied his broken nails and eased a small fleck of dirt out from beneath them, then looked keenly at Azariel, a surge of hope rising inside him. "Stormwolf, you couldn't shift shape and track them in your wolf shape?"

She slid her hand around his waist, the other hand toying with a slightly matted strand of her dark hair. The smooth white of her brow furrowed for a few seconds. "I'm not sure, beloved," she said after a short silence. "The trail's more than a week old now and rain's fallen since then. There was snow that first night, too. I could try. You'd be as likely to draw her with your Gift. Can you, over all this distance?"

He closed his eyes, concentrating on the place in his heart where the mare was bound to him. *Surely I would have felt it if she had died.* He bent his energy on it, tugging on the cord of love and power, but could not feel her respond. At length, he stopped and opened his eyes again. "I can't. She's too far away and I don't even know which direction she's in. Only the King of Heaven, the wind and the stars can see where they are now."

She gasped and her fingers drove the links of chainmail into his stomach suddenly. "You're right," she said, half laughing. "Why didn't I think of that? I'll ask him."

"Him?" He stared at her as she slid her arm from around his waist and stood up. He scrambled to his feet after her, brushing the wet gravel off his thighs and buttocks, and shrugging his cloak back into place. "The King of Heaven? Of course, but..."

"The wind," she replied, a small smile playing around her lips.

"What?"

She put her finger to her lips and turned side-on to him so that the warm wind blew her hair and cloak behind her like a river of darkness. He saw her lips move, but the words were blurred by the rush of wind that suddenly strengthened. A faintly animal smell hung on the hot racing air, musky and sharp. A soft noise of something on the gravel came from behind him and he turned. A huge, well-muscled chestnut stallion stood on the gravel in front of them, ears pricked and dark eyes alert. His mouth dropped open as he watched the stallion pace forwards and lower its huge head to press its muzzle against Azariel's forehead. *What a horse! Where did she find him? And how did she tame him?*

"Welcome back, Azariel, comrade," said a deep breathy voice. He started, then saw the lips of the Stallion twitch. The big horse turned his head to look at him. "Who's your friend?"

She held out her hand and pulled him towards the Stallion. Eagerly, he stepped towards the huge horse. "Stallion of the northwest wind, this is Farren Blackarrow, my betrothed."

"Pleased to meet you, comrade." The Stallion pressed a horse-kiss onto his forehead with a whiskery, velvety muzzle, hot musky breath huffing and gusting over him.

"You're magnificent!" he blurted out, running a hand down the silky hair on the Stallion's thick neck. "I wish I could get a foal or two from you."

The Stallion whickered and bunted him lightly in the chest. "Well, thank you! But I won't breed with any of the mares you could find me. I'm spirit. Never trust a spirit who tries that with a mortal, and you should know, eh?" He bunted Farren in the chest again.

"But I can touch you," he said, admiring the massive muscles on the Stallion's forequarters. *I'd give anything to ride him, even if it were only once. What a horse!* Unthinkingly, he ran his hand over the horse's muscles, stroking the smooth coat and breathing in the smell of the horse.

"You could touch Crajaval, too, couldn't you? What's touch for telling mortals from spirits?" He swung his huge head up. "But what's up? I've got to go soon, and the Wolf will be running above the Kingdom. Why did you summon me?"

"Do you know where our horses are?" asked Azariel. "We need to go home."

The Stallion nodded, mane billowing and whipping like cloud. "I do. They have fallen in with some of my other mortal friends. They're what you might call the *minyasti* of the horses, swift and strong. I'll send them to take you to your own horses.

Kahral and Veranath. They'll take you. I can't do it now." The Stallion raised his head. "The Wolf's coming! I must leave you. May we meet again, comrades." He reared, huge hooves pawing the air. He vanished in a roar of thunder from the clear sky, leaving only a cloud of fine yellow dust. The wind dropped abruptly to gentle eddies that swirled the dust and sent dry leaves scattering across the ground.

"Where did he go?" He scanned the sky, where a single soft grey cloud drifted northwards. A cold breath of air brushed his cheek.

"Wherever the northwest wind goes when the southwester blows." She slipped her hand into his softly. "Come on. Let's make ourselves comfortable while we wait for the raven and the leaf to come."

"The raven and the leaf?" He glanced down at her.

"You know the Old Tongue better than that! Kahral and Veranath – the two horses."

He nodded. "Are you hungry? I am. It's a pity you couldn't have caught something to roast over the fire while it was still hot enough to cook things. But I'm starved after lugging all that gear around."

"Crabapples, then." Her hand clenched his firmly, their rings clicking together. "I hope you don't mind."

"When all you've been living on for over a week is flabby tasteless cakes, anything different is welcome. Let's go."

He lengthened his stride to match hers as they walked to the swinging bridge. The sunlight glittered off the metal of the gong. "Damn," he said. "Look what we forgot to pull down." He pointed at it. "And all those runes and pictures all over it, too! What's going to happen if someone rings it?"

"I am afraid Madam is not available," Azariel said, mimicking the voice of a nobleman's servant. "She is indisposed. No, good sir, I do not know when she will be up and about."

"Never again, I hope," he said, then burst out laughing. "Well said, Azariel! But I won't say you missed your true calling."

She laughed with him, head tossed back and all her strong white teeth showing. "We'd better stop laughing before we try crossing that bridge," she said. "You'll make it buck uncontrollably."

"Thanks, Stormwolf," he said, slipping his arm around her shoulder and walking onto the bridge. It rocked and quivered under his feet. "I haven't had a good laugh for far too long." He held the chains on the side of the bridge with his other hand to balance himself, the rusty metal jabbing little splinters into his hand.

They sat underneath the apple trees, his back against the tree and her back pressed into his chest. They ate and talked together, the cold south wind beginning to undulate the tussocks and stir the branches above them. Grey clouds swiftly streamed north overhead in long fleeces. They marked the face of the sun and the air began to chill. After a time, a sound of hoofbeats drummed on the grass. Two stallions, large as carthorses but without any trace of coarseness or feathering about the fetlocks, cantered towards them, one glossy black and the other light chestnut. The chestnut sported a small crescent-shaped patch of white on its forehead and the black had a tiny snip between its flared nostrils. The two stallions stopped ten paces away and turned their heads to look at them, ears pricked and dark eyes inquisitive.

Azariel felt Farren's arm tense as it lay draped warmly around her middle. She tilted her head back and looked up at him. "They have come," she said. "Kahral the raven will be the black, and the chestnut must be Veranath. Knowing you, you'll take Veranath."

"How are we to guide them?" He shifted backwards behind her and his arm left her waist. She edged forwards and let him scramble to his feet. "Or rather, how will you? I can ride any horse without bridle or saddle, but you haven't my Gift, Stormwolf."

She took his hand and leaned on him as she stood up beside him. A lock of her hair wandered into her eyes, blown by the wind, and she flicked it back behind her shoulder. "I don't think we'll need any tack. They've been sent to us. They know where to go and we don't."

He nodded and walked towards the horses, hand outstretched. The horses both stepped towards him and snuffed at him. She watched him for a few moments as he petted and caressed the two stallions before she walked towards them. One of the stallions, the black, turned his head to her, whickering softly. "Hello, Kahral," she crooned, stroking his face from forelock to the silver snip on his whiskery muzzle. "Have you come to take us away?"

"These ones don't talk, Stormwolf," Farren replied. "But they're very intelligent all the same. I can feel it." He brushed the black and ginger horsehairs off his hands. "We had better not waste any more time. Let's mount and see where they'll take us."

She placed her hands on Kahral's high withers and knotted her hands through his mane. The familiar homely smell of horses rose to her face. *How big is he? He must be at least sixteen hands, if not more.* She leaped up, pressing on the black's heavily muscled shoulders and straining to get her leg over his back. She slipped down, landing heavily. She drew a deep breath, then glanced over her shoulder. "Farren, can you help me up? He's a big horse."

He knelt beside her, chuckling. "For once, you'll let me kneel at your feet." He cupped his hands beneath her knees, secure and firm. "Ready?" She nodded and vaulted up onto the black stallion's back, propelled by him as he got to his feet, thrusting her upwards. She swung her leg over Kahral's back, rolling into place.

She settled herself on the stallion's back, then twitched and shrugged her cloak back from where it hung awry. He swung himself up and onto the chestnut's back with a small groan of effort. He glanced over at her, and she flashed a smile at him. She leaned forwards and knotted her hands through the horse's warm wiry mane again, thighs tight around his flanks and ready to nudge him with her heels.

Before she could spur him, the big horse wheeled around. His ears pricked ahead towards the west and he began to canter. She clenched her knees and thighs against the horse's sides, swaying and pivoting with the rock of his gait, his spine digging into her. Veranath ran beside Kahral, matching each other stride for stride. Farren bent over the chestnut's neck, smoothly blending his movements into the horse's. Veranath's mane whirled back in his speed, almost touching Farren's hair, chestnut blending with auburn. She shook her own hair back to fly free with her cloak behind her. A wellspring of delight bubbled up inside her, whipped into a peak by the cold wind. *I'm riding with my beloved again.* She laughed, then began to sing, a little breathlessly, as she rode, relishing the cold, the strain of her leg muscles holding the horse, and the smell of grass and mud in the air.

The horses cantered downstream a short way then headed westwards into the hills, following the winding course of a small stream. Fingers of sunlight reached through the oncoming southwest cloud, gilding the tussocks and casting shadows over the curving line of flowing water. A tang of rain blew in the air, a cold clean smell. Azariel watched the rise and fall of the land between Kahral's ears. *That hill. That's where the stormdemons attacked me before I met Menkalinan.* She looked at it, then at the approaching grey blanket of cloud from the south. *But that's natural rain. The Stallion said that the Wolf was coming.*

The horses veered southwards short of a small wood as the first drops of rain fell. She reached behind her for the edge of her cloak and wrapped the warm wool around herself. The wind tugged and worried at it with teeth of ice, trying to tear it from her. Through screwed-up eyes, she looked across at Farren, the details of his face and body blurred and indistinct through the tears snatched from her eyes by the cold wind. "I'll wager you wish you were back sleeping in those caves tonight," she called.

"Never," he shouted above the rush of the wind. "Even if snow falls, I'd rather be out of that dungeon."

"Don't speak too loudly of snow." She looked up at the dark smudged underside of the clouds. The air felt exhilaratingly cold, leaving her skin tingling. The head of the clouds towered to the pale blue sky, dark, swirling bitter blue-grey. "It may come yet."

The horses cantered on, only slackening their pace slightly as the sun sank behind the hills ahead of them, staining the oncoming clouds with scarlet. The stallions turned from the stream and began to climb through rolling scrub-covered hills. Mountainthorn, broom and gorse raked at her legs and cloak. A claw of gorse tore over her with a low, tearing sound across her leg. She glanced down. Snapped thorn-twigs were caught on her trousers and boots, and the black leather had a deep gouge across it. She sighed. *We've got a lot to do when we return.*

Kahral edged ahead of Veranath as they trotted up a steep slope. She leaned forward, holding onto his mane as she felt herself slip slightly backwards. The black horse's sides were heaving as he reached the top, a flattish place below a higher peak where a small tarn nestled among the grass and tussocks. Raindrops dappled small circles on the tarn's surface and the wind ruffled the water. The black stallion stopped suddenly, pitching and jerking her forwards onto his neck. She raised her head from his hot, black, sweaty mane. Then Kahral heaved, pitched and bucked, whipping her backwards and forwards. She clung to him fiercely with hands, legs, arms, everything, then felt herself slide and fall to one side. She crashed into the ground, rolling over and over, mud and thorns under her hands and bare forearms. Panting and heart pounding with shock, she watched the big stallion leap clear of her, then vanish down the crest of the hill. "Stop!" she called, bunching her legs under herself in a crouch. "Kahral, come back!"

Veranath whinnied and squealed, and she heard his hooves scrape on the soil. She turned her head, looking through the matted strands of her hair. For the space of a heartbeat, she saw Farren keeping his seat on the plunging chestnut stallion, hands knotted through Veranath's mane. Then the horse leaped and bucked like a hooked fish. Farren rolled to one side, still clinging to the stallion's mane. He regained his footing, holding the horse and pulling at it, sinews on his left arm standing out like ropes. The big stallion reared again then wheeled away, his mane whipping free. Farren staggered before he sprawled on the tussock. Veranath snorted and galloped down the slope after Kahral.

She picked herself up and went to Farren, brushing the mud from her aching hands. "Are you all right?" she said, kneeling beside him and gently stroking his back.

He rolled over, gasping and clasping at his midriff. "Hit... a... rock... when... I... fell," he panted as he slowly regained his breath. She ran her hand over his forearm as he stared up at her, gently ruffling the chestnut hair on his arm. He closed his eyes and she saw his larynx rise and fall as he swallowed. "I suppose I'm all right," he said at last. "Just winded. More bruises just after I've lost the old ones. What did he do that for? It's as if they were telling us they'd carried us far enough."

"Perhaps they have." She raised her head and looked down the slope. "How else could they tell us that we've arrived?"

"Hmm. I can think of a few ways." He reached up and took one of her hands. Rain was falling, beating onto her back and trickling down both their hands and forearms. "It felt as if the tameness wore off and they became wild again. They are wild horses, after all. I could feel it in Veranath's mind. It's hard to explain, but it's got a different texture from a gentled horse. I wasn't expecting it and didn't have time to use my Gift on him."

"I'll take your word for it," she laughed. "I can imagine, but I don't suppose I fully understand, any more than you'd understand what it's like being a wolf."

"So what is it like?" His brown eyes sparkled at her and a smile played around the curve of his lips. He blinked as a drop of rain splashed onto his face.

"Fun." Water dripped from the ends of her hair across her face and she wiped it away. "Are we going to sit here until night falls? This is where Storm and Princess should be, but I can't see any signs of them. We'll have to search – and find shelter, too."

He raised her hand to his lips and pressed a kiss into her palm. "I've got enough breath. I'll call them." He rolled over and got to his feet. She saw his chest rise as he raised his forefingers to his mouth. He whistled, long and shrill.

She put her arms around him from behind as silence fell, resting her head on the warm broadcloth of his cloak and breathing in the acid smell of the wet wool. The rain fell, hissing and drumming on the earth and water, and the south wind blew in little eddies around the bulk of the hill ahead of them. Faintly, she heard a neigh blown on the wind. She tensed and looked up, feeling his shoulders stiffen under her head. Another whinny was blown on the wind, and a crashing, rustling sound came from the broom and thorns ringing the tarn. She flicked her eyes about the tangled scrub, watching the path-gaps that opened into the dense growth. An eddy of wind blew a flurry of wet hair across her face. She wiped it away.

Princess and Storm pushed through the scrub, ungroomed and with matted manes, battered tack still clinging to them. The two horses trotted to them, whickering warm welcoming breaths all over them. She let go of Farren and hugged Storm's neck, leaning her head against his shaggy mane. "Storm, old fellow, I'm so glad to see you again," she crooned, gently easing a gorse twig out of his mane. "You're all safe and sound."

"We'd better take their tack off." Farren looked across Princess's neck at her. "We won't be going anywhere else tonight and it must be hurting them. It's a shame we couldn't get it off them before we parted company."

"If there's a way I can stop to unsaddle my horse while I'm being knocked off mid-gallop, I shall be certain to do it," she said dryly. "But you're right." She reached for the buckles under Storm's cheek and unfastened the bridle before easing it off over his ears.

"Oh, no!" She heard his voice behind her and spun around, Storm's bridle dangling from one hand and the other resting on the saddle. Farren was standing with both hands on Princess's saddle and the mare had her neck arched around so that her muzzle nudged into the small of his back. He ran one hand along her neck, then looked up at Azariel, eyes wide and dismayed.

"What's up?" she asked.

"My bow," he said softly. "It's been knocked out of the grip. I thought the grip would have kept it in place firmly enough."

"In all this tangle of gorse?" She felt for the girth buckles underneath the skirt of Storm's saddle. "I'm not surprised it's been knocked out."

"But where is it?" He laid his head on the saddle. "I don't want to go home without it. There are three things that are precious to me: the first is you, my sweetheart, the second is Princess and the third is my bow. And I want to go home with all three!"

"Beloved, the light is fading and soon we'll hardly be able to find enough fuel for a fire, let alone something to eat."

He sighed. "We'll hunt for it in the morning, then. Will you be able to use your nose?"

"I'll try." She eased the saddle off Storm's back, wincing as she saw the chafed and raw places where the leather had rubbed him. "Poor old fellow," she murmured to the gelding, patting his neck. "That must be sore. Enjoy yourself without the saddle for a while. It won't be long until you're back to your nice stable and grooms to see to you. I wish I could find something to put on it."

She rested the saddle on the ground. "I'll start looking for a place for the night," she said, and pushed into the gorse and broom, carefully looking at each large bush. *Is that one thick and large enough to shelter us from the rain and wind?* Farren's footsteps thudded behind her and she paused. *No. Not that one. It's too low to the ground to sleep under comfortably.*

She pushed a switch of broom out of the way, then held it back as Farren caught up to her. "Thanks," he said, nodding.

She let the small branch spring back into place and walked on, twigs snapping underfoot. *No hope of hunting anything tonight. We're making enough noise for a herd of cows. Everything within half a mile will have fled.* She rounded a bend in the animal-trail and found a heap of rocks piled and clustered together. A hummock of rock lay on the south side of the pile, its northern flank pale grey, unlike the rain-slick black of the other side. Kneeling, she felt the ground and the coarse grass beneath the biggest rock. "It's dry enough to sleep on, even with the rain," she said, turning and looking back up at him.

"Two walls are enough of a house, if we use all the blankets out of the saddlebags. Now to find dry fuel."

"There's no lack of that." She squeezed a jabbing prickle out of the back of her hand with a small twinge of satisfaction as the small sliver of black slid out of her skin. Then she pushed determinedly back through the scrubby growth, gathering up dry and broken twigs and sticks, ignoring the scratching along her bare skin. *Gorse burns well, but I wish it didn't have so many thorns!* She brought out an armload, scraps of gorse dangling in her matted hair.

She dumped the load of fuel at the end of one of the boulders. Farren had heaped up a small pile near the shelter of the rocks with a ring of small broken hunks of stone ringing it. His tinderbox scraped a few sparks up and eventually, a thin trail of white smoke writhed up from the pile, the lower end glowing a faint gold. The yellow flames grew and crackled, and the small circle of yellow light shone onto the cleared ground and a few odd bundles. "What's that near the fire?" she asked.

"Food from the saddlebags," he replied. "I got it while you were fetching wood. It'll be somewhat stale by now, but it'll save us trying to hunt." The yellow light shone over his face, sparkling off his eyes, his even white teeth and the beads of moisture lingering on his face. His ivory skin took on a golden tone, the sharp lines of his jaw and nose softened, and each short red hair, each pore glowed in the firelight. She smiled, gazing at him. *I could look at him forever; he's so handsome.* His dark eyes met hers and she felt her heart melt inside her. Drawn like a lodestone to iron, she knelt beside him and kissed his cheek softly. Then she turned away, reining in her desire. "I had better fetch more wood," she said quietly.

"I'll get more, too," he said. "Let's see who can carry the most." He winked at her and scrambled to his feet.

After they had collected a large supply of wood, they came back to the fire. She sat down with her back against one of the rocks, her legs deliciously warm with the heat of the fire. She gnawed on the dry bread and leathery dry fruit, almost gagging as she swallowed the hard crumbs. She finished then leaned her head back against the wet rock, listening to the wind and falling rain mingling with the snap and mutter of the fire. Farren got up and took the blankets out of the saddlebags. He passed some to her then lay down with his blankets wrapped about him, resting his head on her outstretched legs just above her knees. "Now," he said. "Tell me all that you've done while we've been apart. You've told me about the hellhounds. Then what happened?"

She wrapped the blankets around her shoulders and gently rested her hand across his chest, lips twitching into a smile as she felt his chest slowly rising and falling, the links in his chainmail gleaming one by one like fish scales. Staring into the fire, she told him her story, but stopped as he began to twitch and breathe more deeply and slowly. She looked down. His eyes had closed and his head felt heavy. She lunged and twisted to one side, reaching for more fuel for the fire, then leaned her head back against the rocks. The fire crackled gently, and the rain and wind hissed through the scrub and lulled her to sleep.

She awoke with a start, muscles cramped and one shoulder chilled. The fire had dwindled down to a mere heap of dull red embers in the darkness and her blanket had slipped from her shoulder. Farren's head had rolled from her leg and now he lay sleeping on the ground. She drew her sword and leaned over to gently kiss the top of his head, the warm smoky smell in his hair lingering in her nostrils as she laid the sword between them. She lay down, pulling the blankets about her, a comfortable warmth creeping back into her shoulders as she drifted back into sleep.

***

Farren shivered as he woke. The ground beneath him felt damp and his legs were uncomfortably chilled. Breathing in the clean outdoor smell of wet earth and grass, he opened his eyes and saw the ashes of the fire in front of him. He stretched and yawned, the sound of his breath drowning out the shrilling of the birds for a few moments. The wind hissed through the mountainthorn, gorse and broom, but the patter of rain on the rocks had stopped. Something was digging into his spine. He rolled over and reached around for it. *Have I been sleeping on a rock all night?* His hand met the lump in his hood and he smiled. *Of course. The Stone of Water. We really do have it. And even something as legendary as that is uncomfortable to sleep on.*

He sat up, yawning and stretching again. Azariel still lay asleep on the ground by the rock, her drawn sword lying beside her, and the cloak and blankets heaped around her shoulders. A few threads of black hair meandered across her pale face, gently lifted and stirred by her sleeping breaths. Tenderly, he leaned over her and softly brushed the smooth skin of her cheek with his lips. *I want so much to have her in my arms as she sleeps. One day soon, and the day's drawing nearer.*

He got up and went to the tarn to drink. A light clammy grey mist hung over the hills, drifting and swirling over the tussocks as the wind drove it. On the far side of the tarn, the two horses were grazing. Princess whinnied to him and he chirruped to her before he turned and pushed his way back through the scrub, collecting firewood as he went. He found Azariel awake, sheathing her sword and yawning. She looked at him through tousled black snakes of hair, and smiled. "Good morning, Farren, beloved," she said, half-yawning again.

He laid down his armload of thorn twigs and leaned over to kiss her. "Good morning to you, sweetheart. Sorry I fell asleep while you were talking to me."

"Oh, never mind," she said. "I'll tell you as we ride today." She got to her feet. "My turn to go and drink. Do you want me to fetch any more wood?"

He shook his head. "This will do to warm us a bit while we eat whatever's left in our packs. After that, well… I'd like to find my bow before we go if we can."

He built the fire and fished around in the saddlebags for some of the remaining food. He found a few hard rounds of bread, a cheese with a thin layer of green masking the yellow, several withered and wrinkled apples, a dozen walnuts and some strips of dried salt beef. He put the bread and meat back into the saddlebags, then carefully trimmed the mould off the cheese before slicing it. He divided the slices in half, then sat back against the rock and waited for her to return, listening to the sounds of the birds and the rush of wind through the gorse.

She returned and they ate the cheese and apples in silence. As he ate, grimacing at the strong taste of the old cheese, he closed his eyes. *Master,* he prayed silently, *you know where my bow is. Show me, please. Because what is an archer without a bow?* He nibbled at the floury apple, eyes closed. He hurled the core away into the bushes and heard the words *the creek* drifting through his mind. "Master?" he whispered.

"What's up?" asked Azariel.

He opened his eyes and looked over at her. "I asked where my bow was, and the only answer I got was 'the creek'. I don't know of any creek." He ran his fingers through his hair, then inspected his nails. "But using common sense, the creek will either lead into or out of the tarn."

"So let's search around the tarn." She flicked her hair back, then lightly sprang to her feet.

He stood up beside her and stamped out the small fire. "I only hope it's not in the tarn. It would float, being made of wood and horn, but I'm not thrilled with the idea of swimming naked to get it." He ground the embers to black powder, the last heat of the fire coming through the sole of his boots.

"I'm sure you've got nothing to be ashamed of." She smiled sidelong at him and winked, running her hand over his arm. ":I'll have to resist the temptation to peek at you."

"Stormwolf!" He tweaked her hair lightly, a warm flush spreading up over his face as he saw the glitter in her eye. He bowed his head, uncontrollably grinning. *I'm glad she wants me. I know I want her. One day, one day...* He let out a long slow breath, then stamped out the last tiny spark in the smoking ashes. "We'd better go. Bring Storm's saddle with you. We'll leave them by the tarn while we search."

He scooped up Princess's saddle and walked with it to the tarn. He set it down under a twisted broom bush and straightened up, looking across the small mountain lake and among the yellow-brown rain-beaded tussocks. *The creek isn't flowing down that slope behind us into the tarn, so it must be flowing out. And if it's flowing out, then it must lead to the Illin-Ast. So the creek should be on the eastern side of the tarn.* "This way," he said aloud, walking around the shore and using the wind and what he could make out of the sun to judge the direction.

Azariel darted ahead of him. "Can't you hear it?" She strode in front of him on her long legs, hands parting the broom. He walked swiftly and softly after her, ears straining to catch the sounds above and below the hiss of wind through the scrub. The wind dropped and he heard it: a gentle rush and chatter, only slightly distinct from the noise of the wind. He drew level with her and slid his hand through hers, pressing against the broom and gorse on the left side of the trail.

The stream fell away from the eastern edge of the tarn, a small waterfall gushing through large boulders then winding down through a narrow break in the scrub. "Here's the stream," he said. "Now to look along the trails for my bow." He sat down on one of the rocks, then slithered down the short drop. He landed awkwardly, slipping to one side. He winced as he struck into one of the boulders, knocking an old bruise on his arm. Azariel smiled wryly down at him, then lightly and neatly clambered down beside him. "You search this bank, beloved," she said, "and I'll search the other. Look for hoofprints on the wet ground to see where they've come to drink – shod hooves."

"Right." He regained his balance then slowly and cautiously picked his way downhill and downstream, following the steep slope. Once or twice, he knocked his knuckles painfully against the stones and once he slipped one foot into a pool in the stream, chilly water splashing into his boot and leaving it irritatingly wet inside. He slithered and shuffled down the slope, peering around rocks and pushing apart the small shrubs and tussocks that grew beside the stream, watching for the familiar curves and wood-grain of the bow. *I've hunted for arrows like this plenty of times. I never thought I'd hunt my bow.* He saw a flicker of wood the right colour and thickness and stooped for it. He yanked it free from the tangle of wet grass, then snorted in disappointment when he looked at the piece of old gorse in his hand. Irritated, he threw it away, then walked on, prying and searching, eyes darting to and fro.

"Here it is!" He heard her voice and looked up from the cluster of mountainthorn he was peering under. She stood in a narrow gap between two enormous boulders, her back towards him. He tugged his cloak free from the thorns and scrambled across the rocks to her, a tingling thrill going through the soles of his feet as he slipped and lost his balance, sending his other foot into the cold water.

He squeezed between the boulders, breathing hard. She turned to him, the bow in her hand and gave it to him. "Thank you," he murmured. "It's good to see it again." His right hand slipped around the grip and his left ran over the curves and recurves of the limbs, relishing the touch of the polished wood, studying the whorls of wood-grain that showed through the deep stain. "Welcome back, old friend," he crooned to it. "Are you all right?" The bowstring had snapped and it dangled uselessly from each end. He plucked the twisted sinew off and threw the pieces away. "Just as well I always carry a spare string in my quiver."

He unclipped each of his six arrows and slid the cover of the little square compartment in the middle out of its groove. Two arrowheads and a coiled sinew tumbled out and he picked them up quickly. Holding the string under his chin, he replaced the arrowheads and each arrow in its copper clip in the quiver. He put the loop at the end of the sinew into place on the lower limb of the bow, then bent the bow, pressing on it with his weight, his arms, his legs, straining and striving against the power of the seasoned wood and horn. Muscles aching, groaning with the effort, he fitted the upper end of the string into place, then let the bow glide fiercely into place, turning his face to one side, wary of the untried string snapping. The sinew held and he relaxed, straightening up.

"Are you going to test the new string?" She cocked her head towards him, eyes sparkling.

He looked around at the rocks, tussocks and thorns, then shook his head. "This is the best place I can think of for losing arrows. I'd like to test the new string properly, but not here." He slid his right hand around the grip and felt it nestle snugly into his palm. "Now we're ready," he said, holding out his left hand to her. "Let's go home."

She bent her head and kissed the knuckles of his left hand as he held it out to her. "Keep your hand free for climbing, beloved," she said as she straightened up. "You'll need it."

She turned and lightly climbed up through the rocks and scrub, swarming up the slope as easily as she could climb a staircase. He made his way up behind her, hampered by the bow in his hand. His breath came hard and fast, and his heart pumped the blood loudly in his ears. He scrambled up the last few yards, then halted on the shore of the tarn, waiting for his breathing and heartbeat to return to normal. The back of his mouth felt sticky and he knelt on the wet grass and tussocks to drink.

He stood, wiping the drips away from his mouth. The leather trousers had become wet at the knees, cold and heavy. He picked a few pieces of broom and gorse off his clothing then put his fingers to his lips to whistle up the horses. Whickering and snorting, tossing wet manes, they came to him.

They saddled the horses and strapped on the saddlebags before mounting. Farren took the Stone of Water out of his hood and tucked it carefully deep inside one saddlebag. The wind blew keenly from the south, but the low cloud over the hills was beginning to break up and lighten, changing from grey to soft white patches on pale cold blue. The valley where the stream flowed trailed down towards a high line of hills and mountains that ran roughly north–south. "There's the Illin-Ast gorge," he said, pointing to the mountains. "Let's follow the stream down." He put heels lightly to Princess and headed her down one of the trails through the gorse into the valley.

By nightfall, they had reached the pine-filled valley where they had encountered the phantoms. The wind blew up the slope into his face, rich and fresh with the green scent of sap and needles. "No mist now," Azariel said beside him, her chest rising as she breathed deeply. "Or that smell of death. They've gone."

"We'll get a peaceful night's sleep. I'm ready for it." He yawned. "It's a shame we don't have the tent anymore."

"We can make do without it. Come on. We'd better find fuel and get something for supper."

"Not the carcass of that alphurrhn at the top of the next slope," he chuckled. "If it's still there by now." He reached down and took his bow out of the grip on the saddle. "Time to test the string. Hunt with me, Stormwolf. There's plenty of fuel around, so the fire can wait for later." Bow in hand, he swung off Princess's back.

"With pleasure." She dismounted beside him and slid into wolf-shape. She turned her shewolf's head towards him, one golden eye winking, and her tail bannered over her silver back.

He laid his hand on her head. "What can you find, sweetheart?" he murmured.

She raised her muzzle to the wind and he saw her nostrils quivering. Silently, she turned and trotted slowly along, making her way through the trees. He followed, stepping carefully behind her. She led him deeper into the forest, zigzagging from tree to tree then pausing behind a young pine. She stopped, stiffening and pointing with her muzzle into a space broken in the pines by a huge fallen tree. A small area of grass surrounded the massive tree trunk, dotted here and there with broom and bramble. He followed the line of her muzzle and stiff body with his eyes and saw a rabbit beneath the brambles. It was nibbling grass thirty paces away, well within shot of his bow. He smiled. *So that's what she was doing. Not only showing me game, but taking me to cover to shoot from.* He nocked an arrow to the string. *Ten times – a hundred times better than any hound. My Azariel.* Silently and smoothly, he dropped to one knee, keeping his eye on the rabbit. It had begun cleaning its face with its paws, one ear bent over as it worked busily. The string bit into the fingers of his left hand as he drew. He raised the bow, tilting it slightly, eyes fixed on the rabbit. His wrist touched his cheek, then he anchored his fingers in the corner of his mouth.

He released the string and the arrow flew free. The string hummed faintly; the rabbit looked up and darted away. He saw the arrow strike with a thump into the grass where it had been. At the same moment, the warmth of the shewolf at his side left him and Azariel darted through the young pine and bramble at a gallop. He heard her crash through the undergrowth then heard the bloodcurdling death-shriek of the rabbit. He grinned and went to retrieve his arrow from the grass. *Well, the string shoots well enough. Too bad the rabbit jumped the string.* He brushed the dirt and moisture off the arrow then fitted it back into the quiver. Azariel came out from the tangle of blackberry with the rabbit in her jaws, holding it by the neck and shaking it violently.

The shewolf dropped the limp body of the rabbit at his feet then changed back to her own shape. She looked up at him as she knelt beside him, wiping her mouth. "I should have drunk something before shifting shape," she said. "Ugh! There are still hairs in my mouth."

"It's not a hare; it's a rabbit. Rather a lean one, but it'll make a decent meal." He stooped to pick up the carcass, then held a hand out to her. She leaned on him and got to her feet beside him. "Come on," he said. "Time to collect fuel and make a fire."

They lit a fire and cooked the rabbit stuffed with pine-nuts and the end of the old bread. Belly filled with warm food, he rolled himself up in his blankets and lay down to sleep under the shelter of the low-sweeping branches of a pine, drawn sword lying beside him. The last thing he was aware of was the lapping sound of the flames and the smell of the needles rising from under his head.

CHAPTER SEVENTEEN

Farren felt his shoulder being shaken. Drowsily, he woke and opened one eye. The air had turned bitterly cold and what he could see of the sky looked like the half-dark before dawn on a cloudy day. A slender shape knelt over him among the branches of the trees, hair cascading down and tickling his cheeks. "Stormwolf?" he mumbled.

"It's starting to snow," she said softly. "If I hadn't woken you, you could have slept forever. We'd better ride on so we can get to better shelter before we freeze." She bent her head and he felt her cold lips press onto his cheeks.

He pushed the blankets back from himself and sat up. Something cold and soft fell through a gap in the branches and onto him. He brushed it off with a shudder. Quickly, he folded up the blankets and sheathed his sword. "It's freezing," he shivered. "How long has it been like this?" He got to his feet, found the saddlebags and stowed the blankets away, touching the Stone of Water carefully once to reassure himself that it was still there.

"I don't know. I woke up to find it snowy. I've lit a fire and there's a bit of rabbit left for you; I've had mine."

He ate quickly, huddled over the fire. He saddled Princess, fingers sore and stiff with cold as he tightened the girths around her. Soft rustling sounds came from the forest around him, mixed with one or two bird calls. In the half-light, he found the stirrup and mounted. He settled into the saddle, blowing over his numb knuckles to ease the painful cold. *What happened to my gloves?* Steam from his breath blurred the dark shapes and shadows of the valley. "Stormwolf?" he said through chattering teeth. "Are you ready? Let's get moving before we all freeze here."

"I'm ready." Her voice shivered slightly. He heard a small squeak of leather and the light tap of her heel against the gelding's flanks. Storm moved off, hooves thudding on the earth and rustling through the grass. He nudged Princess gently and headed her up the slope behind Storm, snowflakes dusting his hands and arms.

They crested the hill as a pale band of light showed through the clouds to the east. The south wind drove flurries of sleet and snow into his face, bitterly cold and singing in his ears. He brushed it away and peered ahead, shielding his face with one hand. The hillside dropped away to the dark dawn plains of the Kingdom in front of him. Here and there, he saw a few points of distant lights: farm houses, villages, tiny townships. A pang of homesickness shot through his heart as he looked down the line of the Illin-Ast, a faint silver line through the patchy grey and navy blue. *My childhood home's down that river. Maybe even some of the lights I can see in the distance are Mother and Father's.* He buried his hands into Princess's mane, seeking the warmth of her body. *Rest and warmth at last tonight – in comfort instead of stone or bare ground. I think I deserve it after all I've been through. We both do.*

Princess tossed her head restlessly, snorting steam up into the cold air. A light dusting of snow lay over the tussocks beneath her and she stamped and scraped at it, pulling at the reins and straining her neck. He let the wet leather slip through his hands to let her graze and looked over at Azariel. She sat with her cloak wrapped about her, hood up and the tip of her nose showing past the swathes of black. "Sweetheart?" he said above the howl of the wind. "All silent. What are you thinking? Why stop here where the wind's coldest?"

"I was wondering whether we should go to the Watchtower of the South first to set the Stone in place, or to the capital."

"It's too far to the Watchtower. I suggest we go to Lebhern-y-Domastin," he said, rubbing his hands together. "We'd better show Janna what we've found."

Her white hand reached up and pushed the black hood back from her face slightly. "But he won't be there in the capital. He'll be in the Watchtower of the West instead of us. The acolytes with him, too, probably." She shrugged and the hood fell back from her head. "I don't know why he thinks he has to go there, seeing as the Stones aren't there for him to look after."

"Training the acolytes to look after the Stones, no doubt. But General Alpherastin will be at the capital and we'd better show him. As I said, it's too far to the Watchtower of the South. But we'll be at the capital tonight and the sooner, the better."

Fire flashed in her eyes, barely visible in the cold dawn light. "I'll race you across the border into the Kingdom." She thudded heels into Storm's sides and headed him down the hill in a spray of light snow and water that had been kicked up from the tussocks. He laughed and caught up the reins, shifting his weight backwards as Princess raised her head and bounded down the hill after Storm. His heart pounded with exhilaration, throbbing in his ears, a rhythm beneath the scream of the cold wind that tore tears from his eyes with the speed. The ground beneath him passed in a blotched blur of dark blue-grey and white. Whinnying, the horses reached the foot of the hill and kept cantering a few paces, hooves drumming on the Kingdom plains.

He checked Princess to a brisk walk and patted her neck. Blood tingled in his cheeks and arms, hot and insistent in the cold air. "Which way will we go? Down the river and along the highway again, or cross-country into the wind until we reach the capital?" He pulled his cloak about him, trapping the warmth.

"Cross-country," she replied. "It'll speed our journey." She sat easily in the saddle, one hand on the reins and the other toying with a strand of her hair. "It's a shame we can't go all the way to the Watchtower tonight."

"It's far too far for the horses," he repeated. He settled into the rhythm of riding and rode on through the rain in silence, listening to the squelch of mud beneath the horses' hooves, and the squeak and jingle of the tack.

***

The sleet had eased to rain by the time the grey walls of the capital became visible. Azariel slid her feet from the stirrups and stretched her legs for a moment, then settled back into place, moving easily with Storm's walk. *Nearly there, and I'd wager the horses are more tired than we are. I'm wet, cold and hungry.* She turned Storm through the gates, his hooves and Princess's clopping over the cobblestones. *Here we are again. We've done this so many times the horses should know their own way to the barracks.* The wind dropped inside the shelter of the city walls, but the rain kept beating down onto the roofs, the streets and her hood. Here and there, lights were being lit at the windows of the houses they rode past. At one window, two small children waved and smiled at her. She waved back and sighed as she rode on. *They'd never believe where we've just been, or what's happened if we told them.* A small pang of regret shot through her. *We'll never be able to tell our own children, even. There'll be none to tell now.* She smiled and looked over at Farren, his head and face muffled in his hood. The barracks were in sight, thick mud brick walls dark in the gathering night. *My poor beloved Farren. Those hellhounds must have hurt him so badly.*

"Who rides there?" the sentry above the barracks gate called. "Oh. You're some of us. Hang on a few moments and I'll be down to let you in." Then sentry's face vanished from above the wall, leaving only the point of a spear bobbing above the stones then vanishing. The handle of the gate turned and the gates opened.

She nudged Storm through the gate. *Home at last, at least for tonight.* She shrugged her stiff shoulders, a small fingertip of cold air reaching through the neck of her armour as she moved. She headed Storm across the pockmarked and patterned mud in the bare courtyard. Under the half-shelter of the big slablike office building, she reined him in. "Good old fellow," she said, clapping his neck and getting a palmful of wet black horsehair. She slid her feet from the stirrups and swung herself down into the mud.

"Better get their saddles off and blanket them if we can," Farren said. He dismounted and began to busy himself with Princess's saddle. "Poor things, they need time to heal those saddle-sores. I know you're going to laugh again, but I still wish there was some way to have taken the tack off them before they bolted." He lugged Princess's saddle off and carefully balanced it beside the wall underneath the tethering rings. "The saddles will get wet, but they need so much work already that a bit more water won't hurt them much." He unstrapped one saddlebag and carefully lifted out the Stone of Water from inside it.

"I agree." Storm's saddle lay heavily over her forearm, smelling strongly of sweat. She looked at the battered brown leather, seeing small cracks in it marring the patterns worked on it. She set it down beside the wall and fetched out a rope from the bags. She looped up Storm's reins through the bridle, then tied the rope around his neck. The big gelding snuffled at her and tried to scratch his head on her armour, jerking and jolting her as she fastened the knot and passed the other end through the old iron ring in the wall.

She heard voices crossing the courtyard and looked up. Two cadet soldiers were crossing the patch of open ground, covering their heads with their arms against the rain and talking loudly as they went. *Thank the Power! Now our horses can get a drink while we're with the General.* She cleared her throat. "Hey, you two!" she called. "Over here."

The two cadets stopped and looked up. "Yes, ma'am?" called one of them as the two teenaged boys began to walk towards her.

"Are you busy at the moment?" she asked, looking from one cadet to the other.

"No, ma'am," they chorused.

"Then please go and fetch two buckets of water for these horses, one for each horse. And do you know if the General is in his office?"

"No, we don't, ma'am," said one. "But we'll fetch the water, ma'am."

"Thank you." She turned away from the two lads and looked at Farren. "Polite, aren't they? Remember the days when we got whistled for like that?"

"Very well indeed. So well that I've never grown used to ordering cadets around." He ducked under Princess's neck and came to her, putting his arm around her shoulders, heavy and comforting. "Come on, Stormwolf. Let's show the General one of the lost treasures of the Kingdom." He wrapped the skirt of his cloak about the Stone, hiding its light.

She walked beside him, shortening her long stride slightly to keep pace with him. The flight of stairs at the end of the corridor sloped up in front of her. "More stairs," she said quietly. "As if we haven't had enough of them after – when was it?"

"The day before yesterday. It seems like eternity already."

She nodded silently and trudged up the steps beside him, the heels of both their boots clattering in unison on the stone floor. They climbed to the third floor and wheeled around to walk down the tapestried corridor to the General's office. The door stood closed. Farren leaned forwards and knocked lightly on the wood.

"One moment, whoever you are," grunted a voice behind the door. On the other side of the door, something scratched and shuffled followed by the soft scrape of a chair over floorboards. "Right, now you can come in."

She felt for her sword and drew it above her head in salute as they walked through the door. The General looked up at them, an astonished stare slowly spreading across his reddened face. "You two!" he gasped, rising from his chair as they lowered their swords. "I didn't think I'd ever see either of you back here alive. Janna told me where you were headed. You're back! What happened?"

She turned to Farren. "Give it to him," she whispered.

"You do it." His hand brushed against hers as they went to the pouch at his side. "You're the arch *minyaster*." He turned sidelong to the General, angling himself so that his right side was turned away from the desk. A flash of blue showed between his fingers and light made the flesh of his hands glow purple-red. She turned to him and he slipped the smooth, warm, silver-wrapped ball of light into her cupped hands. Pulses of energy prickled her fingers where they touched the glasslike surface. Her mouth felt dry and a lump hardened in her throat. *What shall I say in a moment like this?* Every detail in the room seemed clear: the smells of paper, ink and burning wood; the sounds of the small fire; and the rain and wind outside. She cast around in her mind for words, heart bounding with a sense of ritual. She drew a deep breath and turned towards the big burly soldier behind the desk. "General Alpherastin, I, Azariel Stormwolf the arch *minyaster*, present you the long-lost Stone of Water," she said. She dropped to one knee and held it up to him.

"Get up and hand it over; I can't reach it down there." He scratched the mole on the end of his nose and grinned. "But I'll forgive you the fancy language. This is... pretty important."

She rose and walked around the desk to him, cloak brushing the papers as she pressed past it. She put it in his callused hands. He nodded and held the Stone up, the blue light casting a purplish colour across his weather-beaten face. "Well, well, well. So this is one of the Stones of Protection. Where are the rest of them?"

"The King of Heaven knows," she said, shrugging her shoulders. "Our task isn't done yet."

"Don't you have to have all four to make that boundary thing?" said the General, handing her the Stone. "From what you two and Janna told me, I thought that was what they did."

She took the blue globe of light and cradled it in both hands relishing the warm tingles coming from the ball. "We do need all four. But for now, we'll put this one back in the Watchtower of the South. Could you think of a better place to keep it while we hunt for the rest of them?" She chuckled and flashed a sly smile at the General. "It'll mean that the *minyasti* at the Watchtowers will have something to do."

"You would say that, wouldn't you?" General Alpherastin stepped around his desk and folded his arms. "You both look pretty battered, not to mention wet. Go and take a rest. I'm afraid it will be cold and empty at your *minyasti* headquarters, as I don't think there's any of you lot there. Off you go and grab yourself something to eat from the common room next door. I haven't heard the servants in there, so there should be a few bits and pieces left. Don't bother to salute."

"Thank you, sir." She handed the Stone back to Farren and watched him slip it into his hood. Then she held out her hand to him and slid her fingers through his, pressing her shoulder into his with a clink of chainmail as she turned towards the door.

They left the General's office and opened the next door along the corridor. The superior officers' common room stood empty, apart from the luxuriously padded leather-covered seats and a small round table. Half a fruit tart sat on the table, a few crumbs lying on the polished wood beside it. She bit her lip and glanced around nervously. *I don't belong in here. I hope nobody walks in. I expect they'd scold us merely for being here, not to mention helping ourselves.* "I suppose it's all right to take it," she said aloud, fighting back a faint quiver in her voice.

"Well, the General did say we could," he said. "Let's hurry. The longer we stand here staring, the more likely we are to be caught and have to explain ourselves. Even though you are the arch *minyaster* and probably have the right to be here."

"You're right." She stepped to the table and eased the tart out of the platter. "Let's go to our headquarters. No matter how cold it is, it'll be luxury compared to rocks and open country."

***

The sound of the bugler woke Farren the next morning. He rolled over in the voluptuously warm sheets and stared drowsily at the elk's head on his wall near the door. Every muscle in his body felt relaxed, warm and weak as string. He yawned and tugged the blankets underneath his chin again. A heaven of warmth and softness surrounded him and he murmured with wordless pleasure. *There's no hurry to go anywhere. We can take the Stone to the Watchtower any time.* He rolled over and fell asleep again.

The sound of a door knocking jerked him back out of the depths. "Are you going to stay in bed all day?" Azariel's voice called from through the door. "I've been waiting for you for hours."

He blinked and scratched at his bristly cheeks. "Hours? Reveille was blown not that long ago." He stretched and yawned, easing his shoulders out from the sheets and folding his arms lazily behind his head. "You can come in."

The handle turned and she walked in. Her hair hung in a rich, smooth fall over her shoulders and he faintly caught the scent of rosemary wafting from it. Her black trousers shone with a dull gleam of new leather. Only her boots and black cloak showed the scuffs, tears and fraying of travel. She put her hands on her hips and shook her hair back from her face. "It's nearly noon, beloved. I don't blame you for sleeping late after all you've been through, but we haven't finished our job yet."

He grinned at her, a small spark of mischief flickering inside him. "Why hurry? We won't be able to hunt the rest of the Stones until after winter's over, anyway. Why not stay in bed and enjoy myself?"

"You're trying to tease me and I know it. Get out of bed – after I've gone!" She smiled and twirled a lock of hair around one finger. "And that was an order from the arch *minyaster*. I'll overlook the fact that you've slept late when there was work to be done, but don't try me too far." She wagged a finger at him mock-scoldingly. "Anyway, I don't know what you would have done this morning while I was making arrangements."

"Arrangements?" He glanced away from her and out of the window. What he could see of the sky loooked grey and cold, and he could hear rain beating on the roofs outside.

"We are going to stay with the Stone at the Watchtower of the South for a few days until Taramaritan is able to come back there. That was what I was arranging. But hurry up. I've had the horses saddled already. All I need now is you."

"I'm coming." He sat up slightly in the bed, pushing the covers down his bare chest, but careful not to let them fall too far. Her eyes flickered down, then met his again. A gleam played in the blue-grey depths and a spot of pink had risen in her cheeks. "You'd better leave me to get ready."

She left the room and he got up swiftly. His spare uniform clothes in the wooden chest underneath the elk's head smelt of camphor and several mothballs rolled out from his woollen undershirt. He pulled the clothes on, battling the dull ache at the back of his head and the stale taste in his mouth. *I really did sleep too long. I hope she'll leave me time to wash and shave.* He looked at the door, then at his chainmail folded neatly on a chair under the window. *I'm going to do it. I'm going to be showing the Stone of Water to everybody down south, and I may as well look good enough to accompany it.* He left his leather tunic unlaced and padded barefoot out of the door and down the corridor to the men's bathroom.

Washed, shaved, dressed and every muscle in his body feeling new, he met Azariel in the common room. She had a thick book open in her lap, but she closed it and looked up as he came into the room. "At last," she said, smiling. "And you look as handsome as ever." She paused to put the book into a satchel, then rose and walked over to him.

He put his arms around her and kissed her, breathing in the smell of her hair and body. "I'm sorry I've made you wait, sweetheart," he said softly. "Will you forgive me?"

"There's nothing to be sorry for or to forgive," she said, smiling up at him, eyes shining.

"I've got something else I need to say sorry for, too." He slid his hand into the scented black silk of her hair. "I'm sorry I lost my temper with you back at Moonlady Falls when you were having trouble with Storm. There's few things I've done that I've regretted more. If I had gone to help you instead of staring at Crajaval and totally losing my wits, then maybe—"

Her lips pressed over his fiercely, cutting off his words. "Don't talk about what might have happened," she said when she pulled away. Her eyes flashed and her lips parted, baring her teeth slightly. "Done is done, and there's nothing we can do to change it. Let's go. The horses are waiting for us." She kissed him again, softly, then turned out of his embrace to pick up the satchel.

"What do you have in there?" He strode to the door and opened it for her.

"The *minyasti* archives. I'll tell you more as we ride."

Princess and Storm were waiting saddled and bridled, tethered in the rain outside the *minyasti* headquarters. The chestnut mare raised her head and whinnied to him as he shut the door behind Azariel. "There you are, my lady," he said. "Ready for one more journey?" He untied her from the hitching ring and slid his foot into the stirrup before swinging himself up onto her back with a squeak of tack.

They rode out of the barracks and out of the open city gates, headed into the wind and riding south on the King's Highway. The rain spattered down in fitful gusts, getting in his eyes and hair, and down his neck. He shivered and drew his arms further back under the shelter of his cloak. The rain tapped and drummed softly on his hood and he bowed his head to keep the pelting rain out of his eyes. Princess's hooves thudded and squelched on the mud and dirt beside the cobbled highway, the steady triple-beat of a canter and the tack squeaking to keep time. He raised one hand and wiped the rain off his face. "You said you'd tell me about something once we were riding. Here we are. Tell me."

"I've got the *minyasti* archives with me so we can write up the account of what we've done."

He ran his hand over Princess's neck, rubbing and stroking the shaggy winter hairs. "That's your job as arch minyaster, isn't it?"

"There's such a thing as an amanuensis." She caught his eye and winked. The south wind blew the hood and hair back from her face.

"Will you ask me to be yours?"

She reached back for her hood and pulled it back over her head. Her hair fell down each side of her face, the ends whirling around in the wild wind. "Of course. You know my pen-work looks like a drunken spider has fallen in the inkpot and crawled across the vellum. Will I let a good pen-man like you sit idle?" She pushed one of the curtains of her hair back inside her hood. "And I think you'll enjoy the work."

The two horses' hooves beat steadily on the beaten muddy ground, eating up the miles, canter, trot, walk, then back up to a canter again. One or two other travellers passed them, splashing through the pools of water spread over the cobbles. The rumour of hooves and wheels faded into the whine of the wind and the constant rumour of rain. Somewhere to the left, a bull bellowed a challenge to the low grey sky. Noon passed and the afternoon wore swiftly. The rain was still falling as the light dimmed and the brighter patch behind the clouds sank towards the smudged grey western horizon. *The mountains and the Watchtower of the West are over there somewhere if we could see them in all this rain.* He drew a deep breath, the smell of mud and wet wool filling his lungs. He shrugged his damp shoulders and looked between Princess's ears again. The thick grey finger of the southern Watchtower stood ahead of them on the shores of the rainwashed lake. Beside him, Storm raised his head and snorted, shaking his mane. "He wants his stable, doesn't he?" he said. "I know I'm ready for mine."

"I hope we've come early enough for them to find us some food and somewhere to sleep after we've handed the Stone over." She glanced around the corner of her hood at him. A lock of hair was plastered to her cheeks and white brow by the rain. "But even so, anywhere dry and warm will be welcome."

He nodded and let Princess trot ahead of Storm. The tall grey tower grew closer, and he rode around it to the wooden door that opened towards the lake. No faces looked over the battlements, and soft yellow light shone out from the topmost windows. He shivered, suddenly aware of the cold and the ache of hunger inside him, and longing for the warmth of the tower. Smoke billowed out from the chimney-vents near the top of the grey stone column. *A warm fire indoors at last.* He swung off Princess's back, squelching and slipping in the mud as he landed, then turned and knocked on the wooden door.

The silhouette of a man's head and shoulders appeared at the window above. "In the name of Caph Domastin, who's that?" a brusque male voice demanded.

"Farren Blackarrow and Azariel Stormwolf," he called up. "Hurry down from your dinner and let us in," he added softly to Azariel. He stepped back and put his arm around her. Her head slumped against his shoulder, soft and heavy.

He stared at the door, listening to the small sounds inside the tower. She caught the sound of feet on stone steps and ground, coming steadily closer. Something bumped and rasped on the other side of the wood then the handle turned. In the half-dark, he saw a broad-chested man in his early thirties with close-cropped blond hair. "Come in! Come in from the cold, you two. Glad to see you." He threw his arms around Azariel, then let her go and slapped him hard on the back.

He groaned and staggered forwards, supporting himself on the door-sill as the bruises on his back throbbed. "Thanks for your welcome, Colonel Annan, but please don't hit me so hard."

"Blackarrow!" The Colonel closed the door behind the horses as they filed into the tower. "What's up? Been a bad boy and collected a few lashes across your back?"

He shook his head and shrugged his shoulders, the ache fading. "Badly bruised from falling off a horse. It's a long story and it's to do with why we're here."

"Really? Tell me about it. See to your horses and come on up. We've only just finished dinner and you're in luck – there's a bit left over." He paused, whistling softly and crackling his knuckles. "Or rather, just come on up and tell your tale. You look as wet and cold as drowned kittens. I'll yell for someone to see to your nags." He went to the foot of the stairs and cupped his hands to his mouth. "Get down here, someone!" he bellowed. Then he turned to them and grinned. "That'll bring them. Come on up."

Farren paused to wash his hands under the pump, then trudged up the stairs after the Colonel. Azariel was waiting for him and he slipped his arm around her waist as he drew level with her.

"Ready to put it back where it belongs?" he asked, brushing the delicate curves of her ear with his lips as he whispered.

She nodded and leaned her head on his shoulder, the soft silk of her hair brushing under his chin and the gentle fragrance of rosemary rising from it. He pressed back against the wall as another soldier came down the stairs. The soldier paused to speak softly to the Colonel, then nodded and raised his eyebrows to them in greeting as he continued down the spiral stairs.

Warm light spread over the cold grey stone of the steps as the Colonel pulled the rope to open the hatch into the common room at the top of the tower. "Clear a space, lads," he said. "Here's a pair of *minyasti* come to finish off what's left of our dinner. Take a seat, you two, and I'll get you something to drink while you tell us what you're doing here."

He sank down onto one of the stools beside Azariel at the table, gently putting his arm around her shoulders as she leaned forwards, running his fingers along the line of soft skin and hairs at the top of her chainmail. *Warm shelter, warm food, company and good drink. It's been a long time, and I never realised how much I've missed them all.* He smiled contentedly and shuffled around on his stool slightly. The Colonel came over from one of the cupboards against one wall, carrying several bottles and beakers. "Are you off duty this time, Farren?" he asked. "If so, then you'll be able to have a glass or three." He set down the beakers and began uncorking the bottles. "See what you think of this cider – bottled this season and only just ready yesterday. I brewed it."

"You and your cider, Annan," he chuckled, catching the big man's eyes and winking. "I don't know if I'm off duty or on it, but I'll only have a few." Azariel sat up and dug him lightly in the ribs, her finger pressing a link of metal into a bruise on his side. He laughed. "And I'm always a *minyastin*. Don't try me too hard in front of the arch *minyaster!*"

"Very well." The Colonel poured the pale gold liquid into the beakers and handed it to them. "Now. Tell us what you're doing here. Another invasion? Or have you been posted here now that good old Taramaritan is in the guard house east of us?"

Azariel reached for the beaker the Colonel handed to her. Her other hand rested on Farren's knee, gently kneading into the stiff muscles above it. "Neither," she said, smiling at the other man. Farren caught a gleam of mischief in her eyes. "What we're here for will probably mean that Taramaritan will have to come back. As a matter of fact, I've ordered it."

"Oh, good." Colonel Annan's blue eyes glowed and flicked eastwards. "It'll be good to have… a woman here to keep the place tidy and give us some decent cooking."

"Be honest, Colonel," one of the other soldiers said. "That's not why you want her here."

He flushed pink. "All right, all right! I do fancy her. She's a nice girl, Taramaritan. Get on with your tale, you two. What are you going to do?"

He looked over his beaker at the other man. "We've got the Stone of Water to put back in its place here." The sweet-sharp cider washed around his mouth and down his throat, leaving a trail of glowing embers behind it.

"The what?"

Still drinking, he caught Azariel's eye. "The Stone of Water," she said. "The reason this Watchtower was built. We'll be here to guard it until your Taramaritan comes. Then keep it safe, because if or when we've got the other three Stones into the other Watchtowers, they'll make a border around the Kingdom to keep enemies out."

The Colonel whistled. "Show me."

He loosened the strings of his belt pouch. "Shall I put it where it belongs, Stormwolf?"

"You may as well." She threw her head back as she raised her beaker to her lips, then set the cup down on the table.

He stood up, unlacing his belt pouch. He reached inside and touched the silver tracery over the Stone and the smooth, warm, tingling surface underneath. He drew it out. Shafts of blue light shone out from between his fingers, dulling and drowning the yellow light of the candles. The Colonel raised a hand in front of his eyes, squinting. "It's bright!" he said.

Farren smiled and walked to the alcove in the southern curve of the wall where it looked as if a window should have been placed. The shadow of the little plinth in the middle of the alcove stood back against the grey stone behind it. He held the Stone in both hands, looking at the plinth. *That's where this one goes. The first of the four,* he thought. He drew a deep breath. "In the name of God Incarnate, here it is," he whispered and put the Stone on the plinth.

Brilliant blue light burned and blazed up from the Stone of Water in a fountain, dazzling him. Instinctively, his hands flew up to shield his face until the fire dimmed. He looked at the Stone, orange-red after-images crawling in front of his eyes. The brilliant fountain and dazzling intensity of the Stone had faded, leaving bright fingers and little lightnings flickering inside the glassy blue globe. He noticed that the stone slabs of the wall beside the alcove were glowing faintly, soft as candle-light but cobalt. Slowly, he turned, heart thumping, scanning the flickering lights inside the grey walls that bathed the common room in blue light.

"Put out the candles," ordered Colonel Annan. "I don't think we'll need them any more. Is it like this all over the tower?"

One of the soldiers went to the door and looked out. "Stairs light as far as I can see," he said. "Even the steps are shiny. If anybody trips downstairs now, they're the clumsiest idiot alive."

"That'll save us candles," said the Colonel. "Finished your drinks, you two? Have some more, and one of you lads go and get them the remains of dinner. Afterwards, you can tell us where you found that shiny ball."

He lingered over his meal, but Azariel finished quickly. She pushed her plate aside and stood up, bumping his elbow. "Stormwolf?" he asked. "What's the hurry?"

"Sorry," she said, resting a hand on his shoulder. "I'm going to fetch the archive book I brought here. We may as well write it up now while we tell the story." She ruffled his hair, then glided out of the room.

He finished his meal and sat sipping a second beaker of cider, watching the flames burning in the hearth in the north curve of the wall. The hatch opened and closed softly, and he looked around. Azariel had the satchel in her arms, one hand unstrapping it. She slid a thick book out of it. "Here it is. The archive book for the *minyasti*. Janna hasn't written much in it yet, apart from odds and ends about us *minyasti*. Not very interesting to an outsider!" she added with a laugh. "The leather's still quite new, but here's your place – after an account of Janna's retirement and my appointment as arch *minyaster*." She put it and the satchel down in front of him.

He ran his hands across the crisp new page then looked in the satchel. A quill pen lay curled inside it, the soft parts of the big feather crumpled and pressed up against two bottles of ink, one red, one black. He took the pen out and unscrewed the pottle of black ink. Quill poised in his left hand, he looked over at her. She was lying stomach down on a sheepskin in front of the fire, a blue-black cascade of hair falling down beside and over her face. A new log crackled and snapped in the grate behind her, casting a few highlights of gold onto the blue sheen from the walls shining onto the long lines of her back and legs and the folds of her cloak. His heart kicked with tenderness and longing. *She is so beautiful*, he thought. Rain drummed on the roof above him and the wind howled around the tower. "I'm ready," he said softly.

She smiled warmly up at him, then her eyes flicked briefly towards the Colonel. "Here goes, and don't interrupt me. She closed her eyes for a few moments then opened them, looking straight into his, lightning flashing in their storm-grey depths. "In the seventh year of Caph Domastin…"